PRAISE FOR KILL NOTICE

"KILL NOTICE is a real nail-biter of a thriller! Devious, fast-paced and packed with relatable characters. Highly recommended." — **Jonathan Maberry**, New York Times bestselling author of DOGS OF WAR and PATIENT ZERO

"Marta Sprout is on her game in KILL NOTICE. The authenticity is evident on every page of this red ball express of a thriller. Detective Bowers is today's protagonist, a pro with nothing to prove as she faces off against Washington, DC crime and bureaucracy with justice on her mind." —**Mitch Stern, former FBI Special Agent**, author of THE RESIDENT AGENT

"Marta Sprout's KILL NOTICE resonates with Dean Koontz and John Sandford. Looming dread and sharp suspense make the prose like a Doberman at your heels." — **Kevin J. Anderson**, New York Times bestselling author of STAKE

Kill Notice

Michele,
Thank You for All
You and Your Family
Does for this Community —
Best wishes,
Marta Sprout

The New Bowers Thriller Series

Kill Notice

MARTA SPROUT

DEEP BLUE PRESS

Copyright © 2019 by Marta Sprout
All rights reserved.

KILL NOTICE is a work of fiction. Names, characters, locales,
and incidents either are the product of the author's imagination or
are used fictitiously. Any resemblance to actual persons, living or
dead, events, or locales is entirely coincidental.

No part of this publication may be reproduced, distributed, or
transmitted in any form or by any means, or stored
in a database or retrieval system, without the prior
written permission of the publisher.

Published 2019 by Deep Blue Press

Cover Design by
Stuart Bache at Books Covered

ISBN: 978-0-9857973-5-5

First Edition

Printed in the United States of America

For Denny

FORGED IN FIRE

If one face in a crowd were that of a killer,
you'd look into his eyes and a switch deep inside would click
as he drew near. Call it gut instinct or intuition.
It would warn you. Or would it?

It Begins

DEVIN WALKER KNEW what he'd seen would stick in his mind for a long while to come. Like something dark and oppressive. Foreign and disturbing. No doubt about it. Something bad was coming.

On that day, he'd been well paid for a West Virginia high school boy. His mission had been to stack hay in a rancher's barn and to remove the accumulated leaves from the basement's window wells around the man's house. By the time Devin finished bagging the debris, the sun hung low on the horizon and the air had grown chilly. Dusk cast a pall of gray over the dry grass and dormant bushes.

Through one of the newly washed basement windows, a flicker of orange caught his eye.

He lay flat on his belly and peered inside where a dark-haired boy about ten years of age sat on the bare concrete floor, nearly naked. The kid's knees were drawn up to his chin and his arms were wrapped tightly around his long, spindly legs.

A furnace, with its access door hanging wide open, stood a few feet away from the boy and almost directly below the corner window.

Dressed only in a pair of ragged, stained briefs, the kid stared at the dancing orange flames as if daydreaming.

He shifted on the hard floor. His spine tracked down his narrow back like a string of mountain ridges between prominent ribs that looked more like a skeleton than the torso of a living, breathing child.

Devin swallowed hard at the sight of the dark purple bruises covering the child's body and his boyish face.

No little kid should look like that.

Wishing that the dim, bare bulb hanging from the ceiling were brighter, Devin cocked his head and tried to get a better view.

In profile, the face Devin saw appeared soft and smooth the way children are at that age.

As if the boy's mind were miles away, his small mouth pulled into a tight slit and his big eyes remained locked on the fire.

Devin felt for the kid as a meager patch of warm light from the furnace washed over the boy. Sadly, the cheery glow of the flames seemed the only cozy spot in the entire dreary basement.

As if mesmerized, the boy sat very still.

Heavy footsteps clomping across the main floor broke the silence. The door to the basement banged open with a loud *smack*.

The kid blinked. His shoulders tensed.

"I know you're down there." The big rancher's voice boomed down the stairs loud enough for Devin to hear.

The boy's eyes continued to focus on the rectangle of roaring orange flames. Both hands reached up as if to embrace the heat emanating from the access door.

"I know what you did, goddammit," the big man yelled. "You ought to be ashamed of yourself. The damned dog is better house-broke than you. There ain't no call for someone your age to be wettin' his bed. Ya hear me? There's something wrong with you, boy."

Kill Notice

Devin couldn't see the rancher, but he knew his voice and could hear the sound of his steel-toed boots kicking at something solid like a doorframe.

"Son of a bitch. I'm gonna hang your piss-soaked skivvies on a post at the bus stop for everyone to see."

As the man stomped away, the boy searched the floor, picked up a pocketknife, and poked at something next to him.

When Devin shifted to get a better angle, he saw a flashlight and a modest pile of what appeared to be small toys. They were hard to make out in the shadows.

The boy's elbow methodically moved back and forth as if he were sawing on something.

Curious as to what the kid was doing, Devin pulled himself closer until his nose nearly touched the glass.

The boy held up the head of an action figure. He inspected it closely in the shimmering light and twisted the head onto the end of a stick. Like a marshmallow on a skewer, he carefully poked the head into the crackling fire. As it burned he sat on his feet and rotated the stick and watched the plastic melt away.

Clomping footsteps returned to the basement door. "Boy! Git your worthless ass up here. Pronto. You ain't goin' to bed until those damned sheets are clean."

By now, the plastic head was no more than smoke.

The boy pulled the smoldering stick out of the furnace and dropped it on top of other charred twigs scattered over the floor. He used pliers to close the access door.

The rancher grunted. "Don't make me come down there. You know what I'll do."

The kid repositioned his flashlight.

"Ya got two minutes to get your ass up here."

The beam of light fell upon his pile of toys.

Devin couldn't help but stare. One at a time, the boy jabbed the tip of the knife into the dismembered parts of the action figure and dropped each into a bright red lunchbox decorated with colorful cartoon characters.

3

"Ya got one more minute." The big man cleared his throat. "You're just like your good-for-nothin' mama. Glad she's gone. Yes I am. She shoulda taken you with her."

The boy methodically tucked something else, something nasty and gnarled, into the lunchbox.

Devin twisted his shoulders and craned his neck trying to see. His chest tightened.

The yellow circle of light from the flashlight fell upon knots of brown fur, tiny legs that were stiff and curled, and small heads covered in something crusted and reddish brown.

He felt the bump in his pulse the moment his brain made the connection. The boy's toys were the mutilated bodies of dead rodents. Their condition made it hard to identify the species, but Devin figured they were probably field mice.

Or what was left of them.

The hair went up on his neck. A queasy feeling swirled in his stomach. His eyes opened wider.

Like watching a train wreck, it was both terrifying and spellbinding.

Devin's breath had steamed up the window. With the cuff of his flannel shirt, he wiped the moisture away in time to watch the kid pick up his last toy. A kind of glee lit up every corner of the kid's face. His eyes sparkled in the ambient light.

By one ear, the boy dangled before his eyes the severed head of a cat.

MESSAGE MURDER

THREE HUNDRED MILES away and twenty-five years later, it was early morning and still dark outside when the knock came.

In that one second, D.C. homicide detective Kate Bowers knew her entire world had shifted.

She stopped in the middle of a set of pushups and listened. With sweat dripping from her face, she quietly stood and rubbed the goosebumps on her arms.

No doubt. The worst kind of evil had found her.

She tried to calm her breathing. No longer could she deny that a psychopath had her in his sights.

She also knew someone else had died.

Bowers held her .40 caliber Glock 22 with both hands. In bare feet, she silently rushed around the stacks of U-Haul boxes in her new apartment. Armed with a full magazine, she braced her back against the wall next to the front door and strained to hear any sounds outside. She heard nothing.

Bowers swallowed hard and eased open the door.

Cautiously, she scanned the walkway before leaving cover. Creeping outside, she stood in the shadows a few feet from her door.

The concrete felt cool and hard under her toes and balls of her feet. Her head jerked as something moved.

A white cat scampered away. Other than that, nothing stirred. Not a person. Not a blade of grass.

Before returning to face her front door, she knew what she would find. There at her exact eye level hung one small button taped to her door.

Soon she'd get another call about another body..

BATTLEFIELD

BOWERS WATCHED a fellow detective take a report and a CSI tech document and collect the button taped to her front door.

After they had left, she hit the shower and began dressing for work, which was no easy task. Most of her clothes, or at least the clean ones, were still in boxes.

She put down the box cutter. *Why does the thing you need always have to be in the last place you look?*

Moments later as she secured her belt and badge, Bowers glanced at the pile of mail next to her laptop. Knowing it contained bills, she felt a twinge of guilt, but there was no time to deal with that. She pulled her brown hair into a ponytail and left the mail untouched.

Until recently, she'd been working hard and enjoying a few days off here and there until a killer had decided to step up his game by leaving buttons on her door. Now it seemed that her days were exclusively filled with work.

She had moved with the intention of disappearing from this madman's sights. Instead, the unfamiliar spaces had left her disorganized and feeling more vulnerable than before.

In the kitchen, the fridge was nearly empty, except for bottled water, a beer, one mummified lime, and a cup of yogurt. She ate the yogurt. After being forced to munch on bugs during Army survival training, anything tasted pretty good and she wasn't picky, except about her coffee.

She left to find a Starbucks.

While locking the front door, she glanced at the black fingerprint powder smudged all over the surface. *That'll impress my new neighbors.*

She jiggled the doorknob to make sure it was locked. Work demanded that she stay focused, but today she felt scattered as if she'd walked into a room and forgotten why she'd come there.

Maybe an extra shot of espresso in her morning coffee would help. *Then again, maybe not.*

Bowers stepped onto the walkway and saw two big brown eyes peering at her from under a red cowboy hat. The neighbor's eight-year-old hid behind the trunk of a sapling, seemingly unaware that the tree wasn't big enough to cover him. "Pee-kew. Pee-kew," he said with his hands pointing at her in the shape of an imaginary pistol. "Bam. Bam. Hold it right there."

Bowers enjoyed the kid's stern expression, which seemed an amusing contrast to his Toy Story hat, camo pajamas, and Superman slippers.

"Morning Trevor," she said. "Come here a second." As Bowers knelt, the boy wandered over, still without smiling.

"Semper Fi," he said with conviction.

"You know what that means?" she asked.

"Sure. It means I'm a tough guy."

Bowers bit back a smile.

Her vest had flopped open and the boy's eyes were locked on her badge.

"I want to have a badge and be cool like you someday."

Bowers wasn't sure she wanted anyone to be like her.

"Let me show you something." She turned the boy around by the shoulders so that she could kneel behind him.

"Aim," she said.

Kill Notice

He did.

Bowers put her arms around him and covered his small hands with hers as if teaching someone to shoot. The kid smelled of bubble gum and peanut butter.

"Brace your wrists," she said, "and keep your elbows up." She leveled his imaginary finger-gun at the tree, quickly shifted her aim to a bush, and finally pointed at the grass. The boy's stance showed he took this as serious business.

"Always aim at the ground or a tin can," she said. "Never at a person or a car or a building. Okay?"

He twisted to look at her. "But... If you don't shoot 'em, how da ya catch the bad guys?"

"Mostly," she said, "you use your training." She pointed to his head. "Ya gotta use what's up here, be smart."

The boy smiled just as his mom darted out of the door next to Bowers'.

"Trevor, get back in here!" she shouted. "What are you doing?"

Bowers stood. "He's just playing." She gave him a high-five.

"He's a real handful," the mother said.

The boy ran off pointing at the flowerbeds and sprinkler heads. "Pee-kew. Pee-kew."

The mother held a baby girl on her hip. "You're good with kids." The woman's blonde hair rode high on her head in a messy bun.

Bowers laughed. "I grew up with younger brothers."

"I've seen you with that gorgeous man in the FBI jacket. You'd make a cute couple. Just saying."

Bowers' brows raised.

"I'm sorry," said the neighbor. "We've just met and already I'm playing match maker."

"Don't worry about it." Bowers checked the time. "I need to get to work." Before leaving, she waved to Trevor, who was busy assaulting dandelions.

BOWERS STOOD in line at Starbucks, anxious to get back to investigating her latest case. The button on her door had thrown her off schedule, and she still had one last stop to make before going to the station.

The dense aroma of deeply roasted coffee filled the air. In front of her a trim woman wore a backless shirt that revealed a sports bra, tanned back, and athletic muscles. She leaned into the man next to her, who rested his hand on the bare skin at her waist. Everything about them seemed as relaxed as a hammock strung between two palm trees.

Despite pretending to be patient, inside Bowers felt anything but at ease. She mulled over the knock on her door, the button, and this morning's conversation with her neighbor. The FBI agent her neighbor had alluded to was Steven B. Riggs, Bowers' ex-lover and best friend. Last year, she'd backed away from their relationship even though they'd been good together. That had never been the problem.

She picked up her drinks and headed to her car. Her phone rang seconds after she'd started the engine. The call came from the nursing home where her uncle lived.

A woman with a soft voice spoke, "He says you're late."

"He's right," said Bowers. "I'm on the way."

"Just so you know, he's developed a cough and is grumpy."

Bowers chuckled. "He's always grumpy."

She ended the call and merged into traffic. Despite her stab at humor, watching him grow old and frail tugged at the things she feared most.

Uncle Marvin had always been her anchor, the strong one who'd listened even when she didn't know what to say. It had been his distinguished career in the Army that had inspired her to join. Neither of her divorced parents had come to her boot camp graduation, but Marvin had shown up in full-dress uniform. He'd also been there when she'd left the Army and needed to sit on his porch and reset. Never saying anything that hadn't needed to be said.

Now she wanted to be there for him.

Up ahead the nursing home came into view. She pulled into a

Kill Notice

parking slot and eased out of the car. The three-story building's fresh coat of white paint and bright red geraniums in neatly mulched flowerbeds were a stark contrast to what she knew would be inside.

This was the last stop for those who'd lost their independence. Her stomach knotted. Inside the front door, she balanced the two cups of coffee and took the familiar trek up the elevator to the third floor.

Bowers marched down a hallway that smelled of industrial disinfectant. Long accustomed to military-issue, no-frills accommodations, she never expected a veterans' facility to be any different. But even to her, the polished floors and occasional potted plant did little to bolster any pretense that an institution could feel like home.

Uncle Marvin had never married. After retirement, a stroke had left him with few options. He'd accepted his fate and the nursing home like the consummate soldier he was, saying he didn't want to be a burden. In her mind that took more guts than being on the battlefield.

The clunking of her boot heels echoed in the corridor. Three feet away, his door stood open a crack. She stopped outside.

The unit across the hall appeared newly vacated. Even the plaque that had once displayed the name of Marvin's friend had been removed. All traces of him had been scrubbed away.

"Shit," Bowers murmured to herself.

Marvin's voice boomed through his door. "I can hear you," he said. "Might as well get on in here, and say hello."

When she stepped inside her uncle's room, the big man's green eyes brightened and one bushy brow went up. She set the coffees on a side table within his reach. After giving him a hug, she took a seat next to his wheelchair.

"They feeding you okay?" she asked.

Marvin snorted. "The C-Rats they gave us in Nam were better and that ain't saying much."

Bowers remembered the military's ready-to-eat meals she knew a MREs and Marvin's generation knew as C-Rations.

"Maybe this will help." She slipped a roll of his favorite peppermint Lifesavers into his plaid shirt pocket.

One corner of his mouth curled into a slight grin. "Mightily obliged. Missy." He patted her arm.

He coughed, covering his mouth with the back of his right hand. The left one lay limp in his lap.

They both sat in silence, squinting at the bright sunlight pouring in the window while watching outside at what looked like a hawk hovering in an updraft.

She gripped his hand. "I'm sorry about your friend."

"Me too." His barreled chest heaved as he cleared his throat. "You never told me why you moved."

She took a sip of her coffee. "I didn't come here to talk about me."

"Might as well. Things around here are about as exciting as a dissertation on floor wax." He squeezed her arm and let go. His broad hand, which had once crushed beer cans as if they were made of paper, now wore a Band-Aid and age spots.

"Do you remember," she asked, "when we used to sit on your porch?"

"Sure do. I also remember the day you turned ten and went after that bully up the street, who'd been picking on your little brothers. I hauled you home, still swinging."

Bowers laughed and then let her voice fade.

"You okay, Missy?"

"Things are complicated," she said. She couldn't tell him about the button on her door and wasn't sure that she'd put her thoughts together well enough to talk about Riggs.

Marvin waited and listened like he always did.

Bowers watched him. "I understand how to nab a perp or how to 'find the hill, take the hill.' It's everything else that I suck at. I can't cook to save my butt." Bowers stretched the tight muscles in her neck. "The Army was easier."

"You got that right." He peered down at his puffy left hand. "We didn't have time to think about what tomorrow would bring."

She glanced at his still hand. It killed her that there was nothing

Kill Notice

she could do to protect him from the damage the stroke had done. Helplessness was worse than being shot at.

"So, why'd you move?"

"I needed to be closer to work."

"Bullshit." He grunted and scrubbed his one useful hand across his grizzled cheeks. "I know of only a few things that would make you turn-tail and run. Which one was it?"

She shrugged.

"It's better to face an enemy," he said, "than get shot in the ass while running away."

"My job has risks."

He sat forward, twisted, and stared at her. "As if that's ever stopped you."

She reached for her coffee and stopped. "I think I've screwed up something important."

"You mean Riggs?"

She nodded. "Each day is filled with uncertainty." She rubbed her palms together. "He hunts down fugitives."

"So do you. Ever wonder how he feels about that?"

"But what if something happens to him and he—"

"Doesn't come back? Now we're gettin' down to pay dirt." A lock of white hair fell to the middle of his forehead. "He or anyone else you care about could be gone, today. Tomorrow. Or maybe three years from now. And you can't stomach that." He dipped his head as if affirming that his suspicions were correct.

Bowers bit at a hangnail. Talking with Marvin was a bit like standing in front of a mirror, naked.

"Have you told this man that you love him?"

Bowers didn't know what to say to that.

"Don't you think he deserves the truth? Let me tell you something, Missy. What if he is gone tomorrow? That would mean you'd missed the opportunity to share whatever time you did have with him. Once he checks out, it's too late."

She cocked her head and glanced at him. "You never married."

"And it was a damn foolish mistake I sorely regret."

Bowers sucked in a deep breath. "Pain in the ass." She felt the weight of his hand on her shoulder. "I came here to cheer you up. Instead, you gave me a swift kick in the pants."

"You're welcome." His one-sided smile returned. "Now, do you have any sugar for that coffee?"

DARK STREETS

AFTER SUNSET the streets of downtown Washington D.C. had become a little cooler. Bowers caught the 9:00 p.m. Metro line toward McPherson Square and held onto a metal handrail inside the train as it rumbled down the tracks.

A few feet from her stood a man in a familiar camouflage uniform. His boots were tightly laced. His hair recently cut.

"You're Army," she said to the soldier who carried his folded cap neatly tucked under his belt.

"Yes, ma'am, military police," he said. "You?"

"I used to be Army. Now I'm a cop."

"You've got that vibe," he said with a knowing grin.

As the train rocked back and forth, she put a hand in her vest pocket and felt the corner of her phone, which held images of the button left on her door.

So much had happened today that she had little time to reflect on this morning's conversation with Uncle Marvin. Bowers withdrew her hand from her pocket and reviewed her new case. Three days ago she'd received another button. Hours later a corpse had been reported. When she'd arrived on scene, the smell of burnt flesh had told her this would be a bad one. She'd been right. The victim had been torched.

Bowers stared blankly at the reflection of the soldier in the dark windows of their fluorescent-lit cocoon as it sped down the Metro tracks.

Today the M.E. had reported finding burns and smoke in the victim's lungs, which meant the man had been breathing when he'd been forced into the trashcan and doused in lighter fluid, seconds before a match brought his life to a writhing end. His charred face hung in her memory.

"Long day?" asked the M.P.

Bowers nodded. "That's an understatement. There's nothing like working homicide in a September heat wave."

"Roger that," said the soldier, who stood as if he were about to face an inspection.

She'd been all squared away like that—once.

The train pulled to a stop.

A minute later, she exited the bright Metro station with the need for a cold beer and a few hours of downtime before heading home for some sleep.

Up ahead, lively music and the smell of burgers from a local eatery's patio had drawn a crowd of customers. She listened to the beat of drums, clatter of forks, and rumble of conversations. At 15th Street NW, she headed toward The Old Ebbitt Grill to meet Riggs.

Six minutes later, she saw his car sitting triumphantly in a parking spot in front of Ebbitt's entrance. "Lucky bastard." She dug her hands into her vest pockets and quietly chuckled to herself.

Once again he'd demonstrated his uncanny ability to find parking, which was no small feat in D.C. He was probably waiting at the bar, ready to rub it in.

Blowing off steam with law enforcement personnel, who hung out at the legendary tavern, had become a ritual. Having the best crab cakes in town didn't hurt either.

The din of horns and traffic echoed off the stone buildings. The people around her hurried up and down the tree-lined street with their eyes locked on their phones. They appeared oblivious to the shabby-looking character in a black T-shirt who scanned the crowd as if sizing up those walking by.

When she neared the White House Gift Shop, Bowers heard gasps of alarm. She glanced over her left shoulder and caught sight of the man in the black T-shirt as he raced toward a lone woman with a large purse. Bowers pushed the middle-aged lady out of the way before he could snatch her purse and felt his long arm grab her waist from behind. His other arm came over her shoulder, brandishing a knife in front of her face.

"Hey babe, why you in my business?" asked the man with his mouth next to her ear. His breath left a putrid, boozy odor in the air.

Out of sheer habit, Bowers sized him up as about her height. Six feet. Give or take an inch. Young, but not a teenager. Wiry. Black. And desperate.

The sharpened steel glinting inches in front of her face sent a surge of adrenaline through her system.

The women who'd nearly lost her purse stared at Bowers and ran. A couple of startled tourists clutched their smart phones and selfie sticks and backed away.

Bowers slipped a hand under her vest and flipped off the safety on her hip holster. People were still driving by and coming out of shops. Her pulse pounded in her ears. Even the retreating crowd was within firing range, which meant this was a lousy place to discharge her service pistol.

The Old Ebbitt Grill stood on the opposite corner. At this hour at least a half dozen law enforcement types or more would be inside. They might as well have been in North Dakota for all the good it did.

Keeping an eye on the knife as if it were the head of a snake, Bowers balanced her weight. Fear was there, but combat mindset had taken hold. "I'll do you a favor," she said. "You get one warning. *Back off*. Go home. Now."

"Pretty lady, you's gonna do me a favor, all right. See, dis be my dick—" He waved the knife around. "—and I be using it, if you don't do what I say."

He took a whiff of her hair. "You be something fine. How 'bout we go have us some fun?"

"I'd rather have nail fungus."

"Guh," he said. "Why you hafta say sum-thin' like dat?"

Up ahead she saw Riggs stick his dark-blond head out of Ebbitt's front door. A few seconds later, he stood on the sidewalk, insistently waving to someone inside.

Her attacker pressed himself against her and flipped the stiletto knife horizontal. She calculated the distance between the thin, sharp blade and her throat.

He was right-handed, which meant the left arm around her torso was his weaker side. Bowers wiped her palms on her pants and took a long steady breath.

"Don't say I didn't warn you."

In the moment it took for a cabbie to zip past, she locked onto his right wrist with both hands. Slammed the back of her head into his nose. She ducked under his arm and drove his hand to the left until the blade nicked his chest.

"What the—" screamed her attacker, who'd been thrown off balance. "Shit, man."

She continued twisting his arm. The pain must have been fierce as the pressure threatened to dislocate his shoulder. He dropped the knife and crumbled to his knees.

She pulled his arm behind his back. Using her weight as leverage, Bowers forced him to the pavement, face-first. She pinned him to the ground with her knee squarely between his shoulder blades. She felt his boney spine and ribs cradling her shin as she slapped the knife away, well beyond his reach.

He nearly bucked her off until she pulled out her Glock and pressed the muzzle against his temple. "Let me introduce you to *my* dick. Mine against yours any day, hotshot."

Sweat trickled down her back. She glanced around to make sure this guy didn't have a buddy. To her back, she heard Riggs yelling.

Running feet pounded the sidewalk. Three familiar faces surrounded her with their weapons drawn on the perpetrator.

Kill Notice

"Get this crazy bitch off me, man."

Riggs knelt down, secured the knife, and eyed her attacker. "What do we have here?"

The perp stared up at the three men as if he couldn't believe his own eyes. "Who the hell be you?"

Riggs chuckled. "The woman who just handed you your ass is a homicide detective." He cocked his head. "Boy, did you pick the wrong person to mess with."

"No shit."

Her attacker tried to push himself up, but Bowers leaned forward, deliberately putting more weight between his shoulder blades.

She gave him enough room to breathe, but made it nearly impossible for him to move. "Choose carefully," she said. "I don't give second warnings."

The suspect hesitated.

Riggs stowed his weapon. "To answer your question, I'm special agent Steven Riggs. FBI." He nodded to the tall, black man next to him. "My colleague is also FBI. And that fellow—" Riggs pointed to a Hispanic man with big shoulders. "He's her boss."

"Damn," said the perp as he pressed his forehead against the pavement.

Bowers holstered her pistol, cuffed the subject, and pulled him to his feet. The man wobbled slightly. He still stank, but at least he wasn't resisting.

She studied his dark eyes and the beads of sweat dotting his upper lip. "Here's how this works," she said while watching him closely. "You assault me, and I will take your ass down. Show respect, and I'll treat you with respect. Your call."

"Ain't no cop gonna show me respect."

"Try me," Bowers said while her sergeant patted down the subject.

The man moaned as his phone and wallet were removed from his pockets. "Hey. I gotta call my bro. How is I gonna do dat?"

Bowers pulled out her phone. "What's his number?"

The man frowned and gave her the information.

She tapped it in and held the phone to his face.

"Leon, dis is Reggie. I been busted. What? I jumped dis woman 'n' she turned out to be a cop. Shit man, I know."

Bowers almost felt sorry for the guy. She hadn't expected Reggie to be dumb enough to confess in front of two cops and two FBI agents and give away the number of an associate. She glanced at her boss and the other two men, who were holding back smiles and trying not to laugh.

When the call was over, Bowers handed her phone to her boss and took her assailant by the arm.

"Reggie," she said. "What the hell were you thinking?" She pointed at the Treasury Building across the street. "Do you have any clue where we are? The White House is within spitting distance. There are more cops per square foot right here than any other place on the planet, and *this* is where you decide to jump somebody? Seriously?"

Reggie grunted. "Papa G gots it all tied-up on the Southeast side. Where else am I supposed-ta go?"

"You might try honest work," she said.

Reggie shrugged his boney shoulders.

She grabbed his jaw and held up her flashlight. A quick sobriety test showed that this guy's dilated eyes were jumping all over the place. Reggie was clearly hammered. That explained a few things.

Bowers groaned. "Reggie, you just cost me a hard-earned night off and tons of extra paperwork." She wanted to sit down and not have to think about anything for a couple of hours. That was now out of the question.

Her boss, Sergeant Charles Mitchell, caught Reggie when he stumbled backward. "I've got this one. Maybe a night in the bullpen will help him reconsider his ways. I'll take him in."

"Mitch, are you sure?" asked Bowers.

As two units with strobes and wailing sirens pulled up, Mitch, who'd been unusually helpful, flashed her his trademark smile and handed her phone back.

Kill Notice

"Gotta keep my arrest record up," he said. "Go enjoy your night off, but have a report on my desk tomorrow."

She nodded toward Reggie. "After he sleeps it off, get this man some food and a toothbrush."

SPECIAL AGENT STEVEN B. RIGGS sat at the end of Old Ebbitt Grill's mahogany bar and listened to the cheers and heckling over Bowers' takedown. She pretty much ignored it. A beefy guy with a red mustache sidled up next to her. "Bowers, you are my kind of woman." The man waved to the bartender. "Get this lady a drink on me."

Riggs could see Bowers' discomfort with the praise. She hesitated and then accepted the beer. "Thanks, Fred, but the perp was drunk on his ass. My seventy-year-old uncle could've taken him down."

She shrugged off the hoorahs. To others she might seem invincible, but Riggs could see her hands had a residual tremor from the adrenaline. He hadn't realized he was staring until she'd finished off most of her beer and turned toward him.

He blinked and glanced up at one of Teddy Roosevelt's hunting trophies hanging overhead.

As much as he loved this place and the bartenders who knew him on sight, he had no doubt—it was Bowers who kept him coming back. It was neutral ground, where they could relax away from her apartment or his. He raised his bottle of Heineken, took a long draw, and let the icy bite wash down his gullet.

After the assault, he'd returned to the bar with Bowers. She'd conceded victory over his parking prowess and congratulated him with a hug. Her face had brushed against his five o'clock shadow and left him with a thirst no beer could quench.

He popped out of his thoughts and glanced up to find her gazing into empty space. She flashed him a smile, but he knew she had something on her mind by the way the dimple at the corner of her mouth puckered while she toyed with her nearly empty bottle of Negra Modelo.

"Your sarge cut you some slack back there," he said, trying to get her to talk. "Maybe he likes you."

"No. He likes taking credit." Bowers bit at a hangnail. "Don't get me wrong, I greatly appreciate not having to do a booking tonight."

Riggs took another sip of his beer. "But?"

"Mitch can't help sticking his nose into our cases, especially mine. The guy watches me like a hawk and micro-manages the crap out of everything."

Riggs signaled the bartender, who brought her another beer. "Maybe he just wants things done right."

"Maybe." She tapped her bottle to his. "Next time, I'm buying."

He watched her tuck a long strand of brown hair behind one ear and secure it with a bobby pin. Her shirt was scuffed with street grime. Riggs found himself hung up at her fitted trousers. Even for Bowers, the tie-dyed fabric and provocative cut were over the edge.

He pointed to her pants. "I see your taste in clothing hasn't changed. I thought CID wanted their investigators to blend in."

"Most of my clothes are still in boxes. Besides, who's going to suspect I'm a cop in these?" She slapped her thigh. Her athletic legs extended from the edge of the stool all the way to the floor.

He glanced up to see her hazel eyes focused on him.

"This is nice," she said, bumping her knee into his thigh. "So is the beer."

Riggs grunted and rocked in his seat. So many things about Bowers worried him. For one, there was the black hole in her past he knew she wasn't inclined to talk about. For another, he'd been sorely disappointed when she'd ended things between them. He'd had his share of women, including an ex-wife, but Bowers had been the first one who'd ever walked away from him.

He swallowed another sip of beer along with his ego.

She seemed tired. He knew Bowers had moved into a new apartment north of Rock Creek Park and closer to the Metro PD on Georgia. He'd offered to help, but she'd declined.

"How's your new place?" he asked while studying her face. Something had changed.

Kill Notice

She shrugged. "It's fine."

"Then what's eating at you?"

She tapped on her phone and put it on the bar in front of him. "He's back."

The screen showed a close-up image of a fancy gold button embedded with tiny rhinestones.

Riggs sat up straight. "When did you get this?"

"This morning." Bowers showed him another picture. "As you can see, I found it taped to my front door. Obviously, changing my address didn't help. He found me anyway."

"But you've only been there four days." Riggs zoomed in and studied the pictures. "This asshole is stalking you."

FOUR KILLS

BOWERS SAT in the passenger seat of Riggs' silver Subaru as he pulled up in front of her apartment building. She felt both grateful that he'd insisted on giving her a ride home and a little annoyed with herself for needing one.

Through the car's windshield, she watched the nearly empty sidewalk. Moisture in the air had left a halo around the streetlights. Her keys rattled as she pulled them from her pocket.

"Thank you," she said. "For everything."

The expression in his eyes softened. "You're welcome."

The harsh light cast deep shadows on his hardened features. She glanced down at the black console, where her fingers were only an inch from his, and recalled what her uncle had said.

Without saying a word, she stared out at her apartment building. The sky and most of the windows in the complex were dark. Tenants were still coming home after a night on the town.

Even with lights illuminating the walkways, her apartment appeared less than welcoming. Being alone tonight felt about as bleak. She rested her head on the seat back and toyed with the idea of inviting him in.

Kill Notice

"How's your wild-child friend?" he asked as if searching for something to fill the silence.

She knew he'd asked about Berti, her friend who had a habit of trusting the wrong kinds of men. She always seemed to be recovering from the latest heartbreak.

"I don't know. I haven't heard from her in a while." Bowers rocked her head toward Riggs. "I've tried to talk sense into her, but she's not hearing it. It never dawns on her that dangerous men can be handsome."

"You calling me badass, Bowers?"

She laughed. "Don't push it."

"Seriously," said Riggs. "Why do you put up with her?"

"She's a great volleyball partner. And she's not as cynical as me. Guess I'm a sucker for lost puppies." She shrugged. "It's hard to give up on someone you care about."

Their fingers were still only inches apart, but Riggs was focused on something outside his side window as if he hadn't noticed. "That's four buttons," he said. Riggs pulled his hand away and stretched. "The one before this was three days ago?"

Bowers nodded. "He left it on the windshield of my car. Apparently, he hadn't found my new address, yet."

"It's time we track this guy down. Either go to your sarge or I'll open a case at the Bureau and do it myself."

"Riggs, I've tried talking to Mitch, but he won't put resources on it until I can prove the cases are connected. What am I supposed to do here?"

His jaw muscles flexed as he chewed his gum.

"Even Major Crimes doesn't want it," she said. "There's something strange about these murders. Random, but not. I can't explain it." Bowers felt a chill in the small of her back. "This guy is different."

"I don't give a crap what Mitch says." Riggs twisted toward her. "I want to know what you say."

"We've got ourselves a serial killer. One that's highly advanced in his craft."

"We need a task force on him, now." Riggs rapped his thumbs on the steering wheel and slumped back into his seat. "He picked you for a reason. Why?"

"When you arrest people for a living, it doesn't exactly endear you to folks." She paused. "Other than that, I have no clue." They sat in silence and watched an older couple, arm-in-arm, as they passed the car and strolled on down the block with their scruffy, white dog.

She felt the warmth of his touch as Riggs ran a thumb over the back of her hand. "I still care about you."

"I know."

DIRTY BUSINESS

THE DISTRICT OF COLUMBIA, Maryland, and Virginia were known to the locals as the DMV, but to Bobby Black it was the place he called home. The cops and the politicians might own the streets across the Anacostia River, but here on the Southeast side he and his homeboys had it tight.

Bobby hurried toward the Metrobus stop. Along the way, folks enjoying the night air sat outside in their sleeveless shirts, smoking and listening for gunshots to pass the time. He felt their eyes watching him.

In the dark, the streets didn't seem as rough as they did in the light of day, but that didn't mean they were any safer.

Bobby heard footsteps behind him, coming up fast.

His pulse jumped.

Up ahead, the Metrobus pulled in.

The door whooshed open and the interior of the bus lit up like a welcome wagon.

Bobby bolted for the open door.

One step away, he felt a hand land on his shoulder.

He spun around, ready to go one-on-one, but found a familiar face grinning back at him. Bobby knew the guy as a regular on the bus.

"Shit man, don't be doin' that," Bobby said as he shoved the hand away and climbed the steps.

Once inside, the driver, who looked like he'd been eating too much of his mama's fried chicken and grits, frowned at them. "Don't you two be givin' me no trouble," he said in a deep voice.

The door whooshed closed.

Bobby pulled at the hood of his sweatshirt to hide his swollen face and found a spot by the window. The dude who'd grabbed his shoulder took the seat in front of him. He eyed the tattoos and scar on the guy's neck. At almost sixteen, Bobby wondered if he'd look like that in another four or five years.

The man twisted around. "You 202 or 703?"

The district had crews instead of gangs, who were known by their area codes and street names.

"202, Southeast," said Bobby. He knew he lived in one of the more dangerous areas, at least at night.

"Shit, man. That's heavy. I hear there be a crazy dude out killing brothers of the 202."

Bobby felt his puffy cheekbone. "Homeboys is sayin' it's Crips and the Bloods tryin' to move in."

The dude bugged out his eyes and jerked his head toward St. Elizabeth's, a psychiatric hospital they were passing on their left. "Or maybe they let loose some crazy-assed doper who's flat-out savage."

"I dunno, man." Bobby felt uneasy.

Bad luck had always followed the ladies of the streets, but lately dealers had been put down, like the dude called Shank who'd been crammed into a trashcan and lit up.

Things had always been tense when deals got done, but now with a record heat wave and a rise in the killings, folks were on edge. Even the cops were taking hits. One of them had been shot in the face just a few weeks ago.

As their ride moved on, Bobby tried to ignore the smell of sweat and the grit under his shoes. He stared out the window and

Kill Notice

thought it weird how a place with so many churches had so much hate.

A few minutes later, the bus' brakes sighed as it pulled to a stop and dropped him off at his corner.

Tourists never saw this side of D.C., or what went down across the street in the park. Most folks think of parks as grassy places for picnics and kids. There was plenty of grass for sure, but not the kind they were thinking about. Hookers did their business there, too. Bobby couldn't blame anyone for not advertising that.

One of the girls he recognized worked her pose and called out to him. "Hey Bobby, I could teach you a few *thangs*," she said. The ladies wore cheap heels and low-cut tops like they were some kind of uniform.

Bobby ignored her and cut across Malcolm X Avenue to join members of his crew and to avoid some shifty-looking dudes in a parking lot.

He slipped into the shadows next to a liquor store. The red-brick wall to his back felt rough, but solid. While Bobby waited, he watched for signs of trouble. Anyone passing by could be an undercover cop, or something worse.

A short time later, the silhouette of a huge man wearing a knit cap like a crown ambled toward Bobby.

The man entered the sub shop next door. Bobby waited for a few minutes and followed.

Inside, he spotted the big man seated at a table. His dark eyes peered out from under heavy lids and kept a close watch on the door and the action outside the windows.

"Hey," said Bobby, feeling his palms sweat. He stood out of respect and waited for an invitation.

The big man nodded.

Bobby slid into the hard bench seat across the table from Papa G, the boss of the X Crew and the man who controlled this part of their namesake, Malcolm X Avenue.

Papa G's big hand pushed Bobby's head to the side. "Your face looks a mile better than dis mornin'." Papa G hunched closer. "Like I told you, I want you to play it smarter tonight. Ya hear me? Last night didn't turn out too good for you."

An encounter with a man wearing black had left Bobby's face messed up. The whole thing still had him spooked. "What if that dude in black was the 202 Killer?"

Papa G waved his big ole hand in the air as if to dismiss the idea. "Ain't no killer. I told you, outside gangs be tryin' to scare us. Dat's all."

His shoulders tensed as his eyes followed something outside. A moment later, his attention refocused on Bobby. "They go off killin' cuz some dude's shoes is red or blue. That shit's a waste. We ain't doing it like dat. Dis be business." Papa G tapped his finger on the yellow tabletop a couple of times to make his point. "Hear what I'm sayin? We's here to make money. That's it."

Bobby nodded, but he still felt scared.

"You do dis good," said Papa G, "My boys will be watchin'." The big man pushed a sub and six packs of cigarettes in front of Bobby. "Step it up tonight. Call me when you be done."

Bobby waited until Papa G had clasp hands with his cousin behind the counter and left, before picking up the sub and pocketing the cigarettes. He went back to his spot against the brick wall and ate the sub before it went cold.

At the corner, a man with bad teeth and stringy, gray hair tried to talk some locals into buying him a bottle of booze, until someone from the crew chased him off.

Buses and trucks zipping by offered the only breeze.

The bitter smells of exhaust fumes, rancid trash, and the stench of old grease from the restaurant across the intersection hung in the air.

Bobby didn't have to wait long before he saw some action. A short dude with blond dreadlocks came around the corner. "Hey, man. I need a smoke," he said.

The cigarettes in Bobby's pocket had been dipped in PCP, and the guy was a regular.

"Dude, I'm low on cash," said the man. "Can you cut me a break?"

Kill Notice

Bobby hated it when folks pleaded with him. "It's twenty-five. Nothing else I can do," he said to the man, who grunted and slipped him a fifty. Bobby dropped two dippers into the man's hand.

"Yo, dawg," said Bobby. "You need to be gone." He didn't want this dude to light up right there and go off acting crazy. You never knew what PCPers would do. They felt no pain. Sometimes they'd run down the street buck naked, scratch out their own eyeballs, or kill their own kids until someone locked them up.

With his face still throbbing, Bobby was in no mood to mix it up with anybody. Not tonight.

The dude with the dreads pocketed his dippers and moseyed off with an extra bounce in his step.

For the next few hours the exchanges went smoothly. Some customers were so casual about it that they would send texts like they were ordering pizza.

One dude, who must have been new at this, showed up in a ball cap and sunglasses. The fool tripped on the curb. Wearing shades at night was dumb enough, but his heavy coat in this heat really gave it up. Wanting no part of that, Bobby sent him away and told him to come correct next time.

At 1:00 a.m. trouble came in the form of screeching brakes. Two big men jumped out of a decked-out Buick and charged at Bobby. When they were almost upon him, he heard the snap of an opening blade and knew they were after his cash and dope. Bobby held onto his pockets.

One guy flashed his brass knuckles and landed a fist into Bobby's gut. Before he could catch his breath, four members of the X Crew jumped in. They quickly disarmed the two men and added the knife and brass knuckles to their own collection. The crew dragged off Bobby's attackers.

The Buick peeled out and sped away.

As the hours passed, the more nervous Bobby became. He still needed to make one more sale, which meant he would once again be out after the bars closed.

He didn't like drunks. They were a lot more unpredictable. Bobby waited. Watched. And worried as folks went past. Sometimes he felt so alone on that stinking corner and wished he had someone he could talk to about this stuff.

He rubbed his sore belly and thought about yesterday and a dancer known as Sapphire.

Papa G was right. Last night hadn't turned out so well for Bobby. It had been slow, like tonight. He'd worked the same corner, around the same time.

The bars had already closed when he'd spotted Sapphire coming up the street. Man, she turned heads. In this hood, where drunks slept in doorways, Bobby thought she stood out, like one of those stars on TV.

He often saw her walking alone toward the park on her way home after work. Sapphire always wore flashy dresses and fancy shoes. Do times two, they called it. This time she looked fine in a dark blue number that shimmered in the streetlights. A long pearl necklace swayed in rhythm with her hips. As any sixteen-year-old would, he took notice of the cleavage on display.

Bobby wasn't sure what to make of that, or of her. Most guys, when they found out that she was transgender, would either beat her up or make fun of her.

Her deal wasn't his, but he'd seen her call a cab for a friend who'd been in a bad way. Bobby let it be. He figured her doings were none of his business.

Sapphire strolled up, dazzling like a shiny page from one those fashion magazines that ladies read.

"Hey, Bobby. Slow night, huh?" she said, pulling out some bills. Her voice sounded deep and smooth. The exchange happened quickly. Before leaving, she handed him an extra ten bucks. "Sorry. It's all I can spare tonight," she said.

"Yes, ma'am." That surprised Bobby. Tipping didn't happen in this business. "Thank you."

Sapphire went off down the street toward her place. A moment later, a man dressed in black stepped out of the shadows and followed her toward the park.

Kill Notice

"Hey," yelled Bobby.

The man-in-black stopped. His back stiffened.

Sapphire waved at Bobby, and shot him a smile. He held up his hand, not sure what to do. No one from his crew was in sight. They wouldn't help her anyway, and he'd get a ration of shit for asking.

Bobby watched the man-in-black take Sapphire's arm. At first she laughed in that deep, warm, and infectious way. Bobby figured the man must be a friend, or maybe she liked picking up extra business on the side.

He watched the pair standing near a streetlight.

Bobby wasn't worried until he glanced back and saw she wasn't laughing anymore.

Sapphire pulled her arm away.

Without thinking, Bobby ran toward them. In the last few seconds his speed accelerated into a sprint as he narrowed in on the man-in-black.

He was two steps away when the tall man did an about-face.

Bobby would never forget the black glove coming at him or the stunning impact of that fist against his jaw.

NAKED

A SIREN OUTSIDE startled Bowers awake.

The bed felt like hers, and yet each time a car drove by its headlights sent a streak of yellow across the dark wall. This living on the ground floor would take some getting used to.

She rubbed her face. No doubt the hammering inside her skull came from last night's beer. She'd needed the break, and appreciated the way Riggs had driven her home as if it were no big deal.

Loud snoring from the other room broke the silence and brought her crashing back to reality.

Coming home to find the bartender she'd been seeing passed out on her couch had pissed her off. Judging by the volume of empty beer cans scattered about, Eric had been too toasted to drive home. Bowers ended up leaving him on the couch in her living room and locking her bedroom door.

Allowing him to help her move had been a bad idea. Obviously, he'd kept a key and had a few presumptions she would soon set straight.

Bowers glanced at the time on her phone. First light wouldn't come for another hour.

She yawned and slipped out from under the sheet and stood

naked in the breeze from an overhead fan. Goosebumps rose on her skin as she glided her fingers over her ribs and the hard scar on her left side. She winced, and went to the open packing boxes by her closet.

After slipping into a sports bra and a silky pair of spandex undershorts, she unlocked her bedroom door and wandered down the hall and into the kitchen.

In the fridge she found a cold bottle of water.

Bowers leaned against the breakfast bar and scanned the open room that included her kitchen and living room. The large space made an otherwise small unit seem bigger and gave it an airy feel. It all seemed right, except Eric's invasion of her couch.

She took a seat across from him on the soft cushions of her recliner and considered cuffing her uninvited guest, but with her luck he'd probably enjoy it.

After several swallows of water, she pressed the cold bottle to the side of her face. A few drops of condensation dribbled down her neck, over her collarbone, and disappeared into the deep groove between her breasts.

In the dim light, she watched Eric sleeping.

Another snore rattled in the air. It bothered her that he'd invaded her home without asking.

Stripped down to his boxers, Eric lay on his back with his legs splayed. One hung limply off the couch with his foot on the floor. His arms were flopped at odd angles, and his mouth gaped wide open.

"That's attractive."

A greasy pizza box lay empty and open on the carpet next to three spent cans of Bud Lite. Two more empty cans had been left on her glass coffee table.

Surrounded by stacks of U-Haul boxes, she sat in the darkness and thought about the killer who'd left the button on her door. Riggs hadn't needed to tell her the dangers of being stalked. Feeling displaced in her own apartment only made it worse.

"What am I doing here?" she whispered.

Bowers finished the water, picked up Eric's pizza box and left it on the counter, and went to take a quick shower.

Flipping on the light in the bathroom, she discovered his muddy boots in the bathtub and his jeans hanging over the shower rod. On the floor lay her new, white towels, which looked as if they'd been used to clean his dirt bike.

She moaned. "Are you kidding me?"

At first Eric had seemed outgoing and witty, but lately he'd acted more like a frat boy who expected her to come running every time he wanted to party.

She brushed her teeth and went to her closet, where she slipped on a shirt and a pair of black-and-red pants that matched her mood. She also wore a black vest that would conceal her pistol and handcuffs.

A few moments later, Bowers heard footsteps in the hall. Her back tensed when Eric walked up behind her and wrapped his arms around her waist. With last night's assault still fresh in her mind, she held in check the impulse to deck him, but barely.

"Come to bed." He pushed his hips into her. "Then you can fix me breakfast. Later, we can go kayaking."

She removed his hands. "Stop, I have to be at work in an hour." Bowers slipped on her belt, checked her Glock, and slid it into her hip holster. She tried to skirt around him, but he blocked her path. She shot him a warning look.

"Eric what are you doing here?"

He sported a provocative grin and tried to unbutton her top.

She pushed his hand away. "I've got to go." She snapped her badge onto her belt. "And I need my key back."

"You know you want it," he said, pumping his biceps and swiveling his hips. Obviously, he hadn't heard a word she'd said.

"Cute." She held out her hand. "My key?"

He tried to grab her. Big mistake.

With a swift kick she buckled his knee and snapped his arm behind his back.

"What the hell?" he yelped.

Kill Notice

"You aren't listening," she said as she leaned close and spoke into his ear, "so let me make this clear. You are out of here." She let go of his wrist. "Hand over my key. Now."

Eric rose to his feet and stormed into the bathroom. Seconds later, he returned with his mud-caked boots, which he dropped on the carpet. With his jeans in both hands, he shook them out and jammed one leg in and then the other.

When he glared at her, she held out her hand for the key. "Next time ask before coming over."

With an expression as cold as a headstone, he zipped up his fly and stormed toward the living room with his boots and shirt in hand. He tossed her key over his shoulder. It landed on the floor of the hallway with a plink.

A second later, Eric was gone. Her front door gaped wide open.

THE PORCH-LIGHT SHOWN like a tiny beacon under the night sky when the Escalade dropped Bobby off on the sidewalk in front of his place. He stood on the sagging porch and quietly unlocked the front door. Much of its brown paint had peeled off a long time ago.

He slipped inside and found his grandmother snoring softly in her old recliner. In the muted light, he studied her dark profile framed in tiny gray curls. It was the one face he'd known all of his life.

A twinge of guilt made him step back. Things were messed up no matter what he did. He'd told her the money he earned came from helping out at a warehouse where the local boxing club held their matches. He didn't like lying, but telling the truth about where he went at night would have torn them both up.

After draping a quilt over her shoulders, he went down the hall and found his fourteen-year-old brother, Tommy, asleep in the bedroom they shared. Everything seemed perfectly in place and all wrong at the same time.

Bobby went outside and sat on a broken, plastic chair that

wobbled. He liked the quiet before dawn. Workers weren't up yet. The hookers and dopers and drunks had all wandered away to sleep it off. It seemed peaceful, as if the whole world had called some kind of truce.

The cash in his pocket should've made him feel better, but it didn't. It had trouble written all over it.

He glanced at their ragged porch and the pot of daisies his grandma fussed with each day. Bobby picked at a rough callus on his thumb and stared at the sad, little yard within the rusted, chain-link fence and busted gate. He skipped down the steps and pulled at a few of the weeds, as if that would help, and tried to swallow the lump in his throat.

His eyes burned. It bothered him that his grandma insisted on sleeping in her recliner so he and his brother could have her room.

Soon even that would be gone.

Like all the other cracker-box units on his street, their home would soon be torn down to make way for nicer houses that folks like him and his grandma couldn't afford. It was called gentrification. A nice word for kicking poor folks out. Ever since they'd gotten the notice, Bobby had worried about where they would go.

He watched as a skinny dog wandered up the block. The pup stopped to paw at an overturned garbage can and sniff at the debris in the road.

Bobby figured he could survive on the streets, but it wasn't the life he wanted for his little brother, and he had no idea what would happen to his grandma or her pot of daisies.

The sky had started to brighten, but all Bobby could see were the dark things that haunted him.

After the man in black had laid him out, Bobby remembered waking up at Papa G's place, which meant he'd overslept and missed school, again.

Papa G had given him a can of ginger ale to settle his stomach, and told him how the man in black had left with that dancer when the crew had moved in. Papa G had also given Bobby twice as much cash as his usual cut, and a pistol.

Kill Notice

"You'll repay me," Papa G had said.

Bobby had a sick feeling about what that might mean.

He also worried about how to take care of his family. Each month his grandma's Social Security check only paid for some of their expenses. Grandma hated to say no to his little brother. She'd eat cereal for a week just so he could have a pair of cleats for track.

Bobby knew the cash in his pocket would cover rent and help them get by for another few weeks, but not much else. He told himself that if it weren't for his brother and his grandma, he'd return the cash and the gun and go somewhere else. Just walk away.

He didn't want to stand on that corner anymore, but for his family he would do what he could to take care of business, and avoid being beaten up again. Maybe.

Wondering about what had happened to Sapphire had stuck in Bobby's mind. He'd seen the man in black's face, which meant the guy had seen him, too.

Bobby gently touched his tender cheekbone. The man must have been a boxer, or something like it. The strength of the blow and the hardness of those knuckles still had Bobby rocked.

He heard the squeal of brakes and watched as a car swerved. The stray dog bolted from the street and scampered through their open gate.

The little mix-breed sat on their walkway staring at Bobby. He stared back and wondered what he'd gotten himself into.

MAN ENOUGH

B OWERS BOLTED through the Metro PD's first floor on the way to the elevator. Up ahead an officer in the hallway stood at attention before the End of Watch Wall where the pictures of fallen officers were mounted in neat rows.

She stopped out of respect and waited as the officer slowly drew his hand into a salute. The man's jaw clenched. Knowing she'd stumbled upon a highly personal moment, Bowers stood aside.

The newest frame on the wall held the portrait of Detective Paul Green, who'd died in the line of duty a few weeks ago. She'd been to the funeral and recognized the officer saluting Paul's picture as his younger brother.

When the young Officer Green passed by Bowers, she called to him. "Officer, hold up," she said. A black mourning ribbon stretched across his badge. "Your brother was a good man. I'm honored to have served with him." Bowers shook his hand. "He was proud of you. Spoke of you all the time."

Officer Green's eyes turned red and watery. He squeezed her hand and walked on down the hall while clearing his throat and shaking his head.

40

Kill Notice

Twenty minutes later Bowers dodged a few detectives and took a seat in the back of the briefing room. She scanned the faces hoping to find Mitch, but he wasn't there.

The clatter of chairs sliding over the polished floor and the usual banter seemed subdued this morning.

Norman Clawski marched in, wearing a rumpled, yellow shirt that didn't seem to want to stay tucked in. He eyed up the empty chair next to her and took a seat across the room.

She'd made Detective Grade 2. Clawski hadn't passed the test and was apparently still sore about it. Bowers ignored him and continued to think about why the killer had chosen to announce his kills to her.

She glanced up at the detectives gathered in middle of the room. Several of them were watching her. Heckling her about her pants had become routine.

"Hey, Bowers," said a detective who sat on the corner of a long table. "I hear the guy outside of Ebbitt's was sweet on you."

More heads turned. Now they all stared.

Bowers fired back. "What's the matter, Doug, you jealous?" Laughter rippled across the room.

Mike, a detective ten years her senior, came toward her wearing a frown. "I heard about the button on your door. Are you okay?"

She shook his hand. "Thanks. I'm still here."

"Morning," said her baby-faced partner, Johnny Torres, as he reached around Mike and handed Bowers a cup of coffee.

When she recognized the fancy logo on the tall paper cup, she wondered why Johnny had gone out of his way to stop at an expensive coffee shop. She also noticed his new pair of shoes, which were mostly black with thin, neon-green stripes and thick soles.

"*Gracias, mi amigo,*" she said, holding up the coffee. She'd started to say *shukraan*, but she rarely ever spoke Arabic anymore, and Johnny wouldn't have had any clue what she'd said anyway.

Clawski sauntered over and circled Johnny while looking askance at his new footwear. "Hey, Guacamole," said Clawski. "Wearin' that shit in taco town might work, but it don't cut it here. *Comprende*?"

"Good God, Clawski," said Bowers. "Shut up."

Johnny's face tightened. "The name is Torres, Johnny Torres. Go look in the mirror, man. The back of your head looks like a crop circle. Before you start giving out advice on style, maybe you ought to learn how to use a comb."

Clawski's neck stiffened as he stormed away.

Bowers quietly chuckled and took a cautious sip of her coffee. "I think you pissed him off."

"What a shame," said Johnny. "The guy needs to mind his own business and learn some manners."

At first she hadn't been thrilled with the idea of tuning up a new detective, especially one this young. And yet, she couldn't help liking Johnny even though keeping him out of trouble had led to a few tense moments. No doubt the offering of coffee came as an apology for the pissing contest he'd gotten himself into yesterday with a patrol officer.

Johnny was engrossed in a conversation with Detective Karen Reeves when Sergeant Mitchell strode through the door and slapped his legal pad down on a long table up front. He popped open his Coke. The noise level in the room dampened.

At six-two, his big shoulders and shaved head made for a commanding presence. He adjusted the cuffs of his black, long-sleeved shirt and scanned the room with a bright smile that made the skin at the outer corners of his dark eyes crinkle.

Everyone took a seat except Johnny. Bowers grasped the tail of his jacket and yanked him down into the chair next to her. "Shhh," she whispered.

Johnny continued yapping.

"Torres!" Mitch's commanding voice silenced everyone, including Johnny who ducked his head. When all eyes were on her boss, his grin indicated he'd enjoyed Johnny's reaction.

Bowers relaxed back into her seat and watched Mitch's dynamic energy light up the room. She had to admit the guy had the looks of a

Hollywood actor. Apparently, she wasn't the only one who held that opinion. Despite Mitch's wedding ring, a disproportionate number of female detectives had gathered at the front of the room.

As soon as this was over Bowers planned on telling him about the latest button.

Mitch clapped his hands. "Listen up, folks. Our murder rate has skyrocketed in the last six months. Murder runs are coming in faster than we can close them."

Stand by, you're about to get another one.

Mitch pumped his fist like a football coach and gave a rousing update on current cases. Bowers shifted in her seat. Inside she felt like a runner anxious to get off the starting blocks.

When the meeting had come to an end, Bowers stood as Police Chief Dan Bowman barreled into the room. Behind him came a wave of people, some of whom were from the Metro PD. He gestured for everyone to remain seated.

Bowers dropped back into her seat.

The chief's tightly cropped, silver hair and tan, square face fit the mold of a man in charge. He stepped up to the wooden podium, with its Metro PD's blue-and-gold emblem proudly mounted on the front, and nodded to a man with a camera.

Bowers hoped this would be quick.

"We have guests with us," he said, "from The Washington Post. I expect y'all to tone it down and behave yourselves," he said with subtle smile.

As several detectives chuckled, she glanced at Mitch and realized he'd been watching her. She listened as the chief left the podium and strolled along the front row where he made eye contact with each person.

"Detective Green's sacrifice," he said, "reminds us of the risks we all take to protect the people of D.C. This community thanks you."

The chief stood for a moment of silence and then raised his head and gestured toward Sergeant Mitchell whose smile broadened as he stood.

"I only have one more announcement," the chief said.

Thank God.

"We'll have a ceremony at the end of the month to present your sergeant with the Homicide Detective of the Year Award. I'd like y'all to come out and show your support."

Applause rose when Mitch shook the chief's hand and flashed his white teeth for the cameras.

Detectives swarmed around Mitch as if he were a celebrity. Watching him lapping up the glory didn't bother her. She didn't care for the limelight. The only thing on her mind was getting the green light to go after the man who'd left the button on her door. Maybe the arrival of the latest button might sway Mitch to investing resources.

She made her way to the front of the room, where her boss posed for pictures and talked with the chief. When Bowers stepped forward, Chief Bowman warmly greeted her with a vigorous, two-handed shake.

As soon as Mitch returned from speaking with a reporter, she caught his attention. "Sarge, I received another—"

Clawski cut her off and inserted himself into the conversation. "Anchorman Marc Davis just did his *Crime in the City* segment. The dipshit told all of America that we have a serial killer running loose on the streets of D.C."

Bowers wanted to smack him. "Clawski, hold on." The guy wasn't helping her cause.

Mitch stared at the floor with his arms folded. "I've heard they're calling him the 202 Killer."

Clawski wedged himself in front of her, with the back of his head in her face. Bowers peered at the man's fair skin and rust-colored hair and smiled. She remembered a guy with similar features at the academy, who'd given her a hard time until she'd put three rounds from a .308 sniper rifle in a quarter-sized target at two hundred meters. She bumped into his back and forced Clawski to take a step forward.

"Sarge," said Clawski, "this is bullshit. We gotta shut this rumor down. If we don't, we'll be dogging down dead-end leads all day long. We don't have time for this shit."

Kill Notice

While Mitch backed away to speak with a lieutenant, Clawski faced Bowers and hiked up the waist of his trousers.

"Listen, sweet-cheeks," he said, "how about you go sit down and let the big boys handle this one?"

Bowers took a long, steady gaze into his squinty little eyes. "What's the matter, Clawski? Aren't you man enough to go after a serial?"

Mitch returned to the conversation.

"Sarge," said Clawski, "it's not the same guy. It can't—"

"Hold on," Mitch said. "Let's hear what Bowers has to say."

Bowers ignored the flush of red on Clawski's neck. "I'm certain that at least four of our cases are connected, but I need resources to prove it."

Clawski grunted. "This is bull crap."

The detective who'd come to her apartment yesterday joined them. "No it isn't. We've got a problem here, sir," he said. "The killer left another button on her door."

Clawski's hands flew up. "What the hell are you yammering about?"

Mitch's eyes took on a sharp intensity. "When?"

"Yesterday morning," she said. Bowers stepped out of the way as the chief and his entourage filed by. "If the pattern holds, another body should turn up any minute."

Her boss cocked his head. "I thought you'd moved."

"I did," said Bowers. "But obviously that didn't stop him."

Mitch stared past her. His phone buzzed and he stepped away to take the call. After a few seconds he nodded, and went into action. He dropped the phone into a pocket and urgently waved Bowers closer. "You were right. We've got another body."

Clawski raised a hand. "I'll take it." He started waving at his partner.

"No so fast," Mitch said. "If Bowers is so sure there's a connection, she deserves a shot at proving it."

Clawski shouldered past Johnny and tromped away.

"Get on it, Bowers," said Mitch. "You're lead. Go."

Bowers signaled Johnny and started to leave, but Mitch's hand on her shoulder stopped her. "One more thing." He lowered his voice. "I know you have a friend in the FBI. Just remember all murders in the district are ours."

WRATH OF MAGRATH

BOWERS SLID INTO the silver, unmarked Chevy Tahoe assigned to her by the Metro PD and fired up the engine. As she waited for Johnny, she scanned the black interior of the cab, powered up the laptop, and tested the sirens and lights.

She would have preferred a dark exterior, but a big, black SUV would've made it hard to do surveillance without being spotted.

She and another detective had scored a Tahoe. The selection process had been luck of the draw to see who'd test the two new units. Even so, it was another burr under Clawski's already cantankerous hide.

Thirty feet away, the station door flew open. She watched Clawski hurry toward his personal vehicle, a black pickup. There he snagged his gear and tossed it into an unmarked tan sedan.

Johnny tapped on the back of the Tahoe and hopped in the passenger seat. Within seconds they rolled out of the PD's masonry walled, parking enclosure with Clawski not far behind.

"Can you believe that guy?" said Johnny. "It's like he doesn't want cases solved." Her partner stared at the side mirror. "Why is he so down on you?"

Bowers chuckled. "If a guy like Clawski starts liking you, run."

She banged a left onto Georgia Ave. "Last year, they accused him of evidence tampering. Internal did an investigation, but deemed his screw-up to be poor judgment instead of willful disregard. They put him through more training, but he still barrels in without thinking."

Johnny tugged at his seatbelt. "The guy's a pig."

Bowers kept an eye on traffic. "Sometimes he does okay. Other times he is about as useful as a back pocket on a T-shirt. We lost a case because he decided a death was a suicide not worth investigating. By the time the coroner ruled it a homicide, any evidence was gone or so contaminated it was worthless."

"Why isn't the sarge all over his shit?"

"Let it go," said Bowers. "We don't work for Clawski, or the sarge. We work for the victims and the people of our community. Trust me. That's the only thing that makes this job worthwhile."

Johnny fiddled with his wedding ring.

"You nervous?" She could see it written all over him. The rising body count hadn't set well with anyone.

Johnny exhaled loudly. "I couldn't sleep last night. I kept thinkin' about that guy in the trashcan. And the smell. I'm not eatin' BBQ ever again." He straightened in his seat. "Even the crews don't go that far. Who'd do something like that?"

She passed a Metrobus and raced down Georgia Avenue. "It takes a psychopath or extreme rage."

"I know," he said. "I just don't understand *why*."

"They're not wired like you and me."

At a light she glanced at Johnny, who stared at a slick black limo dashing through the intersection with a motorcycle escort.

The light turned green. Bowers hit the gas. "So, when we get to the scene, just focus on the facts. Our top CSI, Jackie Magrath, will be there. She'll kick your ass if you do what Clawski does."

Johnny popped a piece of gum in his mouth. "Is the wrath of Magrath as bad as I've heard?"

"Only if you screw up." Bowers nudged him and kept her eyes on the road.

Kill Notice

He rubbed both palms on his black trousers and blew out a long, slow breath.

"Remember," she said. "Magrath is a New Yorker. She calls it as she sees it. Don't let her intimidate you, she's got a heart of gold and is as honest as they come."

"How do you do it?" asked Johnny.

"Do what?" Bowers zipped past a liquor store that had street art painted on the exterior.

Johnny shrugged. "I wanted to punch Clawski's lights out. You stayed cool. How'd you do it?"

"People are like bombs. The bad ones go off prematurely and self-destruct. The trick is staying out of their path and not ending up as collateral damage."

He laughed. "Bowers, you crack me up."

"Look, I've come close to busting his chops, too. Just do your job. Don't worry about him."

"But how do you put aside his crap and station politics and stay so focused?"

She thought about his question for a few seconds. "While in the army, I talked a fellow soldier and EOD into teaching me a great deal about explosive ordinance disposal. A week later, that knowledge saved me and several guys in my unit. You learn real quick to control your emotions and stay on task."

"That's spooky," said Johnny. "I can't blame you for leaving that shit behind."

She could feel him watching her. "My unit wasn't thrilled with having a female on board, especially one who wanted to do EOD and have sniper skills. They wanted to keep it all balls. I decided I could do more good as a cop."

They rode for a few seconds in silence.

What she'd told him was partly true, but telling Johnny the rest of that story wouldn't happen, ever.

Bowers winced. She hadn't realized that she had been rubbing her side until she felt the twinge of pain under her scar. Images of smoke and muzzle flashes seeped into her thoughts, along with the smell of dust. She hated dust.

She kept an eye on a group of people on the corner who were waving signs. Now was not the time to dredge up the real reason she'd left.

"Weren't you scared?"

Bowers blinked. It took her a second to realize he'd asked about the risks of getting up-close and personal with IEDs that were fully capable of blowing your head off and liquefying your insides.

"Always. In a situation like that, anyone who isn't aware of the danger is either lying or stupid. That's not the kind of person I'd trust to have my back." She glimpsed at Johnny. He'd stopped twisting his ring.

"Listen," she said. "You're a solid detective. When we get to the crime scene, just slow down. It's not like the victim is gonna get any deader. Take your time. Focus on what you see. Think through each detail. You'll do fine."

Over the next few minutes they rode without talking. The only sounds were the radio squawk and the thunderous vibrations of rap coming from a nearby purple low-rider with its side mirror held together with duct tape.

Twenty minutes later, they approached the murder scene. Strobes from emergency vehicles lit up the red-brick church like opening night at FedEx Field.

Her phone buzzed with a call from Jackie Magrath. "Come to the small lot and look for my van. We need to talk."

BOWERS PASSED the big lot at the front of the church. When she turned the corner, she spotted the CSI van.

It seemed as if a carnival had been set up on the street. Marked units, two fire trucks, an ambulance, and press vehicles cluttered the road. Reporters pointed their cameras at Bowers as she pulled to a stop.

Kill Notice

"Will you look at this shit," said Johnny.

"Welcome to the rodeo," she said.

The entrance to the parking lot had been blocked by one of the press vans. Bowers hopped out of her unit.

"Take the wheel," she said to Johnny.

She approached WJDC's vehicle and banged on the hood. The driver rolled down the window. Bowers recognized him as Alex Keller, a reporter who'd pulled this stunt before.

"I'm with the press," he said. "I'm on a public street and—"

"Come on, Alex, we've been through this," said Bowers as she waved over a patrol officer. "Get him outta here."

"Sir," said the officer, "you need to move your van so it's not blocking the entrance. I suggest you park in the main lot at the front of the building."

Bowers turned to leave, but Alex's complaints grew louder and more persistent. "I have a right to..."

This guy is not getting the message. Bowers returned to the van's open window, and stood inches from the reporter's face. "You have the right to report on any goddamn thing you want. You do *not* have the right to block our access to a crime scene. Move this vehicle *now,* or you can explain to your boss how you were responsible for getting your van towed, and missing your deadline because you got yourself charged with impeding an investigation."

One corner of the officer's mouth curled into a grin.

Alex blinked and kept his mouth shut.

After he reluctantly rolled away, Johnny pulled in and parked next to the CSI van and got out. Bowers shoved her hands into her pockets and took a moment to scan the throng of spectators and give her temper a few seconds to simmer down. The D.A.'s presence meant a warrant to search the property had already been executed. That was prompt.

"What are you doin'?" Johnny asked.

"Focusing. You know the saying—you only get one shot at a crime scene. Let's make sure we don't screw this up."

The press and bystanders stayed on the sidewalk, a hundred feet from the scene. Ten feet beyond the lot were two rows of yellow crime-scene tape, indicating that the area had been roped off—twice. That had likely come from Magrath stepping in and widening the perimeter. It wouldn't be the first time.

"Let's go." Bowers nudged Johnny. "Follow my lead."

They ducked under the yellow tape.

RIPPED

L IKE ALL COPS, Bowers had seen more than her share of violence. And yet, seeing the worst day of a person's life captured in rigor mortis still seemed like the ultimate train derailment in stop action. Watching a tech with a clipboard standing next to that always seemed surreal to Bowers.

Before being distracted by the body, she viewed the entire scene, which covered an area approximately eighty feet by sixty feet in size. The church's red-brick exterior trimmed in white appeared crisp and clean in the morning sun. Three brightly-colored, stained-glass windows on the side of the building drew the eye up toward the steeple and the clear blue sky above. To the right were five concrete steps and a wrought-iron handrail leading up to an open door near the back.

Bowers spotted a pair of panties.

They had been draped over a small, ironwork angel at the edge of the neatly tended flowerbed. The hair went up on her arms.

She'd found a similar display at the scene of the trashcan man's body and several others. That signature was one of the few consistent things about these cases.

Moments later, she heard Jackie Magrath's New York accent. Her purple gloves and fiery auburn hair made her easy to spot as she vigorously dressed down a young officer. While a photographer videoed the grounds around her, Magrath punctuated everything she said with hand gestures. Today they were both going.

"Officer," she hollered, "what part of 'show up, call it in, and don't touch' don't you get? Ya killed my scene." She pointed to the parking lot. "Get outta heah."

The officer hustled away with his jaw set and his ears burning bright red.

Magrath glanced up at Bowers. "EMTs tromped all over any footprints we might have had. I got a newsflash for them: a decapitated vic don't have no pulse—*give it up*."

Magrath seemed even more animated than usual. "And then there's the pastor who thought it would be a great idea to put a tablecloth over the body so's nobody gets embarrassed, and that greenhorn allowed it. Are you kidding me? Now cookie crumbs from their last bake sale, or whatever the hell was on it, is dusted all over my vic. I hate rookies."

Magrath eyed up Johnny. "Who's he?"

"My partner," said Bowers. "Johnny Torres meet Jackie Magrath."

Magrath handed them both booties. "Keep a leash on him, I've had enough evidence destroyed for one day."

After they put on booties and gloves, Magrath led them into the primary scene, cordoned off with red tape. The body lay in the flowerbed with her back sloughed against the brick exterior, about twelve feet from steps leading to a side door.

If there were such a thing as a typical murder, this wasn't it. This one had an unnerving edge to it. There were no signs of greed or passion that had run out of control. Just the opposite. Like the other cases, it appeared that every detail had been controlled without any emotion.

The amount of swelling indicated the victim had been alive when much of the damage had been inflicted. Maybe it was the brutality or the way he'd kept the victim alive to suffer, but what she saw reminded Bowers of the man in the trashcan.

Kill Notice

The right side of the victim's skull bore severe blunt force injuries. The hands were contorted by multiple fractures and defensive wounds. Bowers had no doubts that the victim had fought hard for her life.

"Shit." Johnny gagged and looked away.

"It's a freakin' bizarre one, huh?" asked Magrath.

Bowers studied the remains. "That's an understatement. What the hell happened here?"

At first glance, the victim appeared to be an attractive black woman who'd been nearly decapitated. A pearl necklace had been wrapped around her neck so tightly that much of it was embedded in the wound.

Strange, gelatinous material protruded from her mouth. A maroon wig lay in the flowerbed next to her. The neckline of her dress had been torn open, revealing large breasts, one of which had been dissected. These were the moments when Bowers wished real murder scenes were as neat and odorless as the ones on TV.

Magrath ran through her findings. "This individual appears to be around thirty-five years of age. Much of the rigor mortis has already resolved."

Bowers calculated the effects of the current heat wave. "So, she's been dead for about twenty–four hours?"

Magrath nodded. "Probably closer to thirty. Coroner might be able to tell us more. Cause of death obviously could have been the wound to her throat, but I can't rule out the head wounds or suffocation."

Johnny frowned and stared at the body. "What in God's name am I looking at?"

Magrath flashed him a stern look. "This, detective, is a transgender person who died before finishing the last portion of her gender reassignment surgery. As you can see, her skirt has been ripped open to display the remaining portion of male genitalia that hadn't been altered yet. They use a technique called a penile inversion—"

"That's enough," said Johnny as he held up his hand and bent forward slightly. "That's sounds excruciating." He made the sign of the cross and grimaced.

Magrath glared at him. "You have a problem, Torres?"

He scowled at her. "Yes, ma'am, I do. No matter what her sexual identity was, I can't believe that some asshole thinks he has license to torture and take the life of another human being because she's, what? Different than him? Yeah, I got a big problem with that. No one should die like *that*!"

Magrath studied Johnny's face. "You're okay, kid. I like you."

Bowers enjoyed seeing Johnny all fired up and taking a stand for the victim, instead of stewing about Clawski.

They stood a yard from the corpse's feet on a tarp that gave them access to the body without disrupting trace evidence. Bowers nodded at the deceased. "It looks like the perp was trying to humiliate her by exposing her."

As the sun rose higher the smells and flies grew worse in the increasing air temperatures.

Bowers knelt on the tarp for a closer inspection. Part of her wished she hadn't. The musky odor of hot iron hung heavy in the air. She hated the smell of blood. She studied the victim. Considering the injuries, there should have been more blood.

"She was killed somewhere else," she said.

The woman's outfit had once been a showpiece of the type worn by performers. Now it lay as rent and ruined as the victim herself. Bowers caught Magrath's attention and pointed out a few tiny seeds and debris stuck to the back of a sleeve and the skirt.

"She's barefoot. Did you find the shoes?"

"Nope," said Magrath as she did a visual inspection of the area around the victim's feet.

Bowers leaned in close. "What did you want to talk with me about?"

Magrath lowered her voice to a whisper. "You saw the panties, right?"

Bowers nodded. "Remember how we found the trashcan man's

underwear on display too? This has to be the work of the same guy. We need to keep this quiet so it isn't leaked to the press. Okay?"

Magrath scowled over the top of her safety glasses. "Seriously? When have you ever seen me this quiet? Never." Magrath grunted and returned to her work. "As soon as the photographer finishes up, I'll bag the underwear myself and get it outta heah."

"Thanks," said Bowers. She found Magrath's honesty a refreshing change from the politics of Washington.

The scene was still at the look-don't-touch stage of the investigation. After everything had been captured on film, documented, and measured, the evidence would be bagged, boxed, and carefully removed. Then Magrath would personally escort it all the way to the lab and the evidence vault, and insure that it was properly logged-in.

Magrath moved to the left along the vic's side. "Ain't this a surprise, she's missing some buttons."

Bowers frowned. "Where?"

"Check it out. Looks like they were cut off."

Bowers studied the row of tiny, pearl buttons and the space where many of them were missing. "Wrong type," she said. "The one taped to my door was gold, but it's possible this guy took more than what's on this dress."

"When you find him, honey," said Magrath, "I'll bet you'll see he has a whole collection."

"Excuse me," said Johnny as he bent close. "We've got company."

Before either of them could intervene, Clawski tromped into the flowerbed and leaned over the victim. He pointed at the body. "Well, look at this. DRT. Dead right there. Looks like another perv is outta commission."

"What the hell are you doing?" yelled Magrath.

"I'm just lookin' to see what killed—"

"Clawski!" Bowers stood and barked at the man. "Get back on the tarps."

Clawski threw up his hands. "I didn't even touch nothing." He backed up and knocked over the ironwork sculpture. The panties fell into the mud, and he stepped on them.

It was one of the few times Bowers had seen Magrath speechless. The silence didn't last long. "Clawski!" Magrath threw up her arms. "You did go to the academy, right?"

He poked his fingers into a pocket. "Don't get your drawers in a knot." He grimaced and reached for the panties with his pen.

"Don't touch that," said Bowers, bolting toward him.

Clawski didn't listen. Bowers grabbed his wrist and slapped his hand against his chest. After pulling the pen out of his fist, she stuck it into his shirt pocket.

"When I say don't touch," she said. "I mean *don't touch*. Got it?"

Clawski's eyes narrowed. His lips pressed into a slit. After peering down at the ink mark on his yellow shirt, he cocked his head and smacked his gum. "Watch your ass, split tail."

"You're done here." Bowers pointed to the parking lot. "Leave. Now."

"What's going on?" asked Mitch.

Bowers flinched. She hated his habit of sneaking up on people. "If Clawski can't restrain himself from destroying evidence, he shouldn't be here."

Mitch wearily waved Clawski closer. "Come on. You heard Bowers. You're done for the day. I want you in my office, tomorrow morning at six. We clear?"

Clawski glared at Magrath as he went by. "Trash collector," he said.

"Button it!" Mitch said as he escorted the detective away. A few minutes later the sarge returned. He stood on the access tarps with his arms folded. "Sorry," he said to Magrath.

Bowers smiled to herself as Magrath wagged her finger at him. "How do you expect me to secure evidence that will hold up in court with that bozo trampling all over everything?"

Mitch snapped on a pair of gloves. "I'll talk to him. In the meantime, do your best. We both know no one is better at this than you."

Magrath grumbled to herself as she went to retrieve the panties.

Mitch carefully stepped closer and stood next to Bowers. "I don't blame you for being upset with Clawski." He leaned in closer. "But

Kill Notice

next time, how about you try not to get into a brawl with your colleagues in public."

She stared straight ahead. "Next time, how about Clawski stops destroying evidence?"

Mitch shrugged. His eyes were on the victim.

"If Clawski gives me anymore lip," said Bowers, "I promise he'll regret it."

Her boss rocked forward slightly and smiled. "Can I watch?"

Bowers chuckled.

"So what have we here?" Mitch asked.

"As you can see," she said, "there's a lot of overkill. Her artificial nails have been ripped off. There's no doubt he tortured her."

Magrath returned. "Your perp posed every detail like a window display on Madison Ave."

Mitch surveyed the corpse closely. After a few moments he spoke. "The unsub saw the subject as a fake."

He knelt and pointed to a strip of false lashes that had fallen to her cheek near a small scar. "Fake eyelashes, fake nails, fake hair." He pointed to her mouth with a gloved hand. "That's a breast implant from the fake boobs."

Mitch leaned his head to the side and examined the neck injury. "Fake pearls." He stood. "Subject appears to be female, but clearly has male anatomy. He saw this individual as a fraud."

Bowers watched him closely. "So, you're saying that the perp killed her because of the way she dressed?"

"No." Mitch wagged his finger in the air. "He killed the subject for pissing him off. She lied to him. The manner of dress led him to believe he was obtaining the services of a woman. He felt played when he found out otherwise."

Bowers could see his point, but the extreme violence suggested something else. "But, sir. He could have dumped her in the woods." Bowers pointed to the dense swath of trees at the back of the church. "He wanted us to find her like this. This guy wanted to shock us. He's sending us a message."

A STRANGER'S CALL

BOBBY HEARD THE FAMILIAR WAIL of sirens as he hustled toward his grandma's church. As on most of the other streets in the area, he passed run-down brick apartment buildings and old cars parked at the curb.

As often happened, he wore the same clothes as the day before. Only this time his whole body ached. After sitting on the porch until dawn, he'd stretched out on his bunk with a pillow bunched under his head and had listened to the sounds of his brother's breathing, but sleep had never come.

Terrifying thoughts had made his brain feel as if it were on fire. Most of all he wanted to find someone he could trust. Someone he could talk to. His grandma loved him, but what could she do? Telling his little brother would be pointless. Bobby was already in too deep with Papa G. Asking him for help didn't seem like a great idea. And nobody in his neighborhood dared to talk to the cops. Papa G would bust him good if he did.

Besides, talking to the cops would be stupid. They'd know he'd been out after curfew. No way could he explain hanging out on the X Crew's corner at 2:00 a.m. selling dippers. That would only get him time. Then who'd take care of his family?

Bobby hoped the pastor at his grandma's church might be willing to help him. The man had shaken his hand a few times and had seemed cool. He knew clergy couldn't talk about things said in confidence. They had some kind of privilege thing, like with lawyers.

After what Bobby had seen, Pastor Bairns' sermons about hell's fire and damnation had seemed not much different from a normal night on the streets. Bobby didn't pay that no mind. But the pastor had also preached about the church being a safe harbor. Bobby liked the sound of that.

He peered over his shoulder as a biker pedaled past.

In his experience, adults talked a good game, but it didn't account for much. His mama had said she would be back in a few weeks. That was ten years ago. He'd never met his papa. Maybe this time would be different. Maybe Pastor Bairns would listen and be a man of his word.

Bobby turned the corner and stopped.

Even on holidays he'd never seen the church this busy. Cops had the street shutdown. Flares and flashing blue-and-red strobes lit up the whole place.

Something was messed up.

Bobby pulled up the hood of his sweatshirt and shoved his hands into the pockets of his jeans. Moments later he melted into the crowd. The folks around him were talking about a cult killing and the work of the devil. Bobby had no idea what that was about.

He watched the pastor talking to a tall woman in wild-ass, black-and-red pants. She was something fine, like an athlete. He knew what badass looked like, and that lady had it all over her. When she pulled a card out of her pocket, Bobby caught a glimpse of her badge and gun.

Badass for sure.

He'd never seen reporters filming before, but there they were, staring into cameras and talking into microphones. This must be something big. A van pulled in with a coroner's sign on the side.

Like ants on a candy bar, serious police types were hitting the place hard.

Bobby felt uneasy with so many cops around. He started to leave, but like everyone else he wanted to know what had happened.

He shimmied up a tree at the back of the parking lot and stood on a sturdy branch. As soon as he had his balance, he pushed leaves and twigs aside so he could see over the cars and the heads of those mingling about.

Not far from where the bus dropped his grandma off every Sunday, Bobby could now look down on the area beyond the yellow tape.

At the center of the cops and cameras and crime scene tape lay Sapphire in her blue dress.

A burning sensation hit him in the chest.

His breath seemed to stick in his throat. He wasn't sure what had been done to her, but it looked real nasty. He felt sick. An aching kind of sadness weighed down on him. He'd seen guys beaten up bad, but never had he seen anyone dead.

His eyes watered as he remembered the warm, deep sound of her laughter and the way she'd helped a coworker into a cab. She'd been the only one who'd ever given him a tip. The blue dress had been her favorite, but the people putting brown bags on her hands didn't know that.

He wanted to run, to go anywhere but here. Bobby slipped and nearly fell off the branch. He scrambled to the ground and pressed against the hard, smooth trunk.

Desperate for an explanation, Bobby scanned the crowd.

He glanced from one face to the next. Most were curious. Some wore serious expressions. One looked right at him. No way could Bobby forget that face.

It was the man in black.

As Bowers interviewed the pastor who'd found the body, she became aware that the D.A. had been keeping an eye on her. He nodded toward her as he spoke with Mitch. A few minutes later, he waved her over to join them.

As they stood in a huddle on the concrete walkway under the shade of a large oak tree, her phone buzzed. When she reached into her pocket the D.A.'s face grew dour. Knowing he took a dim view of interruptions, she withdrew her hand and ignored the call.

Bowers glanced down at the D.A. The little man with his bulging eyes reminded her of a Chihuahua, who had no idea he ranked low on the intimidation scale. She imagined what he would do if confronted by any one of the terrorists she'd encountered, and subtly smiled to herself.

He took a step back and peered up at her with his thinning dark comb-over fluttering in the breeze. With his hands on his narrow hips, he stood there in his trim, white shirt, stepping on a trail of ants traversing across a crack in the concrete. As he spoke, he tried to off them with the edge of his heel.

"The press is all over us." He glanced over at the media and went back to crushing ants. "We can't let this get out of hand. We need to do this right."

"Yes, sir," said Mitch as he shook the D.A.'s hand. "I'll have our public information officer handle the press."

With a scowl, the D.A. brushed a leaf off his trousers. "We also can't allow this to fall apart in court. Do this by the book." He pointed at her. "That means you, Bowers."

Tell that to Clawski. "Yes, sir," she said.

She bit her lip. If the damned D.A. had let her run with this months ago, like she'd asked, this victim and perhaps the trashcan man might not have died.

Until now, the D.A.'s office had shown little interest in the deaths of dealers and hookers, and even less for the homeless. With the press watching, all of the sudden this hit top priority. Bowers took a deep breath.

She did agree with him on one thing. There was nothing like the twisted mutilation of a transgender dancer to spark the interest of reporters.

Johnny rushed toward Bowers with his phone held high. "I'm sorry to interrupt," he said. "But this is important. The PD has something. They want you."

Bowers took his phone.

"We have an anonymous tip," said a female voice from the Metro PD. "He asked for the detective in charge."

"What did he say?"

"I'll patch him through and he can tell you himself."

Bowers' pulse jumped. "Who is this?" She heard the kind of halting breath that comes from a chest shuddering with emotion.

"Her name is Sapphire. She was a dancer at the Junk Box."

The line went dead.

THE JUNK BOX

BOWERS DODGED PEOPLE in the crowd, hurried around a kid in a dark sweatshirt, and jumped into the Tahoe. The pain she'd heard in that young voice had to have come from someone who'd cared about the victim or was scared.

The clothes and now the name *Sapphire* fit with what an entertainer would use. Her place of employment, at a notorious nightclub, came as no surprise.

Bowers started the engine and flipped open the laptop. Her fingers tapped the keys until she found the address for The Junk Box.

Johnny swung open the passenger door. "I take it we're going somewhere?" he asked as he slid into the seat.

"Our victim worked as a dancer at a club known for having drag shows. The owner is Wally Chung. We're gonna do a little knock and talk."

Bowers clicked on her lights and carefully wove through the crowded lot. A patrol officer waved her through one of the barriers and held back reporters.

To warn people as she came through, she flipped on the sirens, which alternated between a high pitched whine and a blaring series of beeps.

Out on the street she shutdown the sirens and passed a Metrobus. Bowers raced up interstate 295, which took her across the Anacostia River toward the club on Half Street SW. It took less than twenty minutes to reach the nearly deserted parking lot.

Obviously, daylight hours weren't their peak times of operation.

A handyman truck sat out front. That and an old, white Cadillac and a faded, red pickup parked near a side door told her that at least three people would be inside.

The club appeared to be a refurbished brick warehouse in a long line of sad, unkempt buildings that now appeared to be used for storage. The club's exterior had been painted flat black.

Bowers frowned at their sign and shook her head.

The graphic of a giant, toy jack-in-the-box outlined in neon lights stood tall above the entrance. The extremely long-necked clown popping out of the box made Bowers grimace.

Despite its colorful costume, the symbolic representation of a male organ couldn't be missed.

"That's *subtle*."

Johnny frowned at the sign. "You're gonna tell me we have to go inside that place?"

"Yup." Bowers locked the Tahoe and approached the entrance. She tapped on the window next to the door and stared through the glass at the purple velvet curtains that blocked her view. She tapped again. This time she heard movement inside.

Fingers pulled back the heavy folds of fabric and a pair of small, dark eyes squinted at her.

"What do you want?" a muffled male voice asked.

Bowers held up her ID. "Police. I need a word with you."

The man's head turned away as he spoke to someone.

Johnny peered in the window. "Just want to talk. It'll only take five minutes."

A series of deadbolts clicked. The door swung open. Bowers gazed down at a short man with a seriously receded hairline. The way he blinked in the bright light reminded her of a mole coming out of his burrow.

Kill Notice

"Are you Wally, the owner?" she asked.

"I am Mr. Chung, the proprietor," he said with a dramatic bow of his head. He gestured for her to come in.

Another man, built like a vending machine with a scrawny ponytail, followed them down a dark hallway past the central bar and main stage.

The place reeked of stale beer and cigarette smoke.

They marched across a dance floor. A head popped up from the bar where a man appeared to be working on the beer taps. Moments later they skirted around cases of canned beer and down a hallway where they entered a small office in the back. The posters on the wall fit somewhere between a low-budget Vegas production and a high school talent show.

"How may I assist you?" Wally asked as he settled in behind a white desk with gilded trim.

Bowers took in his Hawaiian shirt, black nail polish, and abundance of gold chains. "Did you have a dancer here that went by the name Sapphire?"

Before the man answered, she saw recognition in his eyes, followed by concern.

They heard a sound outside. Wally nodded to the bulky man, who left his post at the doorway and went to investigate.

Wally fidgeted with a shiny gold pen. "She's our lead dancer," he said. "We also depend on her to train the new ones."

"Do you have a picture?" Bowers asked.

Wally pointed at the wall to their left, where a large poster showed a tall, smiling woman in a dazzling gold gown, standing in a spotlight.

The corpse they'd left at the church had been a wreck by comparison, but Bowers could see it was the same person.

"You used past tense. Why?" asked Wally.

Even though Bowers didn't care for this man's career choices, she hated delivering this kind of news.

"Mr. Chung," she said. "We think there's been foul play involving Sapphire." She watched his eyes, the corners of his mouth, and his hands for a reaction. "We won't know for sure until the medical examiner finishes his—"

"She's dead," he said. It wasn't a question, just a simple statement of fact. Wally didn't seem surprised. His brows crested in the center and his eyes grew misty. The pen rested motionless in his hand.

"We have a body that we think is her. I'm sorry."

Johnny stopped jotting down notes and waited.

When the big man returned from checking on the noise outside, Wally cleared his throat and motioned for him to take a seat. He gazed at his bouncer.

"Sapphire's gone," said Wally in a barely audible voice. "I knew it. When she missed work last night, didn't I say something was wrong?"

The big man nodded.

Wally nodded in kind and rubbed a hand over the back of his neck. "I've been waiting for her to come in this morning and pick up her pay." He shook his head as if in disbelief. "She didn't show. I called her, but she never answered."

"Do you know her real name?" asked Bowers.

Wally shook his head again.

Bowers frowned. "What do you put on her paychecks?"

"There's no need to put a name on cash."

Bowers felt a headache coming on. "What about an address?"

"No clue. I don't ask those type of questions."

BOWERS LEFT her card and told Wally to call if he remembered anything useful. He wouldn't. Operators like him wanted nothing to do with cops. Whenever authorities began checking into the business practices of such operations, they were notorious for folding up shop and disappearing.

At her car, she gripped the warm, metal handle of the driver's door and was about to get in when a wisp of white paper on the windshield winked in the sunlight.

Kill Notice

After a quick glance at the note, she scanned the potholed trail of asphalt that had once been a road. On one side were overgrown reeds and bushes. On the other, the row of dilapidated, brick warehouses.

Along the edge of the road walked a lone figure in a black sweatshirt.

"Hey," yelled Bowers.

The figure bolted. Bowers went after him.

"We've gotta rabbit," said Johnny.

She could see that the subject was male and agile and fast. She broke into a sprint and heard Johnny breathing hard behind her. Bowers adjusted her footing and leapt over a pothole.

The dark silhouette slipped between two buildings and vanished. Bowers held her sides and paced in a circle, trying to catch her breath.

"What's on the paper?" asked Johnny between gasps.

"I think it's our victim's address."

Twenty-three minutes later, Bowers and Johnny approached a three-story motor inn. The sign stated that they rented by the week, month, or hour. They found the office's entrance next to an ice machine bearing a sign that read: "Out of Order." The front door had been papered in more disparaging signage about noise, checkout times, and the penalty for looting towels. The notice that read: "NO SMOKING rooms include Pot" made Johnny's eyebrows go up.

He laughed. "Somebody slept through freshman English." Obviously, this wasn't the Hyatt, but it was the right address. Bowers still needed a room number.

A bell tied to the door handle jingled as they went inside. Behind a waist-high wall made from water-damaged particleboard, a big man in his thirties sat in a heap behind a cluttered desk.

He glanced up, appearing none too pleased. The armpits of his rumpled, gray T-shirt were sweat-stained. A burger and fries were laid out in front of him, and a small fan in the corner swirled the vinegary scent of ketchup into the air.

He slipped one hand inside a drawer to his right.

Bowers kept a close eye on that hand. She braced her foot against the half wall and rested her palm on the cool steel of her weapon. He sat four to five feet from her and that flimsy wall offered no protection. She felt the ridge of the holster's safety strap and flipped it off.

The man's eyes flashed between Bowers and Johnny and back to Bowers. He slowly removed his hand from the drawer and grabbed a napkin.

"I'm the manager. Whaddya want?" he asked as he crumpled a napkin into a ball.

Bowers still hadn't taken her hand off her Glock.

"We're looking for the room number of someone I think lives here. She goes by the name Sapphire."

"I'm busy right now," said the man. "How about you call for an appointment?" He tossed a wad of fries into his mouth.

Bowers showed him her ID. "How about you make time?"

The guy dredged another bundle of fries through the ketchup and offered up a half-assed grin. "Can't remember anyone by that name."

Bowers was running slim on time and real low on patience.

Johnny leaned over the wall. "Sir. We're investigating a homicide and would appreciate your cooperation. Did Sapphire live here?"

The man continued chewing as if he hadn't heard a word. His big hands snatched up the burger.

Bowers glared at him. "I've had enough of this bullshit." She pulled her phone and tapped on a photo from the crime scene and held it in front of the man's nose just as he opened his mouth for the next bite.

He stared wide-eyed at the close-up of Sapphire's mutilated head and neck. The burger fell from his fat hand and landed with a splat on the desk.

"Goddamn." The man put up a hand. "I don't wanna see that shit."

Kill Notice

"Someone spent a *long time* torturing her," said Bowers. She pulled her phone back. "He might come back, looking for you. I'd like to stop him, before someone else dies." She flipped to another picture and started to show him the screen, but stopped. "Did she live here or not?"

"Room 215. Second floor. Last one on the left."

WORD OF WARNING

B OWERS AND JOHNNY stood watch at motel room 215.

"Which picture were you about to show that guy?" he asked.

She showed Johnny a photo of her with one of the PD's K-9s and laughed.

"Are you shittin' me? You were bluffing?" Johnny continued to give her a hard time as they waited for the D.A. to bring over the search warrant.

The premises had the sad appearance of a place that had seen its popularity come and go forty years ago. Repairs were makeshift. The faded, red doors showed the dings and scrapes of years of abuse. While pacing, she saw Johnny back away from a peeling wrought-iron handrail that had gum stuck to it.

She took a deep breath and studied the door. She thumped it with her knee. "You have no idea how badly I want to break this down."

Johnny stuck a thumb in his belt. "The D.A. said by the book, remember?"

Bowers stepped away from the door. "I'm going to get a coffee," she told Johnny. "When I get back, you can take a break."

A few minutes later, she drove up the street to a place with a

Kill Notice

drive-through and picked up a large coffee, black. Bowers took a few sips and dialed Riggs, but it went to voicemail.

As she drove back to the motel, Bowers began to worry. What if this wasn't Sapphire's room? What if the D.A. and Magrath were hustling to get over here for nothing? The man at the desk wasn't exactly a pillar of credibility.

She parked in a space near the room and went up to the second floor.

Johnny had stayed at his post. "I'm gonna take a look around back," he said as he headed toward the parking lot.

Bowers checked the doorframe and front window for signs of a forced entry and found none. She listened for any movement inside, but heard nothing.

Maybe the contents of the room would tell them more about Sapphire and why anyone would want to hurt her.

The formula Bowers had learned in training ticker-taped through her brain. How + Why = Who.

That worked for ordinary people who had genuine emotions, but for psychopaths *why* didn't exist as far as the usual motives of sex, drugs, financial gain, or revenge.

She recalled Mitch's list—the fake hair, implants, and so on, and yet Bowers knew by the marks on the body that there had to be more to this case than the way the victim presented herself.

At first, what had been done to the victim had seemed like overkill, but the more she thought about it, she realized that each action the killer had taken was for a reason.

CSI always bagged the hands of homicide victims in hopes of finding DNA under the nails. She suspected the reason the perp had pulled off Sapphire's nails wasn't because of some hatred of artificial nails. He knew they might contain evidence and removed them to cover his own tracks.

Things like her teeth and fingertips were intact. So were the implants. All of which were traceable. This guy made no effort to conceal her identity. This killer was very sure of himself.

One thing glared at Bowers. If this were their serial killer, he killed for the simplest and most heinous of all reasons. He enjoyed it.

Bowers sipped her coffee while guarding the room.

When Johnny returned, a fresh troop of patrol officers rolled in to guard the perimeter. As they assembled in the parking lot, two motel doors opened. One on the first floor and one two rooms down from Sapphire's place.

Two couples made a streak for the parking lot. They had no luggage and appeared to have dressed in a hurry. One man had his shirt on inside out.

Bowers hailed down one couple. Johnny corralled the other. Neither couple claimed to have seen or heard anything unusual. Considering that they both had only been there for a few hours, they were probably telling the truth.

When Bowers returned to watch room 215, she heard a faint tune from the 60's coming from the unit next door and knocked.

An elderly man opened the door and emerged from the room. His bent back spoke of someone who'd worked hard jobs all his life. Bowers found it interesting that his fingertips were heavily calloused, and yet the nails were meticulously clean and filed. Milky, blue eyes stared at her from behind his thick-lensed glasses.

"Can I help you?" he asked.

Bowers showed her badge. "Sir, did you hear anything unusual Thursday night or early Friday morning?"

He brushed off the front of his brown T-shirt with long thin fingers. "Miss, I learned to mind my own business a long time ago," he said in the raspy voice of a long-time smoker. "But I did hear someone crying around three in the mornin'."

The old man paused and nodded as if he'd run it through his memory bank a second time, just to be sure.

"As I remember, me and my guitar had a gig at the corner bar." The man cocked his head. "Say, I may have to write a song about that."

"Sir?"

"Sorry. I came home late, as usual, and couldn't sleep. That

Kill Notice

happens when you're old as dirt like me. It started with a thump on the wall. A woman seemed upset. Sounded like an argument. Then the TV came on real loud."

Bowers liked the old guy. "Anything else you recall?"

"Yeah. Before dawn this morning I smelled bleach."

"Bleach?" Bowers had a sinking feeling that they were in the right place but too late. "Are you sure you smelled bleach?"

"Yes, ma'am. I cain't hear so good like I usta, but the sniffer works just fine. It was bleach. I assure you that."

MAGRATH'S VAN pulled into the motel's parking lot, followed by the D.A. and his entourage. Bowers watched him marching toward the office with an envelope in hand. Two uniforms flanked him. Bowers chuckled to herself. She could just imagine him in his stuffy white shirt presenting his search warrant to the fries—man.

A few seconds later, a caravan of news vehicles rolled in. This time, officers were there in force to keep spectators and the press behind the line. The D.A. returned, rubbing his hands together. He dropped a tiny bottle of hand sanitizer into his pocket and motioned to one of the officers to toss Bowers the key.

"Thank you for waiting," he said. "Your restraint is appreciated."

Bowers caught the key and didn't respond. Her full attention shifted to getting everyone lined up. While Magrath examined the exterior and the walkways, Bowers sent two officers around the back.

After signaling for Magrath to step back, Bowers waved in Johnny and an officer named Thompson.

"Okay. Open it," she said.

Johnny and Thompson drew their pistols and stood on either side of the door. Two more officers lined up next to the window. Bowers used the key and kicked open the door.

"Police. Don't move," yelled Johnny. He and Thompson cleared the room. Bowers followed them in with her Glock drawn. Johnny nodded to her. "We're clear."

Bowers holstered her weapon, and sent him and a couple of officers, and a scene tech to investigate the Dumpster on the side lot.

Bowers stood in the middle of the dark-blue carpet and waved Magrath inside.

The old man had been right. The scent of bleach made her eyes water. That wasn't a good sign. Every light in the whole unit had been left on. That wasn't a good sign, either. Neither were the other chemicals she could smell.

A disturbing thought crept into Bowers' mind. What if the killer had turned on the lights because he wanted them to see every inch of this place?

The room appeared to be perfectly in order.

They began the first careful walk-through while the forensic photographer documented everything on film. Bowers put on gloves, and blinked as camera strobes flashed.

Even in the small sitting area and mini-kitchen, the surfaces were spotless. The bastard, it seemed, had known what they would be looking for and enjoyed flaunting his ability to outwit them.

She studied each item in the room. The bed on their right had been neatly made. On the other wall next to Bowers stood an entertainment center and a large TV. No doubt it was the one the old man had heard.

Crime scene techs moved in to dust for prints and were quickly frustrated. No fingerprints were found. Not even a smudge. It was as if no one had lived there.

The D.A. glared at Bowers before tromping away. Inside, she groaned. This was way too clean. Even the trashcans were empty.

She followed Magrath toward the back for a closer inspection of the closet and the bathroom. Bowers pointed to a bleach stain on the carpet near the bed. Magrath nodded.

An open purse left on a small, round table caught Bowers' attention. She peered inside. On top lay a wallet with a driver's license sticking out.

Magrath nodded the go ahead.

With a gloved hand, Bowers carefully opened the purse and

pulled out the license. The name on the card read: "Danielle Fisher." The makeup and hair were toned down in the photo, but Bowers recognized the small scar on the left cheek. Unless Sapphire had an identical twin, the license had to be hers.

"We're in the right place," she said, with some relief.

Once again, the killer had made no attempt to hide the victim's identity.

Bowers shifted her focus to the contents of the small closet. A gold gown that had been tightly wedged between other garments caught her eye.

"Magrath," said Bowers. "Check this out."

Magrath signaled for the photographer to take close-ups of the garment before touching anything. She pulled out the dress and hung it so that the low back was visible, along with its row of gold buttons embedded with tiny rhinestones.

Bowers recognized the gown as the one Sapphire had worn in the poster at the Junk Box. Several familiar-looking buttons were missing.

"I think we found the source of your button," said Magrath as she carefully examined the dress' shimmery fabric and seams. "This wardrobe far exceeds the budget of someone who lives in a motel. They're custom made." She pointed to a sewing machine on the closet floor. "Whaddya bet Sapphire made her own clothes? Which means—"

"This dress is unique," said Bowers. "The odds of my button being from this dress just went up."

"Exactly."

Bowers continued searching under and around the tables and other furnishings. A small dresser drawer had been left slightly open. She approached it with caution and slid it open. The drawer was empty.

"This is maddening," said Bowers. "Something from the killer must have been left here."

She glanced up to see Magrath urgently waving her toward the bathroom. "He left us something all right," she said. "Look at this."

Bowers marched toward Magrath. "What've you got?"

The small bathroom gleamed in the overhead lights. "Wanna bet," said Bowers, "that this is the cleanest this room has ever been?"

"Except right here," said Magrath, pointing at the wall behind the sink. Bowers stepped in and realized that the large mirror contained an unnerving message encircled in panties.

She had seen underwear hung on doorknobs and hooks at the other scenes, but nothing like this. Panties, some of them soiled, had been taped along all four sides of the mirror.

She glanced from one pair to the next. "So, this is probably not her laundry hanging out to dry."

"Honey, you got that right," said Magrath as she examined blood splattered all over the mirror. "This isn't spatter, it's planted."

Bowers heard Mitch's voice. To her right, he filled the doorway.

"You gotta see this," she said.

Bowers turned back to face her reflection and that of Magrath standing next to her. They were both framed in the collection of panties and blood.

In the middle of the mirror were large, red letters that read: "NEVER LIE TO ME."

BEWARE

RIGGS WAITED OUTSIDE Bowers' apartment. Knowing she'd planned to use her day off to unpack, he'd called and offered to stop by and bring over dinner.

A few faint splotches of black fingerprint powder still covered her door. The rectangular outline where the button had been taped could still be seen. Next to it hung a crisp, yellow Post-it note and a message in Bowers' handwriting that read: "I will find you."

Leave it to her to fire back with a message of her own.

He noticed a potted plant and a new deck chair about ten feet from her door. Both sat against the exterior wall on a section of concrete intended as a small patio. He did a double take. It wasn't like Bowers to go domestic.

Riggs knocked. It still bothered him that she lived alone, despite his knowledge of her black ops training.

He rocked on the balls of his feet. Still concerned. Still staring at that note. No matter how smart or skilled, a bullet could stop anyone.

Her skills intrigued him, but it was her ability to react under pressure and her steadfast sense of purpose that had spurred several attempts at recruiting her—to no avail.

He knocked again and took a deep breath. The two new deadbolt locks on her door made him feel a little better.

This time the door opened. Bowers stood there in a black tank top that revealed the definition in her arms. Her wet hair glistened as she greeted him with a warm smile and a hug.

"Sorry, I was in the shower," she said.

Inside, he noticed a pile of new keys and an electric drill sitting on an end table.

"I would've helped you with that, if you'd asked," he said, enjoying her arm around his waist and her clean scent.

Bowers shrugged. "I was in a hurry."

"You're always in a hurry."

"Did you see the camera?" she asked.

He stopped. "Where?" If she'd already put in a surveillance system, that took one item off the list of things he wanted to discuss with her this evening.

Bowers hooked her finger for him to follow her back outside, where she stopped next to the flowerpot.

"It was Mitch's idea," she said. "He sent out techs who installed it this morning."

Riggs knelt and took a closer look. "Where's the power source?"

"It's battery powered," she said.

He studied the small camera hidden among the flowers. The Bureau used a wide array of devices like this one. "Feed goes to an app on your laptop?"

"Nope. Even better, my phone."

Riggs put an arm around her. "Sounds like you got your boss to pay attention."

She took the bag of Chinese takeout from his hand. He followed her back inside.

When she leaned over and put their dinner on the glass-topped coffee table, he couldn't help appreciating how her yoga pants graced the firm muscles of her thighs and butt.

"This smells wonderful," she said, hovering with her nose over the bag.

"I thought you might like it," said Riggs. He knew Bowers avoided cooking whenever possible.

The last time he'd been over, the apartment had the ambiance of a storage unit. This evening the boxes were gone and it looked as if someone actually lived there. He peeked through the blinds on the front windows.

He wasn't surprised to find she'd already made sure they were latched and locked. She'd also jammed doweling into the sliders as a backup.

"You might want to—"

"I know," she said. "They're coming out next week to install the security system."

Riggs took a seat next to her on the big couch. "I'm amazed at what you've done with one day off. When was the last time you ate?"

"I have no idea. How about now?"

"Dig in," he said.

Bowers opened the cartons and pulled out the packets of soy sauce and fortune cookies.

Riggs pushed away the chopsticks and went to the kitchen for a fork. He opened one drawer and chuckled when he realized it was filled with ammo. *Only in a cop's apartment.* In the next drawer, he dug at the utensils with no dividers and found a fork. "What did your forensic lab make of the button?" he asked.

Bowers had already started eating. "They confirmed it's a match to the gold dress in the dancer's closet. There's no doubt it was hers."

Riggs eased down into the cushions and enjoyed the smile on her face. It faded quickly when she saw the cut on his arm.

Bowers gripped his wrist and examined his hand. She pointed to the number seven drawn on his palm. "I see you're still superstitious."

"I am not. I bet another guy I could make seven hits in a row. It's a ritual, like a batter stepping up to the plate. He cocks his head. Adjusts his helmet. Pulls on the strap of his glove. Same order each time. It's good luck."

"Looks like your ritual didn't work." She inspected the bruise on the side of his hand and the wound on his arm.

81

He couldn't help chuckling. "We did joint training with SWAT and the bomb squad. Had a hell of a good time blowing shit up."

Bowers laughed. "You guys are nuts."

"Speak for yourself. You've done the same thing." When she shrugged, he took her hand and held it between both of his palms. "Listen, Bowers, there's something about your case that has me up at night. Please tread carefully."

Her eyes told him she'd gotten the message.

He let go and watched Bowers go back to poking at her meal with chopsticks.

"I think he's challenging us," she said. "With this killer, it's always what you don't expect. He knew we'd assume the button would match the clothing on the victim's body, not something from her closet."

Riggs wiped his mouth. "What's his game?"

"That is exactly the point," she said. "This is his game and he's setting the rules. At both scenes he proved that he's smart enough to leave no evidence except what he wants us to find. In the motel room he left all the lights on as if he were showing off what he'd done."

Bowers rubbed her neck. "The button is a test. He wants to see if we're good enough to find the source. I need to find this guy."

Her words *he wants to see* lobbed through Riggs' brain. How would the perp know if they had discovered the source of that button? How could he possibly see that?

"Bowers, are you being followed?"

She stopped eating and appeared to be thinking. "He didn't have any trouble finding my new apartment." She chewed slowly. "He's bold, that is for certain. The lab says the tape used to display the victim's underwear on the bathroom mirror is the same brand used to tape the button onto my door. Traces of cornstarch were found on both. He used gloves."

"Is the cornstarch traceable?"

"Hardly," she said. "It's the most common lubricant for exam gloves in the country."

Riggs touched her arm. "The unsub has to be male. Just look at the force it took to sever the vic's throat like that."

Bowers wiped her hands with a napkin. "Most of the time we see a killer's emotions at the scene. You've seen how they cover the victim's face or body because they know the person and guilt is eating them alive. You can almost see their fear of getting caught in the way they try to hide things or clean up. Not our guy. This one makes a show of it. Takes his time. He's so cool it's as if he doesn't know fear at all."

"Be careful," he said. "He's too close."

"I want him close." She glanced at him. "Close enough to slap on cuffs."

"Him coming to your door and sending you messages could easily spin out of control." The weight of worry rode heavy and yet he loved moments like this when they could talk about a case. With her, he didn't have to filter out anything, including the gruesome details of violent crimes. Even over dinner. "You find anything else useful?" he asked.

She took a sip from her bottle of water. "After CSI bagged the bedding, we turned over the mattress."

Riggs expected to hear about a significant amount of blood that had soaked the bed.

"*Nada*. No blood," she said. "But we did find a note that said: Nice Try."

"You're kidding? This guy does have a set. So, where'd he kill her?"

She glanced at him with a slight grin. "On the bed."

"But you just said—"

"This time, it's what's not there that matters. I had a chat with the motel manager, who didn't want to talk, at first." She chuckled and shook her head. "Anyway, he said that they'd had a problem with bedbugs. Covers that were both waterproof and air-tight had been put on the mattresses, sealing the bugs inside."

Riggs grimaced. The thought made his skin crawl.

"Apparently," said Bowers, "they saw it as being cheaper than replacing all the mattresses. But when we got there we found the cover missing and no spatter. Nothing on the ceiling or walls. There's only one reason for that."

"He killed her on the bed and used the cover to protect the mattress."

Bowers nodded. "And to wrap the body for removal."

The perp's resourcefulness didn't add to Riggs' comfort level. "What about the floor? Did Magrath pull up the carpet?"

"Are you kidding? Since when does Magrath leave anything unturned?" Bowers licked her lips and then used a napkin. "The carpet came up too easily and it smelled of chemicals. Before we took a look we knew the killer had beat us to it. There was nothing left to test. He obviously knows enough about forensic science to use the right agents to remove all traces of blood. Even Luminol didn't help."

"What do you make of that?"

She set down her chopsticks. "It has to be a cop. Maybe ex-law enforcement or someone inside a forensic lab."

Riggs had lost his appetite. "You find anything at the church?"

"We found a lot of scene contamination, mostly by first responders. Magrath was hacked about it. I had to eject Clawski. The chief and Mitch are losing patience with how he gets things totally back-ass-ward." Bowers tossed Riggs a fortune cookie.

"What about the display on the mirror?" He chewed on a toothpick. "What the hell was that about?"

She cracked open her cookie. "He knew I'd be looking at that mirror and would see myself surrounded by the underwear and his message, which was exactly at my eye level. Just like the buttons on my door. This guy knows too much."

Riggs leaned close to her. The warm scent of her skin drew him in and made the facts of the case even more disquieting. She slumped into his shoulder. They were nearly eye-to-eye.

"Bowers, was his message directed at the victim or you?"

She dropped the fortune without reading it. It fluttered down and landed on her leg. The distant look in her eyes and the dimple at the

Kill Notice

corner of her mouth told him she was analyzing the meaning of the message on the mirror.

He picked up the tiny strip of white paper.

The fortune read: "Beware of the friend who is not."

———

THE NEXT MORNING Bowers awoke ten minutes before the alarm on her phone. Remnants from her dream echoed in her mind, including the voice of a mother screaming for her child.

As she sat up, she realized she'd been lying on her couch, covered in a quilt. The vague memory of falling asleep while a football game played on the television tumbled through her head. Bowers still had on the same clothes from last night.

Riggs was gone. In the kitchen the cartons from their dinner were in the trash. Next to the sink she picked up the clean fork in the dish rack and shook her head. Only Riggs would do things like this.

She tested the door. It was securely locked. When she realized a key was missing, she knew Riggs had used it to lock her safely inside.

His ways tugged at her and made her wish he'd stayed. After a few minutes she pushed the thought from her mind and shifted her attention to catching the killer. While wolfing down a protein shake, she clicked on the news, and caught Marc Davis' interview with a woman, who claimed to have the inside scoop on the minds of killers. The segment was mostly speculation and talking heads. Davis insinuated that the PD had been less than forthcoming with information.

"That's bullshit."

As proof, they aired a clip of Bowers ordering the press vehicle to move, but never showed how Alex Keller had blocked investigators from entering the lot.

"Great. I'll get an earful about that."

As she thought about it, something far more worrisome nagged at her. Riggs had questioned whether someone might be following her. She clicked off the TV. No doubt, something more than news cameras had been watching.

Her phone buzzed with an incoming message from Riggs: *Let me know if you want to run this by a profiler.*

Bowers replied: *Thanks, but Mitch would kill me. PS: Thanks for last night.*

If she went around Mitch, there would be hell to pay.

AFTER A HARD WORKOUT at the police gym, Bowers drove her personal car, a yellow Xterra, down Georgia. Her phone buzzed with an incoming call from her uncle Marvin.

"Are you okay?" she asked. "You never call me at this hour."

"Ornery as ever," he said. "But it's not me I'm worried about. According to what I'm seeing on the news, you have your hands full."

"Sorry, I should've called you. I'm fine," she said. "You'll be happy to know I had dinner with Riggs last night."

"Good." Marvin paused to catch his breath. His cough sounded worse. "Listen, how about we have breakfast sometime soon? I'd like to blow this coop for a few hours."

"Sure. We'll do it. I promise." Though he'd never say so, she knew his birthday was coming up soon.

Bowers ended the call and arrived at the station ten minutes later. There she found a horde of reporters clogging the sidewalk and milling around out front. She waited for two officers to clear a path so she could enter the back lot. Cameramen and people with microphones ran toward her car.

As soon as a hole opened, she slipped inside to the area off-limits to the public. She quickly parked in the row behind Clawski's black pickup.

When she arrived upstairs, Johnny met her on the way to her cubicle. "You're about as popular as my dog when he cuts one loose under the dining room table."

"What did I do?" asked Bowers.

"Everyone's scrambling over this 202 Killer thing. Reporters are clamoring for interviews. The phones are lit up with people calling in

Kill Notice

with stories about a white van seen leaving the church. We're overrun with leads."

"Let me guess," she said. "Clawski is torqued up because he has to get off his ass and do something?"

"Yup," said Johnny. "Follow me, there's something you need to hear."

The station was abuzz with activity as they hurried toward Dispatch. Phones rang in the background. Eyes glanced up and watched them go by.

The sounds of their footsteps echoed off the polished linoleum floors. Johnny turned the corner and waved for her to come.

They rushed down another hallway. Clawski passed by and bumped her shoulder. When he glanced back, she shot him a look that clearly said "Back off."

They swept through a door into a large, dark, carpeted room that hummed as if it were some kind of electronic beehive. It felt as somber as a command center. Dozens of computer monitors and tiny, red and blue lights illuminated the sound-absorbent cubicles.

It was remarkably quiet, considering that at any given moment at least one dispatcher could be involved in a life-threatening incident.

Most of the dispatchers were completely focused on incoming calls. Many of the people dialing 911 were hacked off at a neighbor, pranksters, or drivers who were pissed off at someone who'd cut them off.

The ones that stirred things up were the desperate calls for help. The air in the room felt heavy with concentration as raw panic and chaos were met with calm assurance, and an extraordinary ability to direct resources toward the more serious scenes within seconds.

One dispatcher, a black woman with a wise face and the demeanor of a seasoned mentor, waved at Johnny. They shook hands. Bowers had no doubt that this woman could handle almost anything. Johnny passed Bowers a headset while the dispatcher cued up a recording.

"You gotta hear this," said Johnny.

Bowers put on the earphones. At first she heard fast breathing as if the caller had been running. Then came the voice of a young black male.

"I, umm," said the voice that sounded familiar.

Bowers cocked her head and listened.

"I saw the dude who took Sapphire. I tried to stop him, but he laid me out. He's tall and wears all black." She heard a pause and more breath sounds. "I saw him at the church too. He was watching you."

WATCHING EYES

BOWERS PULLED OFF the headset and handed it back to the dispatcher. "Thank you," she said.

The words *he was watching you* rang in her ears. Her mind had been so locked on that recording that she almost missed the call from Mitch.

"We're having a special meeting on your killer," he said. "I need to talk with you beforehand." His tone sounded flat. She couldn't tell if he was busy or hacked off at her for missing this morning's briefing. While Johnny went off to get his notes, she headed back down the white-walled hallway toward the briefing room.

Moments later she heard a television and news report echoing in the corridor.

Inside the briefing room, Mitch seemed preoccupied by the report on the 202 Killer. She expected him to say something. Instead, he held one finger in the air, gesturing he'd be with her in a moment, and went back to watching the TV.

She suspected he'd called her in to give her a dressing down about the media putting the incident with her and the reporter on the air. It wouldn't be the first time he'd lectured her about the department's image.

89

Bowers slipped into a chair a few feet away, but Mitch kept his eyes on the news station that had switched to a sports report.

"Look at this loud-mouthed putz," said Mitch. "I hate guys like that."

The camera focused on Jayzee Armel, a receiver for the Washington Redskins. He tossed back his dreadlocks and flashed a big toothy smile at reporters, who were comparing him to Jerry Rice and praising his season's stats.

Their showdown with New England would play out next week and reporters were all over Jayzee about last season's bitter defeat. They all threw questions at him.

A tall woman in a red jacket asked, "How can you be so sure you'll beat New England?"

"Because I am the best there is," said Jayzee. "Git that ball to me and I'll show 'em how it's done."

Mitch snorted. "Have you seen how he strikes a pose after he catches a pass? He acts like the game is all about him." Mitch turned his eyes on her.

The screen switched to an image of a reporter standing on the banks of the Euphrates in Iraq. A somber sort of unease settled over her. Nothing would ever make her forget the hot sun beating down on her and being *in the bubble*, staring through the scope of her sniper rifle. The smells of dust and burnt flesh came back along with the heavy, hot iron scent of blood. The reporter in his bulletproof vest and helmet said something about ISIS, but all she heard were the mortar shells in the rubble well behind him.

Bowers felt a hand on her arm and jumped. Instinctively, she pulled her arm back. It took practiced self-control to dampen the reflex to strike back.

Mitch's dark eyes stared at her as if fascinated. "You were special ops or something, weren't you?"

He had no clue what she'd done. On her record it showed that she'd served in the Army. It also showed a blank stretch of three years when she'd been dragged into covert missions. She wouldn't talk about that, especially with anyone at the PD. "I was just a soldier, sir."

Kill Notice

Mitch nodded. "You see things. You know things we didn't teach you at the academy."

She'd become skilled at sidestepping such questions. "Magrath has taught me a lot, sir."

Mitch seemed to be studying her face. She wasn't sure if he'd believed her or not. "I hear you've been busy," he said.

"We have a serial on our hands. Four buttons have been sent to me. The lab thinks they came from the same perp. Same tape. Same method of delivery. That can't be a coincidence. I guarantee it's not four different killers."

***

BOWERS STOOD when the chief entered the room.

He addressed her immediately. "Mitch tells me we've got ourselves a real bad boy on the loose. If Major Crimes gets involved, you sure as hell better be right. If you're wrong, we're gonna look like idiots."

"Understood, sir," said Bowers.

"How sure are you?" he asked.

"Positive," she said. "It's one man with some type of law-enforcement or forensic training."

The chief ran a hand over his head. "That means we need to be even more careful. The chief's eyes narrowed. She could feel his concern. He leaned on his fists. His thumbs pressed into the hard surface until the knuckles were as white as the tabletop. "I don't want us standing around red-faced if this goes south. We get enough bad press as it is."

Bowers heard tapping and glanced toward the sound.

Mitch beat his pen on the table. "We're buried in calls," he said. "An elderly man called in, claiming the 202 Killer was knocking at his front door. Across town a waitress swore her ex-boyfriend had to be the 202 Killer." Mitch yawned. "We sent out cruisers on dozens of calls. They all turned out to be a FedEx guy doing his job or regular people going about their day."

91

"We need resources," said Bowers.

The chief sat on one of the long tables. "It's time Major Crimes steps in."

"Sir," said Bowers, "the FBI could set up a task force and assist us. We'd still have lead and have access to their forensic lab and software—"

"No." Mitch wagged his finger in the air. "All murders in D.C. are ours."

Having Major Crimes involved wasn't happy news. If the chief gave this to them, she'd be out. This felt like being in the Army all over again. Bowers stared at the floor. "The FBI would be a huge asset."

Mitch didn't respond to her comment. "What else have you got on the unsub?" he asked.

"We have witnesses," she said. "One says he saw the man who abducted the dancer. He claims to have seen the same man watching us at the church. Another witness at the motel reported a workman hauling out some bulky bedding. I think it's fair to say it was the perp removing the victim's body."

Mitch remained focused on rolling his pen between his fingers as if thinking. "So at the church he was in the crowd watching us. Did either of your witnesses get a good look at him?" he asked. "Maybe we can get our sketch artist on this and ID the guy."

Bowers wished she knew where to find the kid. "We've had trouble locating one of the witnesses. The other one, the woman who'd seen the man with the bedding, said it was dark. She didn't see his face."

Bowers heard voices in the hall. The noise level in the room rose as Johnny and a handful of detectives assembled for the meeting.

"Listen up," said the chief as he stood. "It looks like we have a serial killer on our hands. All info on this matter stays in this unit. Just to be clear, anyone leaking details will end up on crossing-guard duty. Bowers is gonna give us an update."

She hadn't seen that coming.

Mitch and the chief stepped back. Everyone stared at her. Clawski yawned and sat with one arm flopped over the back of the chair next to him.

Johnny pushed a whiteboard closer to the podium and tossed her a dry marker. As he went back to his seat, she toyed with the smooth black marker and stared at the blank expanse of the white writing surface.

A tall man in a black button-down shirt and mirrored glasses shook hands with the chief and slipped into the back of the room. Bowers suspected the man had come over from the Major Crimes Unit to hear about the case. She scanned the faces of those present.

"Okay," she said. "I did some digging. Currently, we have at least nine unsolved murders that I think are the work of one unsub. Our timeline shows he's killing more frequently. And he enjoys sending us messages."

She listed the names of the victims on the board, ending with Sapphire. "In the last four cases, the symbolism is apparent. We have a white hooker who was strangled and left in a Dumpster, as if she were trash."

Bowers pointed to the next name. "We found this forty-year-old man who'd been involved in a domestic dispute, stuffed into a dog crate as if he were an animal. The wife had refused to press charges for the black eyes and broken jaw from the assault. When the man was removed from the crate it was apparent he'd been viciously beaten to death. His injured and petite wife wasn't physically capable of this level of violence."

She tapped on the third name. "A twenty-year-old dealer known as Shank had been forced into a trashcan and torched. We know this man as James T. Ward, who we've arrested numerous times in the last three years. Each time, he'd shown up in court with top-shelf attorneys. The charges never stuck. Someone with deep pockets obviously had his back until witnesses say they saw him walking in the alley and talking with a tall man dressed in black."

The man in the back jotted down a few notes.

Bowers continued. "And the latest one, a black, transgender dancer had her throat cut. Her body was found posed at a church."

Bowers put down the marker.

"Seems to me he's doing a fine job of cleaning up our streets," said Clawski as he chomped on his gum. "Can we hire him?"

As chuckles rose around the room, he cocked his head and popped his gum.

Bowers ignored Clawski's snide grin, but suspected that the killer might see his actions as doing what he felt the courts couldn't.

She pointed to a detective, who'd raised her hand. "I don't get this," she said. "Strangled, beaten, torched, and throat cut? Bowers, how do you explain the variations in the modus operandi?"

The man in back watched Bowers through those mirrored glasses.

"This guy's different," said Bowers. "He leaves behind no prints. No DNA. No hair," Bowers stared at the man in back. "He is clearly smart enough to change up his MO."

Comments flew like popcorn.

Mitch spoke up. "He doesn't seem to have a type," he said. "Bowers, where is there a pattern?"

Bowers pointed to the names on the board. "The pattern doesn't reside with the victims. To him, they're merely game pieces on his chessboard. His real interest is with us. He knows our methods and what we're looking for."

One of the detectives grunted. "That's disturbing."

Even more unsettling was knowing this guy wanted to make them all look like bumbling fools.

Bowers continued. She told them about the note under the mattress that read *Nice try*. "This guy is so confident we can't catch him that he's taunting us."

"I ain't buying it," said Clawski. Several detectives began whispering to each other. The chief motioned for them to quiet down.

She knew the perp's propensity for displaying underwear would strengthen her conclusions, but she couldn't reveal that with Clawski within earshot. He'd blab it to the world.

"Some of the deceased were big fellas," said Mitch.

The chief nodded. "That's pretty ballsy to take on adult males with your bare hands."

Kill Notice

Bowers nodded. "He's extremely strong. My guess is he uses his charm to get close. By the time the victim sees the danger, it's too late. And you're right. He doesn't use a gun or any weapon that keeps him at a distance. It appears that he prefers getting up close and using his hands."

The chatter in the room quieted down while everyone chewed on that bit of information. The man in back scribbled something in his notebook.

Mike, the detective ten years her senior, spoke up. "I'm worried about his communications with you." That brought all comments to an abrupt halt. Everyone focused on her, especially the man at the back of the room.

"Our killer has a thing for buttons," she said.

Clawski sighed loudly and rolled his eyes. Johnny kicked his chair leg.

While the chief glared at them both with an unmistakable warning, Bowers continued. "Our perp alerts me to each of his kills by leaving me a button from his victim. Usually he tapes it to my door. In the case of the dancer, the button matched a dress in her closet."

"That weren't no woman," said Clawski.

"Good God," said Johnny. "Shut it, man."

"That's enough," said the chief. "Clawski, one more word and you're outta here."

Mike jumped to Bowers defense. "Before Bowers joined us, I remember a killer who did a similar thing. He'd leave snapshots on Paul's windshield. It got too personal, we ended up reassigning him. Those cases are still open. It sounds like the same killer."

"It has to be one guy," said Johnny.

All but Clawski seemed to agree.

"Can any witnesses," asked another detective, "give us a description of his appearance?"

Bowers knew this would come up. "He's described as a tall male wearing all black." Several of those seated in front of her matched that description, including the guy in back. A wave of chuckles rose as one, then two more men stood as if modeling.

Mitch rolled forward and out of the folding chair. "Do I need to remind you that this is serious?" he asked. The chatter fell silent. "One of our own is in the crosshairs. Needless to say, we have some work to do. Talk to people. Find leads. Look through camera feeds. We make our own breaks. Let's do this."

After the briefing, the room cleared. The man in the back hesitated in the bright hallway long enough to dial a number and then strolled away with his phone to his ear. Bowers stood in the doorway and watched him stop and lean against a wall. While he spoke on the phone his other hand toyed with a button on his shirt.

The hair went up on Bowers' arms. She slipped back inside the room and found herself surrounded by Mitch, her partner, and the chief, who paced the floor.

"We need help," said chief. "Maybe Bowers is right. We need the FBI in on this."

"I have a better idea," said Mitch. With his left hand, he grasped the dry marker and circled Sapphire's name on the whiteboard. "We know that this guy has already returned to the scene at the church. We also know he's watching us. It stands to reason that he'll show up at the funeral."

Outwardly, Bowers masked her disappointment. She'd hoped to get Riggs in on this.

Mitch checked off each name on the board. "The M.E. says the body will be released to the sister. The funeral is on Thursday." He smiled at her. "I think Bowers and I should go."

NEW IN THE CREW

THE SPECIAL BRIEFING on the killer hadn't brought in the FBI as Bowers had hoped. Even so, she shook the chief's hand.

"Keep me informed," he said. On his way out, the chief hesitated. "Mitch, keep Clawski on a short rope. He needs to keep his trap shut and do his job."

Seconds later, the chief left.

Mitch stopped Bowers as she and Johnny were about to return to their desks. "Torres," said Mitch. "Go back to work, I need a word with Bowers."

She took a seat. Mitch clearly wanted something. He slid into the chair across from her and waited until Johnny's footsteps could no longer be heard.

He leaned in close. His dark eyes watched her closely. "What's your real take on this killer? There's something you're holding back."

She studied his face. He seemed eager and a lot like her, fully absorbed in the job.

"Mitch, this guy is remarkably adaptable, but what worries me is his depth of knowledge about police procedures. He's four steps ahead of us."

"Any idea who he is?" he asked.

She shook her head. "I can tell you who he is not. This isn't the recluse in his mother's basement like the news would have us believe. The guy we're looking for is smart."

"What else do you know that connects the cases?" he asked.

"He leaves underwear at each of the scenes. He gets gratification from inflicting pain. Most of all he seems to enjoy humiliating his victims. Look at how he posed Sapphire. The trashcan man was naked from the waist down. He made Shank strip down right there in the alley before climbing into the trashcan. Can you imagine how vulnerable that man felt?"

Mitch leaned on his elbows. "Something seemed to be distracting you during the meeting."

"Didn't you see the guy in the back?"

"That was Russ Parker from the Major Crimes Unit. Why?"

She bit at a hangnail. "I don't want to lose this case to them. And besides, the guy bothers me. He wouldn't take his eyes off me."

One of Mitch's brows went up. "That's hardly a crime. A lot of our guys enjoy eyeing you."

She ignored the teasing. "Do you have any ideas as to who our killer is?"

"Maybe he's the Jack the Ripper of D.C. He'll disappear one day and we'll be talking about him for generations to come."

"No," she said, "that's not gonna happen. He doesn't just get to walk away. When he left his crap on my door, he signed his own warrant. I will dog his ass down. I don't care how long it takes."

Mitch stretched back in his chair and scratched the back of his head. "So who are you looking at?"

"I'm certain," she said, "that we're looking for a cop or ex-cop. Maybe someone who was fired or is disgruntled. Or it could be someone who wanted to be a cop who is now a forensic-buff. That would make sense of the way he toys with us and tries to show how he is smarter than we are."

"Watch your back, Bowers." Mitch stood. "I have high hopes for you. I'd hate to see you hurt." He marched through the door and left.

Kill Notice

She heard him humming in the hallway. Bowers reached in a pocket for her phone to call Riggs, but it buzzed with an incoming call from Magrath.

"Honey, have I got something for you. We went through the dancer's purse. She had dippers in a side pocket. Fresh ones. Whoever sold them to her might know something."

Bowers' phone buzzed again. "Thanks. I'll look into it. Listen, I've got another call coming in." She heard voices in the hall and closed the door, ended the call with Magrath, and picked up the next one. Bowers sat back in her chair and crossed her legs.

Johnny sounded excited. "I know where the anonymous calls came from."

"Where?" She ran a thumb over the smooth surface of the table.

"The guy used a burner, so we have no data on the owner, but we were still able to tell which towers the signals bounced off of and when. Get this. One call came from the Southeast side near Martin Luther King and Malcolm X. And you're gonna love this. The first call came from somewhere close to the church. Bowers, he was right there! We probably looked right at him and didn't know it."

Bowers sat up straight. "Nice work. That's something we can work with. See if you can track down footage from security feeds, the press, or cell phones. I'll meet you at my desk in a few minutes."

BOWERS CALLED OFFICER NICK PEREZ, a colleague and member of the narc unit. If anyone knew the southeast neighborhoods, it would be him.

"Can you meet me at my desk?" she asked him. "I've got something to run by you."

"On my way," he said.

After hanging up she realized that she had a text from Berti that read: *Lunch tomorrow at Paul's?*

Bowers replied: *Sure. See you then.*

It was about time she heard from that girl. Bowers wondered what kind of mess she'd gotten herself into this time.

A few minutes later, Bowers hurried through the cramped spaces toward her desk. Within the occupied cubicles, detectives studied their files, made calls, or chatted with each other. Most of their banter revolved around lamenting the amount of paperwork they had to do, but she also heard about some stunt Jayzee Armel, the NFL's badboy, had done.

When they reached her cubicle, Perez and her partner were waiting. Johnny wedged in a third chair so each of them could sit.

Bowers went right to it. "Perez, you know the Southeast. We've got a murder victim whose purse had two dippers in it. She lived near MLK and Malcolm X. We have an anonymous male witness whose burner pinged off a tower in the same area. What does that tell you?"

The narc officer leaned forward on his elbows. Bowers knew he'd been on the job a long time. He tapped his thumbs together. "Bowers, do you have a time when this happened?"

"We're thinking the victim was abducted on her way home, around 2 a.m."

"Bad place to be at that hour." Perez ran a finger over a scar on his chin and grimaced. "You're looking at the corner of MLK and Malcolm X. I can almost guarantee she got her fix from someone in the X Crew. They control that corner."

"Who's the witness likely to be?" she asked.

"Maybe it's a hooker," said Johnny, "or a dealer. Or it could be another customer who was there for a fix?"

Perez chewed at his lower lip. "He's not likely to be a male prostitute. They're across the river. Could be a dealer, but they aren't known to be Good Samaritans. A client isn't going to tip off police that he was anywhere near that corner. My best guess is that he's a BG, a baby gangsta, someone new in the crew."

"How do I find him?"

Perez shrugged. "You gotta be careful. They don't know you. They'll be suspicious. The person who would know your witness is

Kill Notice

Papa G. He has his thumb on everything within his turf. He doesn't tolerate intrusions on his corner."

She remembered hearing that name from Reggie, the guy who'd jumped her outside of Old Ebbitt Grill. "Where do I find this Papa G?" she asked. "Can you get me a picture?"

"I'll do better than that. I'll introduce you."

STANDOFF

RIGGS SAT AT THE BAR at Old Ebbitt's Grill and swirled a slice of steak through a puddle of Worcestershire sauce and popped it in his mouth. He'd gotten a call from Bowers, who'd been teed-off about Major Crimes butting in. Rachel, the bartender, brought him a beer. A few minutes later, a man in an expensive shirt slid onto the barstool next to him.

"You wanted to talk to me," the man said. "What's this about?"

"Thanks for coming." Riggs washed down his last bite with a mouthful of beer and picked up his plate. "Follow me."

The man trailed behind him down the steps into Old Ebbitt Grill's dining room, where Chief Bowman sat at a table sucking down an iced tea that had a half-inch of sugar settled at the bottom of the glass.

Riggs took a seat. The man slid into the booth next to him.

The three stared at each other. Riggs knew both of them were used to running their own show.

The man in the fine clothes reached out a hand. "I'm Russ Parker, Major Crimes."

Riggs shook his hand and went back to his steak. When he shoved the next bite to his mouth, he realized Parker watched as he

Kill Notice

chewed. Bowers had said the man was odd, now he could see why. The guy had a strange habit of staring at people. He also had a swagger about him that annoyed Riggs.

"Now that you've met," said the chief, "we need to sort out our investigation on the 202 Killer."

"Protocol is straightforward," said Parker with his head pivoting between the chief and Riggs. "Now that we know this is a serial, the case comes to us at Major Crimes."

The chief set aside his linen napkin and folded his hands together. "Parker, this case entails more than you know. Special Agent Riggs has some information you need to be clear on."

"I sat in on Bowers' presentation," Parker said, as he toyed with the empty glass in front of him. "We want this case. It's that simple."

Riggs took another bite and chewed slowly. He'd seen guys like him before. Over-confident. The big cases were the notches in a detective's belt, which earned serious stripes. Parker acted the part of a man who thought he had the world by the ass.

"The best option," said Riggs, "is to put our task force on this. We can do it as an assist. I don't give a crap who gets credit. All I care is that we track down this killer as soon as possible."

Parker's blue eyes narrowed. "It's our jurisdiction."

Riggs dropped his fork and wiped his mouth. "Look. If you don't care to listen, know that I'm the twelve-ton gorilla in the room and I can step in and do whatever the hell needs to be done."

The chief put up a hand. "Gentlemen, we're on the same side here. The only thing I want is for the killings to stop and to hang this psycho's hide on the highest tree for what he's done."

"What do you want?" asked Parker.

Riggs pushed his plate away. "For now, I want you to use the best asset you've got."

Parker frowned. "What asset?"

"Bowers," said Riggs.

Parker shook his head slightly. "No way. Why would I do that? She's personally involved, for God's sake. You should have pulled her off this a month ago."

"Hold on son," said the chief. "We had our reasons—"

"Listen up," said Riggs as he toyed with a toothpick. "Look at the old cases she's connected. Every time a detective got close, the unsub made personal contact and the detective was then taken off the case. When you do that, you start all over and lose the one person who knows the case best. You lose continuity. Classic mistake."

Parker looked like a kid who'd just lost his birthday cake. "So why Bowers?"

"She knows more about this killer than all of us put together."

"How can she possibly know more?" scoffed Parker. "My guys have been at this long before she was a cop. I've checked her background. She did a little time in the Army and went to the academy. Big deal."

The chief glanced at Riggs. The corner of his mouth twitched.

Riggs took a sip of his beer. "Bowers has a particular skill-set that she didn't learn in either of those places. She will find this guy, with or without any of us."

"Not on my watch," said Parker. "I'll sideline her ass." As if he owned the table, the restaurant, and the entire damned block Parker grabbed Riggs' water glass and poured most of it into his own glass before handing it back.

The chief eyed him with one brow raised. "Careful, son, unless you have a hankering for humble pie to go with that glass of water."

Parker appeared uneasy, if not puzzled.

"Here's the deal," said Riggs. "If you sideline Bowers, I can just about guarantee she will disappear, where no one can find her, and in time so will your perp. You'll never know what happened to either of them."

Parker polished off his water. "So that hole in her past wasn't from shacking up with some guy?"

"Nope," Said Riggs.

"Can you tell me what she did during those years?"

"Nope."

"Shit." Parker flopped back in his seat. "How am I supposed to handle her?"

Kill Notice

The chief put a fist to his mouth.

Riggs chuckled. "You don't," he said. "You follow her. You give her what she needs and you get the hell out of her way."

When their server appeared and bent to drop off their check, Parker stared at the woman's chest. After she left, he nodded. "So what you're saying is that you want us to step back."

Riggs tapped the table. "You can join the party. Just don't get in the way."

Parker seemed to be choosing his words carefully. "What happens if the killer comes after her and she panics?"

Riggs sat back. "You've worked with the K-9 unit."

Parker nodded his head. "What has that got to do with anything?"

"Then you know," said Riggs, "what training and inherent temperament can do. A friend of mine is a K-9 handler. One of their dogs lives with him. The animal is gentle and playful with the man's kids. I visited him one day when someone, who wasn't supposed to be there, walked up the driveway. Before the intruder took one step inside the garage, the dog reverted to his training and made it damned clear. Not this house, asshole. The dog didn't panic. Neither will Bowers. I guarantee you that she's seen worse than serial killers. If she didn't flinch then, she won't now."

The chief nodded. "Until further notice, Bowers stays in the lead."

LATE THAT NIGHT, the sky was clear when Bowers briskly crossed the PD parking lot with her bulletproof vest slung over her shoulder and slipped into the passenger seat of Perez's black Mustang. She set the vest in her lap.

"It feels weird not driving," she said.

Perez grinned and ran a hand over the dash. "You ain't driving this baby."

Bowers laughed. "I do know how to use a stick."

"I don't doubt it." Perez shifted in his seat and glanced at her as if he were measuring the words he planned to use. "Look," he said, "I've spent years learning who hangs out down on that corner, who their baby mamas are, where their mothers and cousins live. We have a kind of mutual respect. They'll talk to me because they know I'm doing my job and that I will be fair." Perez watched a marked unit pull in. "I don't care about Papa G. With so much available online he's a dying breed, but I do want his suppliers. That means I can't blow this."

"Come on, Perez." She clicked her seatbelt. "This is me, remember?"

"I know." He revved the engine. "Just making sure we're clear. You need to follow my lead."

As they drove out of the lot and into the night, Bowers told him about the case. After dark, the streets made a striking transformation. Bars filled up. More young men hung around in groups of three to six. Ladies' skirts grew shorter, their heels higher. Late-model cars cruised around the same blocks.

Perez kept his eyes on traffic. "I heard talk about your cases at the station. It doesn't sound like the X Crew's kind of thing. We'll see what they have to say."

Bowers felt the weight of the heavy vest in her lap. "You crampin' my style, Perez?"

"Just put it on. I want us both to come home tonight."

"I will," she said, "when I get out of the car."

Thirty minutes later they arrived at the corner.

Perez pulled up across the street from a liquor store.

"This is King's Corner," he said. "Anything can happen here." Within seconds, his whole persona changed. Everything about him turned hard, edgy, and alert.

Bowers watched a man on the sidewalk stumble past the car. His head jerked and he acted as if he were talking to someone. The guy stripped off his shirt. The sweat on his face and skin glistened in the glow of the streetlights.

Perez nodded at the man. "He'll end up in the ER or a gutter tonight. He pulled off his shirt because the PCP is making his temperature skyrocket. His brain is fryin'." Perez used his radio to call for a cruiser to pick up the man before he hurt himself or someone else.

She gripped the vest. "Ready when you are."

"Tonight we're just talking. No arrests. No takedowns, if we can help it." Perez took his time. He checked his watch and waited. Ten minutes later, a big, black man wearing a knit cap strolled up the street. The hem of his shirt swayed as he walked.

"That's Papa G. He has an apartment two blocks away."

The man went into a sub shop. Through the shop's front windows, Bowers could see him leaning against the counter and talking to someone.

"Who's the man behind the counter?" she asked.

"That's his cousin. See the guys in the shadows near the liquor store? They're members of his crew. There will be at least two more somewhere close by, probably more. The man in the jacket with his hands in his pockets is a dealer. Papa G is very protective of his men. Whatever you do, don't show fear or weakness. You sure you're up for this?"

"Hell yes," she said.

They stepped out of the car. While Perez locked the Mustang, she hoisted up the heavy vest. Putting it on had always reminded her of saddling a horse.

"We good?" asked Perez.

Bowers nodded and they crossed the street.

She kept an eye on an old, brown pickup in the liquor store's parking lot. Three men in the back were watching them.

When they marched past one jumped out of the truck bed. "Lawdy, lawdy, I wanna git me some of them pants."

She heard the snickering.

"I like what's in 'em too," said another. "Shit, man. Ain't nobody be callin' her shawty."

"Keep it to yourselves, gentlemen," said Bowers as she and Perez hurried by. She ignored their cackling, and focused on Papa G's men.

As they approached the sub shop, two crew members moved in to cover the door. The light pouring through the shop's front windows did more to illuminate the sidewalk than the few streetlights that weren't broken or burned out.

The air on the corner reeked with the smell of old grease.

Perez entered the shop with no problem, but two from the crew stuck close to Bowers' side. Inside, the shop a strange combination of garlic and orange scented air freshener hung in the air. Papa G sat at a table with his back to a wall.

"Whatsup, mo?" he said to Perez.

By the way Papa G shifted his eyes, Bowers could see the big man had taken notice of her.

Perez stood close to the table with his back against the wall, where he could keep an eye on the door, Papa G, and his cousin behind the counter.

The two crewmembers muscled in close to Bowers. One smelled of sweat, the other of sauerkraut. They stood shoulder to shoulder and attempted to keep her on the other side of the shop.

Packing heat had a funny way of giving young men an inflated sense of their own power. Bowers smiled to herself and leaned back into the counter near the cash register. She could challenge them, but Papa G probably wouldn't be too pleased. Neither would Perez. Violating his trust was something she wouldn't do.

"Don't be rude to my partner," said Perez. "She's come all this way to talk to you, man."

Papa G glanced her direction. "What you want wit' me? I'm just a po' man waitin' on his supper."

"I'm looking for someone," Bowers said. She pushed past the two men flanking her. "Thought you could help. I hear you know things." Bowers took a seat across the table from Papa G and held the big man's gaze.

"I'm listenin'," said Papa G, as he slid his hand under the table. Perez stepped closer and slowly reached toward his weapon. One of Papa G's men slipped a hand inside his jacket.

Bowers leaned forward until the armored plate in her vest pressed against the yellow tabletop. "Don't disrespect me. Put your hands on the table," she said. Slowly she showed him her hands. "You ain't afraid of a lady are you?"

"Bowers, walk easy," said Perez. "We didn't come here to bust chops."

She knew she'd pushed it a little, but respect both given and received was a language she could see Papa G understood. She kept her eyes on the big man and smiled. When he laughed, his belly jiggled.

One of Papa G's men stepped closer.

"Put it away, Dray," he said. "We ain't got no beef. Take it outside."

The two men left. She caught a glimpse of them on the sidewalk, constantly watching the traffic and glancing back at their boss.

Perez took his hand off his weapon and stood close to the table.

Papa G pressed fists with him. "I like a woman who knows what it's about," said Papa G as he put both hands on the table. "Y'all excuse my mens. They took one look at you, mama, and got themselves all 'cited."

"Come on," said Perez. "Let's get down to business."

Papa G grunted. "Who you be lookin' to find?"

"A kid who works for you," she said without blinking. "He saw something important. I need to talk to him."

"Lots a kids out there seein' shit dey shouldn't. I don't rightly know which one you be interested in. Dey all looks alike—"

Bowers deliberately interrupted him. "Think hard, my friend. If I don't find this boy, the man in black will."

She watched his eyes. They narrowed. Clearly he knew exactly who she was talking about.

Her vest pinched when she leaned forward. "If the kid I'm looking for dies, you lose your BG and I don't get the information I need to put his killer away. So there's nothing stopping him from coming around again."

This time Papa G did the staring. She knew she'd hit a nerve. Bowers pushed him a little harder. "I can tell you he has an appetite for stuffing dealers into trashcans and lighting them up for the hell of it."

She felt Perez put a hand on her shoulder to signal they were done. Bowers stood and peered down at Papa G, who wore a thousand-yard stare as he gazed out the window.

In a deep voice he said, "Maybe I'll ax around. If I find dis kid, maybe he'll be talkin' to you."

FLASH BANG

A T 4:00 A.M. THE SKY above Riggs was black as a tomb. Months of surveillance and planning had come down to this one moment.

He hunkered down in an armored command unit in a Northwest section of D.C. The heavily wooded neighborhood suited him just fine. He swallowed the last cold, gritty mouthful of his coffee.

Riggs rifled through the data one more time. Warrants, check. The address, triple verified. Intel on those inside, had been confirmed twice in the last five minutes. What they were about to do weighed on him. Success required getting all the details right.

HRT, the FBI's elite Hostage Rescue Team, had gathered into in a huddle. No doubt they were doing their last-minute checks, too. In full gear, they seemed ready and able to take on just about anything.

The SWAT commander sat down next to Riggs. "We're ready to go hot," said the commander. The man was a big guy, sandy-haired, calm, and armed to the teeth. "Our targets are inside."

They were parked half a block away from the ranch-style home, tucked back off the street with a good view through the trees. The windows in the house were dark.

Riggs knew exactly who was inside. His primary concern was the nine-year-old girl, Lizzie, who had been abducted from North Dakota by her father. He'd recently been let out on probation after serving time for child pornography.

The father, his girlfriend, and two of his partners were inside. A fifth man guarded the front door. Tonight would be a twofer—the opportunity to solve an abduction and take down a child-pornography ring in one operation.

These agents were about to put their lives on the line. Surprises were bound to happen, but Riggs and everyone on the team minimized such things by making sure they knew more about the men inside than they knew about themselves.

One of the FBI's computer wizards waited quietly in a corner seat sipping a Gatorade. The man's butch haircut and muscular build gave little clue to the genius that resided behind his body-builder's exterior.

The SWAT commander, who'd moved next to the door, kept his eyes on Riggs. "We're set. You ready?"

Riggs gave him a nod. "Let's do this."

He spat out his gum, wrote *Lizzie* on the palm of his hand with a ballpoint pen, and checked his ammo. He looked forward to shutting down the kingpin of one of the biggest child-pornography rings on the east coast.

They quietly hustled out of the unit.

In the dark, Riggs couldn't see the rest of the team, but he knew they were in place. He tugged down on his bulletproof vest, gripped his Heckler & Koch MP5 sub-machine gun, and checked his watch before kneeling behind a solid tree.

His earpiece crackled. "Package is in the basement, plus one unidentified child."

That was the first surprise. He hoped there wouldn't be more. Through his night-vision binoculars, Riggs kept an eye on the first subject they would encounter—the big man guarding the front door. The fool had nodded off.

Son, you have the surprise of a life-time coming.

The chain-link fence around the property warned of a dog on the premise. While the pooch slept off chunks of flank steak doctored with mild tranquilizers, their animal control unit waited two blocks away, ready to move in once the scene had been secured. A block away, the special SWAT Medic Unit waited on standby.

Riggs felt the flutter in his gut. Nerves. Energy. Anticipation. His earpiece crackled again.

"We are a go," said the commander.

Riggs responded. "Affirmative."

Within seconds, three SWAT agents silently crept up on the sleeping guard.

Riggs knew this would be worth watching. In a coordinated maneuver, one agent covered the man's mouth, while the other two secured his arms. They carried him, chair and all, to lawn to avoid a ruckus on the concrete at the front door that might wake someone. The startled man's spastic gestures offered little resistance as SWAT swiftly immobilized him.

Meanwhile, two teams rigged the front and back doors for a breach.

The armored unit rolling up in front of the house was Riggs' signal to move in.

Simultaneously, the front and back doors exploded off their hinges. Flash-bang canisters blasted through all the windows. Deafening pops, crackles, and furious flashes lit up the interior of the house.

SWAT streamed into the house, with Riggs bringing up the rear. His night-goggles allowed him to see in the dark, but he had also memorized every room, closet, and crawl space.

Two SWAT members took down a man in the living room while the rest of the team stormed down the hall with speed and force.

"FBI. Hands up. Now!" yelled the man in front of him.

Teams of two cleared each room. Riggs and his partner checked one of the bedrooms. A mound of blankets on the bed moved. An arm and then a leg emerged.

"FBI. Don't move!" Riggs shouted and took cover. His partner stood on the other side of the doorway, backing him up. Everything happened in a split-second and yet time seemed to have slowed down to a crawl.

The subject's head and another arm appeared from under the blankets. The pale face and limbs belonged to a large man, who reached under the bed.

"Don't do it," yelled Riggs, aiming for center mass. "Stop!"

The man didn't listen. He dragged an assault-style rifle from under the bed.

"Drop it! Now." Riggs ordered.

The man continued bringing the rifle up. Riggs waited until he was almost into firing position and offered one last warning before pulling the trigger.

His MP5 let loose a two-round burst. Hot, yellow flames blasted from the muzzle. The recoil pressed into Riggs' shoulder. A rapid *boom-boom* echoed in his ears as he watched the man's arms go limp. His blood-spattered rifle clattered to the floor, followed by the thump of his body hitting the carpet.

Riggs had no time to process how he felt about that. Not now. He secured the rifle and marched down the hall. Screams came from the next room.

Riggs, followed by his partner, passed a pair of SWAT agents in the hallway serving as rear guards. He entered the room where he'd heard the ruckus.

Inside, three agents had found a middle-aged man in bed with a naked woman.

Riggs pushed up his night-goggles. "Lights on." He flipped on the wall switch.

The woman had a mass of tangled, bleached-blonde hair and tattoos running down her back. The man sported a scruffy beard, a hairy chest, and boxers. Two agents ordered the pair into a sitting position on the edge of the bed. The third agent held a semi-automatic pistol aimed and ready.

The SWAT commander entered the room. "The missing girl is in the basement. HRT is down there with her."

Kill Notice

Riggs picked up the wallet on the nightstand and opened it to a driver's license.

The commander leaned in and stared at the photo. "This you?" he asked the man.

The bearded man stared at the floor and nodded.

They confirmed that he was the father of the abducted girl. Two agents allowed the couple to put on clothing before they were cuffed.

The woman spoke up. "I just met this guy. I had nothing to do with this shit."

Outwardly, Riggs showed no emotion. Inside, he wanted to belt the guy across the room. *What kind of dirt bag turns a child, especially his own kid, into a porn star?* He left the room as they were read their rights.

A few minutes later Riggs entered the living room. He glanced through the open door and saw the man who'd been guarding the front door face down on the front lawn. He still appeared shell-shocked as two agents hauled him away.

Riggs heard a whimper.

Two HRT agents came up from the basement with a tearful girl, wrapped in a blanket, and a dazed little boy who appeared to be around the age of eight or nine.

Riggs called in the medical crew. They went down the hall to attend to the man he'd shot. It was a formality. Riggs rarely missed. He knew the man who'd attempted to shoot him was beyond benefiting from medical care.

The guy had been warned.

All in all, it had been a clean arrest. Fast and hard. Riggs liked it that way. He would have liked it a whole lot better if there hadn't been any casualties, but people do stupid things. They don't listen. The guy he'd shot sure hadn't.

Riggs left the house and went out onto the front lawn. The cool breeze against his sweaty face and neck felt good. The air smelled cleaner out here.

Two hundred feet down the street to his left, a small crowd had gathered. Officers had blocked off the road and kept spectators behind the barricades. The press would arrive any minute.

At the house, staging lights had been setup.

A paramedic and a specialist within the Hostage Rescue Team attended to the children. Riggs rubbed a thumb over the name he'd printed on his palm and thought of the girl's mother and the boy's parents and how relieved they would be. He knew this wasn't over for the kids. Their recovery would take years.

Maybe decades.

Riggs checked his watch. The effort of six months' work and hours of careful setup had allowed them to apprehend the suspects within minutes. He unfastened his vest and lifted the weight off his shoulders.

A special agent approached and waved Riggs over. "The boy has been missing for forty-eight hours," he said. "The kid was abducted from a convenience store in Bethesda." The agent smiled. "His parents are en route to the hospital. The girl's mother is catching the next flight possible."

"Thank you," said Riggs. He shook the man's hand.

While the K-9 unit cleared the home, Riggs entered the command unit and checked in with their agent, who'd already begun exploring a recovered laptop.

"We've found something," he said. "They did the filming in the basement. We're gonna have a shitload of stuff to haul away. Might even need another van."

Riggs went to do a walk-through of the house with their Evidence Recovery Team, and see for himself what they had found. In the basement, cash, computers, and stacks of DVDs were photographed, meticulously documented, and loaded into evidence boxes.

Lights and cameras were focused on a bed in the middle of the room, where a child's Teddy bear lay.

Riggs felt a cold knot in his gut. He spoke to the lead scene tech. "This makes me ill."

She nodded. "Go out to my van. There's a bag of new toys in there. Give the kids something to hold on to."

Kill Notice

Riggs went to the van and selected the friendliest-looking ones he could find and gave them to the children. The girl hugged the baby doll and cried. The boy examined the long-eared dog before staring up at Riggs as if he were lost.

Riggs knelt to speak with the children. "I won't let them hurt you again. You have my word."

The boy buried his head into Riggs' shoulder and sobbed. The girl fell forward and threw her arms around him. When he felt her squeezing as hard as she could, he swallowed hard and forced down the lump in his throat.

CORNERED

BOBBY'S GRANDMA had the blinds drawn so she could see the TV without the glare of the morning's sunlight. Bobby sat on the couch, shoving a big spoonful of corn flakes into his mouth and wiping off the dribbles of milk with the back of his hand. He took extra care not to knock her porcelain owl off the side table.

Grandma sat in her frayed green recliner, watching the morning news. Bobby pretended to ignore the reporters chatting it up about the 202 Killer, but his ears heard nothing else.

The anchor introduced a woman who claimed to be a social worker and some kind of expert on killers. Bobby didn't see anything social about someone who would go around killing folks, or why she'd be so interested in them. Even so, he wanted to hear what the white lady in the fancy glasses had to say about Sapphire and the murderer.

"He's a white male who feels powerless."

Bobby frowned and took another bite.

"He still lives with his mother or a family member. He'll shun people and doesn't fit in." The lady kept on talking as she fiddled around with the papers in her hand. "He's unemployed or under-employed."

Hell, everybody I know is looking for work or better pay.

The lady smiled at the camera and took off her glasses. "And he probably has a lisp or some other trait that makes him stick out."

She had it all wrong about the man in black. No one would be catching him with her saying stuff like that.

The corn flakes in Bobby's mouth suddenly tasted like stink. His gut tightened, and he ran to the kitchen sink.

A few minutes later, he hugged his grandma, and hustled his brother out the door to catch the school bus before Grandma started hashing over what that lady had said.

On the bus, Ty, Bobby's best friend eyed up a new girl. "Man, she's some serious bait."

Most of the time, Bobby didn't mind riding the bus, but this time he knew trouble would be waiting for him at school. He thought about that and picked at a hole in his jeans.

"What's up wit' you?" asked Ty.

Bobby shrugged.

A kid wearing a skullcap stood in the aisle and struck a pose. "My name is Sapphire," he said. He moved his shoulders all around, and acted all breathy and stupid. Ty and the other kids snickered. They must have been listening to the news, too.

Bobby wanted to slap them all.

"Dude," said Ty, "I heard she had a dick. That's sick, man."

Sapphire was a whole lot nicer than the kids who were making fun of her. They didn't know her. Didn't know she worked hard or that she was good to people. They hadn't seen her dead body or what had been done to her. That was something Bobby would never forget.

The more the kids came down on Sapphire, the more Bobby wanted off that bus.

He thought about that lady on the news who'd described the killer as messed up. The punch from the man in black nearly took his face off. That hadn't come from some helpless loser. That was for sure.

Bobby stared out the window and wished he were somewhere

else. Anywhere would've suited him, as long as it was out of here. A piece of gum on the floor stuck to his shoes.

The boys continued yapping about the 202 Killer. The kid in front of Bobby smacked a fist against his chest. "I'd bust his ass if he messed wit' me."

Sure you would, thought Bobby, while using the leg of the bench in front of him to scrape the gum off his shoe.

Another boy twisted around in his seat. "I tell you what. We'd be banging his butt all over town." As always, they were chopping it up about stuff they knew nothing about.

Bobby ignored most of it. The 202 Killer wasn't the only thing on his mind. He still had to deal with the bully at school who would be waiting.

The buses rumbled onto the circular drive in front of the school. Brakes sighed as they came to a stop. The door whooshed open and the kids streamed out.

"Watch your back," said Ty before he disappeared into the crowd.

Being a month shy of turning sixteen made Bobby the youngest junior in his high school, and a target. On the way to his locker to drop off his history book and pick up the one for algebra, a big kid everyone knew as Jimmy grabbed him from behind and shoved him down the hall and into the boy's restroom.

A dude at the sink grabbed his backpack and bolted for the door.

Bobby had expected Jimmy would pull something like this. Being on the varsity football team, meant he got away with all kinds of shit. He pushed up the sleeves of his baggy shirt and showed Bobby a leather wristband with its big, brass clasp. More than one kid at the school had scars from that thing.

Teachers never did anything about it.

Jimmy stood there with his bushy red hair and a stupid grin like the whole world was in his back pocket, but this time Bobby saw things different. This time, Bobby knew what it was like to stare into the face of someone far worse than a high school bully.

He'd seen the man in black's empty eyes, and felt the power

Kill Notice

behind his punch. Compared to that, Jimmy looked like chump change.

"Gimme your cash," said Jimmy, as he twisted his bracelet so the clasp stuck out. "Or I'll bust your face in good."

Bobby backed toward the door. He gripped his thick history book, ready to use it to deflect a blow. "Take your crazy shit somewhere else, man."

Jimmy swung. Bobby ducked, and swung back with the hefty textbook. It clocked Jimmy in the nose and sent him stumbling backward, where he crashed into one of the urinals.

When two boys entered, Bobby saw a clear path and bolted out the door and down the hall. He barely made it inside the door of his algebra class before the final bell. At his desk, he rubbed his fingers over the new crease on the cover of his history book and smiled.

As the teacher called attendance, Bobby realized he didn't have his algebra book and hadn't done the assignments. He combatted the teacher's disapproving scowls by slumping down in his seat. Coefficients and exponents didn't mean a hell of a lot when every day was a struggle to survive and care for his family.

At lunch he went to check on his brother, who'd been let out a few minutes early along with the rest of the freshmen. The halls rumbled with the sound of slamming lockers and students shouting. Kids were bumping into each other and rushing in both directions.

In the hallway leading to the cafeteria, the nasty smell of cooking cabbage made Bobby hold his breath. To his right he caught a glimpse of his brother hurrying away with another boy.

Bobby followed.

He had ditched school many times, but seeing his little brother doing it hung him up. Bobby didn't have a choice. Tommy did. The whole point of working the streets had been so his brother could stay in school. Bobby had told him often enough, but Tommy didn't get it.

Bobby waited until no one was looking and left the building. The time had come to have a chat with his brother.

In the cool air outside, he saw the other boy sneak away along the wall next to the library and meet up with a girl. Tommy darted across the street, heading toward the convenience store.

Before Bobby could get through the snarl of traffic, his brother had passed the red-and-white store with black bars on the windows and its pallet of canned sodas outside. When Bobby hit the curb, he watched Tommy peering into the dark space between the buildings and then jumping back as if something had spooked him.

Bobby picked up his pace.

From the sidewalk he saw Tommy duck between the buildings. He could think of several reasons to hide in an alley. None of them were good. He guessed that Tommy was once again looking for a place to light up a smoke.

Through the clutter of leaves and trash, Bobby crept up the sidewalk and leaned on the graffiti-covered wall next to the alley. He heard a conversation, but couldn't make out the words. He crept close enough to hear.

A deep voice spoke. "I've been watching. You come here almost daily," said the male voice that wasn't his brother's. The voice sounded hard and cold.

Bobby heard the higher-pitched sound of his brother. "Sorry to interrupt, sir. I won't bother you no more. I'm gone. The alley be all yours, man."

Bobby stepped away and hid behind a sign advertising lottery tickets. To his right a beer truck pulled up to the curb. He poked his head out and watched his brother backing out of the alley.

A tall dude followed him out of the alley and onto the sidewalk. Dressed all in black, the man turned toward Bobby and stared directly at him.

Goosebumps rose on Bobby's skin. The familiar face set his pulse to pounding.

Seeing the man in black only an arm's length from Tommy lit up something inside Bobby. Pictures of Sapphire raced through his head. Nothing mattered beyond keeping that man away from his brother. Without thinking, he ran for Tommy with everything he had.

He pushed his brother out of the way. "Run," he yelled at him. "Run! Get help."

The man grabbed the sleeve of Bobby's sweatshirt.

Bobby struggled and tried to pull away, but the man threw an arm around his neck. When Bobby screamed for help, the driver of a Budweiser truck at the curb jumped out and stared at them.

The man in black pulled down his cap to hide his face, let go of Bobby, and disappeared back into the alley.

Like a sign post, Tommy still stood in the same spot. He hadn't run. He hadn't called for help. He'd just watched with his eyes bugged out and his mouth open.

Bobby slapped his brother. "When I tell you to run, you run," he said as he grabbed his brother by his backpack and hustled him up the street. "Why didn't you go for help?" He yanked him around a trashcan over-flowing with soda cups, plastic bags, and a torn-up shoe.

Tommy stumbled and glanced back. "Why'd that dude grab you, man?"

Bobby breathed hard. The sweat running into his eyes stung. "What're you doin' here?"

Tommy pulled away and tripped over a hole in the sidewalk. "I was lookin' for a place to do my homework."

Bobby grabbed Tommy by the jacket. "That's bullshit."

"Get outta my face, bro," said Tommy. "You ain't my daddy."

"Why'd you come here?" Relief and anger and nightmarish fear were all tangled up in Bobby's head. "You been sneakin' off to smoke again, ain't you?"

Bobby patted down his brother and found a joint. "I knew it. What would Grandma say if I showed her dis?" He tossed it down a grate in the rain gutter at the curb and glared at his brother.

"Chill, man," said Tommy. "A dude hasta have some fun."

What was he supposed to do now? Even to Bobby, telling his brother to stay away from drugs when he'd been out selling dippers seemed pretty lame. "How do you know that dude in the alley?"

"Ain't never seen him before," said Tommy, "but he sure knows you." His brother pulled a photograph out of his pocket and handed it to Bobby. "Dude told me to give you this."

When Bobby glanced at the picture, he recognized their living room. His face dropped.

He stared at the photo of his grandmother asleep in her recliner.

PIANO WIRE

B OWERS HAD SPENT the last fifteen minutes sitting at a table under the square, black umbrellas of Paul's outdoor eating area. Sitting outside in the open air felt great. The wide-backed chairs and small, white tables had a classy-comfortable style that she could easily envision on a sidewalk somewhere in France.

While she waited for her friend Berti to show up, Bowers watched tourists enjoying the day by strolling up and down Pennsylvania Avenue. Many stopped at the huge circular Navy Memorial not far from her table that depicted milestones from Naval history. A handful of sparrows pecked at the ground and squabbled over every crumb dropped by customers.

The birds scattered as a server arrived at Bowers' table. The waitress placed a tray with a freshly baked croissant, raspberry jam, and a steaming mug of coffee on the table in front of her.

Something about the warm sides of the glass mug and the rich aroma made the world around her feel a little more normal.

It seemed that she'd been in a state of high alert for so long that it had become normal. For the next hour she wasn't on surveillance. She wasn't apprehending a killer, calling for a body bag, preparing for a firefight or worrying about Major Crimes taking over her case. For now, she felt like everyone else enjoying a normal afternoon.

The illusion faded when her phone buzzed with an incoming call from Magrath, who spoke fast as always.

"Bowers," she said, "we confirmed the dancer's identity. In New Orleans she was born Daniel Fisher, and then she went off to D.C. and became Danielle Fisher. And there's something else of interest."

"The killer's fingerprints?"

"I wish. Listen. That was a good pickup on the debris on her sleeve. They're seeds from white avens. They're related to a wild rose."

The name meant nothing to Bowers, but Magrath acted as if it were big news. "We caught a break," she said.

Bowers sipped her coffee. "What's so special about—"

"Avens? They're unique. The seeds dry hard and have an arm with a hook at the end. Little buggers dug right into the fabric and held on for the ride."

Bowers frowned. "None of the flowerbeds at our scenes had anything that looked like wild rose bushes."

"Exactly," said Magrath. "It's something from the killer. He had to transport her to the church in something. Maybe he has a truck that parks under or near a white avens and the seeds blew into the bed."

"Great. Now all I have to do is find him and his vehicle and his damned rose bush," said Bowers. "And enough evidence to tie him to the murders."

"Honey, listen to me. You'll find him. I can tell you one other thing. He used a big knife."

"Straight-edged or serrated?"

"Little of both. Look for something that has weight to it like the kind hunters use. Maybe a Smith & Wesson. They make a serrated drop-point blade."

Bowers ended the call. She tore off a bite of her croissant and watched food trucks gathered along the curb. She couldn't help but laugh when she saw the blood-shot eyes of a crazed, cartoon tomato on the side of the truck that made wood-fired pizzas.

Looks like me in the morning.

Bowers finished her pastry and coffee, and stood to leave just as her friend emerged from the crowd. Annette Bertolini, Berti for short, was a beautiful girl, but Bowers almost didn't recognize her.

Last time she'd seen her friend, Berti had worn a sweet sundress and bright, pink flip-flops. This time she'd decked herself out in black, leather boots, short skirt, a revealing red top, and dark makeup.

Bowers frowned at the getup. "What's with the new look?"

Berti shrugged as she took a seat. "I needed a change." She peeked around the side of the table at Bowers' pants. "Hey. Speak for yourself. At least I don't have sea horses on my ass."

Bowers glanced down at the fabric's swirling blue and green pattern and shrugged. "Somehow, a dress and stilettos don't work with a Glock and handcuffs." Bowers waved over the waitress.

"Sorry," said Berti. "I'm not hungry. I'll just have an unsweetened iced tea."

After their server left, Bowers leaned forward. "Why aren't you eating?" Her concern rose when she noticed an angry bruise on her friend's arm.

Berti tucked a long lock of blonde hair behind one ear. "I'm on a diet."

Their server delivered Berti's iced tea and refilled Bowers' coffee. Berti stood about five-seven and had gorgeous body. She didn't need to lose weight.

"So, does a guy have something to do with this new diet?"

Berti's brown eyes flashed up at Bowers, then looked away. "I need to lose ten pounds. That's all."

That worried Bowers. "So who's the guy?"

"Jeez, Bowers!"

"What do you know about him?"

Berti blushed. "He's crazy about me." She fiddled with a multi-strand silver necklace. "He gave me this. Isn't it cool?"

The attractive necklace had been professionally made, but

showing a homicide detective neckwear made from piano wire was hardly reassuring.

Bowers lean back in her chair. "So tell me about him."

"He's nice to me. Protective," Berti said.

Bowers frowned at her friend, and the bruise. Berti pulled down her sleeve. *This girl has no idea how vulnerable she is.* "Is he the one who told you to lose weight?"

Berti shook her head, but Bowers didn't believe her. "Good Lord, Berti," she said. "When are you going to learn to stay away from guys like that?"

"Hey, I'm not stupid. I watch TV. Besides, he's too cute to be one of those freaks." A slight flicker of strain flashed through Berti's eyes and then vanished.

Bowers threw down her napkin. "Girl. I don't want you hurt. Trust me, looks have nothing to do with it. You can't go by that." She grabbed Berti's wrist. "Do I have to drag you through D.C. Correctional to show you how many handsome guys do hideous things?"

Berti pulled her arm away. "I have a gut feeling about this one."

"It's hunger pangs," said Bowers. "Eat a sandwich, you'll feel better."

"If he was some kind of creep, I'd know it."

Bowers bit her lip. *This is getting nowhere.* "You gonna tell me his name?"

Berti sighed. "I'll let you meet him, but not yet. When you do, you'll like him. He's tall and gorgeous and we're going out later tonight at this little after-hours place he told me about."

"Why so late?" asked Bowers.

Berti glanced at her watch and sipped her tea. "He works tonight, so do I."

Bowers picked at the crumbs left on her plate from the croissant. What if work had been the reason the killer most often struck after midnight?

"Berti, thanks."

"For what?" One of Berti's eyebrows went up.

Bowers paid the bill. "You reminded me of something important

Kill Notice

that I need to check into." While waiting for the change, she scanned the sidewalk and spotted a black kid in a dark hoodie.

"Excuse me for a minute," said Bowers as she stood.

The boy, who appeared to be about sixteen, stopped and took a step back toward the food trucks. They both stared at each other. Bowers recognized him as the same kid who'd run away from her at the Junk Box.

"Look out," said Berti.

Bowers ducked while a server with a full tray of drinks wove between the tables. When Bowers scanned the crowd searching for the boy, he had vanished.

***

AFTER LUNCH, Bowers went back to her desk and put an alarm on her phone to remind her of this evening's training event. The posted notice claimed that tonight's exercise focused on hand-to-hand conflicts. Maybe Clawski would be there. *That could be fun.* A wicked smile crossed her face.

Bowers sat at her desk and scanned the pictures on her shelf and the letter of commendation, shooting awards, and her Metro PD manuals. She studied the photo of Uncle Marvin proudly standing next to her back when she'd worn her battle dress uniform.

She spent the next hour sifting through her files and timelines. With that data, she began plotting out the hours when the killer had been active.

Magrath dropped by, plopped into the chair next to Bowers' desk, and handed her a folder. "You need to see this."

Bowers glanced at the report inside. "You found something?"

"They're cold cases. Most of them are from before you joined the force," said Magrath. "Thought you'd find them interesting."

There had to be twenty names on the list. Bowers read the brief description of each case. One defining detail jumped out at her. Underwear had been displayed at each scene. The last one on the list was the case of a cable guy who hadn't returned from making his calls. The report stated that the body had been found behind a restaurant, head down in a grease barrel. His underwear had been left over the rearview mirror in his van.

She tapped on the cable guy's name. "What was the day and time of death?"

"He disappeared on a Tuesday," said Magrath, "around 3 p.m. Died around 2 a.m. All the buttons on his shirt had been clipped off. Same with all the others."

TAKEDOWN

AFTER FINISHING her timelines, Bowers studied the list Magrath have given her and the corresponding cold case files. She also checked her computer for a response to the data she'd entered into NCIC, the National Crime Information Center. They had done a nationwide search looking for unsolved cases where buttons were taken presumably as trophies. She'd held back information about the panties. If the killer was a cop, he'd have access to the same resources and she didn't want to reveal how much she knew.

Bowers logged in and clicked on the results. A number of cases fit her parameters. The oldest case among them stood out. The victim hadn't died. She'd been raped. Bowers pulled out her phone and made a call to West Virginia.

A detective by the name of Meeks answered. As luck would have it he'd claimed that he'd taken his lunch at his desk while everyone else had left. Better yet, he remembered the case, albeit vaguely.

She could hear him tapping on a keyboard.

Meeks grunted. "As I remember, we were fit to be tied over this one." She heard a pause. "Yip, gittin' her to talk didn't work. She was scared real bad and wanted no part of talkin' to us. Wouldn't cooperate."

Bowers frowned. "Do you have the files or remember the name of a suspect?"

"Doesn't look like it."

"Why not?" she asked.

"I'll give you what for," he said. "We got a new facility about ten years back. When we moved everything over, some stuff came up missing."

She balled up a piece of paper and hurled it across her cubicle.

"But I tell you what, we got something that might help. We still have the rape kit, if you want it. Never ran the tests. No point without the girl's cooperation. But it's been properly stored all this time. We aren't yokels down here."

"Sir, you just made my day," said Bowers.

"Might take me a few days to git it to ya."

By the time she'd made arrangements for him to send the kit, it was too late to grab dinner.

After chugging down a mug of soup in the breakroom, she returned to her desk and found Russ Parker sitting in her chair, thumbing through her desk drawers and files.

Son of a bitch.

He rifled through her pencil drawer. "You got a pen in here?"

She marched toward him and slapped the drawer shut. "What the hell are you doing?"

Parker picked through her pencil cup, took out her favorite pen, and began to write something from one of the files into his notepad. He started to put the pen in his pocket. She grabbed it and tossed it on top of the desk.

"That's not yours."

He swiveled in her chair and leaned back. Without his mirrored glasses she could see his bright-blue eyes. "I'm just checking on your progress. I have a duty to make sure this case gets solved." He grinned up at her. "How about you give me an update?"

"How about you get out of my chair."

Parker slowly rose to his feet. "I'll play this game for a while, but if you want to remain a homicide detective, I suggest you learn to play nice."

Bowers pulled the file out of his hand. "If you want to talk to me, call. You go digging through my desk and files again and we are going to have a problem."

Parker pulled out his phone and punched in a number. Her phone buzzed.

"Okay," he said, "I called. Now can we talk?" He slipped his phone into the pocket of his shirt.

"No." Bowers dropped the file into her file drawer, and locked it. The alarm on her phone went off. "I've got a meeting I need to be at."

Parker tapped on her desk. "I'll be watching you," he said. A moment later he moseyed away toward the exit.

Bowers kicked back in her chair. *What an asshole.* Her eyes drifted up to the shelf above her lateral file cabinet. She frowned. Her pictures had been moved and her letter of accommodation had been left face down on the shelf.

His words *I'll be watching you* tumbled through her mind.

STILL FURIOUS ABOUT Parker's invasion of her workspace, Bowers went to the locker room and changed into athletic gear. She grabbed her green bag and headed toward the back door.

Mitch waited for her in the corridor. "Are you going over to the training session?"

"Yeah," she said, "I feel like punching the crap outta something."

"I feel like that all the time." He kept pace with her. "You okay?"

Bowers dropped her bag and leaned against the wall. "Mitch, I came back from the breakroom and found that guy from Major Crimes going through my desk."

"That's over-reaching," he said. "What did he want?"

She told him about the confrontation. "The guy is starting to piss me off."

Mitch leaned against the wall next to her. "I'll talk to him. Don't worry." He flashed her that smile. "Now go beat the shit outta something, will ya?"

She waved and headed to her car. Maybe Mitch would talk to the chief.

She pulled into the parking lot for the converted garage where PD personnel had started gathering for the training event. She spotted Clawski's truck and Johnny's car. *Sweet.* This ought to be interesting.

Bowers entered the open garage door and found an instructor she recognized from the academy.

His face lit up when he saw her. The man hurried toward her. "Bowers!" he said as he reached out to shake her hand. "If I'd known you were coming, I would've had you teaching this."

"Hank, it's good to see you, too." She snapped his wrist sideways, grinned at him, and let go.

He gave her a hug and slapped her on the back. "I've missed having you in class. Things have been dull ever since you graduated."

Hank checked his watch and let out an ear-splitting whistle.

Bowers watched him shake his hand and chuckle, as he headed toward the huddle of officers. "It's gonna be a good night, folks. Gather around," he said.

Hank stood in the middle of the thick, yellow mat that covered the floor. Most of the detectives from her unit were there, along with others from the PD. Cybex machines, benches, kettle bells, and racks of weights lined the walls.

As Hank explained the skill he planned to teach, Bowers stood in the back and stretched out. She did reps of biceps curls using dumbbells, and listened to him talk about pressure points. She knew them all and had used most of them.

Part of her wanted to return to the cold cases in her desk, until she spotted Clawski standing in the far corner.

He'd dressed in a Wizards T-shirt, and pair of shorts that revealed his white, doughy thighs. As usual, Clawski busied himself with ogling the female officers. Bowers doubted that he'd heard Hank's pointers.

"Now," said Hank, "if you ever have to face off with a subject who

Kill Notice

is bigger and stronger than you—ladies, listen up—this technique will serve you well. But I warn you." Hank held up his hand. "You *must* use this with extreme caution. As you will see in our demonstration, it is important *not* to put too much pressure on the subject's chest or his sternum will shatter and you will kill him."

All eyes were on Hank, except Clawski's. Bowers knew Hank had noticed. He never let things like that slide. She wondered what he would do in response.

This, I've gotta see. She stood closer to the mat.

"Clawski," yelled Hank. "Front and center."

Bowers smiled. She knew the maneuver Hank had described. *Can't wait to see Clawski at the raw end of that deal.*

Clawski strutted onto the mat and stood next to Hank with his shoulders back.

"Bowers," said Hank, "show us how it's done."

She couldn't believe her ears. After hesitating for a split second, Bowers stepped onto the mat as Hank backed away.

Clawski smacked his gum and stood flatfooted. He flexed his flabby biceps and waved at her to bring it on.

Bowers' mind shifted into her old ways of survival. Concentration took over. The hoorahs and cheers fell into the background. From the corner of her eye she saw fists pumping and everything that moved, including the air freshener fluttering in the breeze from a fan.

Clawski stood in the center of her vision. He extended his arms as if he were planning to tackle her.

Dipshit. You're making this easy.

When she stepped closer, Clawski grinned like a cat who didn't know an osprey circled overhead. Bowers adjusted her balance and harnessed all the power in the muscles of her back and legs.

"Go!" yelled Hank.

Bowers sprung. She punched her shoulder into Clawski's torso and heard his explosive exhale. With a fast, sharp sweep, she jerked his right arm back and kicked his right leg out from under him.

Clawski landed flat on his back.

Before his head hit the mat, she planted her knee into his

sternum and pressed down just enough to cause his diaphragm to spasm.

Clawski coughed, swallowed his gum, and lay there wide-eyed, staring up at her.

The voices around her went silent.

She heard Hank in the background. "This is a lethal maneuver, folks," he said. "Right now she could stop his breathing, but, as you can see, Bowers is bracing her weight on the ground to avoid doing any damage."

She carefully leaned in, face-to-face with Clawski. The veins of his forehead bulged. Sweat dripped from his wet hair onto the mat. His pulse pounded at the base of his neck.

Bowers stared back without blinking. She pushed down on his sternum another quarter of an inch and watched his face turn red. In a quiet voice she said, "Don't ever call me sweet-cheeks or split tail again."

AFTER SEEING his grandma and brother to bed, Bobby sat on the floor in the hallway and flipped opened his English textbook. He slapped it closed again and went back to the kitchen.

He scooped up some kibble from the bag in the cabinet and went to sit on the porch, hoping he'd see that stray dog. He shivered as he sat next to his grandma's pot of daisies, and wished he'd had the nerve to talk to that detective. It had taken him nearly two hours to find her and then, when she had noticed him, he'd chickened out.

He had his reasons. On the news he'd seen unarmed black men shot by the police. Brothers of the 202 had no trust for the cops. Getting too close to them was some scary business. Even so, he needed help and this lady cop seemed different.

The clear night sky had caused the temperature to drop. His cheap sweatshirt had thinned with age, and wasn't much help against the wind.

He could buy another one, but he had other things more impor-

Kill Notice

tant to spend his money on. Like electricity, food, and a little something for his grandma's birthday.

While he pulled weeds out of the cracks in the concrete, the dog appeared. He circled the garbage can outside the chain-link fence. Bobby held out a bowl and shook it. The kibble inside rattled.

The dog's head went up.

"Come on, boy. I gots some food for ya."

Bobby had bought the kibble at one of those dollar stores. He used a leftover container from a tub of butter spread as a bowl. The dog sniffed the air and warily entered the yard. His tail wagged as he came closer. Bobby put the bowl of dog food on the ground and waited.

The stray didn't have to be invited twice.

Bobby listened to the chomping sounds. He felt the animal's ribs as he ran a hand down the brown fur on the dog's back. This one was a pup, maybe a year old. No more.

The sense of doing something good made Bobby feel better than he had in a long while.

Within seconds the pup had licked the bowl clean and continued wagging that tail. Bobby refilled the bowl, this time with water from the faucet in the yard.

While the dog lapped up the water, Bobby went out to the curb, where he tossed out the weeds he'd pulled and bent to pick up the spilled garbage.

When he stood, lights from a big, black vehicle nearly blinded him.

Brakes screeched. Two heavy dudes jumped out.

He heard grunts and the shuffling of feet. The dog snarled and bolted for Bobby.

"What you want?" he asked as strong hands took hold of him.

He tried to pull away. His old sweatshirt tore.

The dog growled and snapped at the pant-leg of one man. Bobby heard a yelp as the man kicked at the dog.

"Leave him alone," he screamed at the men. "Let me go."

Bobby felt his feet leave the ground. The men shoved him into the back seat, next to another guy who smelled like sauerkraut. Bobby didn't know their names, but he recognized each one of them.

"Dude, I'm X Crew," said Bobby. "Why you be doin' this, man?"

"Papa G sent us," said the driver. "He wants to know where you been."

"So, you coulda ax me." Bobby checked his sweatshirt for more damage. "No cause to be kickin' my dog and messin' wit' me like dat."

The guy who smelled like sauerkraut shoved him back in the seat with his elbow. "Shut your face," he said. "Or I'll lay you out myself."

The man elbowed Bobby again. He'd seen these two beat up other guys pretty bad. Being trapped between them had him all undone.

His mouth went dry. His eyes watered.

Bobby held on to his trembling knees and wanted to go home.

MARKED MAN

BOWERS TOOK A LONG, hot shower before climbing into bed. The run-in with Parker still annoyed her, but the way Clawski's bug-eyes had stared up at her had topped off her day just fine. She chuckled.

Bowers moved her Glock to the back of her nightstand and grabbed her phone. She opened the app to see what her surveillance camera had captured. Her eyelids grew heavy as she watched videos that didn't change much. She fast-forwarded. The only visitor to her front door had been the white cat.

She lay back into the soft pillows of her bed. Her hand-painted, wooden chair sat near her closet under framed photographs she'd taken on her many dive trips. Among the purple-barrel sponges, a tiger shark, and sea anemones, the image of a giant manta ray coming out of the dark at her, with its four-foot-wide mouth gaping wide open, had always been her favorite.

Berti stuck in her mind. Bowers sent her a text: *Hope your date goes well.*

She put the phone down. Her bedroom had started to feel more homelike. It had a way to go, but unpacking had helped.

She glanced down at her phone. Berti's trusting nature and

striking features drew men who were happy to use her, especially when they'd discovered that she was a sucker for anyone who gave her attention.

It had happened before.

No matter how many times Bowers had tried to warn Berti, she always seemed to think the next cute guy in her life was "the one."

Bowers remembered what Berti had said. "If I let you frisk every guy I met, I'd never go on a date." She had a point, but then she didn't see what Bowers saw each day. Becoming a little cynical came with the job.

She stretched out under the covers and heard faint coughing from the apartment next door. It sounded as if Trevor's bedroom was on the other side of the wall.

A chirping sound announced an incoming message from Berti: *I'm doing great. Music's loud. Busy dancing. Call you later.*

That's weird.

Berti didn't dance. She hated loud music, and she almost never wrote a text more than four words long, much less four sentences.

Bowers rested on her elbow and sent a reply: *Call me now.*

The phone buzzed with an incoming call from Riggs.

"Hey," she said as she pulled the blanket up and rolled to her side. The sheets felt cool against her skin.

"How's the case?" Riggs asked.

She gave him an update, and enjoyed the deep, muffled sound of his voice, which meant he was in bed.

"Sorry," he said. "I didn't go to Ebbitt's tonight."

"No worries. I didn't either. I had a training exercise."

She told him about the takedown, and Clawski swallowing his gum. The deep sound of his laughter made her smile.

"Your partner hates him," said Riggs. "I'll bet he got a charge out of that."

Bowers chuckled. "Johnny left, grinning from ear-to-ear."

"Are you still going to that funeral tomorrow?" Riggs asked.

"Yeah. It's gonna be a zoo."

"Bowers, the press will be there. I assume you're taking the oppor-

Kill Notice

tunity to get information out of them." His tone had slipped into a gravelly sound, which meant he was about to fall asleep.

She pushed images of him in bed out of her mind before they had a chance to draw her thoughts into places she didn't need to go right now.

"I've already talked to them and gotten some footage at the church." she said. "Johnny's still working on it."

She could hear Riggs stretching. Her own pulse quickened.

"Talk to them some more," he said. "Make friends. They might already have shots of your unsub. See if you can get footage of the crowd around the scenes. Compare that to the film you'll get at the funeral. Look for one person who shows up in more than one location."

"I'm trying to clear it with Mitch. As usual, he's all over my case."

"Tell him to back off," said Riggs. She listened to him yawn. The sound of rustling sheets in the background reminded her of how they used to lie in bed and discuss the world and the things they cared about.

Bowers bunched up her pillow. "Magrath has been nagging on him enough for both of us."

"She still pissed off about Clawski?"

"Apparently Clawski wasn't the only one who left footprints at the church. Mitch and a bunch of others did too and we know how much she hates it when cops contaminate a scene." Bowers lay silent for a moment, while listening to his breathing. "Riggs?"

"I'm here."

"There has been a guy poking around from Major Crimes. I think he's gonna pull the case."

"I heard," said Riggs.

"The guy is a jerk."

"I've noticed," Riggs said. "What did he do?"

"Parker marched in and invaded my workspace. I found him going through my desk and files. He doesn't respect personal boundaries," she said. "He likes taking control a little too much."

When Riggs spoke, his voice had become deeper and more

focused. "Don't worry about it, we've talked to him. The chief and I will keep an eye on him."

***

THE ESCALADE PULLED to a stop at the corner. Bobby had to pee, bad. The blinds were drawn on half of the sub shop's front windows. Behind them he could see the silhouette of Papa G's mountain of flesh seated inside at the same table as always.

A slit in the blinds opened. Papa G was waiting.

Bobby's chest tightened. He wondered if he'd ever see home again.

Big hands tugged at him. He grabbed at the headrest and the seatbelt and anything else he could get his hands on. They muscled him out of the car, anyway.

His knees buckled as they marched him inside.

As the door swung closed, Bobby heard one of the two men guarding the entrance say, "We's closed," to a customer, who hurried away.

His shins and elbows clunked against the hard bench as they crammed him into the seat. Bobby straightened himself out and glanced up at Papa G.

Under the harsh overhead lights, the big man hunched forward and focused on the yellow tabletop, where he twirled a straw in circles.

Bobby prayed he wouldn't pee his pants in front of the guys. "Papa G, they messed me up good," he said as he showed the rip in his sweatshirt to Papa G. Bobby tried to sound tougher and braver than he felt. "I told 'em that if you wanted to see me, all you hadta do is say so."

Like a mist, silence settled around him and the men standing near the table. Bobby heard the rattle of the old air conditioner. He also heard the thumping of his own pulse.

"I don't ax," said Papa G. "I tell. Where you been?"

Bobby squirmed in his seat and crossed his legs under the table.

Kill Notice

"I went to school and my grandma's been sick. She needed my help. A man's gotta take care of his family."

"We's your family." Papa G tossed the straw aside. He grabbed Bobby's wrist and yanked it toward him.

With his other hand, Papa G pulled a knife from under the table. The blade snapped open. He nodded to his men.

Bobby's back went rigid.

The guy who smelled like sauerkraut pinned Bobby's arm to the table. Bobby tried to pull away, but a guy behind him threw his arm around Bobby's neck and pulled his other hand back.

Bobby kicked and twisted, but it only made the arms holding him clamp down tighter.

He yelled at Papa G, "What you doin', man?" His eyes watered as he stared at the knife.

Papa G pressed the thin tip against the flesh.

"What'd I do? I don't understand," shrieked Bobby.

He felt a searing pain as Papa G carved a thin line in the skin over his wrist. Bobby heard his own screams as he fought to get away.

Papa G crossed the cut with another carved line.

Bobby stared, wide-eyed, as streams of red pooled on the yellow tabletop and were smeared by the scuffling. The blood and the X cut in his own flesh made his stomach lurch.

He felt his jeans turn warm and wet. He couldn't stop his chin from quivering. He couldn't see beyond the knot of emotion that had betrayal, humiliation, and being scared shitless all tangled up together in his head.

Papa G sat back. He pinched a bunch of napkins from the table and slowly wiped off his knife. "That's to remind you who your real family is."

Papa G let go of the napkins and let them drop to the table. The man who'd held Bobby's arm gathered up the napkins and pressed them against the wound.

The stale, cold breeze from air conditioner made Bobby shiver. His head spun as someone put white tape around the makeshift bandage. Pulling himself together wasn't easy, especially in jeans soaked in sweat and piss that had started to turn cold.

The room swirled, and Papa G looked strangely far away. Bobby took a deep, quivering breath and tried to clear his head.

"Now that we understand each other," said Papa G, "the police been axing for you. Somebody named Bowers. You don't talk to no police. If you go tellin' her about the crew, you and me's gonna have a beef and next time—" Papa G ran his finger through the blood on the table and wiped it off on Bobby's sweatshirt. "—my knife will go lots more than skin deep. You sees what I'm sayin'?"

Bobby stared at him. The room had come back into focus, but he couldn't stop shaking.

Papa G motioned to his cousin, who cleaned off the table. He then went to the back room and returned with a jacket.

The big man took it from him and tossed it at Bobby. "From now on, you come correct. You wear dis."

Bobby stared at the black jacket. It was a fine-looking Helly Hanson and not something he would ever be able to afford.

"I hear tell," said Papa G. "The man in black gave you something."

Bobby nodded. He pulled out the photograph by the corner and handed it to Papa G, who snatched it up and studied it before giving it back.

"You got dis when?" he asked.

"This mornin'," said Bobby. He could barely croak out the words. "He's gonna hurt my family."

"Give my man here some water," said Papa G. He grabbed Bobby's other hand.

Bobby felt another wave of nausea.

This time Papa G patted Bobby's arm. "I gots your back, but you's gonna do something for me first."

SOUND IN THE DARKNESS

B OWERS OPENED HER EYES and lay perfectly still. She stared up at the ceiling of her bedroom and wondered what had woken her. In the darkness, she slowed her breathing and listened.

Sounds of movement came from her living room.

She reached for her Glock on the nightstand as a surge of adrenaline brought her fully awake. Her hand found only her phone and charging cord.

What the hell? She had left her service pistol, a .40 caliber Glock, on her nightstand. Where'd it go?

Bowers pulled back the sheet and quickly slipped out of her warm bed. The bedroom door stood open a crack.

A sound like a marble rolling across a hard surface came from the kitchen. Goosebumps rose over her back.

After quietly opening her nightstand drawer, she retrieved her backup weapon, a smaller version of her .40 caliber service pistol.

Bowers crept across the soft carpet and carefully eased the door closed. Very slowly, she turned the lock, hoping it wouldn't make a noise. She winced when the tumblers clicked as they fell into place.

The shuffling on the other side of the door stopped.

Bowers stepped back and leaned against her polished wooden

dresser. With her backup weapon in hand, she held her breath and heard Trevor's muffled cough next door, but nothing in her own apartment.

Being naked left her at a disadvantage. The breeze from the fan made her feel even more exposed. She carefully stepped toward the closet, where she set down her gun long enough to slip on a pair of leggings. As she pulled a T-shirt over her head, the doorknob twisted slightly.

She grabbed her gun.

The lock held. For now.

Bowers breathed quietly through her mouth and heard footsteps in the hall. The space under the door showed shadows from the intruder's feet pacing in the dim, ambient light. Her toes felt cold air seeping in.

A thump on her bedroom door made her step back.

She picked up her phone and crept around the bed to the window. While leaning against the wall, she sent a text to Riggs: *NEED BACKUP NOW! Someone is in my apartment!*

She peered through the blinds at the darkness. The only illumination came from the decorative lights along the walkway.

Riggs answered almost immediately: *En route.*

Response time from the station could be two minutes or ten. She rested a palm on the cold pane of glass. The sliders had been painted over so many times the window couldn't be opened, at least not without making huge racket.

A loud, hard thump landed against her door. The doorframe popped and creaked. Another blow like that would bust the door in.

Bowers searched for cover. She held her weapon ready, knowing a stray bullet could penetrate the wall and rip into Trevor's bedroom in the apartment next door. Bad odds, all around.

She backed into the space next to the door.

Seconds later, a louder, more forceful impact hit her door. It burst all the way open and sent splinters of the doorframe flying.

The intruder ducked back into the hall. She could hear him breathing.

Bowers started to move. "Hands up or I'll shoot." She aimed around the doorframe and down the hallway.

She heard a low guttural sound as the figure flinched away from her, and ran.

The sound of running feet echoed down the hallway. She charged after the intruder and caught a glimpse of a tall silhouette as it turned the corner into her living room.

Bowers stopped. Crouching low, she eased into the dark room, and lurched away as a lamp hit the wall next to her head.

She dove at the figure. Size and strength told her the intruder was male. He slammed his elbow into her face. Her head and arm flew back and she lost her grip on her pistol. She heard it crash into something.

Bowers landed a hard punch in his side and heard a grunt. She threw everything she had into a leg sweep, knocking him off his feet.

He careened into the coffee table, scrambled over the couch, and landed on the floor in front of her bookshelf. Bowers rolled away and flipped on the lights.

She gasped for air. Her backup pistol was nowhere in sight. Bowers peered at the space between her couch and bookshelf. The intruder appeared to be gone, and yet the deadbolts on her front door remained firmly locked.

A breeze hit her shoulders. Hair went up on her neck. Bowers forced her breathing under control.

She backed away and found her Glock on the kitchen counter. When she picked it up, it felt too light. She dropped the mag. It was empty. *What the hell?*

She always kept the magazine fully loaded with an extra one in the pipe. Bowers reached into a kitchen drawer and pulled out a full mag. She slapped it into the pistol. As she approached the living room, she racked the slide.

Bowers checked behind the couch, where a handful of books had tumbled off the shelf. She also found smudges of mud and a few dead leaves scattered over the carpet.

On the far end of the couch, near the side table, the lower

window stood wide open with the screen missing. Cold night air poured in.

Bowers backed away and quickly checked the other side of the TV and recliner. One step at a time, she moved toward the polished granite breakfast bar.

She held her pistol close to her body as she scanned both rooms again, before taking a closer look at the counter. Satisfied that the intruder had gone, she approached the breakfast bar.

Like a row of tiny soldiers, sixteen shiny hollow-points stood in a neat line. Now she knew where the .40 caliber cartridges from her Glock had gone.

Even worse. Finding the gun in the kitchen meant that he'd taken it from her nightstand while she'd slept. His message that he could disarm her at will pissed her off even more than it scared her.

She kneed the cabinet under the counter.

I need to buy a Belgian Malinois with a bad attitude.

Bowers began flipping on every light. Other than the window, a broken coffee mug, and a smashed lamp she found nothing out of place until she crept back down the hallway toward her bedroom.

She switched on the hall and bedroom lights, and stopped. The Post-it note she'd left on the front door hung on her bedroom door. Her message "I will find you" had been crossed out in red ink.

Under it had been printed "Can't wait."

Bowers groaned.

A new button had been taped to the note.

BOWERS SLUMPED against the wall in her hallway. After a few seconds, she slid down and sat on the floor with the back of her head resting against the wall.

For a moment she closed her eyes. More than anything else, it rankled her that the killer had invaded her home.

With slightly trembling fingers, she called Mitch. "Sarge, I need help. The perp was inside my apartment. He left a button on my bedroom door."

"My God, are you all right?" he asked.

"I'm fine." She wasn't fine, but she wasn't about to tell him that.

"I'll send a team over. When did this happen?"

"He just left." She ended the call and awkwardly pushed herself off the floor, took a few steps, and braced herself against the wall. After taking a deep breath, she straightening up.

While slowly wandering through her quiet apartment, she held her Glock steady and ready. Thoughts about the unsub filled her mind. This time his message had been far more threatening.

With all of her senses still bristling, every flicker of light through the windows caught her attention. The stippled grip of her pistol rubbed against her palm like sandpaper. Water from the apartment upstairs rushed through the pipes in the wall.

Bowers flinched when her phone buzzed. She took a deep breath, and answered.

"Hey, you okay?" asked Magrath.

"I'll be just ducky once we catch this bastard."

"Honey, sit tight, I'm almost there."

Bowers ended the call and heard voices and a knock. She stood against the wall near her front door. "Who's there?" she asked in a firm voice.

"Metro PD. Bowers, this is Officer Thompson."

Peering through the narrow, frosted panel of glass next to the door, she recognized the blurred outlines of three men in uniform. Even so, she kept her weapon ready as she eased opened the door and let them in.

After sliding her Glock into her waistband, she shook hands with Officer Thompson. The other two stood watch at the door, which they left wide open.

Moments later, Magrath marched in and engulfed Bowers in a hug. "Okay, what did you touch?"

"I live here, remember?"

"I assume you handled your weapons."

"I had to defend myself," Bowers said. She felt her temper rising as she pointed at the row of bullets on the counter. "I wanted to throw those across the room and wipe all the crap off my bedroom door, but I didn't."

"Good girl. Let's get cracking." Magrath waved a photographer into the room. "I wanna thorough walk-through. Make that two. And photograph everything."

"Good thing I did the dishes," said Bowers.

Magrath put an arm around her. "Honey, I know this sucks." Magrath frowned. "You look like crap."

Bowers glanced down. The blood on the front of her T-shirt explained why her face and mouth stung.

Magrath went straight to the kitchen. "Where are your Ziplocs?"

Bowers felt her lip, and pointed to the blue box on the counter.

Magrath filled a plastic bag with ice from the dispenser on the door of the fridge and handed it to her.

"Knowing you, the perp looks worse."

That made Bowers laugh, but not for long. Her bottom lip throbbed something fierce. Her tongue felt the split as she watched a growing troop of uniforms and crime scene techs combing her apartment. One pulled her Baby Glock out from under the couch. It had apparently hit the mug on the coffee table and tumbled underneath the couch.

"That's mine," she told the tech, who ignored her and put the weapon in a brown bag.

Bowers tucked her hair behind her ears. "What am I supposed to use for a backup now?" She grumbled, "God I hate this," and went into the kitchen. Once again, she felt like a displaced person in her own home.

"Did the intruder wear gloves?" asked Magrath.

Bowers nodded.

Magrath's eyes studied the room. "Keep your service pistol. We won't get anything off it anyway."

Bowers pressed the ice against her lip until it became numb. *If only this would work on my brain.* Her racing mind hammered at the details, trying to analyze what had happened and why.

Bowers leaned over the cool granite counter and put her face in her hands. *I don't want to be here. Not now. Maybe, not ever.*

"I need to test that," said Magrath as she pointed to Bowers' shirt. "Maybe we'll get lucky and his blood will be on it too."

Bowers straightened up and went to her bathroom, where she changed tops and avoided the mirror. Seeing the damage to her face wouldn't make her feel any better.

Moments later she opened the bathroom door and handed the bloody shirt to Magrath, who'd been waiting with a brown paper evidence bag.

Bowers heard Riggs' familiar voice coming from the living room. "Get the hell outta my way." He flashed his FBI credentials and barreled straight toward her.

Riggs grabbed her hand. "She's with me." They left the crowded apartment and took a seat outside on a wood and wrought-iron bench, twenty feet from the apartment. The course grass under her toes felt damp with dew.

He held her hand so tightly he nearly cut off the circulation. Even so, it felt good to be with him and out of that apartment.

Light pouring through her open front door left a yellow triangle on the walkway. More scene techs arriving in their white, Tyvek suits resembled aliens drawn inside by the light.

She and Riggs watched people coming and going.

Officer Thompson stood out of the way as Magrath hauled in additional toolboxes of gear. On the horizon, the dark sky had begun to lighten. Riggs leaned forward. Bowers leaned into the nook between the back of the bench and his shoulder.

"What happened?" he asked.

She found his voice more soothing than the ice and told him the story. "Riggs. He was in my bedroom watching me sleep. You know how I wake up at every sound. How'd he do that? And why would he take that kind of risk?"

"To show you how close he could get." Riggs stared into the darkness. "This is about control and power."

Riggs put his right arm around her. With his left he lifted her hand with the ice back to her lips. With a frown, he examined her hand. "You clocked him good. Is it broken?"

Bowers shook her head, flexed her hand, and put the ice on it for a few minutes.

Riggs studied her face. "Why didn't you shoot him?"

She sat forward. "A single mom with two kids lives next to me. Her son's room is on the other side of my bedroom wall. Besides, the guy ran. I wasn't going to shoot him in the back."

Mitch showed up. By his stiff posture she could tell he had on a bulletproof vest under his shirt.

Riggs rubbed her shoulder. "What I don't get is why he broke into your bedroom?"

"I do," she said. "I locked the door. I think that pissed him off."

OUT OF CONTROL

BOWERS BLINKED at the pop of a camera's flash and watched a crime scene photographer taking pictures of the new flowerpot outside her apartment. He disappeared around the corner to the window that had been breached. She could no longer see the man, but his camera's strobe went off like bursts of lightning.

After pulling her phone out of her waistband, Bowers tapped on the icon for her surveillance camera, hoping to see if it had captured an image of her intruder. It should've recorded all the people running in and out of her apartment, but didn't.

The last clip had been timed-stamped at 3:45 a.m., moments before she'd been awakened. Bowers sat forward and stared at the small screen. The feed was a little grainier than she liked, but the angle of the camera had been spot on, until gloved fingers moved in front of the lens. The images jostled and the lens rotated toward something dark. A few seconds later, the clip ended.

Riggs had been watching over her shoulder.

"Shit," she said.

"Looks like he repositioned your camera."

"I hate this guy," she said. The bench rocked when she stood. Her toes were cold.

Riggs rose with her and stayed close by her side. "Where are you going?" he asked as he warded off anyone who got too close.

Bowers stopped on the hard pavement. "I'm getting dressed and going to work. We have that funeral today, and I have a shitload of paperwork on my desk."

Riggs followed her into the apartment. A handful of yellow evidence markers dotted the floor and furnishings. A CSI tech dusted the open window and frame. Bowers watched a cushion from her couch go into an evidence bag, and her favorite quilt go into another. She shook her head.

They passed others picking through her kitchen.

When she approached her bedroom, Riggs pulled her back and stared at the door and splintered frame.

His eyes hardened as he glared at the altered note and the tiny, red button still hanging on her door. She could almost feel his anger trip. Everyone said they were sorry and concerned, but the way he seemed to understand the threat made all the difference.

Bowers stepped into her bedroom. Her closet door had been opened. Mitch stood there staring at her clothes.

"Anything missing?" he asked.

"Not that I know of." She felt her neck flush as she reached in front of him for a pair of plain black pants and a shirt. "I'll be in the bathroom."

She closed the door and started to pull off her shirt. Instead, she sat on the edge of the bathtub and stared at the floor. Outside the bathroom, her colleagues were sifting through every square inch of her home. It was protocol. Necessary. And she hated every second of it.

RIGGS NOTICED his photo laying on her nightstand as he waited outside Bowers' bathroom and listened. He had few doubts about what was going through her mind. When they had been outside on the bench, she'd repeatedly gazed back at the apartment. Bowers had

Kill Notice

worked hard to unpack and settle in. Now she watched it all being disassembled in front of her eyes. It probably wasn't her things she worried about, but she did closely guard her personal space. This had to be pure torture.

Magrath entered the bedroom. Riggs frowned when Mitch picked up the photo and poked around inside the nightstand. The guy had on gloves, but still. Riggs felt his temper ratchet up.

"What are you doing?" he asked.

Mitch shrugged. "Just trying to figure out what happened."

"I doubt the perp left his name and number in her nightstand." Riggs stood eye-to-eye with the man. "Isn't it about time you and I start working together on this?"

Mitch peered past Riggs at the note on the bedroom door and snorted. "Special Agent Riggs, I surely do appreciate that you want to help, but—"

"But what? We're lucky it's the door were processing here and not her body."

Magrath nodded in agreement.

Mitch's mouth remained in that tight smile, and his dark eyes locked on the door.

Riggs stepped forward, forcing Mitch back. "Bowers needs resources to solve this damned thing before anyone else gets hurt."

Mitch blinked. His smile vanished. "We may operate a little different than you folks over at the Bureau, but I assure you I've got this under control."

"Like hell you do. Is that what you call this? Riggs jabbed a finger toward the note. "A serial killer just broke into your detective's home. And you allowed it by not giving her resources. This is out of control."

"What's going on?" asked the chief.

Riggs found the chief standing in the hallway, freshly shaven and in a clean uniform.

"It must be slow over at the Bureau," said Mitch as he rested one arm on Bowers' dresser. "The FBI is once again trying to muscle their way into our business."

Riggs ignored Mitch.

The chief stepped into the room and glared at Mitch.

"It's time," said Riggs, "to reconsider our approach."

Bowers came out of the bathroom and stopped. She studied each of them.

The chief took one look at her and frowned. "Jesus Christ, what happened to you?"

RIGGS HANDED an ice pack to Bowers on the way to his car. After driving her to the station, he pulled into the compound on the north side of the building and stopped near the back door.

The engine rumbled in idle as he wrapped his hand around hers. Bowers' slender fingers felt cool against his palm. Her slim, black pants and pale-blue shirt were unusually subdued, but it made sense considering she'd planned on attending a funeral.

He couldn't get over the balls it had taken for the unsub to have breached a locked window and enter the home of a Metro PD detective.

Riggs had examined the damage for himself. He'd seen that sort of thing before. After the screen had been removed, the glass had been neatly cut to gain access to the lock and to remove the doweling. Once the window had been unlocked and opened, the perp had crawled inside. Those adept at burglary often used this method.

It ate at him that the subject had been in Bowers' apartment. Mitch's presence made it worse. The man had a habit of getting under Riggs' skin, bad.

Bowers squeezed his hand and pulled him out of his thoughts. She dropped the melted ice pack into his palm. He tossed the bag on the floor in back of him and rubbed the back of her neck.

His fingers slipped through her silky brown hair. "You sure you're up for this?" he asked.

She wore that pained, distant expression he hated.

"Where else am I supposed to go? Home?"

She had a point. "You know you're welcome at my place."

Kill Notice

Bowers kissed the side of his face and rested her head on his shoulder. He felt her breath against his neck.

"Thank you," she said. "I don't know what I'd do without you."

Bowers straightened up and pulled out her ID card. "The way I see it, I can either sit around fretting, or I can go to work and do something about it. What would you do?"

He gently brushed his thumb across her bruised jaw. "I'd find the asshole who did this and tear him apart."

"Exactly," she said. "I'll call you later."

He watched her leave the car and disappear into the station.

The red button on her bedroom door meant another murder. With one more added to the body count they'd reach the threshold where the FBI would send in assets whether Mitch or Major Crimes wanted it or not.

At least that gave him something to smile about.

Riggs pulled out of the station and headed toward the field office.

Along the way he passed sleek, modern buildings that towered over old, intricate, brick structures. The number of trees and parks in D.C. set it apart from the other big cities he'd seen.

His phone buzzed with an incoming call from their lead cyber technician. "We've gone over the computers from the raid. Most of it is kiddie porn that you really don't want to see, but we also found some interesting files that contained their client list. We're back-tracing the IP addresses."

"Anyone of interest on the client list?" asked Riggs. He took North Capital Street to avoid tie-ups near Howard University and stopped at a red light.

"As expected, they all used code names. However, one user stood out. He wasn't as tech-savvy as the others. So far, we've been able to determine he's somewhere here in D.C. and goes by the name Hardball."

"Nice work. Find him. I'll be there shortly."

AFTER LEAVING RIGGS' car, Bowers entered the doors of CID and listened to the quiet rumble of the day getting started. Two detectives stopped talking and watched her go past. She ducked into the break-room and found a full pot of coffee that had just finished brewing.

Her mug was easy to spot amid the others on the drying mat. Riggs had given it to her. More than one of her colleagues had commented on the FBI logo emblazoned across the front of it.

The old coffee machine, the boxy refrigerator, and the bulletin board filled with notices hadn't changed. And yet everything around her seemed shifted slightly out of place.

After she filled her mug, Bowers slipped into a seat at the table with her back to the wall. The warmth of the mug cupped in her hands seemed to be the only thing that felt right.

She needed a minute.

The disjointed events from last night hobbled through her mind: the crashing of the lamp against the wall, a face she'd never gotten a good look at, and the intruder's gloved hand. Stark images from Ramadi welled up from the past. With them came the faces of the friends she'd lost.

The warm coffee made her lip throb. She knew Marvin was an early riser. Bowers leaned back against the wall and called him.

He answered promptly. "Morning, Missy."

They engaged in small talk. She listened as he told her about the X-Rays and medication they'd given him for his cough. The conversation came to an end when they called him to breakfast. The conversation had been brief, but the sound of his voice helped.

Bowers heard footsteps and glanced up to find Johnny standing in the doorway. He entered the small room, pulled out one of the blue chairs, and took a seat across the table from her.

"I heard what happened," he said. The flesh between his brows crimped. "I would've come over, but they said you'd already left for work."

She nodded. "Hell of a way to start a day."

Bowers expected him to ask her if she were okay or to tell him the story. Instead he gave her space and quiet, and time to regroup. He waited until she looked him in the eye.

Bowers couldn't help but laugh. "I must be quite a sight." She spread her fingers wide and peered down at the bruised knuckles on her right hand.

His eyes softened as he rocked back in his seat. "Nothing looks better than seein' my partner right here, right now."

Bowers realized there was more to this man than she'd originally suspected. He stared at the white wall behind her and patiently waited.

"Johnny? What do you make of this case?"

He cocked his head and hesitated for a second as if thinking. "The perp knows too much. You'd said he was way too skilled to be a civilian. I think that's an understatement." He picked up a broken plastic fork from the table and pressed its two remaining tongs into a Styrofoam cup. "He's been trained to kill," Johnny said. "That rules out wannabes."

She took a sip from her mug. "He's a cop, who's a hell of a lot more than a patrol officer."

Johnny nodded. "He knows too much about us, and especially you."

"That's exactly what I'm thinking," she said. "He knows us."

Bowers glanced down at the wedding ring on his hand. She knew Johnny had been married less than a year. "Is there anyone out of the area who your wife could stay with until this is over?"

"Already done. She's at my brother's house."

"The one in Maryland who raises German Shepherds?"

"Yup. God help anyone who tries to mess with her there." Johnny crushed the cup and tossed it and the fork into the big trashcan in the corner. "I'm just sorry I wasn't there, Bowers. You're my partner, I shoulda—"

"Thanks, but there's nothing you could've done," she said, picking up her mug. "Let's get to work. Magrath dropped off some cold cases I'd like your opinion."

JACKED UP

A N HOUR BEFORE Sapphire's funeral began, Bowers parked away from the fray on a patch of gravel near the cemetery's exit. As she made her way closer to the dark-green tent and standing sprays of white lilies and gladiolus, she passed the hearse and caught a glimpse of the casket behind the stately curtains.

It all appeared so solemn and understated, and so unlike what she knew of Sapphire. The dark, polished casket provided no hint of the carnage or the chaotic terror of her final hours. Bowers remembered that poster of Sapphire beaming in the spotlight in her gold dress.

She passed one headstone after another and felt the weight of the weapon on her hip. The jobs she had done hung in her thoughts.

One man in black robes came to mind. She remembered staring down the scope of her sniper rifle to watch him wielding a knife. He stood behind his hostage who'd been dressed in orange and forced to his knees.

Bowers knew the American's name and that his only mission had been enduring the unbearable poverty and heat to help feed Iraq's hungry and displaced citizens.

In one hand, the terrorist had held the hostage by the hair. In the other, he firmly gripped his knife. Poised and ready, he waited for a signal from the man operating a camera.

Bowers had wasted no time and took aim. She remembered hearing her own breathing and her spotter whispering to her of a shift in wind direction. After the final adjustment, she exhaled and squeezed the trigger.

She remained still. The only movement came from the familiar recoil thrusting into her shoulder as she continued staring through the crosshairs. Her shot had found its mark. Her hands didn't shake. She'd quietly pulled back the bolt with her thumb and caught her brass and let the hot casing drop next to her rifle.

Later, when asked what she had done afterward, she'd simply said, "Reloaded."

Her bravado was a mask of toughness expected by the Army, but there was nothing about killing that brought her joy. She never counted her kill shots. Didn't want to know. A clean hit was necessary. Important. But not something she celebrated.

She had simply been the last line of defense for that hostage.

It was the same with the 202 Killer. She needed to stop him before others died.

The gravel crunched under her steps as she hesitated near a tombstone for someone whose life had ended at the age of fifteen. That seemed like such a loss.

She'd never seen anything good about war, but it had some sense of fairness. Both sides had a job they'd been well trained to do. Not so when unarmed civilians faced a skilled killer. Their deaths seemed unfair.

Bowers knew the life of a soldier and a cop, but she hadn't really thought about what people like Sapphire faced each day. Bowers didn't condone her drug use, but from what she had pieced together, Sapphire had worked hard jobs and long hours in some pretty seedy operations. She seemed to be making an effort to make her life better. Then a killer had taken everything she'd worked for away.

A cool breeze made Bowers blink and popped her out of her thoughts. A long line of cars had begun queuing in behind the hearse. By the makes and models, she expected that Sapphire's friends were about to liven up her funeral with a little color.

Jacked-up pickup trucks, an old sedan with its bumper held on with tie-downs, a black mustang with purple running lights, and many others came in force.

Wally Chung stepped out of his old, white Caddy. He wore huge sunglasses and an open-necked shirt that had been pressed. Wally wore his best.

Behind him came a troupe of dancers. Their dresses of vibrant blues and greens, rich reds and corals, and hot yellows glimmered in the sunshine. The parade reminded Bowers of peacocks in full plumage.

While a wave of sequin-crusted shoes, beaded purses, feathered hats, and Wally's shiny scalp filled the guest area, uniforms kept an eye on the media lined up on the perimeter.

WJDC's reporter, Alex Keller, whom she'd been waiting to see, hurried toward her. She took the DVDs he handed her and dropped them into her jacket pocket.

Bowers ignored the way he stared at her face.

"What the hell happened to you?" he asked.

"My job comes with hazards."

"So I see." Alex continued to frown as he pointed at her pocket. "Those are copies of everything I've got. What do you want me to do now?"

"Cover this as you would any funeral. Get shots of everyone in the area and give me a copy."

"Will do." Alex leaned in close. His aftershave had a crisp, clean scent to it. "I thought you hated me. Why are you giving me this break?"

"You put yourself on the line. I can relate to that." Bowers forced her sore mouth into a half-smile. "If you want this story that bad, you deserve a chance to do it right."

Alex nodded and started to leave.

"However," she said as she grabbed him by the elbow. "If you

Kill Notice

screw up or cause more harm to these people or my investigation, I'll hang your ass on the communication tower behind my office."

He held up his hands. "Roger that."

She watched him set up on the green grass, at a respectful distance from the tent and the preacher and the grave.

Bowers caught sight of Mitch strolling about and went to check in with him.

"We're all set," she said as pallbearers slowly moved the casket into place.

Mitch yawned and stood quietly watching each person passing by. Knowing that he and many of her colleagues had been in her bedroom still bothered her. Bowers watched the continuing arrival of guests.

Some sat in the folding chairs next to Sapphire's sister, who wore a modest, black dress and a bleak expression. A very elderly gentleman, who appeared lost, sat next to her. His mouth moved constantly as if he had a tremor.

Many of the colorfully dressed dancers had gathered on the other side, near Wally. Everyone else stood quietly in a semi-circle.

While words about Sapphire's life and her loss were spoken, Bowers strolled around the outer perimeter and studied as many faces as possible. She saw a mix of frowns and tears. Heavy voices resonated with grief and disbelief. Clearly there were people who loved her.

Mitch remained in the same spot and appeared to be daydreaming.

Clawski showed up with a detective she knew as his partner. Bowers went to head them off before they reached the mourners. Clawski warily stepped back as she came closer. It didn't surprise her that he had given her a wide berth after the takedown.

Bowers kept her voice low. "Not one wisecrack out of you," she said. "Reporters are here, so keep your mouth shut. Do your job and keep an eye out for anyone suspicious."

He flashed her one of his wise-ass grins.

Bowers left him with his partner and another detective. As she grew closer to the grave, she noticed a man who looked like a college kid wandering the grounds.

She took a few steps toward him. When he held up his head and crossed a clearing she recognized Johnny's profile and gait, despite his undercover disguise. He covered the expanse of dense, green grass and respectfully stayed clear of the somber stone angels and crosses. Each time he moved, he had a different angle on those gathered.

As if on cue, the breeze blew in a scattering of clouds as three women sang something soulful. The air itself seemed to reflect the emotions of the mourners.

Clawski rocked back and forth in his wrinkled, khaki pants and shot Bowers another grin. One of these days, she thought, someone was going to deck that man.

Mitch stood behind three of the mourners and appeared to be watching the crowd. Bowers noticed his eyes shifting from the smooth, polished casket to the tall woman in front of him and then to the reporter filming the event.

Behind those gathered, one of the flashy dancers from The Junk Box contingent stood alone. She frowned at Clawski, who popped his gum and winked back at her.

Bowers waved over a detective. "Go tell Clawski I said to put his eyeballs back in his head and stop leering at that woman."

The detective approached Clawski and whispered to the man. Clawski glared at Bowers and then went back to flirting with the dancer, who appeared to be ignoring him.

You sad sack of shit. Flirting at a funeral, seriously?

Bowers started toward Clawski until she noticed someone in the trees. Johnny had his eyes on him too. Bowers couldn't get a good angle on it, but after shifting a few feet to her right, she caught a glimpse of a black male in a dark hoodie. The boy appeared to be the same kid she'd seen near Paul's and the Junk Box.

Johnny strolled past the hearse and made his way toward the teenager. Before Johnny could get to the boy, the kid disappeared into the woods.

Kill Notice

When the service ended, Bowers watched as mourners stood in huddles and consoled each other.

While the reporter interviewed attendees, Clawski took up a post near a few large oaks well out of the camera's line of sight. The dancer he'd been flirting with sashayed up to him in her fiery-red dress.

Bowers couldn't reach him fast enough to keep him from opened his trap, not without drawing the cameraman's attention. She watched as the dancer eased in real close. A smile of expectation covered his face. His eyebrows went up, so did the dancer's knee. Hard and fast. Clawski's mouth puckered. His face twisted into a knot as he bent forward.

His partner had gone to help keep the media in line and missed the whole thing.

Clawski's skin turned crimson. The dancer, who stood three inches taller than Clawski, put an arm around him as if they were old friends and held him upright. She escorted him a few feet and eased him down onto a bench. Clawski sat on the edge, gripping the armrest, and staring at the grass.

When the dancer put her back to Clawski and squared her shoulders, Bowers wondered if he had any clue that the dancer worked for Wally at The Junk Box or what that meant. After straightening her skirt, she strolled by Bowers with a satisfied grin and winked.

Bowers chuckled. *Saw that one coming.*

A few minutes later, the crowd began to thin.

Mitch had his phone up to his ear. His eyes were searching the crowd. When he saw Bowers, he emphatically waved at her to come.

She reached him as he dropped his phone into a pocket.

"Get Johnny. We've got another body. A female. This one is at the mansion of an NFL big shot."

MURDERMOBILIA

BOWERS FLIPPED ON her lights and sirens and zigzagged through the knot of vehicles on Chain Bridge Road. She drove past the 10,000 square-foot mansions across from Battery Kemble Park.

Johnny's chin dropped. "Look at these places. I couldn't afford the electric bill just to vacuum one of them."

Bowers focused on what she saw up ahead.

"Holy crap," said Johnny. "It looks like every news station on the east coast is here."

He was right. The press had arrived en masse.

At least six vans had their antennas up, and more were arriving by the minute. Fire trucks, ambulances, black-and-whites had reduced the road to one lane.

Bowers glanced in her mirror at the cars with government plates pulling in behind her.

Lights flashed. Cops and the curious were arriving in droves. A patrol officer waved her past a barricade. Bowers pulled halfway into the driveway.

"The damned garage is bigger than my whole friggin' apartment," said Johnny as he popped out of the Tahoe.

Kill Notice

When Bowers stepped out, a news helicopter whooshed overhead. She called over two men in uniform. "Mission one is to secure the evidence," she told them. "Keep everyone but essential personnel out."

Bowers viewed the expansive, cream-colored structure. The word *house* didn't do this place justice. Its three stories, arched doorways, five-car garage, and extensive landscaping had the aura of an Italian villa.

She spotted the line of officers protecting the perimeter. Because of the expansive size of the property, Bowers knew this one would be a challenge.

Johnny rounded up six more officers. She gave them two rolls of crime scene tape from her SUV. "Widen the perimeter," she yelled, as the whomping of helicopter blades vibrated the air and stirred up a series of whirlwinds.

She called dispatch. "I'm on scene. Wave-off the news in the sky, their rotor wash is disrupting evidence."

Redskins supporters in their maroon-and-gold jerseys waved and cheered, "Jayzee–Jayzee!" Bowers ordered them back.

A knot of reporters charged at her with microphones held out like bayonets. She ignored their shouting and grabbed Johnny's sleeve. "Follow me," she yelled over the crowd noise.

While Johnny stationed officers at every entrance, she reminded the one at the front door that no one was to enter the house or leave the premises without signing in and out with him first.

Bowers led the way around the side of the mansion with Johnny at her side. In back, the sound dampened and Magrath's New York accent could be heard loud and clear. As usual, she barked at anyone out of line.

The backyard opened into a sweeping landscape comparable to that of a palace. A raised deck soared two stories high, where white columns glinted in the sunlight and open arches overlooked an enormous, blue pool. A tangle of lush, green trees grew near one side of the concrete deck surrounding the pool. The house had been built on a knoll. Beyond the pool, grass sloped down into a carpet of green big enough to play a descent game of football. Woods surrounded the house, yard, and outlying cottages.

From what Bowers could see, Jayzee had had one hell of a party last night.

The scene could've been a beautiful sight, if not for the empty beer bottles and debris, and the bright yellow tarp covering the body.

"Bowers," yelled Magrath as she pointed at a man and a woman who'd run out of the trees. The pair snagged a few things by the pool and bolted toward the woods.

"Get them," Bowers yelled at Johnny. "They're scavenging." With so much media attention, she wasn't surprised to see thrill-seekers on the hunt for murdermobilia.

Johnny and another officer had already taken off after the couple. They caught up with the thieves six feet from the tree line. Bowers and Magrath hurried down the grassy slope to the duo, whom Johnny had placed face down in the grass.

"Well, this is a clusterfuck," said Magrath.

Johnny handcuffed the pair and made them stand. Bowers eyed each of them closely. Both glanced at her and then hung their heads.

Magrath glared at the pair. "Do you two numbskulls have any idea what you just did? It's pretty damn stupid to go interfering with an active murder investigation, dontcha think?" She threw up her arms. "Do you want the guy who killed that woman to get away with it?"

Bowers noted the man's round face and college kid appearance. He bit his lip and looked away.

The girl shrugged. "We..." Her voice dropped when she glanced up and saw Bowers towering over her.

While Johnny patted them down and Mirandized them, Bowers studied the girl's pale face and dyed-black hair with the brittle ends. Her cheeks were dotted with tiny freckles and she wore a nose ring.

They stood in the shadows of the trees. Overhead the sounds of the helicopter faded to nothing.

"You tampered with a crime scene," said Bowers as she glared down at the girl. "Why would you do that?"

Kill Notice

"I didn't—"

"Like hell. I saw you," said Bowers.

The man spoke up. "Look. We're sorry. We were just trying to make a few bucks."

Magrath retrieved the bloody brick they'd taken. "I should smack yous both with this."

Bowers barked at the pair military style. "That poor person—" Bowers pointed to the yellow tarp next to the pool, "—is dead. Murdered. She had her life ripped away from her. Don't you think that is violation enough without you two marching in to take away evidence that could lead to her killer? If that were your friend, how would you feel about some assholes stealing evidence so they could put some change in their pockets?"

The man's face flushed bright red. The girl's chin quivered, and her eyes filled with tears.

When Bowers had finished, Magrath jumped in. As she bagged the brick and a beach towel they'd pilfered, she explained to them the penalties for their crimes in vivid terms.

Bowers only listened to part of it. Her mind had moved on to what they would do now. The placement of each piece of evidence told a tale. These two yokels had certainly screwed some of that up. Moved evidence became little more than trash.

Bowers sighed. "I'm disgusted with both of you."

The girl frowned at her companion. "Donnie, you didn't tell me about this shit. You said this would be easy money." Johnny pulled the girl away when she tried to kick the boy.

Bowers intervened and pointed at the girl. "Do you want assault charges added to the list?" The girl stared up at her and wilted.

Johnny waved over two officers. "Take them in."

The sounds of the girl still trying to blame her companion faded into the distance as Bowers headed back toward the pool. She caught up with Magrath and stood next to her. Footsteps and whispers could be heard around them. Bowers scanned the trees and undergrowth. A squirrel scampered away. She spotted a tripod and camera, and then another.

Up the hill, techs strung up canvas shields to block the photographers who had stationed themselves in the woods encircling the property.

"This is nuts," said Bowers. "It's like trying to wave flies off dead fish."

Magrath trudged back toward the pool. "The media has whipped this 202 Killer into a front-page saga. It's no wonder the public is out here. Next they'll have 202 Killer T-shirts and costumes for Halloween."

"You're probably right," said Bowers. She slowed her gait to stay by Magrath. "The killer is loving this. The more airtime he gets the more attention he'll seek."

Magrath came to a stop and appeared worried. "Bowers, I've been at hundreds of crime scenes. This guy isn't like anything I've ever seen."

She gestured toward the lawn. "When a mower runs, it has no consciousness. It has no feelings. It doesn't distinguish between grass, weeds, flowers, or an unfortunate snake. It simply chops down everything in front of it. This killer is like that. He's a killing machine that needs a lethal case of lead poisoning, if you get my drift."

Bowers brushed pine needles off her leg. "That would be too quick and too painless. What would hurt him most is to live out his days in obscurity in some isolated cell where each boring day bleeds into the next."

Magrath shook her head. "You're right, but this boy isn't gonna let that happen. He'll go out in a firefight so's he can take as many of us with him as possible. You be careful."

"I promise you we'll get him," said Bowers.

The din of crowd noise continued in the background. Someone used a bullhorn to proclaim something about Armageddon. She and Magrath watched more officers take up posts around the tree line.

Bowers nodded toward the tarp. "Who's the victim?"

"Female, no ID," said Magrath. "Mid-twenties. Come take a look." She marched back toward the body.

Kill Notice

As Bowers followed, she spotted Mitch on the lower deck, scanning the grounds. He came toward her as if he had something to say.

Ten feet from the concrete patio around the pool, Bowers glanced down and came to an abrupt halt. She heard Mitch's voice and Magrath's, but their words seemed unintelligible, like a garbled cell signal.

At Bowers' feet in the green grass lay a bright, pink flip-flop.

Magrath's words *female, mid-twenties* rang in Bowers' ears. She looked up at the yellow tarp and back at the flip-flop. Size six.

Bowers closed her eyes. Her jaw set.

Something deep within her quaked.

She opened her eyes and scanned the grass. Ten feet away, she spotted the other pink flip-flop.

"Not Berti. Please, not Berti," she whispered.

GONE

BOWERS STOOD with her arms folded, staring at the woods until she'd lost all sense of time. Johnny gave her a cold bottle of water.

Magrath put a hand on Bowers' shoulder. "Wait until we verify her ID, maybe—"

"I gave her those flip-flops," said Bowers. "If you look at them closely, they have her initials on them." She gazed at Magrath. "She had a hummingbird tattoo on her ankle."

"Aw, hell." Magrath's lips pressed together hard and she shook her head. "I'm sorry."

Bowers scanned the yard. A beer keg and bright, plastic pool toys had been rolled down the slope. A huge array of paper plates and wine bottles from Jayzee's big bash had been left scattered over the lawn. The body lay by the pool like another discarded party favor.

A bowl filled with condoms sat on a small side-table next to a lounge chair. Bowers looked away and took a few gulps of the water. It helped wash down the lump in her throat.

"Annette Bertolini," she said to Magrath. "We called her Berti. She was twenty-six. Sweet girl. Naive as hell. How did she die?"

172

"You really want to do this?" said Magrath. Her hand clamped down on Bowers' shoulder.

"Either you tell me," said Bowers, "or I'll go see for myself."

"Strangulated, by the look of it."

Bowers felt goosebumps rise on her arms as a breeze blew across her skin.

"She had a necklace made from piano-wire. Did that have anything to do with this?"

Magrath nodded. "It looks that way."

"Dammit," said Bowers. "I warned her." She wanted to kick herself. "I had no idea Berti's new boyfriend was..." A burning sense of fury flashed through her mind. "That son of a bitch gave her that necklace and watched her delight, knowing full well that he intended to use it to kill her. That's not even human."

She threw the water bottle into a trash bin, bit down her anger, and marched toward the tarp. Johnny grabbed her arm. She stood less than a foot from his warm-brown eyes and pained expression.

"You gonna help me," asked Bowers, "or get in my way? I don't recommend the latter."

Johnny let go. "You don't need to do this."

"Like hell I don't. Now is not the time to go soft. That's what this killer wants. He's trying to break me, and it's not happening."

"I'm trying to protect you."

"Don't." Bowers skirted around him and stood by the tarp. She snapped on a pair of gloves and pulled back a corner, exposing a woman's long, pale leg, the tattoo of a hummingbird, and the pink nail polish on her toes. The birthmark on the thigh severed Bowers' last thread of hope of being wrong.

"It's Berti," she said.

Magrath slipped on a fresh pair of gloves and removed the rest of the tarp.

Bowers carefully knelt without touching anything. Her friend's clouded eyes stared up at her as if begging for help. Bowers swallowed hard and inspected the wounds.

As suspected, the killer had used Berti's necklace as a garrote to strangle her. The strands had cut deep into the flesh. A head wound had bloodied her blonde hair.

"Why didn't you listen to me?" Bowers whispered. She wanted to touch Berti's face, but didn't. "I'll miss you."

Bowers stood. Images of Berti at Paul's showing off that damned necklace played in her mind. So did the bubbly sound of her giggle.

As much as Bowers wanted to go get her rifle and shoot the crap out of a target, she knew emotion wouldn't help anyone. She stowed it away, for the moment, and snapped her objective edge back in place.

There would be a time when she'd have to face the loss and outrage, but now wasn't it.

Her friend's skin appeared waxy and gray under the overcast sky. Her skirt had been pushed up to her waist, and her underwear removed.

Bowers pressed a thumb against Berti's neck and arms. They were cold and had begun to stiffen. Bowers glanced away for a few seconds, cleared her mind, and began to study each detail. She noted the defensive wounds, the strap of a lacy red bra, and the same bruise she'd seen before on her forearms. Under Berti's sleeve she found a handprint.

"Magrath. Check this out."

Mitch joined them.

Magrath waved over a photographer. After he snapped a series of close ups, Magrath measured the marks and pointed to the buttons on her shirt. "Those look familiar? Several are missing."

Bowers nodded. "They're the same size, same color as the one on my bedroom door." She surveyed the area as the clues began to form patterns in her mind.

Mitch knelt next to Bowers and put his arm around her. "You okay?"

"Yes, sir," she said. *I'd feel a lot better, if I could strangle the asshole who did this.*

Mitch pointed at the body. "Her fingernails are missing. How do you account for that?"

Kill Notice

Bowers had noticed. "Just like Sapphire, he's covering his tracks. Can't get DNA from nails that aren't there."

Mitch smiled. "Nice, Bowers, I think you're right."

She stood and took a step back. A new realization bloomed in her mind. What were the odds of Berti picking out a new boyfriend that just happened to be the 202 Killer? *Answer: none.*

"Shit," said Bowers.

Mitch watched her closely.

Magrath stepped over. "What?"

Bowers snapped off the gloves and hurled them against the concrete. "The killer could've picked anyone, but instead he took Berti just to get under my skin."

BOWERS LEFT Berti's body in the care of Magrath and went inside the house, where she spent the next several hours interviewing Jayzee's staff and talking with the man who'd found the body. Mostly they were hung over or hadn't been there during the party.

A man came to inform her that while they waited for Jayzee's attorney to show up, the team doc was upstairs with the football star, trying to help him recover enough to sit up and carry on a coherent interview. Apparently, Jayzee had been ralphing his guts out.

Bowers went outside, where the chief kept a watchful eye on the scene. He nodded toward the lawn were an officer corralled a man with a camera, who yelled obscenities while being escorted back behind the yellow tape.

The chief stood at Bowers' side. "Sometimes this is a thankless job," he said. "We put up with crap no one else would tolerate."

"You got that right, sir," Bowers said.

The chief didn't always follow the rules to the letter, but he did what was right and fair and honest and she admired him for it.

Bowers caught sight of the mayor and a group of city administrators who were approaching the body.

"Trouble just showed up," he said. She knew he and the mayor hadn't always seen eye to eye.

Bowers started toward the officials. "Hey, hold up."

The mayor beamed her best politician's smile at Bowers.

"I'm sorry," Bowers said, "but you can't be here. This is an active crime scene. We're still working it."

Magrath's head went up. "Get them outta heah," she yelled, seemly unaware that she'd just hollered at the mayor.

The man with glasses standing next to the mayor didn't appear pleased. Bowers kept on her good-soldier face and ignored the indignant glares. Just as she was about to wave over an officer to herd them away, Clawski stepped in and surprised her.

He shook hands with the mayor. "Ma'am, I'm detective Clawski, let me help you out," he said. "We have a VIP area set up for you near the media. As soon as I have any information, I'll be along, personally, to talk it over with you."

Clawski had risen to the occasion and seemed to enjoy talking with the politicians. She had to hand it to him–he'd been more diplomatic than her own approach. Bowers had no patience for the real reason these officials had shown up. Ducking under the yellow tape amounted to flexing their influence before the cameras and getting free airtime.

"Thanks, Clawski," she said. "Well done."

He still had that wise-ass grin. "No problem."

She went back to standing next to the chief. They watched Clawski escorting the mayor and her entourage away.

"Clawski did good, sir," she said. "Giving them their own space near the press was smart."

"He has his moments." The chief chuckled.

After talking with the chief, she went back to the pool area and watched the M.E. arrive with a gurney and a body bag. To her right she caught sight of Clawski returning to talk with the chief, but it was the body bag that held her attention. The overcast skies seemed to darken. When she headed toward the house to check on Jayzee, she heard Clawski's voice and saw him hurrying up the embankment toward her.

He seemed out of breath and motioned her to the side.

"Bowers," he said, while shoving his hands into his pockets. "Look, I heard you knew the vic. I'm sorry about that." He hesitated and nudge at a plastic spoon on the ground with his boot.

"Thanks. What's on your mind?" she asked.

He lowered his voice. "Did anyone at the funeral see what happened? You know, with that dancer?"

Bowers could almost feel the embarrassment radiating off him. "Nah," she said. "I don't think so." That was mostly true, except for Johnny and one other detective who thought Clawski deserved a wakeup call.

Clawski seemed a bit relieved. "You won't tell anyone will you?"

"Nope." She chuckled. "She clocked you pretty good."

"Damn straight," he said with a scowl. "Won't be riding my exercise bike for a while." He paused. "One more thing," he said, "I appreciate you putting in a good word for me with the chief."

Bowers nodded. "You earned it."

"I'm sorry for some of the things I've said."

"Don't worry about it."

Bowers strolled away and stopped when she heard his voice behind her.

"Hey, sweet cheeks, you're okay." Clawski winked and popped his gum before sauntering away.

For some stupid reason he'd made her smile.

"Pain in the ass," she said. She heard him chuckle.

A moment later, Bowers approached the sliding glass doors, where a pair of bloodstained shoes lay near a large doormat. A scene-tech took close-ups of the shoes and the two partial footprints. Bowers stepped around the area he had blocked off to protect the evidence. The huge athletic shoes had Jayzee's name embroidered on the side.

Bowers used her phone to snap a photo of the shoes and started to go inside, but stopped and knelt for a closer look. The evidence seemed too neat. And far too obvious.

The killer she knew would never have been so careless as to leave these so prominently displayed. Never before had he left a print of any kind, much less one to match a pair of shoes. This had to be deliberate.

Bowers moved on and found the D.A. in the foyer. He turned his back on her and continued a hushed conversation with a tall man in a suit, who looked up and winked at her. She recognized Russ Parker immediately. Seconds later, he slid over within inches of the D.A., who appeared uncomfortable and stepped back.

In the hall, Bowers sidestepped the top of a woman's bikini and took note of the clutter. Seemingly hundreds of disposable cups and plates littered the tables and floors. On the huge circular staircase, a CSI tech adjusted her light and continued dusting the banister for prints.

Bowers stopped at the bottom of the stairs. The sight before her brought an image of Berti's red lace bra to mind. There, over the large wooden knob, hung a pair of red, lace panties.

BOWERS EXAMINED each room of Jayzee's main floor, took notes, and searched for anything that might help identify the killer. Above her were vaulted ceilings and gilded moldings. Below her were Persian rugs and tiles that looked as if they'd come straight from Italy.

In her opinion, the place had all the warmth of a museum.

She stood next to one of four couches in the living room. It sat about three feet from a wall. She felt the soft leather and heard a groan.

Bowers frowned as she peered between the couch and the wall with her flashlight. A flutter of arms and legs bumped against the wall and the furnishings.

A young man with a disheveled man-bun dragged himself to his feet and clung to the back of the couch. "Whoa, dude. That was a trip." He reached down and pulled up a girl with blonde dreadlocks and no top. When the pair noticed Bowers, the girl covered her chest with a pillow from the couch.

"Oops."

"What are you doing here?" asked Bowers.

"Guess we overslept?" said the girl.

Bowers checked her phone. "It's after 1:00 p.m. I don't think so."

The two stared at each other.

Man-Bun rubbed his eyes. "Maybe we got a little too stoned?"

"Yeah," said the girl, with a giggle. "Last night was totally too much fun."

"Seriously?" Bowers called a detective over to take their statements.

The girl's bare chest had caught the attention of several male officers. The younger ones nearly stumbled over each other to assist. The older ones stood back and watched from a distance, as a female officer grabbed a throw from the couch and tossed it over the girl's shoulders.

Bowers shook her head and walked away.

A big man came down the stairs with a Bluetooth in his ear and leaned in to speak with her. "Ma'am. I'm one of Mr. Jayzee's security men." The bodyguard's jacket didn't fully conceal the piece on his hip.

"I sure hope you have a license for that."

"Yes, ma'am. I do," he said as he reached for his wallet.

Bowers put up her hand. "We're good."

"Mr. Jayzee says he'll be down shortly. He's sorry for the delay. We'll bring him to the dining room."

After the big man ambled back to his post by the front door, Bowers went to the dining room, which overlooked the pool.

The room felt more like a banquet hall. Bowers wondered where Jayzee sat when he ate. It must feel strange to sit alone at a table this large.

She stepped over the shot glasses on the floor. An overturned saltshaker lay at one end of the table next to empty tequila bottles and spent lime wedges.

Through the enormous windows Bowers watched Magrath talking with the M.E. In the shade from the second-floor decking, Clawski strolled among the tables and stopped at each one, checking-out the leftover food. He smelled a few of the items and tasted a few more.

Bowers waved over Johnny and pointed to Clawski. "He's at it again."

"That's gross," said Johnny. "Maybe we should let him get food poisoning."

"No. Go get him before the chief sees what he's doing."

Johnny headed toward the back door.

While Bowers waited for Jayzee, she watched Johnny reining in Clawski and smiled to herself. At least this time he'd stayed away from the evidence and had done a solid job with the mayor.

A few minutes later, Bowers heard the sound of footsteps. Jayzee Armel entered the gilded double doors with two men accompanying him.

One shook her hand. "I'm Jayzee's attorney."

The other introduced himself as the team doc.

Jayzee barely made it through the doorway without ducking. Now she understood his fondness for arching doorways and cathedral ceilings.

"I'm detective Kate Bowers." She shook Jayzee's hand, and took a seat at the end of the table opposite from the tequila station. "I have a few questions."

In person, Jayzee seemed bigger than life. Bowers found more things than his height stunning. His smoky-black hair hung in a mass of dreadlocks, which he'd tied back in a thick ponytail. All his features, his nose, mouth, and even his teeth were huge. His hands were the size of dinner plates.

Jayzee's warm, brown skin had turned ashen. He appeared drained and shaken. He collapsed into a chair across the table from

Kill Notice

her, making the normal-sized men to his right and left seem strangely small. Even Bowers felt short next to him. *That's a first.*

"What happened last night?" she asked.

His attorney pulled out a notepad, while someone brought Jayzee a coffee and a bottle of water.

Jayzee glanced at the other end of the table, where the empty tequila bottles lay, and made a weak attempt at a smile. "We had one fine party until I got sick."

The physician spoke up. "I had his security men shut it down around two and send everyone home."

"Your parties usually include murder?"

"Hell no." Jayzee shook his head, and then gripped the table as if he'd realized too late that it had been a bad idea.

Bowers tapped on her phone and showed him a picture of the shoes outside the door. "Are these yours?"

He squinted at the small screen and shrugged. "I suppose. I got dozens of them all over dis place."

"Why are your shoes stained with blood?"

"Lady, I don't rightly know where my dick was last night and you're axing me 'bout some shoes I haven't seen in months?"

The physician blinked. The attorney covered his mouth.

Bowers leaned forward. "Let me see your hands."

Jayzee sat up and stuck out his arms so fast his attorney didn't have time to object.

His big hands were clear. One forearm had a healing abrasion near his elbow. Both of Bowers' brothers had played football and the wound appeared to be of the type common to his sport. Except for that and the Band-Aid where his IV had been, his arms and hands were clean.

Berti had fought back hard, and Jayzee had no scrapes or gouges from fingernails. That confirmed a few things.

As Bowers made a few notes she knew things weren't adding up. Jayzee's staged shoes were incriminating, but it didn't make sense. Last night his house had been filled with partygoers. It would've been impossible to do this in the open with so many witnesses clamoring for his attention.

Berti had once been a volleyball player. She may have been naive, but physically weak she was not. Jayzee was certainly strong enough to overpower her, but not in his condition or with an IV in his arm.

Bowers heard a sound behind her. Mitch stood in the doorway. He brought her a bottle of water. "Things going okay in here?" he asked.

"Yes, sir," said Bowers. "Thanks."

The attorney put his card in the middle of the table. "What was the time of death?" he asked.

Bowers did the dance and handed him her card. "That's for the M.E. to determine," she said. "I'd like to see Mr. Armel at the station to take a statement."

Jayzee reached out a long arm and motioned to his attorney. "Roger, I'll do this."

Bowers stood. "Your cooperation is appreciated." Johnny rushed into the dining room with his eyes wide. He skirted around Mitch with an "Excuse me, sarge" and whispered into Bowers' ear. "We found Berti's car. It's two blocks away."

BAD LANDS

FROM WHERE BOBBY SAT in the old jacked-up GTO, this had bad news written all over it.

He guarded his sore wrist and watched as Papa G's men drove south. The crews of the 301 were only fifteen minutes south of Barry Farm by car, but their turf seemed like an alien planet.

They passed through an area known as Washington Highlands. What Bobby had heard about that place made his neighborhood feel like a field trip. One of the stories had been about a woman who had killed her own kids. Bobby had no idea why people would hate on each other like that. It made no sense to him. He figured hate was like weeds in a good lawn. It choked out everything.

Being this far from home had Bobby on edge. At least in his 'hood he knew how to get around. Bobby twisted in his seat and noticed a black Mustang a couple of cars back. "Yo dude, there's a..."

The two homeboys sitting up front kept on yakking, and ignored him. He shut his mouth and let his voice drift off.

He had no idea where they were going or what they'd do when they got there. Papa G had promised to protect him and his family, but he'd also said, "You's gonna do something for me first."

That had to be what this was all about.

183

Bobby glanced out the back window. The Mustang still hung back behind a panel truck.

He picked at the callus on his thumb. The pistol in his jeans felt hard and awkward. He'd shoved it into his waistband like he'd seen on TV. The dudes in the movies made it look cool and all, but Bobby couldn't find any spot where it felt right. He wasn't sure if the thing could go off by itself or not. Just in case, he kept it in the back, figuring he'd rather have his ass shot off than the stuff in front.

His homeboys were still chatting it up. The one in the passenger seat went by the name Dray. Bobby knew the driver as Captain Crazy. Most of the guys just called him Cap. Bobby didn't trust either of them, especially Cap. The dude was a hothead.

When Dray reached over the front seat and slapped a hand at Bobby's knee, he saw the X-shaped scar on Dray's wrist and the big ole grin on his face. The dude geeked it up like he was all excited. The guy made Bobby nervous.

He shook his head. Nothing about this felt right.

"Dude," said Dray. "This be your first gig, man."

Bobby paid him no mind.

Dray shrugged and the two men up front continued to ignore him for the rest of the ride. That was fine with Bobby.

Ten minutes later they entered some back roads into a wooded area that seemed like a park. The back of his neck prickled. From Bobby's experience, parks were where bad things happened.

While they waited in the car, Dray slapped Bobby's leg. "A truck is coming in from California. We got orders to meet up wit' it before the 30Is get here. All I need you to do is act tough and do what I tell yah."

Bobby listened as Dray and their driver talked about another crew who'd been hitting Papa G's suppliers. Without a fresh supply of PCP, Papa G couldn't make dippers. That had put a crimp in his dealings for sure.

Bobby wiped his sweaty hands on his jeans. Back home, he knew how things went. The crew was there to keep everyone in-check. But facing off with the 30Is seemed like a whole different deal and a real bad idea.

The dudes in the front seat acted like they were heading off to a party. Cap nodded his head in rhythm to rap on the radio. Dray still had that grin on his face as he pounded out a beat on the dash. Bobby had seen Dray dealing and knew he was nearly as crazy as Cap.

Bobby gazed out the window and wished he were home.

"I gots mad-juice for Papa G," said Cap. "But maybe we should SOS these dudes. Put an end to it. See what I'm sayin'?" he said to Dray.

Bobby shifted in his seat. He knew SOS meant shoot on sight. Seeing Sapphire dead had been enough for him. He wanted no part of this mess.

"Nah," said Dray. "Papa G won't rock with dat. He wants his supply. That's all. He told me his-self this is business. But I don't suppose he'd mind if we put 'em in-check before we leaves. Might send a nice message not to mess with the 202 brothers."

Both men laughed and gave each other high fives.

A few minutes later an old pickup rolled in. A dude with cowboy boots stepped out.

Bobby ducked down low in the back seat and heard the car doors creak open.

Cap turned the car off and slid out like some serious badass.

Dray jumped out, all bug-eyed and jittery. Bobby figured he'd been using his own supply. He sure acted like it. Dray opened the back door and grabbed Bobby by his new jacket.

"Hey, man. Hands off." Bobby shoved his hand away. "Papa G gave me dis. He'd be all over my ass if I mess it up." He brushed off the jacket.

They stood on the other side of the car, away from Cap and the cowboy. Dray pulled his pistol and nodded to Bobby to do the same.

Bobby's hands shook when he felt the gun's hard grip. Slowly he pulled it out of his waistband and ducked down. He could see Cap and the cowboy through the windows.

Another truck pulled up. Two guys with rifles got out. The cowboy had come with his own crew.

The idling engines of both trucks told Bobby they weren't planning on staying long.

"Who are you?" asked the cowboy.

Cap puffed up his chest. "Papa G sent us to collect his California sunshine."

The cowboy glanced at his watch. "Sorry fellas. This run is spoken for."

Cap put a hand in his jacket. "You be misunderstanding. This shipment be ours. We'll pay the usual price." He put his thumb in his belt.

A shot rang out.

The cowboy dropped to his knees and fell face-first into the dirt. Cap jumped and ducked.

The rest was a blur. Bobby saw two SUVs pull in. Dust flew into the air. The dudes with the rifles cut loose, and Cap took a bunch of rounds to the chest.

"Shoot," yelled Dray. "Shoot them!" Dray grabbed Bobby's gun and ran off firing with both hands at everything thing in front of him.

Bobby crouched and squeezed under the car. He heard the sounds of big engines and people yelling and guns firing and wondered where all these folks had come from.

The side of his face pressed into the dirt. Sharp pebbles poked at his cheek. From where he lay he could see four guys on the ground, including the cowboy. None of them moved. Bobby breathed fast. He flinched as each bullet hit the car.

More vehicles arrived.

Someone yelled, "Cops!"

Big, black boots ran by. "Hands up! Police!"

Loud pops of gunfire echoed around him. Bobby covered his ears and saw another body fall. Dray lay in the dirt. His open, blank eyes staring right at Bobby.

Getting out from under the car seemed a poor idea. He didn't know what was going down. He wanted no part in mixing it up with the 301 and getting himself shot. He closed his eyes and listened to his heart pounding.

Kill Notice

Moments later, something snagged his foot. Bobby started kicking, but strong hands pulled him out from under the car.

He found himself staring up at a man he didn't know.

BOWERS HAD JUST FINISHED up with Magrath. The evidence they had collected didn't amount to much. They knew one thing to be true. The scene had been carefully staged.

Jayzee never made it to the station. Johnny finished taking his statement bedside while his doctor administered more IV fluids and ordered him to rest.

When Magrath left to process Berti's car, Bowers took Johnny and followed.

Before impounding the vehicle, Bowers and Magrath checked the interior. Berti's purse, phone, and a jacket were still inside. They also found a pink envelope addressed to Bowers in the console.

Bowers waited until Magrath's team had bagged and tagged the items in the car, including the pink envelope and its contents.

Magrath handed Bowers the card. It had been opened flat and slipped into the plastic evidence bag. Magrath gave her a few minutes alone to read the words.

Bowers took a deep breath as she focused on the image of a sunset on the front cover before flipping it over to view the inner flap.

The note was in Berti's handwriting:

> *I'm sorry I gave you a hard time. I know you care.*
> *That means the world to me. Thank you.*
> *Hugs, Berti*

Bowers ran her thumb over the hand-drawn heart at the bottom of the page. She wanted to feel the paper and the indention made by the pen, but the film of plastic barred her from touching the note.

The words *I'm sorry* sounded in Bowers' mind over and over again. She handed the card back to Magrath.

Bowers folded her arms as Berti's last words to her were packed away in an evidence locker.

This morning the security of her home had been torn away by the silhouette in her living room. Now Berti. This had been one hell of a day. Bowers paced in a circle and tried to wrap her brain around it all. She kicked the tire of the Tahoe and then slipped into the driver's seat.

Johnny stayed behind.

Bowers drove back by herself. On the way to the station she stopped at Paul's. The restaurant had begun closing down for the night and the last few stragglers were leaving. Lights inside the restaurant showed workers cleaning.

Bowers ducked under the black umbrellas and circled the table where she and Berti had sat. She stood there for moment, but couldn't bring herself to sit down.

The day played in her mind like a nightmare. She called Marvin. His phone went directly to voice mail, which meant he was already asleep. Bowers listened to his gruff voice telling her to leave a message. "I'm fine. Love you," she said before ending the call.

It was getting late, and she still needed to return the Tahoe and pick up her car before going to find a motel room for the night.

On the way back to where she'd parked, she paused when she saw a man standing at the Navy Memorial where huge stone blocks commemorated a moment in Naval history. The stooped gentleman's white hair shimmered in the light from the streetlamps. He bowed his head and gripped the Vietnam panel with a pale hand that had prominent knuckles.

A lump rose in Bowers' throat. The man removed his glasses and rubbed his eyes with his shirt sleeve.

He straightened to his full height, spotted her, and held her gaze. The sorrow in his eyes seemed to mirror her own.

The man nodded as if he understood.

CUTTING LOOSE

RIGGS STRETCHED BACK in his recliner and watched the fire in his gas fireplace. He wished it were wood burning, but this one had come with the condo. At least the logs resembled the real thing and the flames warmed his toes.

He gazed at the flickering, orange flames and reflected on a day of satisfying progress with his child pornography case. They had found the IP address of the D.C. client who went by the moniker Hardball.

Riggs had begun to drift off when he heard pounding on his front door. The sound brought him to his feet. He grabbed his service pistol and approached the door.

The persistent knocking grew louder.

"Who's there?" he shouted.

"Riggs! It's me."

The moment he recognized Bowers' voice, he yanked open the door.

She stood there wide-eyed.

He pulled her inside and gently put an arm around her. When he felt the tension in her shoulders, Riggs shut the door and engulfed her in a hug.

"I hate that son of a bitch. I hate him," she said.

He knew even before she'd said anything that something had gone bad. Bowers went to the spare bedroom he'd turned into a small gym. He hadn't used it since the last time she'd been there. She faced off with his punching bag and cut loose. Solid thumps and grunts filled the room as her fists, knees, feet, and elbows slammed against the heavy bag.

He watched her biting back tears. She might want to cry, but experience told him she wouldn't. Not until this was over.

While his punching bag took a beating, Riggs went to the kitchen and put down his weapon. When he returned, her forehead pressed against the black cylindrical bag, she gasped for air, and her skin glistened with sweat. She went at the bag again.

He waited until she was spent.

"Come on," he said softly. He handed her a towel and a beer. He always kept a six-pack of Negra Modelo in the back of his fridge for moments like this.

He sat on the couch next to her. She wiped her face on the towel, took a long draw of the beer, and stared at the fire.

Riggs waited.

He poured her a shot of his smoothest tequila and set the glass in front of her. She downed it. Normally, she liked lime and salt with her shots, but at this moment he knew the alcohol served a different purpose.

Her silence wasn't a good sign.

The expression on her face told him she'd hit the wall. Something had beaten her up enough to leave her rocked, and yet she was far too stubborn to give in.

Not everyone could do the jobs they did. They'd both witnessed things that would burnout most people or turn them cold and cynical. He and Bowers were the exception, but it didn't come without personal cost.

Tonight he'd give her whatever she needed. Booze. Silence. Talk all night. Listen. Whatever it took. She'd done the same for him, many times.

He touched her hand. "Shitty day?"

Kill Notice

She nodded. He poured her another shot.

"I'm going to find that bastard." She turned toward him and held eye contact for the first time since she'd arrived. Her eyes glistened in the firelight. "Part of me wants to go back to my apartment and wait for him to return, and when he does..." The muscles in her jaw hardened. "Riggs, you know what I'd do."

"Hey. Come on now." He touched her shoulder. She tensed and he withdrew his hand.

"I know I can't, but that doesn't mean I don't want to."

That had him worried. Not about Bowers falling apart or going on a shooting rampage. He knew she'd purge the worst of it out of her system by tomorrow and be back at work kicking ass. But it ate at him that the perp had hit such a deep nerve. The only way she'd get this hacked off was if he'd messed with someone she knew.

"You want to talk about it?"

Bowers leaned forward and braced her elbows against her thighs. "Berti," she said. Her chin quivered and the muscles in her neck grew rigid. "He killed her."

"Aw, Jesus," said Riggs. He ached almost as if he'd taken a hit himself. He reached out for her, but pulled his hand away. Everything in him wanted to hold her. Truth be told, she wasn't the only one who wanted to pop this asshole.

Riggs took a deep breath and listened. After she'd finished her beer, they talked quietly for the next hour. She told him about the staged scene at Jayzee's house and the media circus, and the mayor.

Bowers yawned and ran a hand through her hair. "Apparently Jayzee threw one hell of a big bash. It looks like the killer showed up right after the party had ended, but he didn't know that Jayzee had a stomach bug. That and some serious indulgence in alcohol had Jayzee sleeping it off with an IV in his arm when—" Bowers paused and took a deep breath, "—when she died."

Riggs reached out. This time he hugged her close and kissed her forehead. "I'm so sorry. I'll help you find this guy. Screw what Mitch wants."

Some of the tension seemed to leave her. He could feel her fatigue.

"I warned her," she said. "If only she'd taken me seriously. She was so trusting."

Riggs quietly listened until she'd said everything she needed to say. It was all he could do. When she grew quiet, they watched the fire in silence.

After a long while, he put out his hand and lifted her to her feet.

"What are you doing?"

"I'm tired," he said. "You're exhausted from a barbaric day. We both need some sleep. I'm going to bed and you're coming with me."

He picked up his pistol and led the way down the hall, pulling her behind him into his bedroom.

"But? Wait."

"Shut up. This isn't about sex. It's about you not going back to your place or a motel alone. Not tonight. You've done enough for one day."

He took her Glock and her phone, and put them next to his on the nightstand. Next he pulled off her boots and his jeans. "You can sleep in your clothes, if you want, or you know where my T-shirts are. Or hell, you can sleep naked. It's up to you."

The dimples at the corners of her mouth puckered. It wasn't exactly a smile, but close enough. He tried not to look when she pulled off her pants and slipped under the covers.

Riggs spooned up against her and reached over her to turn off the light.

"I need to be at work in the morning," she told him.

"Me too. You warm enough?" He felt her head nod.

Riggs put his arm around her and held her close. He closed his eyes and pretended to sleep.

For a long while he listened to her breathing. He enjoyed the warmth of her hand on his arm. When her breathing shifted into the soft rhythm of slumber, Riggs allowed himself to drift off to sleep.

At least for tonight he could keep her safe.

ALL IN

BOWERS LISTENED to the morning news on her car radio. Naturally, the murder at Jayzee's mansion had become their lead story. *Here it comes.* Now the press had another juicy story to hash over in front of the cameras.

Everyone, it seemed, had something to say about Jayzee.

She listened as the man's sister and mother, fellow players, and fans rallied to support him. Critics chimed in and flooded the media with calls and posts depicting him as a lowlife who never should've been in the NFL.

She swerved around a hunk of tire in the road as the league's spokesman reiterated its intolerance of violence. Jayzee's sponsors were dropping him faster than a Maserati could hit sixty. He may not have been a Boy Scout, but he surely didn't deserve a trial by media.

Bowers stopped by her apartment to pick up some clothes. When she arrived at her front door, she found it wide open.

Now what?

She put a hand on her Glock. Even before she peeked inside she heard voices and the buzz and pounding of tools. A middle-aged man with a hammer hanging off his belt glanced up at her.

MARTA SPROUT

"Looks like you're repairing my window," she said.

He nodded. "More like replacing the whole thing. Someone did a number on it. Are you the tenant?"

"Yup," said Bowers. "I stopped by to grab a few things."

She went down the hall and felt a breeze. When she saw the bedroom door, her shoulders tensed. Images of waking up with that man in her apartment flooded back. Bowers peered inside her bedroom and found a workman surrounded by tools and lumber.

He nodded at her and kept working.

It felt as if the entire world had traipsed through her bedroom.

The splintered doorframe had been replaced, but the rest of the apartment was a wreck. Black fingerprint powder covered just about every surface. Workers had tracked in dirt. A list of her things that were now in evidence lockers lay on her dresser.

The entire window in her bedroom had been removed, leaving a gaping hole to the flowerbed and walkway outside.

Bowers threw some clothes into a bag. After taking the photo of Riggs off of her nightstand and tucking it into a pocket, she stepped over the tools and grabbed a pack of bobby pins out of a dresser drawer.

The dark-haired handyman continued sawing two-by-fours.

"Looks like you've got your hands full," she shouted over the noise.

He took his finger off the saw's trigger, and the rasp died down as the blade came to a stop. Sawdust covered the floor. "What?" he asked.

She stepped closer. "Why did you tear out this window?"

The man sat on the construction horse. "We came in to repair the window in the living room, but when we checked this one we realized it wouldn't open. Per code we had to change it out. It's a good thing we did. See this wood rot? I'm reframing the whole thing."

While the man went on about the details of installing a new window Bowers knelt and picked up an orange strip of plastic that held a row of shiny bullets. "These are .22's. What are you doing with snake shot?" She studied the man carefully.

194

Kill Notice

The carpenter picked up a big, red gun-like tool. "They're powder charges for my Hilti nail-gun. See? No cord. No bullet or pellets. It uses the charges to fire the nails into concrete. This puppy can drive a nail right into a steel I-beam.

Bowers frowned at the device. "You could kill someone with that."

"It's happened. The nails have been known to go straight through drywall or a solid wood door and right into someone's head on the other side." The carpenter shrugged. "A hammer could kill a man, too." He went on to explain how he needed it because of the materials in the wall. "You want to try it?" he asked.

Bowers stepped forward. "Sure."

The carpenter demonstrated. "You press straight down and pull the trigger." She heard a loud pop.

He handed her the nail-gun. For something so big, it felt lighter than she'd expected. She aimed it next to where his nail had gone in.

"You sure you can handle this?" asked the carpenter with a smirk.

Bowers pulled back her vest and showed him her .40 caliber Glock. "Yeah, I think I've got this."

BOWERS PICKED up her bag of clothes from the bedroom and headed toward the living room.

The man working on her front window put down his level. "Say, did that guy find you?"

Bowers frowned. "What guy?"

"He was here earlier askin' for you. He looked around, in the kitchen and bedroom, but didn't leave a name, just said he was a friend."

Bowers' neck stiffened. "What did he look like?"

"Tall," said the guy as he flipped a screwdriver up in the air and caught it, "nice clothes. Expensive. And he had these really intense blue eyes."

Bowers wanted to hurl her bag across the room. "I know who it is. Thanks."

"When I asked him for his number, he'd already gone outside. He stood there for a while and talked to your neighbor," said the worker.

"That's just swell," said Bowers.

"Sorry."

"Don't worry about it," she said, "I'll find him."

When she left the apartment, dew still covered the green grass and gray clouds loomed in the sky overhead. Bowers had already begun thinking about the work on her desk.

When she approached her car in the parking lot, she heard the scuffle of feet on the asphalt. Her gait slowed. She quietly sat her bag on the walkway and eased around the car parked next to hers. When she saw the back of a man peering through the glass into her car, she put a hand on her weapon and flipped off the safety strap.

He tried the door handle, twice, but she'd left the car locked.

"You looking for something?" she asked.

The man straightened up and glanced over his shoulder. She recognized the profile.

"Morning, Bowers," said Russ Parker. He turned to face her and nodded at her hand, still on her weapon. "You need to take it down a few notches. Take a few days off. Or give me the case and go take a vacation somewhere tropical. I assume from the pictures on your bedroom wall that you like the ocean."

As he pulled down his sleeves, she caught a glimpse of his bare arms, which bore fresh scrapes and bruises.

"You have no right to go into my home, especially my bedroom." She took a step back. "What the hell do you want?"

He held out his arms and made an attempt at a smile, but those blue eyes were glacier cold. "I just dropped by to see how you were progressing with the case."

"That doesn't give you the right to trespass. No one goes into my home uninvited."

"That's not what I've heard. Apparently, you had an intruder just yesterday—"

"You could have called me. Setup a meeting." She went back to the sidewalk and retrieved her bag.

Kill Notice

He moved closer and reached in a pocket. "I can call you right now," he said as he pulled a phone out his pocket and waved it at her.

"Get out of my way." She pointed at him. "I'm going to work. You want to talk to me, it'll be at the station."

When a FedEx truck pulled up, she brushed by him, got into her car, slammed the door shut, and locked it. As she left the parking lot, she kept an eye on her rearview mirror.

Russ Parker hadn't taken his eyes off her car.

TWENTY MINUTES LATER, Bowers sat at her desk. The warmth of her coffee mug helped her focus.

Johnny passed by her desk and stopped. He checked the time and staggered backward. "You're here!" he said with a grin. "Good afternoon."

"Wise-ass, it's not that late." She waved him closer. "Have you seen Mitch?"

He shook his head. "He left right after our morning briefing. Where have you been?"

"Long story, you find anything on those tapes yet?"

"Nope," he said, "but I'm working on it."

After Johnny went back to his desk, she finished up her paperwork and let her thoughts volley between confronting Russ Parker and where she'd woken up this morning.

Before dawn, she had woken to find Riggs' arm still around her waist. He'd never tried to touch her in an overtly sexual way.

When she'd felt him stir, she'd pretended to be asleep and had remained tangled in the soft sheets. The extra few minutes had allowed her to take in the smell of his skin and the warmth of his arms and shoulders around her.

Mitch's incoming call brought her back to the day at hand. "Come to the briefing room," he said.

BOWERS FOUND Mitch flipping through a file at the front of the briefing room. She took a seat at one of the long tables. He appeared eager to speak with her and slid into a chair across from her.

"What's up?" she asked.

"You've got a good handle on this guy, don't you?" he asked.

She tilted her head slightly. "You might say that. I can tell you it's not Jayzee."

"What do you see? Who is this guy?"

"Well. He knows CSI procedure, how to kill efficiently, and not to leave evidence behind."

"Without forensic evidence, how are we gonna find him?"

"He'll screw up," she said. "When he does, I'll be there."

Mitch nodded as if satisfied. "You might as well stick around, the chief wants to talk to you. Your partner is on his way over."

Bowers leaned forward. "Sarge, I need your advice."

He checked his phone as if pressed for time. "What's the problem?" he asked.

"Russ Parker is driving me nuts. This morning, he went out to my apartment. I wasn't there, but workers were. Mitch, he went into my bedroom." She told him the whole story, while he kept glancing at the time.

He smiled and patted her hand. "Everyone knows he's an asshole."

"I'll second that," she said, "but there's something else. He had what appeared to be fresh, defensive wounds on his arms."

Mitch shook his head. "I know what you're thinking, but it's not him. He helps train police dogs. Marks on his arms are part of the job."

"But, Mitch—"

"Look, Bowers," he said, "Don't worry about Parker. Stay on your case." With that, Mitch swiveled in his chair and clicked on the TV.

Sometimes Mitch just didn't get it.

When he wove his fingers together to cradle the back of his shaved head, she took note of his crisp long-sleeved shirt and immac-

Kill Notice

ulately clean nails. For such a tough guy, he certainly paid attention to the details of his appearance.

On the screen, Marc Davis, the anchor for WJDC, played moderator for a heated interview with Senator Harry Keats about the gentrification project.

"The good people of D.C.," the senator said, "shouldn't have to put up with drive-by shootings and all the other mayhem being perpetrated on our streets. Folks have a right to feel safe."

"Oh, bullshit," said Mitch. "What about the 202 Killer?"

Bowers' leg bounced. The cameras centered on Keats sitting in a big chair. She'd done security for him in the past. She knew the man was abrupt and rotund. The cameras' hot lights cast a spotlight on his sallow skin and bloated belly. His jowls quivered when he shook his head.

"It's high time," he said, "we play hardball and clean up our streets. Take out the trash and make our communities safe for kids."

While Davis took comments from community leaders who opposed the project, Mitch began flipping through his papers.

The camera turned to a civil activist. "This is a war on the black people of D.C. Decent poor folks and the elderly living on fixed incomes are not trash to be tossed out into the streets, Mr. Senator."

Bowers rocked forward to go get a cup of coffee, but Johnny entered the room and quietly sat next to her.

The anchor switched to a report on the 202 Killer.

Johnny leaned forward. "Sarge, I wanted to ask—"

"Shhh," said Mitch, as he hunched forward.

Bowers knew he had made a statement at the press conference, which had been set up on Jayzee's lawn. He seemed eager see how they handled his comments.

Marc Davis took off his glasses. "By our latest reports, I can tell you that killers of this type are sexual deviants. They're cowards, who are incapable of normal human relationships."

Mitch rubbed a hand over his head, but said nothing.

A breaking news story flashed across the screen.

They all stopped and listened.

"The body of Detective Russ Parker of the Metro PD's Major Crimes Unit was found less than an hour ago in Rock Creek Park. At this time, it appears to be a one-car accident. Hopefully, the medical examiner's report will shed light on his tragic death. We'll let you know as details emerge."

Bowers sat back in her chair.

The chief marched in the room and headed straight for her. She stood.

"How are you fairing?" he asked.

That was a loaded question. If she said "fine," he'd know she was lying. If she said what she really felt, he would take her off the case.

"I'll deal with my feelings later. For now, I'm focusing on catching this bastard."

"Glad to hear it. I'm counting on you." The chief's expression softened. "I am sorry about your friend."

"I appreciate that, sir, but what's on your mind?"

The chief stood tall. He glanced at Mitch, and stepped closer to her and Johnny. "It's time for a change in tactics. How would you feel about working with a team?"

"I'd welcome it," she said.

Mitch's eyes narrowed. "What team?"

"We need help," said the chief. "I called ADIC over at the FBI."

Mitch's face fell flat. She briefly caught a glimpse of the fury in his dark eyes before he stared at the floor.

The chief kept his focus on Bowers. "We've given this our best shot, but this has gone on long enough. We're under-staffed. And from what I hear, Major Crimes is busy with their own troubles."

Mitch started to complain, but the chief put up his hand. "Mitch, I respect your opinion, but the D.A. and City Council are on my ass. They want everyone all-in and they want it now."

The chief started toward the door and hesitated. "The FBI will show up any minute. I expect your full cooperation." He tapped on the doorframe and left.

Mitch stared at the open door.

Johnny scratched his head. "Who's the chief calling a dick?"

Bowers started to laugh. "ADIC is short for Assistant Director in Charge. He's the first point of contact for establishing an FBI task force."

RIGGS ENTERED the precinct with a formidable team at his back. He'd selected the top people from the field office.

They marched into the building, flashed their IDs. Seconds later, they swarmed off the elevator and streamed into a large conference room two doors down and across the hall from the briefing room.

He found Bowers waiting for him and handed her a cup of coffee. The surprised expression on her face made the side trip to get it worth the effort.

He watched as three men hauled away the conference table and replaced it with long tables and more chairs. Two men brought in an array of computers and monitors on dollies. They immediately went to work stringing cables.

With the work well underway, Riggs leaned against the windowsill next to Bowers. She kept her hands wrapped around the cup of coffee and her eyes on the techs doing the setup.

"Today any better?" Riggs asked.

"Much." She raised her cup of coffee. "Gettin' better by the moment. Thank you."

Riggs spotted a glimmer of a smile on her face.

"Did you hear about Parker?" she asked. The smile had vanished.

"We'll talk about that, later," he whispered. He left her to finish her coffee while he supervised two techs setting up a bank of phones on a long table at the back of the room.

Riggs caught a glimpse of Mitch pacing outside the room. Knowing how this would piss him off, Riggs slapped a sign on the door that read: "NO ENTRY ZONE, TASK FORCE PERSONNEL ONLY."

Mitch glared at Riggs. "I'm not happy about this."

MARTA SPROUT

Riggs tossed the tape into a box. "I'm not happy about a killer on our streets."

MIND OF A MANIAC

BOWERS SCANNED THE ROOM in amazement. Things that had been on their wish list for months, even years, were there in duplicate. The transformation into a secure communications hub had taken ninety-three minutes.

Special ID cards were given to authorized team members only, which allowed them entrance to the task force room. The chief was the first to get one.

Johnny escorted a woman with FBI credentials to the front of the room. The woman acknowledged those who filled the seats.

The chief stood. "Let's do this, folks." The sound level in the room faded to a whisper. "This is Rebecca Hoffman from the FBI's Behavioral Analysis Unit. She is here to give us a profile on our killer."

Magrath hurried in and took a seat. She and Hoffman nodded to each other. Mitch stood in the back, where he toyed with his new ID and glared at Riggs, who seemed to be ignoring him.

Hoffman brought everyone to attention. "I've heard about the progress you've made in this case. I agree," she said. "Jayzee is a pawn in this, but so are you. Somewhere, this killer is watching the news and planning his next move, but before we can find him we need to know what to look for. That's why I'm here."

All eyes fixed on her. Heads followed her movements as if they were attached to her by invisible threads.

Hoffman proved to be direct. Factual. And Bowers found her remarkably likable.

"I'll grant you that this serial killer is elusive," she said. "You already know he is a highly skilled killer, which means he's well into his career. He's been doing this for a long time. He is organized, meticulous. Takes his time. He is very strong. Serial killers are by definition psychopaths. Very few psychopaths are violent, but our guy is—to the Nth degree. And he is smart."

Hoffman scanned the people listening. "Don't believe the crap on the news. Our guy is the man next door. He is a master at fitting in. He'll live in a normal house, has a wife and kids and a good job. He is charming."

Bowers watched Johnny scribbling notes. Mitch's scowl had relaxed, which surprised her, considering he hadn't wanted the FBI involved.

On the other hand, the chief's neck and shoulders were tense. He listened with his brows furrowed as he scanned the room.

Bowers saw the same familiar faces that had been present when she'd done her own talk. Maybe now they'd listen. This time Clawski sat up and paid attention.

He raised his hand. Bowers held her breath, hoping he wouldn't make one of his stupid comments.

"What's his motive?" he asked.

Several Detectives eyed Clawski. A few murmured to each other.

"Listen up," said Bowers. "Clawski's question is an important one."

At first his eyebrows went up. Then he beamed.

"I agree," said Hoffman as she slowly strolled between the tables. "This is a critical point. Motive requires deep human feelings, which he doesn't have." She paused. "If he does have a motive, it's not one we can easily relate to. Here's the thing you need to understand about the man you're looking for—he looks like you, but underneath he isn't like you at all and I can prove it."

Kill Notice

She picked up a remote and clicked on the sixty-inch monitor at the front of the room where a slideshow of images began to play. Beach scenes faded into swaying palm trees. Sunsets cut to mountain streams and wide-eyed puppies. Gorgeous forests changed into powerful waterfalls.

Bowers knew where this would go.

Suddenly the close-up photo of a man who'd committed suicide by blowing his own face off with a shotgun popped onto the screen.

Bowers glanced away. She heard grunts of alarm and disgust around the room and watched as people jerked back in their chairs.

Hoffman pointed to the screen. "You are feeling a visceral reaction," she said. "Your heart-rate just went up. Your hands are sweating. Maybe you have a knot in your gut."

Hoffman scanned the room. "Do you know what your killer would do?" Her eyes stopped on Clawski. "Nothing. No blip. No recoil. His pulse would thump on unaltered. If your killer had any reaction at all, it would be to lean forward in fascination. Would he be repulsed? No!" She shook her head. "Would he be absorbed? Absolutely."

People began taking notes.

"Your unsub is neurologically different. He doesn't have real emotions. Sure, he can cry at a drop of a hat, laugh, and make grandiose gestures. He can appear worried, when in reality he's merely mimicking behaviors he's witnessed in others. *He does not feel what you feel.* Therefore, his motives are known only to him."

Bowers knew Hoffman was right. "Why is he escalating?" she asked.

Hoffman stopped and stood next to her. "There is some debate on this, but the theory is that the one thing he does feel is the thrill he gets just before he kills his victims. Control over life and death empowers him. Gives him a rush, but it has a limited return."

Hoffman continued pacing the room.

"The high only lasts so long. After a while, he'll escalate, hoping to once again feel the intensity of his first kill."

MARTA SPROUT

The chief spoke up. "But we can't see the inner workings of his mind. What's it like to stand next to someone like that?"

Hoffman clicked on the remote to a picture of Ted Bundy. "Like I said, he is charming and glib. Loves the limelight. He's arrogant."

"We have a lot of those in Washington," said Johnny. "We call them politicians."

Chuckles rose around the room.

Hoffman nodded. "You're correct. Psychopaths are drawn to positions of power. You'll see them in government and CEOs of major corporations. Law enforcement is a powerful draw to a man like that. I guarantee that at least one psychopath is in this building right now."

HARD ROAD

B OBBY KEPT AN EYE ON the clock as he did the dishes. It felt as if his whole world had started coming down on him. Even Grandma had jumped on his case and insisted he stay home today. He didn't take no mind to laying low, but now he had somewhere he wanted to be. Maybe soon she and his brother would fall asleep.

Yesterday had him all torn up inside. The man who'd pulled him out from under the car turned out to be a cop named Perez. The dude had taken him up to the Metro PD for questioning as a witness. They hadn't arrested him. It surprised him that no one had roughed him up or threatened to shoot him like he'd seen on TV.

He had never seen the inside of a police station before and expected a lot of yelling and punching, but it wasn't like that at all. He mostly saw folks sitting at desks and chattin' it up on the phone. He was more worried about Papa G than the cops, anyway. They had bosses and laws. Papa G made up his own rules.

Bobby played dumb as best he could until Perez had said they'd talked to his grandma and someone was bringing her in. He knew she'd have more questions for him than the police.

Awhile later, the door to the interrogation room had opened. An officer led his grandma inside and offered her a chair. She'd worn her best dress and sat in the corner holding on to her pocketbook like someone was about to snatch it. The shame he'd felt was hard to swallow, especially with the way her mouth had been set. "He's a good boy," she'd said to Perez. "Done my best raisin' him up."

Things got worse when Perez had started swabbing Bobby's hands and noticed the bandage.

"What's that?" he'd asked.

"I be playin' wit' my dog," Bobby had said, "never knew puppies had such sharp teeth, man."

Perez let it be, but Grandma never took her eyes off him. He figured that she knew he wasn't tellin' the truth. The cop said the swabs of Bobby's hands and clothes were to check for drugs and for what he called GSR.

"Don't know what that is," Bobby had told him, "but I ain't got none."

Perez had smiled. "We're looking for residue to see if you've fired a gun recently."

Grandma shook her finger at Bobby. "You be dancin' at the wrong end of a whippin' stick, if you been messin' wit' dat."

Officer Perez talked real nice to his grandma and took her to another room. He turned out to be pretty cool.

Even with Grandma out of sight, none of the cops had yelled at him or slapped him around like he'd expected.

With his grandma's permission, Perez and his partner talked with Bobby while they waited for the test results. There wasn't much he could tell them about the 301 crews or the supplier, so acting dumb about that had been easy. Things got tense when Bobby had to explain how he'd gotten himself in the middle of a firefight.

He made up a story. "See Dray owes me money," he told Perez, "dude told me he had to go get the cash. I rode along wit' him and his friend to make sure he wasn't jivin' me, man. But then all that crazy stuff happened. I didn't know what was goin' down."

The story was sort of true. Dray did owe him five bucks. Perez

Kill Notice

gave him a nice cold root beer and wanted to know what Bobby had seen. He told him about the men arguing and then shots and then hiding under the car. He just left out some of the details.

When the tests had all come back negative, Perez had turned him over to his grandma and they'd ridden the bus back to Barry Farm.

That suited him fine. Word of a cop car sitting in front of his house surely would've gotten him into trouble with Papa G.

The problem now was the cop knew where he lived and might be watching him. Papa G wouldn't be happy about the deal gettin' busted. He'd surely have some questions about that. And the man in black was still out there. It seemed that everywhere Bobby turned there was someone waiting to bust him down about something.

The news came on with a report of another black man who'd been killed by a cop. He listened to his grandma and brother talking about it. Bobby watched the jittery cellphone video and shook his head. What he saw didn't look right. And yet, he knew all cops weren't like that. Perez wasn't. Bobby figured it was like the kids at school. Guys like Jimmy were looking for trouble, but that didn't mean everyone was like him.

Bobby popped out of his thoughts about yesterday and rinsed the last two pots in the sink. He glanced up at a commercial on the TV. His grandma yawned. His little brother sat on the couch all wide-eyed and ready to watch another show.

"Hey, Tommy," said Bobby as he wiped out the sink. "You're in high school now. Ninth grade is a big deal, dude. You best be gettin' your homework done."

Grandma clapped her hands. "Bobby's right. Go brush your teeth and git after them books."

Tommy dropped the remote and glared at her. He started to complain, but Grandma pointed to the hall. There was no arguing with her once she had her mind made up.

They could still hear Tommy kicking up a fuss as the water ran in the bathroom. Bobby wished his biggest problem was getting to school with his homework done.

As his grandma shuffled toward the kitchen, Bobby cleaned off the counter. He still felt bad about the cop dragging her down to the station.

Grandma hobbled up next to him and put her head on his shoulder. "Bein' the man of the house has fallen to you. I'm mighty appreciative of all you do to help out."

Bobby nodded. This wasn't the scolding he'd expected. The dog sat on his foot, licking his fingers. He'd grown attached to that silly pup.

His grandma waved at the kitchen and living room. "This may not look like much to a young'un such as yourself, but folks like us has come a long way. There's still a ways to go, mind you. Yet, the opportunity is there for you and that hotheaded little rascal." She pointed toward the bathroom where Tommy had holed up. "Today black folks can be presidents and senators. Dat means you can be whoever you want." The conviction and hope in her voice made him ashamed of what he'd done working for Papa G.

Bobby glanced at her.

"You're a better man than those you been hangin' out wit'."

He didn't know what to say to that.

Grandma's expression changed. She patted her chest. "This old heart needs you to do the right thing, son. Be a good man. Make a good life. Show Tommy how it's done." She gripped the kitchen counter and eyed him up real close through her thick spectacles. "I did the best I could. Show me it wasn't for not."

Bobby felt all squishy inside. He hated it when she did that. He couldn't lie with her staring at him like that.

"Can you do dat for me?"

Bobby picked up a ragged towel and dried the big pot. "It's hard, Grandma. Kids today—"

"Oh, bull-feathers. Kids today got it easy." Grandma patted his arm. "I was a little-bitty thing back in the fifties. The colored drinkin' fountain was broke. Dry as two-day-old toast. I was powerful thirsty. My mama lifted me up and gave me a drink from the whites-only

Kill Notice

fountain." Grandma wiped her eyes with a crumpled tissue and held it over her mouth as she coughed. "Still remember it to this day. Some big men hauled my mama away. They were real mean about it, too. If it weren't for my granny, I wouldn't be here tellin' 'bout it."

Bobby pushed the dog's nose out of the way and stuck the pot inside the cabinet. "What happened to your mama?"

"She came home four days later. They'd beaten her up good and charged her with stuff that made no sense to me. I was too little to understand. I knew she was hurt real bad, but she was strong. She never gave up. Word got around about the beatin' and all, and how she'd stood up and told them it weren't right to leave a baby-child thirsty when water is right there and for the takin'." Grandma wagged her long boney finger at him. "Today those fountains are for every-body, as it should be."

Bobby rested his elbows on the counter. He and his grandma were shoulder-to-shoulder. He felt her thin arm around his back.

"Son, life is sometimes hard on everyone. Don't matter if you're black or white. Moneyed or po'. What matters is that you does what's right. No one ever promised it would be easy."

BOWERS RUBBED her sore neck and checked the time. At 9:30 p.m. she locked her desk and wondered why Johnny hadn't come back. She headed toward the Tahoe.

He'd gone out to drive by Jayzee's and then the cemetery to see if anyone else of interest had returned to the scenes.

She called him. He didn't answer.

Bowers clicked her seatbelt and started the engine. She drove up to the exit of the PD's lot and stopped just before the street. To the left lay the cemetery across town. To her right, awaited the promise of sleep at the room she'd booked for the night. She could go back, get her Xterra, and call it a night.

She turned left.

Forty minutes later, Bowers pulled into Lakefield Cemetery and parked near a big tree. She stayed in the Tahoe. The tent and mourners were long gone. Bowers searched the rows of headstones and didn't see Johnny or his car.

Up ahead she spotted staging lights. Fifty feet from where Sapphire had been buried, workers dug deep into the earth with a backhoe. Apparently they were working late to prepare for tomorrow's business.

Thinking that they might have seen Johnny, she left the Tahoe and jogged toward the lights.

To her right she saw a figure in the darkness.

Bowers stopped. Someone sat on the ground next to Sapphire's grave.

She stepped closer.

The dark figure jumped to his feet.

"Don't run." She recognized him. "Please."

***

GOOSEBUMPS ROSE UP on Bobby's back. His legs felt all twitchy. He knew it was that cop, Bowers. When she came closer he stepped back. Part of him wanted to take-off. Part wanted to stay.

He stared at her. Unsure. In his mind, images of Papa G with his knife fought against his memory of the man in black and those eyes. The trusting face of his grandma was there too, reminding him that it wasn't just his life at stake.

Bobby felt like a roach running from one dark hole to another. He didn't want to live like that.

His grandma's words—*you're a better man than that. Do what's right*—wouldn't let go of him.

"What you want?" he asked.

She stepped closer and stood a few feet from him.

He half expected her to cuff him for not telling Perez the whole story. Instead, the cop knelt next to the grave where a green plastic frame was stuck into the ground. It held an index card with Sapphire's name handwritten on it.

"I don't like it," he said. "It don't seem right. Dey coulda put something better 'n' dat."

The cop brushed pieces of grass off the small marker. "This is temporary," she said. "I heard her boss paid for a nice headstone. It takes time to carve granite. You'll see, it'll be a lot nicer than this."

Bobby glanced down at the cheap sign. He'd read the whole thing in the workmen's lights. The name *Sapphire* had been put in quotes like it wasn't real. Underneath it someone had written Danielle Fisher. He'd never heard that name before and figured that Sapphire changed names, like the actors in Hollywood.

"It wasn't right," said the cop. "I'm sorry this happened." Her words were kind, unlike the kids on the school bus or the guys in the crew. "You knew her, didn't you?" she asked.

Bobby swallowed hard, nodded, and stared at the wilting flowers. "She had problems, but I never saw her hurt no one."

He stepped back when the cop stood.

"You're good at getting around," she said, as she dusted off her pants. "You've been following me. Why?"

Bobby opened his mouth and the words fell right out. "I thought maybe you could be somebody I might talk to." He kicked at the dirt and felt stupid. Papa G was gonna get him for sure.

She cocked her head. "You must have something important to say." The lady cop talked to him like his opinions mattered. That surprised him.

He pointed to her mouth. "Looks like somebody been messin' wit' you."

"Comes with the job. You want to sit in my car and talk for a bit?"

"Yeah, okay," he said. "Can I bring my dog?" Bobby glanced over his shoulder.

"Sure." The lady cop didn't seem to have a problem with that either.

"Come on, boy." Bobby called his pup, who'd been sniffing

around in the woods. When they got to her car, the cop let the pup into the back seat. She sat at the wheel.

Bobby slipped into the passenger seat. It felt real strange to be hanging out inside a cop's car. He sized her up. She had a big, ole pistol on her hip. Up close, she seemed even more badass, but not mean. That surprised him too. He wondered if she could protect him from Papa G and the crew.

"I sat in a police car once," he said, "but I never took no notice of all that stuff." He pointed at the computer and didn't tell her he'd ridden in the back.

The lady cop twisted the laptop toward him and showed him how it worked. She handed him the radio. He laughed when it squawked. Bobby liked the lights.

"Those switches are for the sirens. Hit one."

He couldn't believe she would let him turn on the sirens. Never expected that. When he did, he jumped at the sound. Dawg started to howl. He and the cop laughed at that.

His dog pawed at the clear window that separated the back seat from the front. She tapped on the window. "We call this 'the cage.' It's where we keep suspects during transport." The pup kept pawing at the window.

"Dawg, knock it off," said Bobby.

"You call him *Dawg*, seriously?"

"What else can I call him?"

"Well," she said, "how about we think of someone strong or cool?"

"Like LeBron or Denzel?" He shook his head. "Nah. I can't name a dog Denzel, that's kinda random."

"What about Bo?"

"Bo is seriously cool." Bobby smiled at the dog and knocked on the Plexiglas. "Your name be Bo." He'd laughed for the second time. It had been a good long while since he'd had anything to laugh about.

Then she really hung him up. The lady cop pulled a treat out of the console, got out of the car, and tossed it to his dog.

When she returned to the driver's seat she said, "I'm Bowers. What's on your mind?"

Kill Notice

Bobby could tell by the way she watched him real close that she didn't miss much. "I'm Bobby. Bobby Black. I'm in trouble, ma'am. I did some stuff," he said, glancing up at her.

His gut tightened up. He figured she'd arrest him any second now.

"Bobby I'm not here to judge. I'm here to help."

"You gots to understand, I was only trying to take care of my family. See what I'm sayin'?"

She nodded.

"I live with my grandma and brother and I've been doing some jobs to make cash, but it don't make no difference cuz they gonna take our house away no matter what I do." Bobby stared out the window at Sapphire's grave and the sad little plastic marker.

"Did Sapphire buy from you?"

Bobby knew he was trapped now. "I gotta man-up to that. Yes'm, she did. That's where I saw the man in black. I told you about him, too."

"You're the one who called me?"

He nodded.

"Thank you. That was brave." The lady cop paused, like she'd been thinking about something. "A friend of mine, Officer Perez, said he talked to a boy named Bobby. Was that you?"

Bobby nodded. "Yeah, but I was too scared to tell him much."

"You scared to talk to me?"

He shrugged. "Some. There be folks who don't want me to."

"At least, you're honest." The lady cop stretched. "Tell you what, whatever you say right now is just between you and me. Deal?"

Bobby nodded.

When they shook hands, she didn't let go. Her eyes went from checking out his bandage to staring him in the eye. "What happened?"

He pulled the bandage off his wrist and showed her the bloody X.

She frowned and pulled out her flashlight and took a good, long look at the wound. "I've seen this before. X Crew did this?"

"Yes, ma'am. Papa G did it his-self. Said it makes us family, but it hurts like hell."

"Call me Bowers."

"Yes, ma'am. Bowers."

She glanced up and smiled.

"Papa G says he has my back," Bobby said, "but he wants me to do stuff I don't want to do. He sure don't want me talkin' to you. That's fo' sure."

The lady cop patted his arm. "Stay put. I'll be right back." She went to the back of the SUV and returned with a first-aid kit. While she put some kind of cream on his wrist and a clean bandage, he filled her in on the whole nasty business with Papa G, and even told her about what his grandma had said about doing the right thing.

"If that ain't enough, the man in black is after me, too. I don't know which way to run. I don't much care if he comes after me, but my family." Bobby shook his head. "That's different. I gots to protect them." Bobby showed her the picture of his grandma in her recliner and told her how he came to have it.

"I owe her. Grandma raised me up." He wiped his eyes with his sleeve. "I can't let the man in black hurt her. You can lock me up, but please help my grandma and my brother."

"You have a cell phone?" she asked.

He nodded and pulled it out of his pocket.

"Good. Put my number in your contacts, but give it a name only you know. It's safer for you if no one knows you have my number." She handed him her card. He did as she asked and left the card on her console. Bobby gave her his number, too. He'd never expected to be exchanging numbers with a cop.

Bowers stiffened. She cranked the engine and stared at the rearview mirror. "Bobby, buckle your seatbelt." Her voice sounded serious.

He looked around. "What's up, man?"

She hit the gas. "Seatbelt. Now!" she yelled.

BOBBY SNAPPED HIS SEATBELT. Bowers' SUV lurched forward. Head-

Kill Notice

lights flooded the cab. They were so bright he could barely see. They sped up, and the lady cop took off like nothing he'd ever experienced before.

Gravel flew all over.

Out on the street, he grabbed the door handle each time she skidded around a corner. She went right through red lights. If he weren't so scared, it would've been fun. "I knew you was badass, but shit!"

"I won't crash, I promise," she said as she raced through a parking lot and down an alley. Seconds later, they were on another street, and then another. She pulled under a bridge and stopped. The truck that had been following them had disappeared.

"Bobby, I have a friend in the FBI."

"Shit man, tell me I ain't in that much trouble."

"I wish you hadn't sold dippers, but if you help us find the man in black and tell us what you know about Papa G's operation, my guess is that my friend will take very good care of all of you."

"Papa G is gonna kill me. I know it."

"I won't let that happen. We're gonna get you and your family somewhere safe. Where's your grandma now?"

Bobby blinked back the tears and didn't know what to say. He couldn't believe it. No one, besides Grandma, had ever helped him like this.

When his phone died, the cop let him use her phone to call his grandma. On the way to his house, Bowers charged up his phone and talked to someone named Johnny. After she bitched the dude out for not calling in, she told him to come back her up.

An hour later, they'd picked up his family and were pulling into a motel that even allowed Bo.

While the dude named Johnny checked the room, and helped his brother and grandma inside, Bobby sat in the lady cop's SUV. He saw his grandma staring at him through the front window of the room.

Bowers handed him his phone back. "My guess is that she's going to ask you tougher questions than I did."

"Yes, ma'am. You got that right." Bobby stared at Bowers for a few seconds. "Why would someone such as yourself care about me and mine?"

Bowers stared out the window. He wasn't sure if the look on her face was sadness or being pissed off or both.

"Bobby," she said, "the man in black killed my friend, too. I don't want him hurting anyone else."

IMPROMPTU POSSE

THE OLD EBBITT GRILL was busy as ever. Riggs settled into his favorite seat at the end of the bar, away from the media assembled near the front door. He'd seen the press secretary and some others from the hill enter about twenty minutes ago. Ebbitt's staff were accustomed to the chaos that often followed public figures who frequented their restaurant. Apparently the reporters outside were waiting for the officials to exit after a testy news conference earlier in the day.

Inside, things had settled into the usual nightly banter. Riggs glanced out the exterior glass walls at the front and hoped Bowers would stop by.

His thoughts returned to last night. He'd woken around 3 a.m. and had found her right next to him. Now she was out there in the city, beyond his reach.

He heard an uproar outside.

Riggs signaled the bartender and handed her a twenty. "Save these two seats. I'll be right back."

Riggs made his way down the steps and through the crowd at the hostess desk. He held up his hand to shield his eyes from the popping of camera flashes outside.

He saw Bowers' unit parked next to his car. *That's odd.* She never drove here, unless she was on duty.

Six feet from the entrance, he caught a glimpse of Bowers surrounded by a knot of reporters. They were mostly polite, but competing microphones, camera lenses, and questions fought for her attention.

"Dammit," he said. "She doesn't need this." When Riggs flagged down the head waiter, he realized a few of the guys from the bar were right behind him. Reporters clogged the entrance. One scruffy cameraman shoved Bowers back and pushed his camera lens into her face. The big lens jabbed her in the chin.

That was a critical mistake. Bowers grabbed the cameraman's shirt and hauled his ass inside. She slammed him against a wall next to the banister. The reporters outside jockeyed to see, but she and the cameraman were out of their line of sight.

Riggs pulled the head waiter along with him. The men behind him fanned out and blocked reporters from entering.

"Is she okay?" asked the head waiter as he waved customers out of the way.

Riggs smiled. "She's fine. It's the cameraman who's in deep shit."

Bowers ripped the camera out of the guy's hands and held it over the stairwell that went down to the restrooms. Riggs had been up and down those stairs more times than he cared to admit. If she were to let go, that camera would drop a good twenty feet before smashing into the black-and-white tiled floor below.

She leaned in to the man's face. "Here's the deal. You lay your hands on me again and I'll charge you with assaulting a police officer. You hear me?"

The man's eyes darted between her face and his camera and back again. "Look, I'm sorry." His eyes were wide, and his voice pleading. "I'm just trying to do my job."

"Whadda think I'm doing?" She shoved his camera into his chest with the same amount of force he'd used on her. The guys from the bar appeared amused. "Next time if you want my attention, ask. Nicely." Bowers pointed to the door. "Leave. Now."

"Coming through. Make a hole," Riggs yelled.

One of the men from the impromptu posse escorted the cameraman outside. Two brave reporters tried to enter, but stopped when the guys from the bar lined up like a wall of guard dogs.

One man nodded to where she'd held the cameraman. "Bowers. What the hell was that?"

"Restraint," she said as she walked away.

Riggs took Bowers by the hand. The head waiter escorted them to the rear room called Grant's Bar. Riggs glanced up at the mural on the ceiling and the nude painting hanging on the wall behind the bar. There was no place on Earth like The Old Ebbitt Grill.

They stopped at a secluded table. Riggs took off his jacket and pushed up his sleeves. Table 306 was usually reserved for dignitaries, the elite of Washington, and major players who wanted to eat or talk in private.

"No one will bother you here," said the head waiter as he handed them menus. "I'll send over your server. Let me know when you're finished and we'll take you out the side exit."

"Thanks," said Riggs. He slipped the guy a twenty.

This was becoming an expensive evening.

A tall server with a mass of brown curls arrived with his beer from the bar. Riggs noticed that his half-empty bottle of beer had been replaced with a fresh one.

Moments later, Bowers' ice tea arrived, soon followed by two steak dinners. Riggs slipped the Swiss chard onto her plate. She gave him some of her fries.

"I've got some news for you," he said.

Bowers stared at him.

"I entered the case details into the National Crime Information Center," he said while cutting his steak.

Bowers cocked her head. "And?"

"We got some hits. There are cold cases going back over fifteen years. If this is the same guy, he's killed over fifty people."

She dropped her napkin. "I know. I sent in a request too. I found a case in West Virginia where a girl had been raped. She survived. And they have a rape kit that has never been tested. I had them send it to you. It's a long shot."

"Maybe it will tell us something." Riggs sipped his beer. If it's the same guy, it appears that the early incidents were disorganized, sporadic crimes of opportunity, home invasions, and a little arson. All of the victims had missing buttons."

Bowers ate as if she hadn't eaten in weeks.

"If it's our guy," he said, "the time between kills is diminishing. He's now averaging one every week or so."

"Here's the problem," she said. "He's a cop. My guess is that he's Metro PD, which means he'll be getting real-time updates, which also means he knows everything we know. No wonder he's ten steps ahead of us. He can see us coming a mile away."

Riggs put a finger to his lips and leaned close so he could speak quietly. "That's why I've formed a shadow force. We're working behind the scenes. You're the only one at the precinct who knows about it. Keep it that way."

"What about my partner, Johnny?"

"Have him follow up on leads and callbacks. Meanwhile, we're going to limit what's reported to the press and inside the PD."

"I like it," she said, "but Mitch will know something is up. He's obsessed with the news on this case."

Riggs shrugged. "Won't be the first time Metro has been pissed at us. Sometimes you have to do what needs to be done." He watched her finish her steak.

"What happened to Parker?" she asked. "I haven't heard a word from Major Crimes."

Riggs fiddled with his knife. "The chief and I had a talk with him. He wasn't pleased, but he agreed to back off. As far as his accident, I've got someone looking into it. I suspect his brakes didn't fail for no reason."

"Don't tell me," she said, "he's missing buttons, too?"

"Don't know, but something stinks. Maybe the killer didn't want Major Crimes to take over."

The dimple at the corner of her mouth puckered. "If the killer

Kill Notice

doesn't want Major Crimes involved, I guarantee he won't want you and the FBI on his ass." Bowers stopped eating. "Riggs. Watch your back."

"I always do," he said.

She hesitated as if mulling over something in her mind.

"We have another issue," she said, "that we need to deal with."

Riggs watched her biting at a hangnail. "What's up?"

"I found the witness," she said. "His name is Bobby Black. He's a scared kid who got in over his head. The X Crew and Papa G are manipulating him from one side. Our killer is coming at him from the other. And he is trying to protect his grandmother and brother."

"The killer made contact?" asked Riggs.

"Yup. He cornered the kid's little brother outside his school. He gave the kid a photo of their grandmother asleep in her recliner as a warning. He tried to grab Bobby right there on the sidewalk."

"What stopped him?"

"A truck driver pulled up to the curb to make a delivery and saw the man hide his face and run." Bowers put down her fork. "Bobby has seen our killer's face more than once."

"That's why he's going after this boy. We need to protect him."

"Exactly," said Bowers. "I've already put Bobby's family up in a motel. That's what I came here to talk to you about. Johnny is there now, but I can't keep them there for long. With the heightened security over terrorist threats, visiting dignitaries, and now this hunt for a serial, we don't have the manpower to babysit them. I can't protect him or his family."

Riggs picked up his phone. "I can."

BEING HOLED up in a motel room with a cop was as awkward as anything Bobby had ever felt. He watched Bowers' partner peering outside at the parking lot.

Later on, pounding on the door woke Bobby with a jolt. The feds had shown up and it scared him. At first he'd figured that Bowers had ratted him out, but they turned out to be cool. And she'd kept her promise.

His grandma had wanted to go back to their little house, until two big dudes with serious rifles and big vests had helped her down the steps. She'd winked at Bobby and had said, "With them around, ain't nobody messin' with us."

Their belongings were scooped up along with the dog as they were hustled into a van. It was like something from a movie, except his grandma held onto her pocketbook with both hands.

When their ride came to stop, they stepped out onto the far end of a dark driveway under a bunch of trees. From there they were quickly escorted into a house that sat a long way off the street in what looked like a fine neighborhood.

The safe house was a lot nicer than what they were used to, even so, it felt strange being there. Like they were in the wrong place.

When Tommy saw he had his own room with a TV, he acted like Christmas had come.

Grandma eyed the king-size bed in her room and clapped her hands. "Lawdy, lawdy," she said, "this here bed be big enough to sleep the whole neighborhood, and there be enough food in the kitchen to feed them, too."

After his brother went to bed, Bobby sat up with his grandma. They hadn't talked much since the police station. He'd been dodging most of her questions, but the time had come to tell her the truth. She deserved that much. He told her everything about Sapphire and Papa G. She was none too happy about the dippers.

Bobby felt his grandma's hand on top of his. He stared at her boney, cool fingers and waited for her to pronounce his punishment.

Grandma cleared her throat and nodded. "I know why you did it," she said, "and son, I rightly appreciate dat." She put her arm around him. "But yous need to know dat I'd rather do without than to live on ill-gotten money."

Her words were firm, but gentle, and they stung more than a beating. Shame and regret clung to him like a wet T-shirt.

THE MAN IN BLACK

THE NEXT MORNING, Riggs left his car in the Metro PD's compound. His eyes felt dry and irritated. He'd been up most of the night. It had taken time and pulling some strings, but Bobby Black and his family were securely relocated to a safe house.

Bowers would be happy about that.

He'd also spent a good three hours organizing his shadow task force and setting up a secure room at the field office for meetings.

After showing his badge, he went up to the second floor and wove his way through the maze of cubicles to Bowers' desk. He found her hunched over a cup of coffee and a pile of case files. He took a bit of pleasure in knowing she still used the mug he'd given her.

"How's motel coffee working for you?" he asked. *That should tweak her.*

Bowers kept her eyes on her reading. "Don't ask."

"See? You are a coffee snob."

"Shut up," she said with a grin. She glanced up at him and did a double take. "We're a matching set. We both look like crap. Elbow to the face did it for me. What's your excuse?"

"I've been up all night," he said. "Bobby and his family are in the safe house."

Bowers dropped her pen. "Thank you. I've been on edge worrying about that kid." She stood briefly and gave him a hug.

Riggs took a seat. "We'll pick him up this afternoon and take him over to the field office for an interview and an appointment with a sketch artist. You in?"

"Absolutely," she said. "I called Senator Keats' office in hopes of getting them something more permanent. I couldn't believe the man answered the phone himself. Anyway, I'm going to meet him tomorrow."

"Good. I'll be tied up most of the day." He leaned in close to her ear. Her hair smelled of the same shampoo he remembered. "The shadow task force is operational."

Her eyebrows went up. "My God, you were busy last night."

Riggs' phone buzzed with an incoming call from Johnny.

"Hey Riggs, I've gone over the security feeds from Jayzee's place. We've got a shot of the killer."

"We'll be right there," said Riggs. He ended the call and dropped the phone in his pocket.

He felt her watching him.

Riggs waved for her to follow. "Your partner is turning into a real asset. He found something important. We'll look at it during our meeting. Let's go."

BOWERS CALLED the chief as she headed down the gleaming, white concrete-block corridor toward the briefing room. Along the way, she planned to stop and give Mitch a heads up.

"Chief," she said, "Johnny found something. Riggs says we'll be reviewing it during our meeting."

"I'll be there shortly," said the chief.

She ended the call. Twenty feet from Mitch's office, she could hear him bitching. "Loud-mouthed putz," he said.

Bowers stopped at his doorway.

As usual, he had the news on while going through the reports on

Kill Notice

his desk. He threw a wad of paper at the TV screen. He didn't show it, but she could tell he'd seen her. In the background, Senator Harry Keats stood before the cameras.

"The way that blowhard sucks up airtime," he said, "you'd think nothing else in the rest of the world was worth reporting."

Mitch swiveled toward her in his chair. She nixed the idea of telling him about tomorrow's meeting with Keats. "I stopped by to—"

He stood and welcomed her into his office. "Sorry, I got caught up with all this. How can I help you?"

"The task force is gathering for our meeting. Thought I'd stop by and remind you."

AFTER REFILLING HER COFFEE MUG, Bowers entered the task force room. Riggs and Mitch were on opposite sides of the room. The chief marched in and stood against the wall next to the door. At the table a few feet in front of him sat Johnny, who appeared tired and a little jittery. He wore the same clothes as yesterday. Apparently Riggs wasn't the only one who's been up all night.

A few minutes later Clawski, Detective Karen Reeves, and the rest of the task force filled up the chairs.

Riggs clapped his hands. "We have the security footage from Jayzee's house. Johnny has found something on it that you all need to take a look at." He clicked on the big screen up front.

Johnny queued up the footage.

The chief patted him on the shoulder. "Son, I sure hope this is good. We're sorely in need of a break."

Riggs stood at the front of the room. As everyone watched the screen, Mitch leaned against the doorframe next to the chief and flipped off the lights.

"What you're seeing," said Riggs, "is the south side of Jayzee's house." He nodded for Johnny to continue.

Johnny hit the play button. "As you can see, the time stamp is 2:54 a.m."

Bowers studied the shadows on the screen. Lights from a passing car briefly illuminated a female figure slumped against the house and a tall figure behind her with his back to the camera. The man wore all black, with a cap and hood covering his head. Seconds later another car went by. Berti's face emerged from the shadows and stared up at the security camera.

Bowers flinched and forced herself to remain focused on the screen.

The man in black grabbed Berti from behind and pulled her back into the shadows. She fought him, but was quickly subdued.

Bowers folded her arms. She could almost feel Riggs watching her. She pointed to the numbers in the corner. "Is that time stamp accurate?" she asked.

"Yup," said Johnny. "First thing I checked."

Bowers glanced up and held Riggs' gaze. His eyes reflected a mix of concern and sadness. She knew he understood.

As the tape replayed several times, Riggs paced up and down the side aisle. "As you can see," he said, "our perp is about six-two, strong, and very much in control."

While the chief made a few comments, Riggs leaned against the window ledge next to her. "I'd like Bobby to see this tape," he whispered.

She kept her voice hushed. "We could do it this afternoon, before he sees the sketch artist. Maybe it will jog his memory."

Riggs nodded.

After they finished showing the tape, he went over everyone's assignments. Bowers heard his words, but Berti and her desperate expression remained in Bowers' thoughts.

When Mitch, the chief, and nearly everyone else had left, she sat on the table near Johnny. "Nice job. Good find."

Riggs interrupted. He had his phone to his ear and a very pissed-off expression on his face.

"What's up?" asked Bowers as he ended his call.

He guided her toward the back of the room and stopped. "The family is fine, but Bobby is missing."

Kill Notice

BOBBY'S HANDS were sweating as he stared out the windows of the Metrobus. Any minute he expected a road block, and a bunch of feds to storm the bus and drag him off. Instead, he saw folks outside on the streets going about their business like normal.

A lady with earbuds sat next to him. She listened to her phone and yawned. He could relate. He couldn't remember the last time he'd slept for more than a few hours.

This morning, he'd woken early and had stared up at the ceiling fan. Meeting Bowers had changed everything. She'd kept her promise. That was something. His family was safe and he wanted to be done with the crew. He vowed to himself that he would never again sell dippers.

An incoming text showed Papa G thought otherwise. Bobby read the message: *Come to the corner tonight.*

Bobby nearly dropped his phone when Papa G sent him a photo of the safe house. The next text read: *You know what I'll do if you don't show.*

If he didn't go, the crew would swarm the house looking for him. No telling what would happen to his family if that happened.

He knew Grandma and Tommy would be safer, if he wasn't there. Bobby also knew he couldn't come back unless he faced Papa G and settled this for good.

Saying it and doing it were two different things. With the two security types watching the place, sneaking off proved to be a lot harder than Bobby had imagined. They didn't let anyone in or out without authorization. It felt like school all over again, only worse.

Bobby never expected his break to come from his little brother, but it did.

Headstrong as always, Tommy didn't read the instructions on the bag of popcorn. Ten minutes later, smoke came billowing out of the microwave and filled the kitchen. That set off the smoke detectors, which set Bo to howling. Everything went nuts. Everyone started yelling, most of all Tommy.

Grandma tried to stop him from opening the microwave door, but he didn't listen. The bag of popcorn went up in flames and set Tommy to hollering louder. Before Bobby could get to either of them, the security dudes pushed him out of the way and hustled all of them, including Bo out the front door and away from the smoke.

Once Bobby realized the place wasn't burning down, he saw his chance. While the ruckus kept everyone distracted, he slipped into the trees and darted along the side of the house. He could still hear Tommy yelling on the front lawn. By the time Bobby'd jumped over the back fence and ducked down another street, he heard the fire truck sirens. It had taken the better part of an hour to find a bus stop.

In the seat next to him, the woman with the ear buds began snoring and brought him out of his thoughts. As the bus rumbled along, his leg bounced. With his phone about to die, he bitched at himself for leaving his charging cord at home. When the bus pulled to a stop in his neighborhood, he hopped off and headed toward his old house.

With the weather getting cooler, porches were empty and folks had gone inside. Out here, he felt like easy pickings. The man in black could be around any corner, and Papa G had a strange way of finding him.

Bobby had some comfort in knowing that if he wasn't at the safe house, Papa G had no reason to go there or to hurt his family.

As he approached his old house, Bobby tried to stay out of sight. When he cut between two townhomes a big, black dog charged up and barked at him from behind a fence. That got Bobby's heart pumping.

The closer he came to his place, the more he wondered if it had been left alone or if his neighbors had broken in and helped themselves. Being poor made some folks desperate. It made them do dumb things. He knew all about that. Hooking up with the crew had been stupid.

He jumped a few fences and came up the back. After unlocking the back door, he ducked inside and locked the door behind him. In the living room his grandma's recliner sat there sad and worn. He

Kill Notice

stared at the packed-down cushions. It seemed strange to see it empty. Part of him wondered if he'd ever live here again.

After folding up her quilt, Bobby left it on the seat. He hurried into his old room and plugged his phone into the charger. In the closet, he pushed his brother's junk out of the way and opened the access panel to the bathroom's shower. When he reached in the gap between the wall and the plumbing, the bandage on his wrist caught on a hard edge.

"Shit." The wound stung like crazy.

He dug his other hand into the space and felt around until he found the plastic, hamburger-bun bag he'd snagged from the trash. Bobby pulled it out, counted the cash inside, and dropped the bundle into his backpack.

He stood in the middle of the bedroom. His old, torn sweatshirt lay in a heap on his bunk. He glanced down at his chest and the Helly Hanson logo on his jacket.

Bobby ripped off the jacket and hurled it across the room. He sat on the edge of his bed and buried his face in his old sweatshirt. Everything in him wanted to go back and do this all different. He'd once thought money and fine clothes would fix everything.

"Man, was that stupid."

He'd have been better off if he'd never met Papa G.

THE BLACK TRUCK

BOWERS DROVE by the basketball court at Bobby's high school where a group of kids were playing. She got out of the car. "Hey," she called out to a tall kid.

A gaggle of boys surrounded her. They were sweaty, pimpled, and out of breath. The tall one bounced the ball on the ground, again and again. Each time it made a hollow thump.

"Say, mama," he said, "what you want?" His big grin showed a rack of white teeth.

Bowers smiled to herself. These kids thought they were tough stuff. She talked to them for a few minutes. None of them admitted having seen Bobby recently.

Twenty minutes later, she pulled up in front of Bobby's house. She slipped through the broken gate and up onto the porch, where a pot of daisies had begun to wilt.

The door was locked.

She knocked, and peered through the front window, but didn't see or hear anyone inside. Nothing appeared to be disturbed. Bowers sat on the porch and scanned the street.

This was a tough place for a kid to grow up.

Kill Notice

A small, plastic bowl full of water sat on the porch a foot from her. She dumped it into the pot of daisies and wondered where Bobby had gone.

Back in the Tahoe, Bowers drove toward the cemetery. She knew his family meant everything to him. He wouldn't leave them unless he saw no other option.

Bobby had run for a reason. She hoped he wouldn't try to deal with Papa G or the killer on his own. He'd lose that fight.

She cruised in and around the cemetery, searching for him. "Where the hell are you?"

At a corner convenience store, she took a right and spotted a big black truck behind her.

Bowers sped up and made two more turns. When she came over a hill, a stalled car blocked one lane and three guys were trying to push it off onto the shoulder. She swerved around them.

The next time she glanced in the mirror, the truck drew closer. Each time she turned a corner or passed a vehicle the pickup copied her moves.

He hung back far enough that she couldn't see a face or license plate number, but close enough to be a threat.

She called Riggs. "I'm being tailed. I'm not sure if he's after me or trying to see if I find Bobby."

"Stay on major roads," Riggs said, "and maintain an even speed. Keep him following you. I'll call the PD, they'll send cruisers out to corner him."

Bowers took the shortest route out of the residential area. She passed a Safeway, and toyed with stopping in at the police substation a few doors down, but that would throw her tail for certain.

For now, the truck remained in the center of her rearview mirror. She still couldn't see the license plate, but the vehicle appeared to be a Chevy.

A few seconds later, she stopped at a light and watched a woman push a bike through the crosswalk.

Bowers' radio squawked with chatter from dispatch. Three

cruisers were en route. She heard one officer calling in who said he was two blocks away.

The light turned green.

As soon as the traffic started to move, the black pickup peeled away, and darted down a side street.

DANGEROUS GROUND

BOBBY HAD FALLEN ASLEEP on his bunk. He vaguely remembered someone knocking on the front door or maybe it had been a dream. He sat up slowly and checked his phone. Three messages from Bowers filled the screen. She wanted him to call her, but he couldn't. Not yet. This was something he had to do on his own.

He turned off his phone and stripped off his clothes, flapped his arms like a swimmer, and tried to build up his nerve to go back to the corner.

In the bathroom he stared at the cracked tiles, broken mirror, and the rusted faucet. Oil for the furnace had run out a month ago, which meant there was no heat or hot water.

His reflection showed the same anger and frustration that had led him to Papa G, only now he'd had enough of the X Crew, the man in black, and people like Jimmy who liked to push him around.

Bobby cracked a half-smile. At least he'd set Jimmy straight. His smile faded. Now he had to face Papa G.

The handle on the faucet had fallen apart last year. Bobby kept a pair of pliers on the sink to turn on the water. He shivered as he washed up.

While shaving the bit of fuzz off his chin and upper lip, he pulled back his shoulders and practiced what he wanted to say to Papa G. Finding the right words proved to be a struggle.

After pulling on a clean T-shirt and jeans, he stuffed his toothbrush and charging cord into his backpack. His hand brushed against his old sweatshirt. It felt soft and familiar and had been paid for with honest money from honest work. Money he'd earned flipping burgers.

He'd once been ashamed of it and the dirt-poor life it symbolized. Bobby's jaw tightened. His eyes burned. It wasn't supposed to be like this.

After scooping up the Helly Hanson jacket and stuffing it into his backpack, he shook out his old sweatshirt and slowly pulled it over his head and drew up the hood and stared at himself in the mirror. He ran his hand down the front and stood a little taller, torn sleeve and all. To him the bloodstain meant he'd been in battle and lived to tell about it.

He hoped he'd survive tonight, too.

Half an hour later, he caught the Metrobus heading toward MLK and Malcolm X.

The time had come to return Papa G's cash and his stupid jacket. Dray had taken the gun, now Perez had it. Nothing Bobby could do about that. Papa G would have to take that up with Dray, whom he figured would be laid out in a body bag by now. *Good luck with that.*

The bus rumbled along the dark streets. By 9:00 pm the action on the corner would be starting. He turned his phone back on and checked for messages.

The closer the bus got to the crew's territory, the faster his leg bounced. Bobby kept telling himself that Papa G was a businessman. He might have to work to pay him back some, but he'd be reasonable. Bobby sure hoped so.

When he jumped off the bus a few blocks early, the familiar scents made his shoulders tense. His mouth went dry. Tonight the smells seemed nastier. The dopers seemed even more pathetic. Like having brand new eyes, he saw how bad things really were on the streets.

Kill Notice

His shoes scuffed against the sidewalk grit. His wrist still hurt from the last time he'd seen Papa G. Bobby decided to check out the corner and see who was there before walking into a trap. No reason to be stupid. He curved around the back of the park and stayed out of sight.

Business at the park had gotten under way. Bobby avoided the dope heads and drunks peeing in the bushes. He ignored a few call-outs from the hookers, and shimmied up a big tree until he'd climbed high enough that the leaves hid him from view.

Last time he'd climbed a tree had been at the church, where he'd seen something he wished he hadn't.

He peeked through the leaves and settled into a V between two big branches. Bobby shifted when a twig poked his butt. After a few seconds, he curled up and waited.

From his perch it wasn't hard to see the crew standing watch as usual. Papa G came down the street and disappeared into the sub shop. Bobby pulled out his phone.

After dimming the screen, he tapped on the camera icon and played with the zoom. He took some shots of Papa G talking to the crew. It surprised him when a new guy with crazy red hair went into the sub shop and sat down in front of Papa G.

What the hell? What's Jimmy doing here?

Bobby took a short video and could see he'd already been replaced. Jimmy took three packs of cigarettes from Papa G and went down to the corner.

Bobby took more pictures and a video of Jimmy selling dippers. Bowers would have fun with that, if Jimmy ever messed with him again.

The time had come to face Papa G who was sitting at the table waiting. Bobby dropped his phone into his backpack and slipped out of the tree.

He started to cross the street north of the sub shop to avoid Jimmy. A familiar Tahoe drove toward him. Bobby ducked back into a dense stand of trees and watched the big vehicle slowing down. Bowers sat behind the wheel. Bobby withdrew into the darkness.

The last thing he needed was for her to see him with Papa G and get the wrong idea. If the crew saw her, they might even start something. After the shootout with the 301s Bobby wanted nothing to do with another confrontation.

After she'd driven on, he stayed inside the tree line for a few moments. The headlights had messed up his night vision. He stumbled over a tree root.

Bobby had almost reached the sidewalk, when he heard something soft like a boot in the dirt behind him. A strong hand went over his mouth. The cold hard barrel of a gun pressed against his neck.

BOWERS PULLED into the Starbucks on H Street. Perez pulled up next to her.

She went inside, where the night crew restocked the sugar bins and stir sticks. The place had a cool groove to it. At one of the small tables, two men were playing a game of backgammon.

A few minutes later, she hopped into her Tahoe and handed Perez a cup of coffee.

"Thanks," he said, holding up his cup. "I need this."

"Tell me about it." Bowers took a sip of her coffee. "Thanks for giving me a heads up about Bobby Black."

"I ran into him a few days ago." Perez eased his seat back.

"You know where he is now?" she asked.

"No." Perez shook his head. "I thought you'd found him. What happened?"

Bowers told him the details. "I need him as a witness. He's the only one who's seen the 202 Killer's face and lived to talk about it. Now he's missing."

Perez shifted in his seat and kept an eye on the parking lot. "So he's running from you, Papa G, and a serial killer?" He let out a soft whistle. "The odds are not in that boy's favor."

"You said you talked to him?"

"I did. I've been running surveillance on Papa G. He's in competi-

Kill Notice

tion with the 301 crews over suppliers. PCP is in short supply and he sent out some guys to intervene with an incoming shipment. Bobby went with them. It all went haywire. They shot each other up. We rolled in and shut it down. I found Bobby under one of the cars, scared out of his mind. The kid was clean. Other than being in the wrong place at the wrong time, I had nothing on him other than being a witness."

"You find out anything else about him?" she asked.

Perez laughed. "Bobby is a lousy liar. He pretended to know nothing about Papa G and PCP. And yet, he sat there in ragged clothes and a high-end Helly Hanson jacket. That means one thing— Papa G has his hooks into him."

Bowers put down her coffee. "I think Bobby wants out. If you see him, please bring him in and let me know. I'll come get him."

Perez nodded. "No problem, but I need to warn you. Word on the street is that Papa G is highly torqued off about losing his California supplier. I don't have a good feeling about this."

TOO CLOSE

THE NEXT MORNING, Bowers picked up Uncle Marvin and took him to breakfast. He had no problem celebrating his birthday with big stack of pancakes piled high with fresh berries and cream.

What he did have a problem with were the bruises on her face and told her so. "What happened?"

She told him she'd found a thief in her apartment. He drank his coffee and they talked awhile.

At the end of the meal he put his hand on her arm. "That wasn't some burglar in your apartment. I've been watching the news. I know who you're huntin'."

She stared at her coffee cup, debating about how much she could tell him without causing him too much worry.

"Missy, when I was in Nam it was a different kind of warfare. Couldn't tell the enemy from civilians. They used guerilla tactics and hid among civilians."

She leaned into his shoulders. "Terrorists do the same thing."

"So do serial killers," he said. His voice had that tone he used when he wanted her to listen up. She felt his big green eyes honing in on her.

Kill Notice

"I know," she said. "I'm staying in a different hotel room each night. I'll watch my back, I promise."

BOWERS DROVE through the usual heavy traffic. Marvin's reaction to the set of videos she'd given him about powerboat racing made the commute to work almost tolerable.

As cars slowed to a crawl, she called Riggs to see if he'd heard anything about Bobby, but he didn't answer. He must have been deep into something. The sound of his recorded voice put a smile on her face.

Bowers pulled the small, green stopper from the lid of her Starbuck's coffee and chewed on it. Perez had worked last night until dawn and so far he hadn't called her, which meant Bobby was still in the wind.

Bobby tried to act tough, but him out on the streets wasn't much different than dropping a puppy onto the Washington Beltway. He didn't have a chance.

Fifteen minutes later, Bowers pulled into the station and went up to her cubicle.

Perez sat in the chair next to her desk, waiting for her. "I haven't seen your Bobby Black," he said.

"Damn." She took a seat at her desk. "We've got to find him."

"I did notice something," he said. "I followed a car north almost to Silver Springs. Papa G was in the back seat. They drove up and down streets and around blocks. Either he was casing the area or searching for something."

"That's way off grid for Papa G. Isn't it?"

Perez nodded. "Papa G never leaves Barry Farm."

"Why didn't you stop him?" asked Bowers.

"He knows me. If I had stopped him, he would've known I was tailing him. I still need Papa G to lead me to the rest of his contacts. You were in Barry Farm last night, right?"

"Yeah," said Bowers. "I cruised King's Corner. There were drug

MARTA SPROUT

deals going down around me, but I didn't see Bobby. The second time I went by, someone picked up Papa G and left. He seemed to be in a hurry."

"Something's up," said Perez as he slowly stood.

"Keep me posted," she said.

After he'd gone, Bowers searched her desk and frowned. When Johnny passed by, she waved for him to stop. "Hey, Johnny. Have you seen my mug?"

"Yeah, you left it in the task force room. I picked it up and washed it. It's in the breakroom on the mat next to the sink."

"Thanks. This living out of a suitcase is taking some adjustment."

Bowers went in the breakroom and found her mug upside down on the drying mat. Karen came in and grabbed a yogurt out of the fridge.

"Bowers," she said. "How's the face?"

Bowers lifted up her mug. "Better, thanks..." She stopped and stood there for a second. "Oh, shit!" She backed away from the sink. "Goddammit."

"Bowers, what's wrong?"

Johnny ran into the room. "Are you okay?"

The three of them stared at the mat where her mug had been sitting.

"No way," said Johnny. "Tell me this is another one of Clawski's dumb-assed pranks, because that wasn't there when I washed your mug."

In the middle of the ring, where her mug had been, lay a small pink button.

———

BOWERS PRESSED her thumbnail into the soft Styrofoam cup on her desk. Drinking out of a disposable cup wasn't the same. Her mug and the pink button were now in the custody of Magrath and en route to the FBI's lab.

242

Kill Notice

Bowers speed dialed Riggs. He didn't answer, which didn't surprise her. He had said he would be tied up today.

She knew the pink button signaled another kill. If the pattern held, another body would be found any minute.

She sat at her desk staring at a picture of Marvin in his younger years. Her phone buzzed with an incoming call from West Virginia. "This is Detective Stan Meeks," the voice said. "I found that rape kit you've been lookin' for. Should be at the FBI's lab by tomorrow."

She thanked him, once again.

For now, all she could do was wait. Besides, she had a meeting with Senator Keats. Bowers gathered up her things and hit the road.

It felt as if she were heading the wrong direction. Everything in her wanted to go find Bobby. Hopefully Perez would find him soon.

Across the Potomac lay Virginia and Woodlake Regional Park, where the senator wanted to meet at a fishing cabin. She enjoyed being out of the city and surrounded by forests of oak and sycamores.

When she reached the park, Bowers followed the instructions to the exclusive section that had become popular with Washington's elite. It offered privacy and a getaway not too far from the District.

She watched for a path that led deep into the woods. Up ahead, a narrow road to the right had a posted sign that read: "No. 19." She eased down the long stretch of gravel. A minute later, the riverfront cabin came into view.

Her vision of a cozy cottage vanished. In front of her loomed a large two-story structure made of polished wooden beams, high-end stone, and huge tinted windows.

Cars she assumed were Keats' security detail surrounded the building. That didn't surprise her until she came closer and realized that they were all law enforcement vehicles, federal ones by the look of it.

When Bowers spotted a man in an FBI jacket putting up yellow tape, she knew something was way out of kilter. She slipped out of the Tahoe.

A special agent stopped her. "Ma'am," said the agent, "you'll have to stay behind the line."

"I'm Metro PD." Bowers showed her badge. "I have an appointment with Senator Keats. Where is he?"

"Bowers?" asked a familiar voice.

She scanned the deck. There near the door stood Riggs.

———

BOWERS NOTICED several special agents watching them as Riggs escorted her inside the cabin. In the foyer, she stopped him. "What is all this and where the hell is Keats?"

"He's gone. Why are you here?"

"I had an appointment," she said, "to discuss housing for Bobby and his family."

Riggs waved her forward. Bowers followed him into the main room of the cottage, where he pointed to a loft. There over the railing hung a pair of white-lace panties.

"Aw, crap," said Bowers.

"It's another one. Looks like our killer is now operating in Virginia."

She blinked. "Is the victim wearing something pink?"

"Yeah, how would you..." His eyes went wide. "You got another button?"

"Yup." She showed him the picture on her phone. "Found it in the breakroom under my mug."

His jaw tightened. "He was inside the station? Jesus."

"I told you our guy is Metro PD." She nodded toward the railing. "How did you find out about this one?"

"We didn't. I came down here to serve a warrant to search this cottage. I'll explain in a minute, but for now can you take a look?"

"Sure." Bowers hoped this time it wouldn't be someone she knew.

He waved over a tech from the FBI's Evidence Recovery Team, who handed her booties and gloves. The woman spotted Bowers' ponytail and handed her a cap.

A quick scan of the rooms told her a lot about Keats. "If this is roughing it, sign me up."

Kill Notice

The kitchen had granite countertops. The dense trees and the river could be seen from every window along the back. The massive, stone fireplace dominated the living room. The place would have been gorgeous, if it weren't for the knocked over lamp and the paw prints.

In this area the larger prints were likely from coyotes who moved through the forests like ghosts.

It looked as if a pack of them had been living there. The leather couch had been gnawed on, and most of the items on the lower shelves of the pantry had tumbled out onto the kitchen floor.

All doors were wide open, even the sliding glass doors that opened onto the huge deck.

"Did you open these?" she asked Riggs.

"Nope. We found them this way. We chased a raccoon and two squirrels out of the kitchen."

A rank odor she knew well filled the cabin despite the breeze blowing through. Decomp was one of those odors one didn't forget.

Riggs stood back and watched.

She did a walk-through of the living room first. From the access tarps, she noticed a large backpack next to the couch. A shoe of the type a teenager might wear lay at the bottom of the stairs. Flies buzzed around the room.

"Riggs, I don't like the look of this."

He nodded.

"Something's way off," she said, "I received the button this morning, but there's no way this victim was killed last night." The smell told her that much.

"You're right. She died about three days ago. We're late to the party."

"Mind telling me what the warrant was about?"

He shifted his gaze toward the woods.

"Dammit, Riggs, talk to me."

He leaned in close. "Remember the raid I told you about?"

She nodded.

"We busted up a child-porn ring and confiscated a laptop. It had an app that led us to a burner phone and IP address we traced to here. We had no idea Keats had leased this unit until we served a search warrant on the park's management early this morning."

"Keats is involved in kiddie porn?" said Bowers.

"Either that or he's been set up. The man gets hate mail on a daily basis. It wouldn't surprise me, if he were on someone's radar. I don't know yet if Keats is good for any of this or not."

"Jayzee was set up," she said. "It's possible that Keats was, too. Where's the victim?" She could've followed the scent, but they'd always respected each other's turf and she let him take lead.

"I'll show you."

Bowers followed him toward the stairs. "Good God, tracks are everywhere."

"Trust me. It gets worse."

Bowers studied each of the open doors in the living room. The woods were only twenty feet from the house. Dirt-brown prints came into the room, dark redish ones left. This was going to be ugly.

Bowers ascended part way up the stairs. Signs of a struggle marred the wall. The cream-colored surface bore dents and smudges of blood. The railing showed scuffs. Riggs nodded to a tech dusting for prints. She could see he'd found some on the upper rail, but the lower railing was clean.

She stopped. "Something's wrong. The 202 Killer, wouldn't have left behind any prints on the railing or anywhere else." She carefully stepped around an evidence marker near a tiny gold earring. "He wouldn't have left that either. It might have DNA on it."

They continued up the stairs. Bowers took a deep breath before entering the bedroom. The window, like the doors, had been left open. Bird droppings coated the top of the dresser and headboard.

The carpeting and bed reminded Bowers of a truck stop, with mud tracks leading in and out. Blood spatter on a wall next to the bed suggested blunt-force trauma. It was another example of what the 202 Killer would not have left behind. She wondered if this was a different unsub."

Kill Notice

A rig of the type used by hunters to dress deer had been chained to the rafters. The body hung upside down by both ankles.

"Riggs, she's barefoot and could've kicked her attacker. We might get lucky and find some cells under her toenails."

The victim appeared to be barely more than a child.

The garment, or what was left of it, had been torn from her body. Shreds of the sheer, pink fabric lay in tatters over the bed and carpet. Bowers stepped closer. A piece of fabric with two tiny, pink buttons lay on the bedspread. They appeared to be identical to the one she'd found under her mug. This had to be the same guy, but something had changed.

Bowers grimaced as she studied the body. At least half of it had been ravaged by predation. "I sure hope this poor child died before the animals found her."

Riggs cleared his throat. "Amen to that."

The thought of her hanging there while her body had been torn apart put a knot in Bowers' gut. She glanced away and remembered how Berti's killer had given her a piano-wire necklace and watched her wearing it.

"He likes watching," she said. Bowers stepped back and quickly scanned the room.

"What are you looking for?" asked Riggs.

"That." Bowers pointed at the bathroom. The open wooden door showed a sink and toilet on the left and a large shower with a clear glass door that was partially visible from the room. Bloody paw prints smeared the lower half of the glass. More covered the floor. Goosebumps rose on her arms.

"Good God," said Riggs. "He watched?"

"The coyotes tried to get at him too. Look at how they pawed at the left side of the glass door. That's where he stood, which makes sense. It's the only angle where he could've seen the girl. That also means he had to be real close to the glass. His breath must have touched it. There could be contact DNA," she said.

Riggs stepped outside the bedroom and called downstairs.

When he returned, she asked, "How old was this girl?"

"We're guessing about fourteen." The pissed-off tone in his voice told her that he hated this as much as she did. "We'll know more once the M.E. takes a look."

"You're gonna have a tough time establishing cause of death with so much... missing."

He nodded.

"Hey, Riggs," said a man in a white Tyvek suit. "You wanted me up here?" He stood in the doorway, holding a collection kit in one hand and a brown paper evidence bag in the other.

"Yup." Riggs nodded at the evidence bag. "What's that?"

The tech set down the kit, which resembled a large toolbox, and held up the bag. "We might have caught a break. We found a Coke can in the woods next to some tire tracks. Probably a four-wheel truck of some kind."

Riggs pointed to the shower door. "Bowers just found something. I want everything you can get out of that." He pointed toward the bathroom. "Take the whole damned shower door and anything else you can find."

BURNING FEAR

RIGGS SELECTED the baked-potato soup special from the menu. After what he'd seen today, steak or lasagna were out of the question. With Bowers sitting next to him, he took a sip of his beer, and enjoyed the moment. "I'm glad you stayed," he told her.

Bowers poked at her salad. "Me too, but I'm buying, like I promised."

A crowd watching a football game had gathered at the other end of the restaurant to cheer on their team. He and Bowers had chosen a more secluded corner where the television had been tuned to the news, which meant it was quiet enough to carry on a conversation and had just enough background noise to frustrate anyone trying to listen in.

Table selection with her had always been amusing. He wanted his back to a wall with the entrance in clear view. So did she. They worked out a compromise and sat on the same side so they both were comfortable.

"Mitch is pretty bent about it, but your guys have done a great job with the media," said Bowers. She laughed, but he could see the strain in her face.

Riggs nodded toward the TV. "Here it comes."

A breaking news story flashed across the screen. Anchor Marc Davis stared into the camera. "Senator Harry Keats is nowhere to be found tonight, after a fourteen-year-old girl was found brutally murdered in a cabin he rented. Sources claim that the senator's laptop, which was recovered from the scene, contained child pornography. Senator Keats has allegedly been linked to the same child-pornography ring that was recently broken up by the FBI. His staff has no comment as people from both sides of the aisle are reeling from the news."

"He's in deep shit," said Bowers.

Riggs smiled. "Washington is mired in it." He reached to his left and touched her hand. "Where are you staying tonight?"

Her eyes were focused on her salad. "Haven't thought that far ahead."

Riggs sat back and pulled his hand away as the waiter dropped off the check. Once he'd left, Riggs rubbed his thumb over her fingers. "We're outside D.C. I have the key to a friend's cottage. We could take a night off. I could use a break. How about you?"

FORTY MINUTES LATER, Riggs entered the cottage's kitchen and put a couple of beers in the fridge. Bowers had gone to take a shower. He could hear the water running. He also heard something else.

He hurried down the hall and opened the bathroom door.

The moment he saw her, a knot rolled in his gut. He could see she was using the sound of the shower to cover up the emotions that were surging to the surface. The sight damn near broke him.

She glanced at him, leaned into the tile wall, and wrapped her arms around her head. Streams of steaming water pounded her back and ran over her bare skin.

He pulled off his shoes and trousers and stepped into the shower. When he rested his hand on her shoulder, he felt her body quake. She slammed her fist against the tiled wall.

He'd seen her like this before.

Kill Notice

Riggs knew how the horrors and the pressures of the job built up over time, and once in a while she had to let it all out.

Bowers turned toward him and buried her face in his shoulder so hard she pressed him against the shower wall. He rested his cheek against her wet hair and wrapped his arms around her so tightly he expected her to complain. Instead, she shuddered and pulled her arms in close against his chest. "I should've caught this bastard by now."

He closed his eyes and listened to the rush of water pelting the shower walls. Hot water splattered against him. Steam filled his senses.

After a few moments she lifted her head and pressed the soft skin of her face against his cheek. She slapped her hand on his wet shirt and laughed.

"You dipshit. What are you doing?"

He glanced down at his soaked shirt. "Once in a great while you get to be there for someone you love."

She said nothing. He was almost afraid to look at her. When he did, her hazel eyes made him feel a dizzying surge, as if he were about to tumble off the edge of a cliff.

He blinked when her warm, soft lips touched his mouth. *Hell yes.* He'd missed her for so long that his shirt quickly ended up on the bathroom floor, along with his soggy socks and skivvies. The shower rushed at them until it had run out of hot water.

He grabbed two towels and tossed one of them to Bowers. They ran out of the bathroom and across the hall, where they dove headlong under the king-size bed's velvety, soft comforter. His feet and her legs tangled in the soft, flannel sheets.

He pushed a sea of pillows and down blankets out of the way to hold her. He savored the waves of pleasure and the surge of passion. They whispered and kissed and smiled and laughed out loud. This remarkable fusion had brought him back to her after being apart for far too long.

Afterward, they lay there out of breath.

He kissed her fingers and held her close and took in every

moment, for fear this were a fragile dream that would soon vanish like smoke.

Her eyes were open and honest. "I love you, you know that, right?" she asked. Her voice sounded soft and barely audible.

"So let me in," he said. He took in every lock of wet hair and the blush across her cheeks. He could feel her heart beating.

He kissed her fingers. "I'd take a bullet for you."

"Don't ever say that," she said, frowning at him. "Don't even joke about it. I don't know what I'd do without you."

"I'm serious," he said. "I love you. Always have. Always will. I can't get you outta my head."

A tremor seemed to engulf her whole body.

His tough, resilient, smart, kickass Bowers lay in his arms with tears glistening in her eyes. This was the raw part of her soul she guarded so fiercely.

He swallowed the lump in his throat and felt as if he were treading on hallowed ground. Gently, he glided his hand down her side and over her ribs. The tips of his fingers found the fibrous ridges of her scar.

She flinched and pulled away.

He firmly drew her hand close and pressed her fingertips against the knobby scar on his shoulder. He took a deep breath and stared into those hazel eyes.

"These are our badges of honor," he said, softly. "We need to see these in the mirror each day to remind us that we have faced real evil and survived."

Tears spilled from the corners of her eyes.

After carefully lifting her arm out of the away, he leaned down and softly kissed the scar on her side.

She took in a sharp breath.

Her skin felt warm against his lips. When he kissed her again, goosebumps rose over her ribs. He put a hand on the low part of her back and pressed the side of his face against her torso. He could hear her breathing and feel her pulse.

As she pulled his face up next to hers, he took in every detail from

Kill Notice

her long dark lashes to her tousled hair. Her deep hazel eyes watched him with a tenderness he'd never seen before. This wasn't the kickass cop or the elite sniper on counter-terrorism missions. This was Kate Bowers, the woman. His best friend, and the one person he loved more than life itself.

He kissed her forehead. "Kate, you and I are like my favorite T-shirt. A little stained. A little torn up, but it's always soft and fits just right." He gripped her hand. "This is something I never want to lose."

She kissed him back and chuckled. "At least I don't remind you of those ragged boxers you used to wear."

He watched as her smile faded and her eyes filled with pain.

"Does the scar hurt?" he asked.

She pointed to her heart. "Only in here." Her voice wavered and she swallowed hard. "Berti isn't the first friend I couldn't protect."

Riggs propped his head on his arm and waited.

After a few seconds she took a deep breath. "I was in Ramadi. Randy had been my spotter. Emotionally, we were closer than being married. Our lives depended on each other. We'd been pulled into an off-the-record mission to take out a high-ranking terrorist."

Riggs found himself wrapped in her story. He could feel the anguish as it swelled to the surface.

She stared up at the ceiling. "Our unit was ambushed. It all went to hell, fast. We were fielding fire from other rooftops. A shot ricocheted off the wall and hit me. The bullet tumbled and tore me up good. Another one hit my rifle in a bad spot. Jammed it. I heard rounds ripping past my head."

Bowers choked out her next words. "Randy was hit." Her chin buckled. She put her hands over her face as if wishing she could hide from what she'd seen. "It was a head shot."

Riggs winced. He reached over and took her hand. Her grip tightened on his fingers. Each breath seemed labored. Part of him wanted to stop her. He wanted to pull her away from this, but personal experience told him that burying it would only make it worse. She needed to get this out.

"I can still see the muzzle flashes and smell the dust and

gunpowder and blood. So much blood." Bowers bit her lip, briefly, and continued. "Hostiles were everywhere. I had no time to think. I had no choice, but to wipe Randy's brains off his rifle and go back to protecting my unit. They were taking heavy fire below. I don't know how many combatants I took out, and then this boy," she paused, "God, I hate this." She grimaced as if each word burnt. "A skinny kid, maybe fifteen or sixteen years of age, came around the corner wearing a bomb vest. He ran toward our unit. I had two seconds to decide. One shot to save them. The kid looked a lot like Bobby Black until I pulled the trigger."

She held her side. "I watched my bullet hit. Riggs, I saw his mother run into the street. I heard her shrieking. She kept screaming *tufali aljamil*, my beautiful baby, over and over again."

The pain on Bowers' face moved him in ways hard to explain. Now he understood the real reason she'd left the service. The horror of that memory left them both in a moment of silence.

Riggs pulled her close and held her head in his hands. He drew her into his shoulder and wrapped both arms around her. There were no words for this one.

"I used to catch my brass," she said. "They were hot, obviously. Once they'd hit my hand I'd let my casings drop into a neat pile next to my rifle, until that shot. I slid back the bolt, caught the brass from the bullet that killed that boy, and didn't let go." The skin between her brows crimped. She held up her hand and stared at her palm. "I took his life, I wanted it to leave a scar, but it didn't. At least not one you can see."

Riggs kissed her palm and brought her hand back against his chest. "Bowers. You didn't start their war. They did. They set the rules, not you. They put that vest on that kid. That boy would've died that day, no matter what you did. The only choice left was whether you were going to let him take out your unit, too."

When Bowers took a breath, her chest shuttered. "Randy left his wife and a baby boy at home."

BLOWN AWAY

BOWERS WOKE ten minutes before the alarm went off. The room around her came into focus. The white ceiling above her came to a peak, where the blades a fan whirled in a lazy rotation.

She felt a smile she couldn't suppress. The sun had just peeked over the horizon and was amplified by the buttery yellow walls. The place smelled like sunshine. This wasn't a dream.

Riggs' arm draped over her waist. He cupped his hand and pulled her close. Definitely not a dream.

When she turned her head to look at him she realized he'd been watching her. "You okay?" he asked.

She stretched. "Yeah, I'm okay." She propped herself up on her elbow. "Hey, don't we need to be somewhere."

"Yes," he said. "We need to be right here." He pulled her against him. "I sent a team out to dog down Keats. Briefing is at 9:00 a.m. Hoffman is coming over." He kissed the side of her face. "You hungry?"

"Ravenous."

Riggs chuckled deep and low. "You got that right. I'm exhausted."

By 7:30 a.m. Riggs had crossed back into the District with Bowers following in her Tahoe. He pulled into a bakery he knew she liked and ran inside. While he waited for his order, he watched her sitting in her unit with her phone up to her ear. She didn't look happy.

A woman in a light-blue shirt handed Riggs a white paper sack and two coffees.

As he approached the Tahoe, Bowers reached over and pushed open the passenger door. He slid in.

"One coffee, black." He smiled and handed her the tall paper cup.

She took the first sip. "Mmm. Good. Thank you."

He pulled a foil-wrapped bundle out of the bag and tossed it to her. "Croissant with egg and cheese."

She took the sandwich and studied him. Her eyes had the same soft expression as last night, minus the anguish. "You really are the best," she said.

As they ate their breakfast, Bowers told him about the call she'd made. "I talked to Bobby's principal. She hasn't seen either boy and had tried to call the grandmother, but no one picked up. I told her to not let Bobby go if she sees him, and we'd come pick him up."

"Any of his friends heard from him?" asked Riggs.

Bowers shook her head. "Not that they will admit. What has me worried is that Perez saw Papa G in the Northeast section. He doesn't go up there."

"Unless he is looking for something. Did Perez run the plates?"

Bowers sipped her coffee. "The car was registered to Papa G's cousin who works at the sub shop." She wadded up the foil and tossed it in the white paper sack and brushed the crumbs off her black-and-white pants. "Something tells me Bobby is in trouble."

Inside Metro PD's compound, Riggs parked in a space next to Bowers. He could see that security had been beefed up. However, if the killer were Metro PD, Riggs doubted that would help much.

With a phone to her ear, Bowers opened the door of the silver

Kill Notice

Tahoe and sat with one leg extended all the way to the asphalt. While Riggs waited, he watched people entering.

The K-9 unit patrolled back and forth. An officer with a blonde ponytail stood guard at the door with her Belgian Malinois. The young dog's intense temperament clearly required a strong handler. Out of the corner of Riggs' eye, he spotted Mitch heading into the building.

Back at the door, the Malinois obediently watched each person entering.

Riggs caught sight of Mitch hustling toward the door with a scowl on his face. The dog backed away. After Mitch went inside, the Malinois sat staring after him through the glass.

I'll be damned, thought Riggs. *Maybe the dog doesn't like Mitch any more than I do.*

Bowers put a hand on his shoulder. "That was Perez on the phone," she told him. "He and his partner are still trying to find Papa G and Bobby."

On the way inside they passed the dog, who showed no interest in them. Bowers stopped at the breakroom. "I need another cup of coffee. I'll meet you at the briefing."

Riggs went on. As he approached the task force room he saw the chief up ahead ambling his direction.

"Can I have a word?" asked the chief.

Riggs posted a DO NOT DISTURB sign on the door to the task force room. Inside, they sat facing each other with one of the folding tables between them.

The chief shook his head as he glanced around the room at the whiteboards and timelines. Like a man with a heavy load, Chief Bowman hunched forward and blew out a long breath. Riggs waited while the folding chair creaked under the chief's weight.

"It can't be one of my guys," said the chief. "It just can't. Everyone in this office has had background checks."

Riggs felt bad for the man. "That only means he hasn't been caught." The chief's reaction was understandable.

"Every damned one of them has gone through at least one lie detector test."

"Chief," said Riggs, "we both know a psychopath can defeat a polygraph."

The chief shook his head. "If it turns out to be one of my guys, it'll kill me."

"Who's to say it isn't one of mine?" asked Riggs.

"Hell of a deal." The chief ran a hand over his closely cropped hair. "Never thought I'd see the day."

Riggs felt bad for shutting the chief out of the shadow task force. The man's integrity had never been in question. But who he trusted might be.

The shadow force had been getting results and putting bits of data into a clearer picture. If Bowers was right and the killer was inside the Metro PD, the shadow task force was their only real option. That left Riggs no choice but to operate in secret. The intel had to stay out of the station.

"I keep rackin' my brain tryin' to figure out who it might be." The chief's forehead furrowed. "Johnny is too new. The others are either too young or female. That only leaves guys that have been with me forever. Clawski is a pain in the ass some of the time." The chief chuckled and rubbed his chin. "I'd send him back to the academy but the instructors would revolt. Anyway, he's not capable of something like that."

"You're right," said Riggs. "Clawski nearly jumped out of his seat when Hoffman did her slideshow. No way could it be him." He considered the others. Riggs didn't care much for Mitch, but he wasn't the first arrogant son of a bitch Riggs had encountered in the field. Big egos often came with the job. That didn't make the man a killer.

"Listen, chief," said Riggs, "You have a solid team and some of the finest officers I've seen anywhere. Your CSI, Magrath, is top-shelf. I'd steal her, if I could."

The chief laughed at that. "If she shows up missing, I'll know right where to look."

Kill Notice

Riggs rested his elbows on the table. "How about we work the facts and go wherever they take us, your shop or mine?"

The chief slapped the table and stood. "I appreciate your assistance," he said, "do what you have to do. Just help us find this bastard."

BLOOD SPATTER

BOWERS ARRIVED at the task force room and stood near the windows without looking directly at Riggs. Personnel from the PD and the FBI often dated. Higher ups didn't say a word, if they behaved themselves in public and kept things professional in the office. In her peripheral vision she could see him wearing a slight smile.

While the team filed into the room with the usual banter, she realized she hadn't felt this good in a long time. Uncle Marvin would be pleased.

She watched detectives and agents filing in. They reminded her of a stream flowing between boulders as they bottlenecked at the door and spilled into the room where one after the other poured into the rows of seats. Some of them stopped first at a side table to pick up a coffee or a blueberry muffin.

Riggs strolled over and spoke in her ear. "I plan on showing some pictures of Berti."

"From her phone?" she asked.

"And the crime scene. You can step out, if you want."

"Come on, now." Bowers leaned on the windowsill. "Not a chance, but I appreciate the heads up."

260

Kill Notice

She remained at her spot by the windows and wondered why Johnny wasn't here. Several detectives made a hole and let Mitch through. He seemed to be in a foul mood as he hurried toward the back of the room, where he joined the chief.

Riggs returned to the front of the room. Judging by the way he stood a little taller, she wasn't the only one who'd felt renewed after their time at the cottage. His words, "This is something I never want to lose," had stuck with her.

The door creaked open. Hoffman quickly entered and mouthed, "sorry." She stood against the wall near the door.

Riggs nodded. Hoffman dimmed the lights.

When Riggs clicked on the overhead screen, the chatter in the room dropped to a hush. "Listen up, folks, we've got something we need you to take a look at."

Still photos from grainy surveillance feeds popped on the screen.

"As you can see," said Riggs, "this is our vehicle of interest. It's a black, extended-cab pickup identified as a Chevy Silverado."

Clawski sat back in his chair. "Shoot. I got one of them right outside in the parking lot. Arrest me now."

A couple of guys chuckled.

Karen raised a hand. "There are hundreds of similar trucks in the DMV. Do we have a plate number?"

"Not yet," said Riggs. He pressed the remote button. Even with his warning, seeing Berti smiling at the camera wasn't an easy sight.

"We retrieved these," he said, "from Bertolini's cell phone. Here, she's standing at the tailgate of the truck we are searching for. Unfortunately, her legs block the plate number, but you can clearly see there are some identifying marks, like the orange frame around the plate and a scratch in the bumper."

He flipped through three more pictures of Berti smiling and posing with the black pickup behind her.

Bowers forced herself to see beyond the pink flip-flops on Berti's feet. "Riggs," she said, "it looks to me as if the perp took these." She pointed at the screen. "The plate is obscured in each shot. And the registration and inspections stickers are carefully outside the frame."

261

Hoffman nodded. "That's exactly why we're interested in finding this vehicle."

Bowers knew that several guys in her department owned something similar. It also reminded her of the vehicle that had followed her.

At the back of the room Mitch's expression seemed unreadable as he gazed at the screen and popped open a can of Coke and took a sip.

Hoffman folded her arms. "We've put out an APB and notified the press. Every uniform, shop owner, mail carrier, and paper-boy will be out searching for that truck."

Clawski groaned.

Hoffman glanced down at him. "Calm down, detective, we have six dedicated agents who will man the phones and enter the data into the system."

"A few things have become clear," said Hoffman, "Your killer isn't just escalating. He's evolving. When the press turns to other topics and takes him out of the spotlight, he kills again to regain their attention. He's also changing his tactics. If we look back at the cold cases we believe are his work, the thrill of the kill worked well enough in the beginning. Later on he moved into torture. With recent kills he takes his time and poses the bodies with the clear intent of humiliating his victims and sending us messages. Now that's no longer enough. Now he's doing something we've never seen before."

Hoffman put up scenes from Jayzee's house. "Bowers, walk us through this."

Bowers pushed away from the windowsill. "It appears that some of the people he has killed are not his main focus. Twice now our perp has killed a bystander and staged the scene to implicate his real target, someone high-profile."

When Hoffman put images of Berti's body up on the screen, Bowers felt her temper rise. "To the perp, this woman was nothing more than a prop, a way to ensure the police would get involved.

"So, here's our perp's game. He kills the girl, plants evidence to implicate Jayzee, his real target, and then sits back and watches the press do the rest of the work for him. This is about publicly humiliating his victim. His reward is witnessing the press tearing Jayzee's life to shreds on national news. I wouldn't be surprised if he records it all on his DVR and replays it at night to feed his ego."

Bowers scanned the room. Hoffman nodded as if she agreed. Riggs checked his phone.

"Jayzee has taken a huge hit," Bowers said. "He is taunted even at practice sessions. Social media has trashed the guy. You should see his house. Everything in his yard has been stolen or destroyed. He lost his sponsors, and has cut his bodyguards down to two."

Bowers paced up and down the aisle and stopped at the front. "Meanwhile, our killer is enjoying manipulating all of us for his own twisted game."

Mitch's face had relaxed into a partial smile.

"What's the deal with Senator Keats?" asked the chief. "It sounds like the same kind of setup."

"It is," said Hoffman.

The chief continued. "But how can we catch this SOB if he's always ahead of us?"

"Chief," said Riggs, "even though this guy is good, he isn't perfect. This twist is new territory to him, and because of that he has made some really dumb mistakes."

Mitch's expression caught Bowers' attention. His smile had receded into a vacant dark stare.

"Our perp missed a few critical details," said Riggs. "He knew about the party and had expected Jayzee would be there. What he didn't know was that Jayzee had gotten sick and had gone to bed with an IV in his arm and had a doc at his side during the time period when the victim was murdered. That alone clears Jayzee."

As the presentation continued, Bowers found herself once again caught by the way Mitch glared at Riggs.

"As for Senator Keats," said Riggs, "have you all seen the man? He's an older gentleman who gets winded just walking from his car to the elevator at the capitol building."

Bowers had seen that first hand. Keats was a big guy, who sometimes used a cane. It had been explained to her that he suffered from diabetes and his feet often caused him great discomfort.

Riggs pointed around the room. "Can anyone tell me how in the hell a man that physically limited strung heavy chains and a dressing rig up into the rafters, and hauled a struggling, kicking, hundred and twenty-pound girl up the stairs? It didn't happen, folks. Someone much younger, stronger, and in top shape is our culprit."

Riggs checked his phone again. "I just receive word that we've located the senator. Special agents are preparing to speak with him any minute now. My guess is that the murder charges won't stick. In the meantime, he's going to go through hell. Press is all over him. Social media is calling him Senator Sleaze."

Bowers noticed the corners of Mitch's mouth curling into a smug smile as he sipped his Coke.

Johnny bolted into the room. "Turn on the news!"

Riggs grabbed the remote and flipped to WJDC.

Marc Davis beamed at the camera. "Today we have an exclusive interview with a very special guest."

Riggs leaned on the windowsill next to Bowers and watched with one hand over his mouth. He whispered to her. "Our agents are inside the station."

Bowers watched the screen.

Marc Davis held out one hand. "Would you please welcome Senator Harry Keats."

"Looks like you found him," she whispered back.

Despite the grand introduction, Keats sat slumped in the chair, like a man who'd come undone. He dabbed the sweat from his pasty-white skin. His white hair and gray suit were disheveled. She almost didn't recognize him.

"Senator, in your own words, please. What happened?"

Keats' hands shook as he took a sip from a mug that bore the station's logo. His voice started out low and hoarse. "I admit to all of you, that I'm no angel. I've done some things that I shouldn't have." He grimaced as if the words had gotten stuck in his throat. "I've done a lot of things, but I've never killed anyone."

Kill Notice

"But, Senator, how do you explain the fourteen-year-old girl who was found dead in your cabin?"

"I don't know that girl. I have no idea. I wasn't there." Keats had his hands in his pockets. "Don't you see?" he asked. Keats stared at Davis. "This ruins me and everything I've tried to do for the people of D.C."

His face flushed red. "I hope the asshole who did this rots in hell. I was trying to help our city." His chin quivered. "I tried to clean up D.C. so it's a decent place. You remember that."

Keats grew teary eyed. The camera focused in close on the senator as he blinked and twisted to the side. The view panned back to Marc Davis, who opened his mouth to ask his next question.

"Oh, God. He's got a gun!" a voice shouted in the background.

The camera briefly showed Keats with a revolver up to his temple and then Marc Davis' stunned expression.

Bowers tensed her shoulders. She glanced toward the back of the room.

A loud pop and screams sounded in rapid succession. She took a breath and went back to watching the screen. Marc Davis' blood-spattered face reflected all that needed to be said. Senator Harry Keats had committed suicide on national television.

Bowers turned her head and felt the bump in her pulse when she glanced toward the back of the room.

RECOIL

BOWERS WATCHED as everyone cleared the room. Clawski stopped by the side table, where he snagged a small, brown sack and stuffed it full of muffins before leaving.

Riggs hung back and watched people shuffling out. Before leaving, the chief hesitated and nodded at Riggs.

What that was about?

Bowers eased into a chair and rested her elbows on the table.

"We'll find him," said Riggs. "He's out there."

"No, Riggs. He's right here."

Riggs sat next to her.

"Dammit," Bowers said. She ran a hand through her hair.

"That rape kit you found in West Virginia came in this morning. Our lab is already on it."

She twisted toward him. "When will you get the DNA results back on it and the Coke can you found in the woods?"

"We should have some answers by this afternoon," he said. "Come on over to the field office. You can be there when we get the report. Maybe we could go to dinner afterwards?"

She nodded. "I've got something I need to do first."

Kill Notice

Riggs gripped her hand. "Perez called me. They've spotted Papa G's car. Hopefully, we'll hear something soon."

After Riggs left, Bowers strolled toward the back of the room, where she stopped.

Multiple images poured through her mind as she stared at Mitch's Coke can still sitting where he'd left it. The most terrifying ones were from a few minutes ago. When Jayzee's distress played for the world to see, Mitch had seemed pleased. When the senator had shot himself on the morning news, everyone recoiled. Everyone except Mitch.

He didn't smile, but he did lean forward. His eyes were wide, and his face had gone slack as if he were mesmerized.

"I'll be damned." Bowers felt numb as the implications sunk in. His Coke can still sat on the table where he had left it after drinking the last swallow.

At the side table, she snagged one of the brown paper sacks. After taking a snapshot of the can, she lowered the bag over it. Once she had slipped it into the sack, Bowers held the bag and a notepad in one hand and headed toward the door.

Mitch filled the doorframe. "What are you doing?" he asked, as he scanned the room.

Bowers forced her breathing under control. His dark eyes studied her closely.

"Just cleaning up, sarge."

Mitch glanced at the sack. "What's in the bag?"

Bowers sat down at her desk and put the brown sack in her green gear bag.

"You okay?" asked Johnny.

She flinched at the sound of his voice. He took a seat in the chair next to her desk. "You're jumpy. You know who it is, don't you?" he asked.

"Maybe." She paused. "Yes." She told him about Mitch's reactions and the Coke can.

"Shit," said Johnny. "Did he see you bag it?"

"I don't think so, but he asked me what was in the sack. So I told him I'd taken a muffin for later."

"Good answer," Johnny said. "Let's hope he believed you." He took a red pen off her desk and toyed with it. "Whadda we do now?"

"Keep working the evidence until we have definitive proof."

Johnny's thumb kept clicking the pen. He shook his head. "I'm not surprised."

The sound of footsteps clomping in the corridor behind her silenced their conversation.

Mike came around the corner, nodded, and headed toward the breakroom with his coffee mug. She waited until he'd gone out of earshot.

"Johnny, listen to me. Mitch's reactions don't prove he's our killer."

"I'm not so sure. I found something you need to see. Come over to my desk."

She followed Johnny into the next cubicle. She stood behind him as he put a thumb drive into his computer and swiveled the monitor so only they could see it. Johnny pulled up a video file.

"This is why I was late to the meeting. I put these clips together from the DVDs Keller gave us from Sapphire's funeral. I think they're important." He tapped the play button and sat back. "This isn't the first time the sarge has acted strange."

Bowers watched the screen. The camera focused in on Wally and panned out to scan the faces of the mourners at Sapphire's funeral. There in the background stood Mitch, smiling at the casket. The hair went up on her arms.

"It gets better," said Johnny.

In the next segment, Alex Keller had filmed the crowd breaking up. At the side of the frame he'd caught Mitch leisurely strolling past the casket and subtly gliding his fingers over the rim where the upper and lower sections met.

"Have you told anyone about this?" she asked.

Kill Notice

Johnny shook his head.

"Keep it that way. Not a word."

"There's one more clip you need to see." He tapped on another file.

This time the film caught Mitch standing behind a woman. When the shot zoomed in, he clearly wasn't looking at her at all. Instead, he stared at the long line of buttons running down the back of her dress.

Johnny handed Bowers the thumb drive.

"Thank you," she said. "Good work." Bowers hesitated. "One more thing. Find out what kind of vehicle Mitch drives. Also check all the black Chevy Trucks in our lot and compare them to the license plate reader records. Let's find out where they and Mitch have been."

"Roger that."

She lowered her voice. "Keep a real low profile. I want you to go home to your wife when this is over."

"Bowers," he said. "You be careful, too."

She patted his shoulder and checked her phone. "I've gotta go."

Bowers wasted no time getting to her desk. After grabbing her gear bag, she hurried downstairs toward the exit. What if Mitch didn't buy her explanation about what she had in the sack? He could be waiting around any corner.

The usually quick trip to the car seemed like a marathon. Bowers forced her legs into a normal pace that wouldn't draw attention. Her heart pounded in her chest. She pushed open the double-glass doors and resisted the urge to glance behind her.

After sliding into the Tahoe, she slammed the door shut, and clicked the lock. A flood of relief hit her.

Within seconds, she headed toward the field office.

During her twenty-minute drive fear had settled into determination. She left her SUV on the street and approached the six-story building on 4th Street. Its massive block structure appeared to be impenetrable. The entrance had been fortified with barriers that

269

could stop anything but a fighter jet. On second thought, maybe it could stop that, too.

She spotted Riggs' favorite armored command vehicle parked out front. That stopped her. In their on-going competition for parking, she wondered if he'd parked it there just to make her laugh. She slipped between the barriers and jogged up the steps to the glass entrance.

Bowers knew all the doors would be locked. She waved at the security guard inside. She'd seen him before. As a member of the FBI's internal police force, his duties included keeping their buildings secure.

The exterior panel of bulletproof glass had the thick, heavy appearance of impenetrability. The guard unlocked the glass door on the far right and let her into the security checkpoint. He examined her gear bag and eyed her Glock. "Bowers, mind if I hold on to that?"

She pulled out her pistol and handed it to him barrel down. "Careful, it's loaded."

He snickered. "Come see me when you leave to pick it up." He glanced at her ankles, searching for a backup she didn't have.

"Roger that."

Even before she arrived at the reception window, Bowers saw a head of dreadlocks and knew James manned the desk. She stepped closer and waved at him through more heavy glass. When he saw her, his face lit up with a broad smile.

"Let me see," he said as he stretched up in his seat and peered at her from behind his desk.

Bowers held out her arms and let him get an eyeful of today's pants. These were pretty subdued in her mind. From a distance the pattern appeared to be random black lines on white fabric, but close-up they resembled a bazillion small puzzle pieces fitted together.

"Let me see yours," said Bowers.

The big guy rose from his desk, sporting a Bob Marley T-shirt.

"Nice. Love the dreads, James."

He grinned and handed her a visitor's badge and pointed to the chairs along the wall. "Riggs will be out in a minute," he said.

Kill Notice

While she waited a man in a suit, with a shaved head and a Bluetooth in his ear, entered the building. He flashed his badge to security and went on down the far hallway. The guy had "fed" written all over him. A few minutes later two more people arrived, only this time the woman wore sweats and the guy had on a Hawaiian shirt. Without their badges, no one would have guessed they were special agents.

Riggs appeared and waved her through a low gate. He escorted her down the hall to a room she hadn't seen before.

"Welcome to our shadow task force," he said as he swung open the door.

Bowers nodded at Hoffman, who'd glanced up from a pile of documents spread over the other end of the polished, wooden conference table. She stood and shook Bowers' hand. "Thanks for coming over."

"Any word on the DNA from the Coke can?" Bowers asked as she put her things on the table and took a seat.

"Still waiting," said Riggs. "They're doing us a favor by running it this quickly."

"I'm sure Riggs told you that we've received the rape kit," said Hoffman. "Let's hope the lab in West Virginia stored it correctly. We're keeping our fingers crossed that it will tell us something."

"I tried to find more documentation," said Bowers, "but all we have is the girl's admission that she was raped. By whom she wouldn't say. There is a note from a nurse stating that the rapist left her underwear displayed over a wreath on her front door."

Hoffman wrote a few notes. "The lab is processing swabs from the earring found on the stairwell at Keats' cabin and scrapings from the girl's toenails."

"Good," said Bowers. "What about the shower door?"

"It turned out to be a goldmine." Hoffman smiled. "They found saliva on the glass. Apparently our killer sneezed."

Bowers envisioned Mitch standing in the shower behind the glass door.

"The 202 Killer isn't normally that careless," said Bowers. "A hallmark of his scenes is the way he meticulously cleans up after himself. Until now, he hasn't left evidence behind."

Hoffman frowned. "How do you account for the shift in his behavior?"

Bowers thought for a few seconds. "I think he came back to do his clean up and didn't expect the FBI to show up," she glanced at Riggs, "your arrival with the warrant probably interrupted him. That would explain why you found half of the rail on the stairs had been cleaned. You threw him off his game. He probably dropped the Coke can in his hurry to get out of there and didn't dare go back to retrieve it."

"I'm telling you, Riggs," said Hoffman. "We need to hire her."

Riggs rapped his fingers on the table. "Believe me, I've tried." He started to say something else, but Hoffman motioned to Bowers with the sign of a phone and mouthed *call me.*

"I'll think about it," said Bowers, "but we have something else we need to talk about first."

"I'm listening," said Riggs.

"Did you see Mitch's reactions at the meeting this morning?"

Riggs frowned. "The guy pisses me off so much I try to avoid looking at him."

Hoffman cocked her head. "What did you see?"

Bowers pushed her notepad aside. "Mitch's reactions stuck out. He seemed out of sorts from the get-go, but when we were talking about Jayzee's life being turned upside down and when the senator appeared so devastated Mitch's expression changed into a sly grin."

Hoffman nodded. "Told you there was a psychopath in the building."

Bowers turned to Riggs. "When you said the perp had screwed up, done some stupid things, Mitch glared at you as if he wanted to rip your face off."

Riggs snorted. "He does that on a good day."

"It gets better," said Bowers. "When Keats shot himself right there on TV, everyone in the room grimaced and jumped. Everyone except Mitch. Instead of flinching, he leaned forward with his eyes glued to the screen. He was captivated."

Kill Notice

"Oh, shit," said Hoffman. She stood and began to pace. "It makes sense. He has a legitimate reason to be at the scenes. And he gets to relive his kills."

"Exactly," said Bowers. "And he can explain away any evidence he leaves as scene contamination. He can't do that with the evidence you found at Keats' cabin. Your team investigated it, not us, which means there shouldn't be anything from him there."

Bowers pulled out the brown sack and put it and the thumb drive in front of Riggs.

He frowned. "What's this?"

"Presents."

Riggs picked up the thumb drive. "What's on here?"

"I used the media, like you recommended. Mitch was present at all of the scenes, and at Sapphire's funeral."

Hoffman listened.

"And," said Bowers, "you'll find footage on there of Mitch smiling at the casket and running his hand along the lid. The photographer also caught Mitch ogling the buttons on the dress of the woman in front of him."

Riggs inserted the drive into the computer. "When you said presents, you weren't kidding." He eyed the sealed brown bag. "What's in there?"

"Another Coke can." She showed him the picture on her phone of it sitting on the back table. "Mitch and only Mitch drank out of it during our meeting. I stayed behind and bagged it."

Riggs focused on her then on Hoffman and back to her as if he were stunned.

Bowers sat forward. "I have to know if my boss is our serial killer."

DEAD END

RIGGS ESCORTED Bowers to the lobby. "Listen, I've got a table for us at Ebbitt's," said Riggs. "You still up for dinner?"

"Sure," she said. "Call me later."

Bowers waved at James, picked up her Glock, and left.

After a brief trek to her Tahoe, she fired up the engine and entered the traffic, which hadn't gotten any lighter. She shot through a green light and headed north on Georgia Avenue toward Hemlock. The street name rang a bell, but she couldn't place why.

While driving she thought about the cable man's case. A copy of the job-list for Dick Evans' final day on Earth lay in the passenger seat next to her. Like his life, the list had been left unfinished. There were similarities between his case and the trashcan man. Both men were found naked from the waist down.

According to the reports in the case file, the man's boss had stated that Evans had made it to his first three calls that day. Upon arriving at his forth call on Hemlock Street, he'd checked in with the office, but the residents at that address claimed they hadn't seen him.

That's where the trail had ended.

The next time anyone saw Evans came when a cook, who had been cleaning out the fryers at a local eatery, went to dump used

Kill Notice

grease into the barrel in back and found the man crammed into the container head first.

She wanted to see for herself where Dick Evans had been that day in the hopes that someone might remember him and be able to tell her something.

Bowers kept her phone close at hand, hoping the DNA results would come in soon. That would tell the tale, especially if it turned out to be a match to the saliva on the glass shower door and the can found in the woods.

She passed two cabbies who were honking at each other and using all kinds of creative gestures. Bowers gave credence to what people often referred to as gut feelings or intuition, except when it came to psychopaths. The line between emotion and intuition was a thin one. Bowers put her money on forensics and hard evidence that didn't lie. And yet today, she'd seen Mitch's reactions when he didn't know she'd been watching.

She chided herself for letting Mitch's appearance get to her, but she couldn't deny what she'd seen.

She'd stood face-to-face with killers before. She'd seen the eyes of terrorists just before they'd killed. The one thing they all had in common was the way they dehumanized their victims. They painted themselves as honorable, even noble, and blamed their helpless victims as an excuse for some of the worst atrocities one human being could do to another.

Her mind went back to that morning briefing when the chief had announced that Mitch would receive the Detective of the Year Award. She remembered how he'd reveled in the attention and the cameras and the vigorous handshakes.

Psychopaths craved the limelight.

At the same meeting he'd glared at Johnny for talking.

Psychopaths don't tolerate disrespect.

Mitch had railed at the TV screen every time the news wasn't on the 202 Killer. Nothing was more important to serial killers than their own legacy.

Her pulse quickened. Mitch had been at all but one crime scene.

Not once had he referred to the deceased as "the victim."

Serial killers had no empathy, and always blamed their victims.

Bowers ran her tongue over the lump on her lower lip. She wondered if the silhouette in her living room had been Mitch.

If it had been him, he certainly had a set to come back into her apartment and pretend to be her oh-so-concerned boss. She remembered him staring at her clothes in the closet. "Son of a bitch."

WHILE WAITING for the DNA results, Riggs watched the videos Bowers had given him, twice. As he made a list of things to follow up on, his phone buzzed with an incoming call from James at the front desk.

"There's someone here to see you, sir," he said.

"I don't have any appointments. Who is it? Did he ask for me?"

"His name is Devin Walker." James lowered his voice. "He didn't ask for you, but I really think you'll want to hear what he has to say."

"I'll be out in a minute." Riggs hung up.

He tossed down his pen and rubbed his eyes. Taking time to talk to a walk-in right now was a pain in the ass. Nevertheless, his job required it.

Riggs strolled down the hall and peered into the lobby and immediately saw the tall man in a dark-green uniform. The soldier stood and nodded.

Riggs waved him closer and shook his hand. "I'm special agent Steven Riggs. Follow me."

He took the man to the small conference room near the lobby and gestured for him to take a seat. Instead, the man, who was a few years older than Riggs, stood tall and squared his shoulders. Seven rows of colorful ribbons and medals decorated his chest. Riggs noticed the distinctive star and gold striped insignia on the man's left sleeve. This wasn't any pair of boots. This soldier was a sergeant major.

"My name is Devin Walker, sir, and I have something we need to discuss."

Kill Notice

Riggs slid into a chair and dropped his legal pad in front of him. The soldier neatly placed his beret onto the table before taking a seat.

"Sir, I feel terrible," said Walker. "I should have said something years ago, but I didn't know who to tell and I didn't have any proof and no one would've believed a kid anyway."

Riggs frowned. *What the hell is this guy getting at?*

Walker rubbed a hand over his mouth. "A few days ago, I caught a few minutes of a press conference on the news. Reporters were questioning police officials about the murder at Jayzee Armel's home. I knew right then, I had to come forward."

"How does that relate to you?" asked Riggs.

Walker rested his elbows on the table. "I knew something bad was coming." He shook his head. "Twenty-five years ago, I was a kid in high school. Every chance I had, I worked to earn a little extra cash. Times were tough back then. Rural parts of West Virginia didn't offer a lot of options for a kid."

Riggs frowned and wrote *West Virginia* on his notepad.

Walker continued. "One of the ranchers I worked for was a mean bastard. Old school, white bread kind of guy. He paid good enough, but worked me into the ground."

Walker folded his hands on the table. "That was nothing compared to what he did to his boy. His son had a problem with bed-wetting, right after his mama went back to Mexico. The kid was messed up something fierce. By the time he reached ten, he'd taken to torturing small animals and settin' things on fire. And then one day his papa nailed the kid's soiled underwear up on the post by the bus stop for all the school kids to see."

That set Riggs back in his chair. "You mind if I have a colleague join us?"

"Don't mind at all," Walker said. "I came here to put this on the table."

Riggs called Hoffman. "Come to the small conference room. Now." He also asked James to send in some water.

Almost immediately he heard a knock. James handed him three bottles of water. Behind him stood Hoffman.

She stepped in and closed the door. "They call you yet?" She spotted Walker. "Oh, hello."

Hoffman introduced herself. "What brings you here?"

Riggs couldn't wait to see her reaction to the next bit of news. "He's from West Virginia."

Hoffman took a quick glance at Riggs and settled into the seat next to him. She pulled a pad and pen close, and leaned forward.

Riggs filled her in on what Walker had said so far. Her reaction mirrored his, especially about the underwear at the bus stop.

"Please continue," said Riggs.

Walker glanced over at Hoffman and hesitated.

Riggs understood. "Look, before she became a profiler, Hoffman worked with our Evidence Recovery Team. This woman has scraped stuff off walls that would give most people nightmares. There's nothing you can say that she hasn't seen firsthand."

Walker cleared his throat and nodded to Hoffman. "Ma'am. It wasn't long after that stunt at the bus stop that the rancher's house burned down, with him in it. The place was so isolated that by the time the fire department got a truck over there, nothing was left. Our small-town fire chief said it was an accidental death, but I never believed him. No one did."

Hoffman hadn't taken her eyes off of Walker. "What do you think happened?"

Walker nodded as if confirming things to himself. "I think the kid got even."

"Did you ever see the boy again?" asked Riggs.

"A few times. I graduated and went off to boot camp. The kid lived with an aunt down the road. When I did come home to visit, I heard people around town talking about a fight the kid had with a neighbor who'd refused to let the boy ride his prized black stallion. Shortly after that the man's barn burned down with his horse inside, but nothing could be proven.

"One summer when I came back, my best friend told me about his brother's girlfriend. He said Mitch had raped the girl."

"What?" Riggs sat up.

Kill Notice

Hoffman stopped writing. "What was this kid's name?"

"Charles Mitchell. He's the police officer I saw on the news." Walker's head pivoted between Riggs and Hoffman. "I didn't know he'd become a cop, but I recognized his eyes. They weren't something you could forget. I nearly fell outta my seat when they said his name. Never forgotten that either." Walker held Riggs gaze. "We all knew him as Mitch."

Riggs dropped his pen.

DEVIL'S DEN

BOWERS SLOWED DOWN as she approached a community bank located on the corner of Hemlock and Georgia. A woman in an old, brown Toyota, who'd been following too close, laid on the horn. Bowers glanced up in her mirror and saw her flash an obscene gesture. In response, Bowers flipped on her lights. The Toyota abruptly exited the road into a shopping center.

Bowers chuckled and banged a right onto Hemlock.

Ever since the black pickup had tailed her, she'd kept a keen eye on her rearview mirror. As she searched the sycamore-lined street, she took note of the red-brick homes, most of which were multi-family units.

As a gray squirrel scampered across the street in front of her, Bowers realized that arresting Mitch would be a tricky operation.

Moments later, she curved around a bend in the road and stopped by a huge rhododendron still red with blossoms. After retrieving the list from the passenger seat, she rechecked the address. The duplex to her left was the right number. A tilted FOR SALE sign poked out of the tall grass in the front yard. Clearly, the sign had been there awhile.

Kill Notice

"Dammit." Bowers dropped the paper.

Yellowed newspapers lay scattered over the concrete walkway leading to the front door. The big, red bush seemed the only thing still thriving.

Bowers exhaled and leaned back in her seat. It had been a little over three years, nevertheless, someone might still live here who could recall having seen Dick Evans or his cable van. Maybe someone had heard rumors about who'd kill him.

She glanced at the homes behind and around her. To her right, a grassy knoll covered in trees obscured the house on the corner. She could barely see the driveway that dipped down into a garage. After backing up a few feet, she could see the address on the curb.

As she began to type the street number into her laptop she heard a car engine behind her. She glanced up and watched as a bright-blue sedan drove past her and pulled into the driveway. Within a few seconds it disappeared into the garage.

Bowers watched as two kids darted away from the driveway and onto the grassy knoll, where they chased each other in and around the trees.

She recognized the boy immediately. He had been at Detective Green's funeral. The children were Mitch's son and daughter. The boy appeared to be about eleven, the girl a few years younger. Bowers' laptop confirmed that the address on Hemlock was Mitch's home.

Bowers quickly put the car in gear and drove up the street and around the corner. Her heart raced. The cable guy disappearing right in front of Mitch's house was no coincidence.

She didn't dare call the chief or the station for fear of alerting Mitch. It didn't surprise her that she hadn't heard back about the DNA tests yet. They had a lot to process. She called Riggs, but the line was busy.

Bowers started to put her phone away when she noticed a new message from Bobby that read: *Help me!*

RIGGS FOLLOWED Hoffman down the hall toward their secret task force room. Walker's statement had put a surge of urgency into their steps.

Once inside, Riggs took a seat in one of the bucket chairs and logged-in to the computer.

Hoffman paced back and forth in front of the timeline and photos.

"Out of the damned blue sky," said Riggs.

Hoffman faced the whiteboard. "Everything he said fits. The information about the 202 Killer's thing for displaying underwear was never leaked to the media. Walker has to be telling the truth."

"It all adds up," said Riggs. "We already knew that Mitch was from West Virginia." He opened Mitch's background check. "It says here that he was named after his father, who died in a house fire. His mother was from Mexico." Riggs sat back. "But we still need solid, physical evidence that will stand up in court."

"I'm going to check with the lab." Hoffman hurried out the door, leaving him to ponder their next move.

Riggs finished his water. Bowers had been right.

His phone buzzed with a call from Bowers' partner.

Johnny sounded out of breath, and his mouth was running a hundred miles a minute. "Riggs I took the photographs you brought to our last meeting of that black truck and compared them to the pickups in our lot, we usually have about fifty cars in the compound, and ten of them turned out to be black trucks, and of course I knew that Clawski's pickup would be a match because he drives a black Chevy Silverado, but that didn't mean much because he goes home at night, and sometimes to a corner bar by his house—"

"Johnny, take a breath," said Riggs, "and get to the point."

"Mitch drives a black Silverado. I ran his plate numbers through the database of our license-plate recognition system." Riggs heard Johnny take a deep breath. "Turns out, his pickup was within blocks of each crime scene."

Every Metro PD vehicle had readers that recorded license plate numbers out on the roads. Often the license plate readers picked up other law enforcement plates.

"Johnny, it's a great idea to use the LPR, but we already know Mitch came to each of the scenes. That's his job."

"But, this was *before* the bodies were discovered."

"That changes a few things," said Riggs. "Nice work. Send me those files and keep your mouth shut. Steer clear of Mitch. We'll handle this from here."

"Yes, sir," said Johnny. "Bowers gave me the same speech. I got it."

Hoffman barged in, wide-eyed and smiling.

"Johnny, I gotta go." Riggs ended the call.

Hoffman closed the door and leaned over the table like someone who'd just hit the jackpot. "The lab ran the DNA from the can Bowers had given us. It's a spot-on match to everything else we found, including the rape kit. We've got him, Riggs."

"I never did like that bastard," he said. He thumped a fist on the table and grinned. "I'd like to see him explain why his DNA is all over a murder scene that he supposedly had never been at."

Riggs straightened up in his chair, grabbed a yellow pad of paper and a pen, and pulled out his phone. Arresting Mitch would be a pleasure. The trick now was finding the bastard before he got wind of things.

This much evidence meant he had probable cause and didn't need an arrest warrant. SWAT was the best choice for taking down someone as violent as Mitch. This time he had to call the chief in on this, and have him pull Johnny out of harm's way.

Riggs made the dreaded call to the chief. "Sir, I'm not going to sugarcoat this. Mitch is our killer."

For a few seconds, he heard nothing but breathing. "Ain't that a fine kettle of fish?" The chief sounded disgusted.

"Sorry for the bad news," said Riggs.

"You've got solid proof?"

"DNA. Lots of it." Riggs doodled on his notepad. "I'd appreciate it if you would pull Johnny aside and keep him away from Mitch. He helped us build the case."

"Anything else?"

"I hate to ask you this," said Riggs. "but I'd appreciate it if you would locate Mitch, and keep this between us."

TRIPWIRE

BOBBY WOKE UP shivering on the dusty floor of a warehouse. It smelled old and nasty. The concrete under him felt hard and cold, and seemed to be sucking all the warmth out of his body. He'd been lying there for so long he'd lost track of time. Everything hurt.

Ten feet from him, at the base of the wall, a rat gnawed on a lump of something in the shadows. When he'd finished licking his furry belly and paws, the thing scampered away and returned with another lump. Whatever it was, it smelled rank.

Bobby tugged against the restraints that secured him to a metal pole and awkwardly sat up. Grit dug into the heels of his hands. The handcuff around his left wrist pinched. The other end of it attached to a chain around the pole. He hadn't eaten in nearly two days.

With the air smelling like rotten meat, he wasn't hungry, but he did feel powerfully thirsty.

His grandma's story about being thirty when she was little hit him hard. Bobby would have given anything to hear her stories again and feel her arms around him.

He'd cried a few times last night, but his eyes were too dry for actual tears. He'd yelled, but no one came. One yellow light bulb had flickered above him all night long. Or maybe now was night. With no light coming in, he couldn't know for sure. Most of the time he'd stared at his backpack in the corner. The man in black had searched it and found his phone. Bobby wished he had it back.

He'd rubbed his wrist raw trying to wiggle out of the handcuff. Every so often he would stop and listen.

The smallest noises echoed in the big space. Hours ago, he'd heard a train that sounded close. Bobby rested his head against the cold, steel pole, and closed his eyes, and tried to think of anything that would take his mind somewhere else.

Each time he tried, he couldn't help going back to the park and wishing he'd flagged down Bowers when she'd driven by. "I'm such a dumbass."

He'd also spent a lot of time thinking about the man in black and hoping Papa G hadn't hurt his family when he didn't show up.

Bobby tried to swallow, but his mouth had gone dry. He could see some of the back wall of the building through a large, open, garage-style door. The place had been built for moving big stuff in and out.

His head jerked when he heard keys rattling. The back door, to the right was out of his line of sight, but he heard it creak open.

A man hummed.

Bobby watched as the man in black came into view. The dude made no attempt to cover his face. Bobby knew what that meant. His odds of leaving this building alive weren't good.

A thick feeling rose in his throat. He wanted to see his grandma and his brother. He should never have been in the park in the first place. He should've stayed with his family. He should've asked Bowers for help.

The man in black set a rifle in the corner near a window. The rat dashed away when the rest of the lights came on. Bobby stared at the man, who set a couple of bags on the floor. He seemed interested in the wiring for the garage door.

Bobby watched as the guy messed with a wire connected to the door opener. He laid it out on the floor and pulled a pipe out of his bag and carefully set it next to the electrical wire.

Next he grabbed a white plastic sack. The red lettering on the side

Kill Notice

read: "WOODY'S HARDWARE." Bobby had never heard of the place, but he watched the man dump the contents of the sack onto the floor.

"What you doin'?" asked Bobby.

The man didn't answer. He knelt on the concrete and ignored him. Once in a while he'd glance over his shoulder, but he never anything.

Bobby tried to figure out what he wanted with that pipe. It had been capped off at both ends and had two wires coming out of a hole at one end. That didn't look good.

The man in black seemed real interested in those two wires. He pulled some kind of tool out of his bag and stripped the ends down to bare wire.

The dude took his time tearing open a tiny, clear bag and dumping a handful of alligator clips onto the floor.

Bobby had seen clips before. He'd even found a few under Tommy's mattress a couple of times. Dudes on the street used them to smoke weed, but he didn't think that was what the man in black had in mind.

Bobby had no idea what regular folks did with them.

"Hey, dude. What you want wit' me?" Bobby's voice had grown so hoarse he barely croaked out the words.

He couldn't help eyeing two bottles of water that had rolled out of the bag and across the hard floor. He'd do just about anything to get at that water.

The man carefully used the alligator clips to connect the wires from the garage door opener to the wires sticking out of the pipe.

"Sir," said Bobby, "Please, man. I'm real thirsty. Can I have some of that water?"

The man's big shoulders dropped as he stood and sighed. He snagged one of the bottles of water off the floor and marched toward Bobby. "You're thirsty?" he asked. The dude's tone and crazy-assed eyes had Bobby worried.

He nodded. "Yes, sir. Please."

The man in black cracked open the bottle and poured it on Bobby's head. He opened his mouth and tried to take in as much as he could, but most of it spilled all over him. When the bottle was empty, the dude threw it at him.

The plastic bottle bounced off Bobby's shoulder and fell to the floor, where it spun a few times and stopped.

"What was that for?" he yelled at the man.

"You know what you did," the man said.

"I didn't do nothin' to you. Man, I ain't never touched you. You're the dude who laid me out and tied me up wit' no food or water."

"You should've never interfered," said the man. "You drew attention to me and that freak."

"Sapphire weren't no freak. She never went around killing folks, that's for sure."

"Shut up," shrieked the man in black. He kicked Bobby in the thigh, twice, with the toe of his boot. It smarted something fierce.

The man went back to the pipe and moved it closer to Bobby. He knew he was in deep trouble even before he realized it was a pipe bomb.

BOWERS SAT in her car and watched the traffic passing by. When she checked her phone another message appeared. This time it gave an address.

After merging back into traffic, she raced around a white, box truck. Seconds later, she headed down Blair Road toward an industrial area across the railroad tracks.

The one-mile trip to the location translated into four minutes with traffic. Bobby's words, *Help Me,* made every few seconds seemed an eternity.

The Tahoe bucked over a pothole. While she drove, Bowers couldn't get Mitch out of her mind. The man had been right there in front of her the whole time. As much as it rankled her, it also told her that he ranked with the worst variety of psychopath.

When it came to manipulating other peoples' perceptions, Mitch was a master. However, he did have one weakness. His arrogance. She

Kill Notice

could just about guarantee it had never occurred to him that he might be caught.

She figured that Mitch already knew the evidence he'd left behind could be his undoing, which would force him into a corner and make him far more unpredictable and dangerous.

Looking back, it all made sense. Now she understood why he was so fixated on the news. She remembered how he'd referred to the 202 Killer as the Jack the Ripper of D.C. His legacy was likely one of the few things he truly cared about.

Taking him down would not be easy.

At a stoplight, she kicked herself for not seeing it sooner. The light turned green and she drove on. A serial killer living on Hemlock Street sounded like something from a Sherlock Holmes story. Bowers figured Mitch had probably gotten a kick out of living on a street that bore the name of a highly toxic poison. He probably picked it intentionally.

That irony told only part of the story about where he'd chosen to live. The location off Georgia Avenue gave him quick access to the most direct path south to the station. By itself that bit of information didn't mean much, but in the total context it showed her a man who had thought through each and every aspect of his life. Everything he did had a purpose.

Riggs' intervention at Keats' cabin had up-ended Mitch's routine. For a man so meticulous, that had to have gotten under his skin, especially coming from Riggs.

Bowers imagined Mitch in an orange jumpsuit, behind bars, with nothing but plastic game pieces to manipulate. She knew the idea was pure fantasy. Mitch would never let that happen. He certainly would have an escape plan.

A few minutes later, she made a right onto Maple Street, and stopped at the curb under a large tree. Bowers put a call in to Riggs, but the line was busy.

She waited a few seconds. The address on Bobby's text was down the street to her left. She scanned the road and caught sight of the back end of a black SUV turning into one of the businesses on the right. A moment later, a smaller car rolled out of the shadows and appeared to follow it.

She lost sight of both vehicles. The small industrial park bore the signs of dying a slow death by decay. Tall, chain-link fencing surrounded many of the buildings. At an abandoned boat-storage place across the street to her left weeds grew knee-high. A weathered realtor sign hung askew on the property's locked gate.

To her right, large sycamores dotted an open grassy field. Not a soul was in sight.

Bowers studied the dead-end street. One-way in. One-way out. That and the isolation and the buildings encircled in heavily woods made the perfect setup for an ambush.

She had no idea if that message had really come from Bobby or someone with access to his phone.

This had to be a trap.

MAN DOWN

BOBBY'S WET CLOTHES stuck to his skin. He felt colder than ever, and his thirst hadn't let up. The man in black had gone off to the front door with some tools and wires. Bobby heard him working on something.

A little while later, he returned to the main room, marched across the floor, and stopped. Bobby watched every step. The man in black tossed a bundle of wire to the side and stared at him.

As the man circled the pole, Bobby tucked his bare feet in close to his body and listened to each step on the gritty concrete.

He glanced up at the dude towering over him.

Without warning, the man unlocked the handcuff on Bobby's wrist. He rubbed his arm and wondered why the man had done that. It wasn't to be nice. That was for sure.

"Take off your jeans," he said.

Bobby hesitantly did what the man asked, hoping he'd get an opportunity to bolt.

"Drop them."

Bobby let go of his damp jeans. His belt buckle made a clink sound as it hit the floor.

"No, drop them. Your skivvies."

"Hell, no!" said Bobby. "Take your crazy-assed shit somewhere else, man. I ain't strippin' for you or no one. Freak."

The man stepped back and smiled as if surprised.

Bobby heard a sound at the back door and considered running, but the man in black pulled his pistol. He slapped the handcuff back on Bobby's wrist and hurried down the hall on the left.

Bobby heard him running toward the back.

After shuffling to his left, Bobby stared through the open garage door, which gave him a clear view of the loading area and most of the back of the building.

The man in black stayed in the shadows on the far wall. He shoved his pistol into a hip holster and grabbed the badass rifle sitting in the corner. The dude crept along the outer wall of the platform toward the back door to Bobby's right.

Being tied to a pole while a crazy dude ran around with a rifle wasn't Bobby's idea of a good plan. This time he didn't have a car to hide under. He was stuck out in the open like a chained dog. He heard the back door slam and footsteps, but he couldn't see who had joined them.

"I came for my man, Bobby," said Papa G. "I know he's here."

That startled Bobby. He sure hadn't expected Papa G to show up, especially in this part of town.

Bobby watched the man in black step out of the shadows. He stood in front of Papa G who had three men with him who Bobby recognized from the crew.

"How did you know he was here?" asked the man in black.

"Whoddaya think gave him that phone, bro?" Papa G held up his phone. "I gots an app so's I can find him when I have the need."

Now Bobby understood how Papa G had always known how to find him.

The man in black seemed real uptight. "Did anyone follow you?"

"No way," said Papa G. "No one even knows me up here."

The man in black didn't seem to be buying it. "You better be right. I'm going to check. When I get back, I'll consider giving your boy back, if you stay put." The man held up a small, black device with a

Kill Notice

red button and waved it in the air. "I've got this place rigged. If you try to leave or mess with the kid, I'll turn all of you into pink mist."

Papa G took a step back and stared through the garage door at the pipe bomb.

The man in black hurried toward the back door, beyond Bobby's view. He heard boots stomping up the stairs to the second floor.

Bobby had seen a glimpse of the second floor. It had no walls over the loading platform, which made it easy to hear the man's boots crossing the floorboards. The sounds stopped.

For a few seconds it was quiet.

"Shit, Perez is here," said the man in black.

BOWERS CALLED RIGGS AGAIN. The line remained busy. She sent him a text: *URGENT. Call me.*

The address in Bobby's message matched a business maybe a block down the dead-end street to her left, somewhere close to where the two cars had gone.

Her long gun and a bulletproof vest were in the back. Bowers felt her Glock on her hip. In a sleeve on her left ankle, she wore a knife. Unfortunately, her smaller backup Glock was still in the evidence locker.

The street appeared quiet. The only movement seemed to be a tabby cat that lay nestled in the grass. Its ears twitched as if a sound had caught its attention. The cat lurched forward and pounced on something near an old tire.

Bowers rolled down her window and listened. The wind whistled through the tree tops.

The urge to find Bobby before he ended up like Berti made it tempting to go charging in, but that would be stupid without backup. Bobby might not even be there.

With so many unknowns, she waited.

Her phone buzzed with an incoming call from Riggs. "We've gotta talk," he said. "Where are you?"

She told him her location, and about the text from Bobby.

"Hold on," said Riggs. "I've got an urgent call coming in."

A few seconds later, shots rang out.

Bowers ducked and hunched over the console. The blasts came in bursts of two to three rounds each. Then nothing.

"Dammit, Riggs. Hurry up," she yelled at the phone.

Riggs came back on the line. "Get the hell out of there!"

"Riggs! Shots fired!"

"I heard," Riggs shouted. "Perez called in from your location. He's down. Backup's en route. Do not go in alone. Repeat. *Do not go in!*"

RECON

BOWERS SCRAMBLED over the console and exited the passenger door. She crouched low to the ground and put the Tahoe's engine compartment between her and the dead-end street, where the shots had been fired. Her heart raced.

Riggs had said not to go in, but how could she just sit here when Perez needed help?

The shadows grew long as the sun settled toward the horizon. She weighed her options. None of them were good.

Bowers crept toward the back of her unit. She popped open the hatch and pulled out her gear. In the dusk, she stripped down to a T-shirt and donned her armored vest that weighed thirty-six pounds. It was olive green, standard military issue.

She filled the pockets with ammo, strapped on a flashlight, and grabbed her rifle. In her hands, the AR15-A3 Tactical Carbine felt like a good pair of boots that fit just right.

Kneeling at the tailgate, Bowers lifted the rifle strap and slung the long gun over her shoulder. The weight of her gear reminded her of being back in the Army in full battle-rattle.

If Perez were able to come out under his own power, he would've done so by now, which meant his injuries were severe. Backup would be at least five minutes out. He could bleed out in the interim.

"Shit," she whispered. "To hell with that."

Bowers crept down the street and took cover behind a big oak tree. Recon, with so many places to hide, took her full attention and more time than she wanted.

The little tabby from the abandoned boat-storage place followed her. Farther down the street she spotted the smaller car and recognized it as Perez's Mustang. It blocked the exit to a self-storage building.

She glanced at the closed auto repair shop behind her. In the fading light, graffiti on the boarded-up windows resembled two glaring eyes. One warehouse stood across the street next door to the self-storage business. All but the self-storage building appeared to be boarded up and abandoned.

Bowers glanced at the Mustang and had no idea where the other vehicle had gone.

She listened for the sound of sirens, but heard nothing but a dog barking in the distance. At this rate, darkness would fall before they got here.

After carefully scanning the woods, buildings, and rooftops, she crouched low and crossed the street. Bowers knelt behind the most impenetrable cover she could find, the engine block of Perez's car. The V8 creaked as it cooled. Perez had come here for a reason. Maybe Bobby was here too.

Her pulse pounded as she peered around the front bumper and scoped out the white, one-story, storage facility. Blue letters spelling out SELF STORAGE were painted across the top of the building. The structure had the same address sent to her from Bobby's phone. He could be in there. If he were, Bowers hoped he'd found a hole, out of the line of fire.

The sun had dropped below the horizon, leaving the last fleeting wisps of orange in the sky. She still saw no sign of backup. Security lights around the self-storage building popped on.

The facility appeared to be rows of garage-style units, which

Kill Notice

could be accessed from the wide blacktop driveways on either side. The open gates rendered the chain-link fence useless. Anyone could come and go at will.

Bowers lay flat on her belly, and peered under the car at the pavement along the side of the storage units.

Behind the second row of garage units, a man lay on the asphalt, but she could only see his legs. The building obscured the rest of his body. The boots appeared to be the type law enforcement wore and they weren't moving.

Crap.

With her rifle ready and close to her chest, Bowers cautiously entered the compound. Just like in Ramadi, the shadows became her allies. Time slowed. She used every bit of cover she could find, and carefully made sure her body wasn't backlit.

Riggs would kick her ass for this, but she calculated the risk and couldn't leave Perez there to die. With her back to the storage building, she edged forward. When she drew closer, she realized the boots were too big to be Perez's. She glanced around the corner and saw the rest of the body.

She recognized the man as Perez's partner. He'd taken a round to the neck and lay in a large dark puddle.

Ten feet from him lay Perez. Both men wore bulletproof vests. Their long guns lay on the ground. This had the earmarks of an ambush.

Bowers scanned the upper branches of the trees, and the rooftop of the warehouse next door for a sniper. She saw no movement.

After a quick stop to check his partner for a pulse—there was none—Bowers crept up to Perez's side. He took a shuddering breath. His fingers trembled.

He blinked when she touched his neck. His skin felt cold and clammy. His pulse was weak and rapid. His hands shook. Shock had set in.

Where the hell is backup?

"I've been hit," he said. His voice sounded like a grunt.

"No shit," said Bowers as she did a quick assessment. He'd been shot twice. Once in the forearm. Once in the thigh.

The arm wound wouldn't kill him, but the hit to his thigh could, especially if the femoral artery had been hit. He'd already lost a lot of blood.

She slung her rifle over her back, yanked open the first-aid kit on Perez's belt, and pulled out the tourniquet. Every second wasted meant more blood lost. She applied the tourniquet to his thigh above the wound and kept an eye out for the shooter.

"Perez," she whispered, "where'd the shots come from?"

He struggled to point at the large trees at the back of the warehouse next door. That made sense.

The angle of the divots on the pavement seemed too shallow to be from the roof. All of the warehouse's windows were dark. No movement. No silhouettes. No light from inside. The shooter had probably left by now.

When she tightened the tourniquet, Perez groaned. "I called for backup." He grabbed her arm. "Get out of here."

"Not happening." She secured the tourniquet.

"Go. Now," he said through gritted teeth.

"Shut up or I'm putting one of these around your mouth."

Perez forced a smile. "Pain in the ass."

As long as she could keep him talking, he had an airway and a pulse. Only when they went quiet did things get hairy.

Bowers dug her hands under the shoulder straps of his bulletproof vest and found a good grip. Step-by-step, she pulled him in a long-axis drag toward his car. The vest rode up and cradled his head.

"Perez, talk to me," she said. "You okay?"

"You told me. To button it. Remember?"

Bowers kept moving. "Now who's being a pain in the ass?"

When she reached the car, Bowers thought she heard shouts. They were muffled and sounded far away.

The whine of sirens screamed in the distance. She listened as they came closer.

It's about time.

Kill Notice

Perez's whole body trembled.

"Hang in there," she said. Each second felt like hours. The sirens stopped. The strobes drew her attention to the boxy vehicles amassing at the end of street. It seemed as if the FBI's entire SWAT team and half of the Metro PD had shown up.

"Perez, they're here," said Bowers.

He didn't answer.

"Look, you son of a bitch." She slapped his good arm. "Don't you dare bail on me now. I put my ass on the line for your sorry hide." She felt Perez grip her arm. He still trembled, but at least he'd remained conscious.

She used her flashlight to send an SOS signal to SWAT at the end of the block.

An armored medic unit instantly started to roll. It came up fast, while the others hung back. Three guys in full SWAT gear jumped out, followed by the man she knew as the SWAT Doc. While the three acted as rearguards, the doc knelt down and immediately checked the tourniquet.

"It's been on for three minutes," Bowers told him. "Carotid pulse is over a hundred. No radials."

The doc nodded and glanced at the arm wound. "Nice work, Bowers."

Two SWAT medics joined them.

"This is a grab and go. Do it now," said the doc.

The two medics carried Perez on board. The doc hustled her into the armored unit after Perez.

Inside, the space had been fitted as a mobile ER unit. As the doc attended to Perez, she stayed out of the way and took a seat on a fold-down chair. Bowers closed her eyes and rested her head against a compartment wall.

When she opened her eyes, Riggs stood there in full gear, staring down at her with his arms folded.

MINUTES LATER, Riggs stood at the end of the street and close enough to Bowers that their shoulders touched. They watched the ambulance leave with Perez. "He'll be okay," he said.

Bowers hadn't taken her eyes off Perez until the ambulance doors had shut.

"He's tough," she said. "I've seen him in worse shape." She sounded hopeful, but the crinkle between her brows showed that she was more worried than she'd admit.

Riggs had waited to speak with her until the ambulance had left. Going in without backup had been risky, but sometimes you had to break the rules. He knew why she'd done it. Leaving an injured man to die wouldn't rock with her. *Can't argue with that.*

The commander waved him and Bowers onto the exterior steps of a SWAT vehicle. They jumped on board and clung to handrails as it rolled up in front of the self-storage building. More armored units pulled in behind them. Their headlights cast oval orbs of yellow on the asphalt.

HRT arrived in force.

Bowers jumped off and kicked some mud off her boots at a curb across the street from the storage building.

Riggs stood in front of her. "Bowers?"

She threw up her hands. "I know what you're gonna say, but—"

Riggs pulled her behind one of the armored units, where he leaned in close with one hand above her head on the heavy metal. "Listen. I'm proud of you," he said. "That took guts."

She appeared surprised. "I didn't have a choice."

"I know," he said. "I would've done the same." Riggs rolled away and leaned his back against the armored unit. "You were right about Mitch. Our subject is no longer an unsub." He told her about the DNA results, Johnny running Mitch's plates through LPR, and his talk with Devin Walker.

"I knew it," she said. "I've been thinking about how he was right in front of us the whole time."

Headlights shone on the road at their feet.

The FBI's SWAT commander marched around the corner of the

Kill Notice

heavy vehicle and joined them. "Bowers, do you know where the shots came from? Did you see anyone? Hear anything?" he asked.

"Perez said the shots came from the woods. He pointed to the big trees at the back of the warehouse next door." She recapped what she'd seen and heard. "Watch yourself," she said. "I received a text alerting me to this address."

"I thought Perez called it in," said the commander.

Bowers adjusted her vest. "Perez had been looking for our witness, Bobby Black. He arrived just before I rolled in. Something is going down here."

TRAPPED

BOBBY HAD HEARD the shots. So had Papa G.

"Don't worry," said Papa G. "We's family, like I told you. I ain't leaving wit'out you."

Bobby pointed to the pipe bomb and the garage door. "Don't be walkin' through there or you'll blow us all up. That dude is flat-out crazy, man. I'd run if I was you."

The guys from the crew kicked around the alligator clips on the floor. One of them pocketed a few and picked up the last bottle of water. Bobby couldn't take his eyes off it.

"It's four men to one," said Papa G. "Come on, now. I got this." He snorted like he had this under control. He motioned for the bottle of water. After cracking it open, he handed the bottle to Bobby. He guzzled down half of it. Water had never tasted so good. "Thank you. I was powerful thirsty."

"Like I said, we's family," said Papa G. The big room behind Bobby caught Papa G's attention. He went to check it out.

Papa G returned seconds later with his face all screwed up. "My corner smells a mile better than dis place."

They all looked up when the man in black's footsteps stomped across the second floor toward the stairs. Papa G started toward the hallway.

One of his guys tried to take a shortcut through the garage door. Papa G grabbed the man by the collar and waved the other two from the crew into the hall. Bobby heard Papa G's ragging on his men. "Any of yous git near dat door again and I'll shoot your punk-ass myself."

Bobby ran a thumb over the bandage on his wrist and drank the rest of the water. It surprised him that Papa G had been nice to him. The man in black wasn't like that. That dude was so messed up, he made Papa G seem like one of the good guys.

Clomping footsteps came from the stairs at the back. The man in black hollered at Papa G, like he was real mad about something.

They were in the back chopping it up. It sounded like a serious beef. Bobby knew Papa G wouldn't back down, but then neither would the man in black. This was some dangerous business.

After snagging his damp jeans with his toe, Bobby pulled them closer. While the men really got into it, Bobby wiggled his way back into his cold, wet jeans.

The shouting in back grew louder.

He tried to twist out of the handcuffs, but it only made his swollen wrist start to bleed. Bobby searched for a way out. He pulled on the pole. No way, could he jiggle that loose. It was bolted to the floor and ceiling.

If he could get free, Bobby knew he would have to go right past the man in black to get to the back door. He expected the front door was rigged. Bobby didn't want to find out.

Bobby had noticed a lot of strange things about this place. For one, all of the windows, or at least the ones he could see, had been covered with plywood and the edges sealed with black duct tape. This dude had sure done a lot of work to keep the sunlight out.

He glanced at the rough plywood walls of the room behind him. It didn't have doors, just an opening near some kind of maintenance room. He couldn't see inside, but he'd seen the rats going in there. Papa G had poked his head in and backed away, real quick.

Bobby had no idea what was in that room, but one thing was for sure. The worst part of the stink came from behind those walls.

BOWERS WATCHED MARKED and unmarked police units rolling up at the end of the street. Johnny came around the corner all revved up like he was ready to go hot.

"Where have you been?" she asked.

"We got a call. That news anchor, Marc Davis, is missing. I'll tell you about it later. Where do you want me?"

"Slow down, cowboy," she said. "We're watching from the sidelines on this one."

"But Bowers," said Johnny, "Perez and his partner are our guys. We should be in there."

"FBI's SWAT team is on it," said Bowers. "After they clear the area, we'll get our turn."

They watched SWAT streaming into the self-storage property in full gear, with with MP5 rifles and .40 caliber semi-automatics strapped to their legs. They cautiously covered every inch of the facility. Teams of two broke off to maintain control over the spaces already searched.

Since the shooting, things had been quiet. Bowers suspected that the shooter was long gone. She took a deep breath. Maybe she should have taken Riggs up on his offer to recruit her. She'd much rather be up there doing something than standing back here.

"I want to be in there," said Johnny.

Bowers nodded. "Me too."

The chief strode between two boxy vans and came straight toward her.

"Any word on Perez?" she asked.

The chief nodded. "He made it to the hospital. I expect he's in surgery by now." The chief firmly shook her hand. "The doc told me that you saved Perez's life. I tell you what, Bowers, I'd ride with you any day."

Kill Notice

"Thank you, sir," she said. The chief seemed restless. "What's up, chief? You have something on your mind."

"Dammit, Bowers, how do you do that?" He hesitated for a moment. "You have any idea where the hell Mitch is? No one's been able to find him."

Johnny gave her a sharp frown.

Not knowing whether the chief had been read-in or not, she had to step carefully. "Have you spoken with Riggs?" she asked.

"I heard the whole damned story. That son of a bitch," said the chief. He kicked at a rock on the asphalt. "Seems pretty clear who did the killin'. Tell you the truth, no one wants to take him out behind the shed more than I do."

"I don't know about that, chief," said Bowers. "You could sell tickets for that one."

"I'm in," said Johnny.

The chief scratched the back of his head. "I still can't believe I didn't see that coming."

"No one did, sir," she said. "Blame Mitch, not yourself."

While Johnny and the chief moved in closer for a better view of the action at the storage building, Bowers backed away and stood in the background.

As she crossed the street, her fears of something happening to Riggs came to the surface. She spotted him braced behind a corner and giving cover to others who were clearing the area. Like a badass angel, he had their backs. That's when it crystalized that the risks they both faced were worth the good they did, no matter what the outcome.

She still kept an eye on him.

A mist hung in the air. The flashlights on the ends of their MP5s cut through the darkness. Their constantly moving beams seemed other worldly, like a mass of robotic fireflies.

When a police wrecker arrived, she helped wave personnel back so the vehicle could move Perez's Mustang out of the way and unblock the entrance.

Bowers slipped back into the shadows near the front of the vacant warehouse next door. Through the vines and twigs on the chain-link fence between the two properties, she watched Riggs and the SWAT team's progress.

Two firefighters joined her. They kept an eye on the action too. "I don't know why we're here," said the younger one.

"Protocol," the other said. "Let's go. There's nothing we can do." The two men lumbered away in their big helmets and bulky gear.

When a patrol officer came closer, Bowers took up a position farther down the fence line. Twigs brushed against her pant legs. She peered through another gap in the fence.

This time the view hit her hard. Members of SWAT stood guard over the body of Perez's partner. Despite all the cruelty she had witnessed, she often saw honor appear in the worst of times, and when least expected. She watched an armored unit roll in front of them to provide additional cover.

Another fire fighter stood at the fence with a helmet and visor that covered his face. Like everyone else, he watched the movement next door.

Bowers took a step back and felt something snag her pants. She pulled her flashlight from her vest and cast a light down at the weeds at her feet and stopped. A dusting of tiny brown specs covered her boots and pant legs. She brought up her flashlight and closely inspected the bushes growing in and around the fence. They looked like rose bushes. In the hot circle of white from her flashlight she saw tiny brown seeds, just like the ones on Sapphire's dress. She felt a bump in her pulse and realized the plants were white avens.

"Hello, Bowers," whispered the fireman in a familiar voice. Bowers knew trouble had found her even before she spotted the muzzle of his pistol.

***

Bowers reached for her Glock.

Mitch's voice was unmistakable. "I wouldn't do that if I were you."

People along the fence had drifted back toward the street. She

Kill Notice

pulled her hand away. He'd concealed his pistol in the long sleeves of the coat.

"Looks like your latest victim was a fire fighter."

Mitch flipped up the visor and grinned. "He doesn't need it anymore."

"I shout one word, and they'll be all over your ass."

"But you wouldn't do that," said Mitch. He nodded toward the warehouse. "Come quietly or I'll cut Bobby up into little greasy pieces and feed his sorry ass to the ducks in the reflection pool."

Riggs and his partner made two circles around the storage building and had found nothing. The teams in the woods had discovered no sign of foot traffic, squatters, or snipers.

Something felt off. He returned to the front of the building and waited for the commander. There he found the chief and Johnny. He clasped a hand on Johnny's shoulder. "Chief, this man has done a fine job. Solid work."

Johnny smiled. "Thanks. Wish I could've been in there with you guys."

Riggs scanned the crowd. "Where's Bowers? The last time I saw her she was with you."

The chief pointed to the fence. "She's over there, or at least she was last time I looked."

Riggs ambled over, expecting to see her, but didn't. The only one there was a firefighter. "Hey, did you see a tall woman standing here? Brown hair. Detective."

The short man took off his helmet. "You mean Bowers? I saw her earlier. Then I got busy. Haven't seen her since."

Riggs studied the line along the fence and noticed a flashlight on the ground. He picked it up, clicked it on and off, and frowned.

JAWBONE

BOWERS STOOD a few feet inside the warehouse. It was unlikely that anyone outside had seen her. As Mitch prodded her forward with the muzzle of his pistol, she assessed her situation. No one could out run a bullet. Pound for pound, he was stronger. She knew several moves that might disarm him, but he knew many of the same tactics and would see it coming.

Out of habit, she analyzed her surroundings. The structure's thick brick walls buffered most sounds from within. Shouting wouldn't help. To her left a long hallway led to the back of the building. To her right it continued toward the front where a set of decayed metal stairs gave access to the second floor. Ten feet in front of her, an archway led to the building's core where a dim light shone.

The exterior door shut behind her. The metal-on-metal sound of a bolt closing brought back what she'd learned in survival school. First rule of survival: Mental toughness. *Don't panic.*

Her mind was her greatest asset.

She glanced back at Mitch, who held a pistol in his left hand and ripped the helmet off with the other.

"Eyes forward. Move," he said as he stepped back.

Kill Notice

She needed to appear fearless. "What's the matter, Mitch? You afraid to get too close?"

"Bowers?" She recognized Bobby's voice. "Run," he screamed. "Get out of here!"

"Shut up," yelled Mitch. He shoved her down the hall toward the back. At a storage area he stopped. "Drop your weapons."

Bowers pulled the shoulder strap over her head and rested her AR15 on the floor next to her feet. Mitch kicked it away. She winced at the sound of it scraping over the concrete. "That'll screw-up the bluing."

"Drop the Glock."

She did an about face and found the muzzle of his pistol aimed at her forehead.

"I'll take that," he said. Mitch reached for her belt and took her Glock from the holster. He stepped back and tossed it next to her rifle.

She heard it hit the clumps of broken concrete on the floor and the rustling of him removing the fireman's jacket.

Bowers noticed a lanyard hanging from his neck.

He put a hand over his chest and smiled. "You lookin' at this?" He held up what appeared to be a detonator.

She'd begun to sweat under her bulletproof vest. "You planning on blowing up something?"

"Bobby, if you don't cooperate."

"You don't need to—" Before she could finish her sentence she found her face smashed against the rough brick wall and felt the muzzle against the base of her neck. As he groped around her waist, her muscles tensed. She wanted to cut loose on him right here, but it would be a pointless gesture that would likely get her shot.

Second rule of survival: keep your body intact.

She felt Mitch's fingers. His touch poked at the undercurrent of anger she'd known most of her life. His hands glided down her legs. His fingers worked the fabric searching for anything hidden. At her left ankle he found her knife.

"You came armed for bear. I'm honored, Bowers. I knew you'd be a worthy opponent." His fingers explored her right ankle.

When she twitched, Mitch shoved the barrel of his pistol between her legs. His voice was as casual as if he were discussing the morning's traffic report.

"You could fight me if you want," he said. "But I'll pull the trigger." He paused as if thinking that through. "I've never shot anyone there before. Might be interesting to see what happens."

He took her knife and tossed it in the pile with her Glock.

After forcing her to face him, he pushed her back against the wall. His hand moved over her chest. Even with the vest's armored plates between his hand and her body, the violation made her jaw clench.

She remembered his pattern of humiliating his victims. Obviously, this was about getting a rise out of her. She refused to give him one, and held her emotions in check. She'd done it before. Terrorists in Ramadi had taunted her until she'd shot one of them. Apparently there were no seventy-two virgins in paradise for any man killed by a woman. That day, she became the sniper they feared most—and the one with the biggest price-tag on her head.

Mitch pressed his pistol against the base of her neck.

She stood at attention, and stared straight ahead.

He slammed his right hand into the wall next to her left ear. She didn't flinch.

They were nose-to-nose. "You afraid of me, Bowers?" he asked as he cocked his head and stared deeply into her eyes.

Sweat on his scalp glistened in the light from a bare bulb hanging from the ceiling.

"Answer me," he yelled. His spit hit her cheek. "Are you afraid of me?"

"No." That wasn't entirely true.

His pupils grew wide and dark. "You should be."

Kill Notice

RIGGS SEARCHED the fence line again. He stood and scanned the crowd and saw many familiar faces. None of them were Bowers'.

He used the flashlight he'd found and aimed the beam at an angle across the ground and through the weeds until he found footprints in the dirt. There were too many of them to make sense of any pattern.

"Where the hell is she?"

BOWERS LOOKED for cover and warily watched Mitch reach behind a pallet stacked with bags of concrete and pick up a rifle. He searched a corner and kicked chunks of concrete away from a large hole in the floor.

After tucking her Glock into his waistband, Mitch dropped her rifle and knife through the hole in the floor. She heard the clatter as they fell into the basement below.

He motioned her forward with the muzzle of his pistol. The rank odors of decomp and dust made her shoulders tense. She forced herself to remain focused and stayed a few steps ahead of him. Bowers pulled down on the neck opening of her vest with both hands. The armored plates covered in course fabric offered a little reassurance. Each time he poked her with that damned pistol she wanted to rip it out of his hand and beat him with it.

Bobby was there somewhere, but from the hallway she couldn't see him or the building's interior, which made mounting an effective defense difficult.

At the back of the building, Mitch shoved her into a room where four men were lined up in folding chairs with their hands behind their backs. One of them was Papa G. The other three she suspected were from his crew. Apparently, Mitch had handcuffed them before going outside and pretending to be a fireman.

A shuffling sound to her right drew her attention. Through the garage-style door she could see the interior and a figure slumped against a metal pole.

"Bobby?" She took a step toward the door. Almost immediately she spotted the pipe bomb and stopped.

"No!" shouted Bobby. "Don't go through there."

"It's okay, I see it." She recognized the IED. It appeared to be simple. Crude. And deadly.

Mitch seemed pleased with himself. "Either you cooperate or he dies." He tossed her a key for the handcuffs. Bowers caught it with her right hand.

"Go un-cuff them," he said, pointing at Papa G.

She stopped behind each chair. Because of Papa G's size, he wore two cuffs linked together. One by one she released the men as ordered.

Bowers backed away and kept the key firmly in her grip.

As Papa G stood, he scowled at Mitch. "There's no call to be doin' dat." He rubbed at the grooves left by the cuffs and folded his arms. "I told you I'd be waitin'."

"Bowers, let me introduce you to my guests." Mitch's tone and gestures were grandiose and pathetic in her mind.

Papa G continued glaring at Mitch. "You gots my man, Bobby, and my guns. I wannum back. It's time to deal."

Mitch pointed to a metal railing along the concrete platform. "Bowers, cuff yourself to that rail while I have a word with these gentlemen." He nodded to a pair of cuffs near an open floor drain two feet to her left. She made no attempt to comply.

Mitch aimed his pistol at Bobby. "Do it," he yelled.

"Hey, there be no need for shootin'," said Papa G as he held up his hands. "You shoot him and there will be a price to pay. Give me my boy, now, and we's outta here."

With the key still in hand, she knelt and picked up the handcuffs. As Mitch watched, she fastened her wrist to the railing.

Mitch grunted. "Bowers, surely you don't think I'm that stupid. Toss me the key." He sounded almost insulted.

Papa G's men began to fan out. While Mitch kept an eye on them, Bowers picked up a small bolt from the floor and tossed it into the drain, hoping the dodge would work.

Kill Notice

As the sound of metal plinking against the walls of the pipe echoed in the room, she held her breath and slipped the key between the laces and tongue of her boot.

Mitch hadn't taken his eyes off Papa G. "I knew you'd be a challenge." He shrugged. "No worries. I have a spare."

Bowers exhaled and noticed how the X Crew had grown tense and edgy.

"I've had enough of this," said Papa G. "I've put up wit' your bullshit long enough. Hand over Bobby. Now."

Mitch stepped back as if he were heading for the hall to get him. Instead, he ducked behind a corner wall.

"Let me have Bobby," said Papa G. He began backtracking toward the door. "And I'll go tell the cops I came to get this here runaway and take him home. See what I'm saying? While you make yourself gone, I'll run cover for you, man. All I want is the kid. You can keep our guns."

His three men followed him. One reached for something in his pants.

Bowers hit the floor.

Mitch opened fire.

The instant Riggs heard the shots he crouched and ran for cover. Double-taps were quickly followed by more gunshots. It sounded like a firefight.

The rounds had come from inside the warehouse behind him. Within seconds he and other members of SWAT ducked behind one of the armored units.

Two figures bolted away from the back of the warehouse. One guy continued firing at someone behind him. They darted through a hole in the fence. When they saw the SWAT team, the skinny man dropped his pistol and they both ran with their hands in the air.

Riggs hurried to head them off. When he arrived on the other side, he found a big, black man in baggy pants and a knit cap standing behind the armored unit and gasping for air. His shirt was spattered with blood.

The skinny one cradled his hand, which appeared to have taken a round. The thumb hung at an odd angle as if dislocated. A knot of special agents surrounded them.

Riggs recognized the big man. "I can't help but wonder what would bring Papa G this far north," he said as he stepped up and held the man's gaze.

The commander joined them with a bead on Papa G. "What the hell is this about?"

"Look, man," said Papa G, "I ain't shot no one."

"We've got one dead officer," said Riggs, "and another wounded. You have some explaining to do."

"I didn't shoot your mens." Papa G put a hand on his chest. "I knew Perez was here, but I gots mad-juice for that guy. He a good man."

Papa G bent forward. His wheezing became pronounced as he struggled to breathe. Apparently the stress of running for his life had set him off. He shook his head. "I got no reason. To hurt a guy, like dat," he said between gasps. "I hope he's okay."

The SWAT team took custody of the other man.

"Who's he?" Riggs asked as the thin man was escorted away.

"Dat be one of my homeboys. He got his hand shot when we was leavin'." Papa G glanced down at the blood on his shirt and grew quiet. The big guy wasn't looking so good. He was sweating like crazy.

The commander hauled Papa G inside the armor unit. Riggs followed and tore open a plastic bag containing a re-breather mask and put it over Papa G's nose and mouth. After connecting it to their oxygen tank, Riggs set the flow rate to three liters.

Papa G held a big hand over the mask and concentrated on sucking in air. After the wheezing eased, Riggs handed him a bottle of water and turned off the O_2.

"You all right?" asked Riggs, as Papa G pulled off the mask and took a sip of water. "I can get a medic."

"I appreciate dat," he said. "Dis has been a bad night. If it weren't

Kill Notice

for my man havin' a piece stuck down his shorts, we'd all be dead 'n' gone."

Riggs started to ask him about Bowers, but was cut off by the commander. "What was the shooting about?"

"Lost two of my mens back there. And I tried to get Bobby out. Hell, he just a kid." The big man appeared genuinely sad. "I shoulda done it different wit' him," Papa G said, "then maybe he woulda come to me and I wouldn't be sittin' here in a police vehicle. No offense. Beats being dead, but this ain't my kinda place. You read me?"

Papa G studied the interior of the unit and nodded. "I need to git me one a these. Shit you even got a coffee machine in here."

Riggs hadn't moved. "Answers. Now."

"Guh. Don't be eyeballin' me like dat. I'm a businessman." Papa G settled back into his seat. "I ain't done nothing. It's your Mr. Mitch who's out poppin' folks. He shot your mens and killed two of mine. He's right inside that buildin'. Take your beef to him."

"How do you know Mitch?" asked Riggs. He noticed blood dripping from Papa G's arm. The commander pulled out a first-aid kit.

Papa G leaned forward and held out his arm. "See, I knew the cops was interested in Bobby. Perez and a lady cop ax me about him. Then your Mr. Mitch comes around choppin' it up wit' my crew. You know, he's talking about how he gots to find Bobby. Some bullshit excuse about he owes him. Next thing I knows, Bobby is gone, gone. My crew tells me Mr. Mitch is a cop and he done took my Bobby. I felt bad about that. So I uses an app and follows Bobby's phone on up here. Took me a while to locate dis place. You gots poor reception up here. Anyway, I git here and I tells Mr. Mitch dat Bobby is mine, not his. You dig? Then I run into this mess." Papa G rubbed his face.

The commander put a bandage around Papa G's arm while listening to the story.

Papa G pulled down his cap and took another sip of his water.

"How many inside?" asked the commander.

"Bobby for sure. My shot-up mens. Cain't believe they's dead." Papa G shook his head. "And your Mr. Mitch. You should see for yourself the savage shit he's got in there. Some dude's jawbone is nailed to the wall. That dawg is flat-out crazy, if you ax me."

Riggs caught the look in the commander's eyes.

Papa G leaned over and gazed at Riggs from under heavy lids. "He gots a pipe bomb in there, too."

Riggs sat up. "How do you know that?"

"Saw it myself. Right on the floor 'bout ten feet from Bobby. Bowers confirmed it, so it hasta be true. She's a smart lady." Papa G whistled.

"Bowers' in there?"

"For sure, bro."

NO WAY OUT

WITH HER EARS still ringing from the gunshots, Bowers glanced to her left. Bobby lay on the floor with one arm over his head. Before getting up, she scanned the room and saw the two bodies, but not Papa G nor Mitch.

She dug the key out of her boot and un-cuffed herself.

From behind the corner, Mitch strolled out of the shadows. He glanced at the open floor drain and cocked his head. "You fooled me!" he said as if amused. He leaned against the wall with his pistol dangling from his hand.

"Bastard," she said. She stood and brushed the grit off her hands. It irked her how he ambled over as if he had all the time in the world. When he reached for the shoulder strap of her vest, she slapped his hand away. He jumped back as if he'd been jabbed by a hot poker and aimed his Glock at her face.

"No more tricks or I'll make you watch as I filet the kid." Mitch's right hand rested on his hunting knife. His thumb stroked the hilt. "They scream a lot."

He took the key out of her hand and forced her out of the room and down the hall. A few seconds later, they entered the large room where Bobby sat on the floor, cuffed to a steel support column.

317

The poor kid stared at her. "I'm sorry I left the safe house."

"Shut up," yelled Mitch, who picked up a screwdriver and threw it at him. Bowers grimaced as Bobby hunched his shoulders and pulled away. The tool clanked against the pole and landed a few feet from the pipe bomb.

Bare light bulbs hanging from the ceiling cast a dim glow over the room. Mitch stood motionless as if he were sizing her up. All pretenses of the smiling sarge had vanished. His blank face and dark eyes held no sign of emotion. Nor did they show any fear. This was the real Mitch, not the persona he'd projected for the benefit of fitting in.

"It must get tiring to keep up the act in front of others," she said.

He didn't answer. Instead he waved his weapon toward an inner room where the smell of decomp grew stronger.

With Mitch's pistol at her back, Bowers passed a door labeled BOILER ROOM and stopped next to a work table. Underneath it she spotted several orange buckets filled with tools. In one of them she recognized the red handle of a Hilti nail gun.

Mitch forced her closer to the odd room constructed of metal studs and sheets of plywood. Once inside, it took a moment for her to make sense of the things displayed on the walls and tables. When she saw bloody handcuffs lying on top of a chest freezer, the details painted a gruesome picture. This was Mitch's workshop.

Everything in his trophy room reeked of death.

The hair went up on her neck. Her eyes watered at the smell and she fought the urge to gag. The source of the odor seemed to be a blue, fifty-five-gallon barrel in the corner. The lid sat askew. A rat jumped down from the edge and scampered away. Mitch pounded on the lid until it snapped back in place.

"Sorry. The gases push it open," he said as if embarrassed. His reaction surprised her, but it didn't last long. "Marc Davis said the 202

Kill Notice

Killer was a sexual deviant. A coward." Mitch ran his fingers along the edge of the barrel's lid. "He should've kept his mouth shut."

A pile of clothes lay on the floor next to the blue barrel. Above them, a press pass dangled from a nail on the wall. Next to it was an enlarged photograph of a pair of pinstriped boxers draped over a press van's side mirror.

Bowers nodded toward the freezer. "Why didn't you put the body in there?"

"It's occupied," said Mitch. He glanced at her and laughed.

A few feet from the blue barrel lay a balled-up mass of plastic sheeting encrusted in dried blood. A pair of sparkling pumps lay on top. Bowers nodded at the shoes. "Those were Sapphire's. Right?"

"See? I knew you'd understand." The beaming satisfaction on his face changed in the blink of an eye to casual reflection. He shrugged. "She deserved everything that happened to her."

Each word out of Mitch's mouth made her want to bash his face in. During her duty as a patrol officer, she'd heard many drivers use passive language to avoid admitting their guilt. They'd say things like "the pole hit my car" as if it were the pole's fault. Mitch did the same damned thing. "Bullshit, Mitch. Nothing 'happened' to her. You killed her."

He blinked and tilted his head as if it were a compliment. Mitch nodded toward a wall six feet to her left where he'd mounted a grizzly display of trophies. There in the center of the wall hung a charred human jawbone.

Handwritten words on the plywood wall above it read: "Now who's talking?"

Mitch's face lit up in a kind of twisted glee.

"That's my Daddy." Mitch's voice fell into a West Virginia accent. "There's something wrong with you, boy." He wagged his head in mockery. "Don't make me come down there. You know what I'll do."

He added another piece of tape to a faded picture of a burnt house hanging next to the jawbone. "Old Daddy yelled too much."

The number of hate-filled notes scribbled on the wall indicated that Mitch had spent a good deal of time there carrying on a one-sided rant.

"Your colleagues lack insight," he said. "They are so locked into thinking that there can only be one MO. Good God, folks, have some imagination! There are a multitude of intriguing ways to stop a pulse." He paused. "You were smart enough to see that."

Taped to an adjacent wall were dozens of photos. He handed her one. She glanced at it and refused to take it.

"Come on, Bowers. I made this one for you."

Knowing the picture was of Berti, she left her arms limp at her sides and stared straight ahead.

It appeared that many of the pictures had been taken at the moment when the victims realized there was no way out and they were about to die.

Other images recorded how he'd posed them.

The smells. The brutality. And the loss of life represented by each trophy rivaled the horrors of Ramadi.

One of the things she hated most was the way he enjoyed humiliating his victims. She nodded at the wall of photos. "Why kill the girl at Keats' cabin?"

"That's obvious." He sounded surprised. "Keats was a vile man that had to go."

"But she was a vulnerable kid. Still a child."

Mitch seemed captivated by the wall of photos. "They were weak." His voice graveled with distain.

Bowers took a step back and caught a glimpse of Bobby through the opening. The pipe bomb sat on the concrete floor, fifteen feet from him. She'd seen IEDs like it many times. If this one went off, it would likely kill anyone in a seventy-five-foot radius. Disarming it would be simple enough, if she could get to it without Mitch noticing.

"Don't try to be clever," he said as he unbuttoned his long-sleeved shirt. With his pistol still in hand, he quickly peeled off each sleeve. "That's better." He stood before her in a sleeveless undershirt and his tan tactical pants.

Kill Notice

Bowers had never seen him in anything but long sleeves and could see why. His arms and one shoulder bore a web of tortuous burn scars.

She noted a charred horse's hoof on his wall. "I see you're a fan of arson."

"We all have our scars, don't we Bowers? Mine are on my skin, but yours run deeper. Don't they?"

She ignored him. The injuries covering his forearms had caught her attention. They were consistent with wounds one would get from a victim fighting back. Many of them were smooth white scars. Some were still red. A few were freshly scabbed over.

He glanced between her and his arms and held them out, twisting and turning them, as if showing off. A moment later, Mitch pulled up his shirt to reveal a large, purple bruise covering his side. "You have one hell of a punch. It still hurts to breathe."

"That's what you get," she said, "for invading my home."

"You have no idea how long I've waited for this day." He pulled down his shirt. "I saw your place, now you get to see mine."

The photos, earrings, driver's licenses, and other fragments from people's lives made her wonder how many he'd killed.

Mitch excitedly pushed her to the end of a table and pointed to a framed photo of the trashcan man taken when the flames had just caught his sleeve on fire.

Bowers had seen enough. She searched for a way to disarm him, but he never gave her the opportunity.

While Mitch pointed out other articles as if he expected her to appreciate his actions, Bowers looked to her left and saw something that stopped her cold.

Five feet from her an old dresser had been tucked into a dark corner. On top of it sat a desk lamp and jar. Mitch clicked on the light. Hundreds of buttons filled the jar

MITCH WAVED her out of his trophy room. His excitement seemed to build as they neared a door next to the electrical panel. Bobby sat up and raised a hand as if we were about to say something. She signaled him to keep quiet.

Keys rattled as Mitch unlocked a latch under a sign that read: BOILER ROOM. When Bowers glanced at the Hilti, Mitch's head snapped to the right. He glared at her and the table.

"No tricks," he said as he pulled her into the small boiler room. The space housed a water heater, furnace, and a sink. A mop and bucket stood in one corner, but they weren't what had drawn Mitch's attention.

He pulled a pair of pliers off a shelf and opened the furnace's access door. The roaring, orange flames cast a warm glow in the otherwise gray room.

From the top shelf, he pulled down a child's lunchbox. Its once bright red color and decorative cartoon characters were cracked and faded by time. He gently placed it on the chair. "You'll want to see this," he said. "This is where it began." He opened the lunchbox and gingerly lifted out the white skull of a cat.

Bowers slowly rolled back a step closer to the exit.

Mitch rubbed a thumb over the dry bones and gently returned the skull to the lunchbox. He took in a deep breath and exhaled. "Nothing like the memories of childhood, huh, Bowers?"

She took another half-step back. "I get that you hated your father, but why Berti or these others? They didn't hurt you."

"Berti," he said with a shrug, "showed me how committed you were. Most people would've given in at that point. I'm happy to say you didn't."

When she said nothing, he stopped admiring the skull and stared at her. "You were supposed to understand." His gloat instantly transformed into a scowl. "You disappoint me." His voice rose to a bellow. "I bring you here and show you all of this and you still don't get it, do you?"

Mitch's eyes had turned dark and vacant as he dug a hand into his pocket and pulled out a button and threw it at her.

Kill Notice

Bowers let it dropped to the floor. A wave of nausea hit her as she glanced down and immediately recognized the blue-green button that had come from her sea-horse pants.

BLINDSIDED

PAPA G'S NEWS about Bowers felt like a body blow. Her being inside with Mitch and a pipe bomb had Riggs primed to tear that building apart. Brick by brick, if necessary.

Two agents detained Papa G while Riggs went with the commander to gather the team. Hostage rescue joined them. With binoculars in hand, Riggs scanned each of the warehouse's windows and found nothing of note. Someone from HRT confirmed that the building had power. He hadn't expected that. It appeared dark and deserted.

The FBI's SWAT team quickly reassembled. Teams amassed in the front of the two-story brick structure, which stood a good forty feet wide and a good hundred feet long.

Normally, Riggs saw himself as a patient man. Not tonight. The prep time for entry chafed at him. He wanted to go in now. As if willing them to move faster, he watched a team approach the side door and prepare for a breach. Two others had gone around the back to rig the back door.

The team at the front door had used an under-door camera that showed them an explosive device taped to a panel of glass inside. Breaching that entrance would have been a disaster.

Kill Notice

Riggs groaned as the threat of booby-traps slowed down the pace even more. Their surveillance van reported hotspots in the building, which translated to three people downstairs. Two of them appeared to be moving. Another hotspot showed as a furnace. Two duller spots were likely the bodies of Papa G's men, which gave credence to his story.

The team in back radioed in to report they'd found two vehicles. One black Silverado pickup and a black Escalade.

Riggs lined up with the rest of the SWAT team.

"Hold up," said the commander. "You shouldn't go in."

"Why the hell not?" asked Riggs. "I'm part of this team."

The commander shook his head. "Not this time. Bowers is in there. You're too close to the situation."

"Either I go in or you're gonna have to shoot me. When have you ever seen me be anything but spot-on?"

The commander stared at him for a moment. "Riggs. You're killing me," he said, waving him in. "Stay in the back, will ya?"

Riggs lined up. *Like hell I will.*

WHEN MITCH REACHED up to put away his lunchbox, Bowers bolted out of the boiler room and slammed the door shut behind her. She grabbed the bucket with the Hilti. As the door began to open, she threw her weight against it and caught his hand.

"Goddammit," yelled Mitch. A shot ripped through the door, just missing her. Each time he drove his shoulder into the door she looked down at the Hilti in her hand as the energy of the impact rocked her body.

Bowers wedged her foot against the floor and used her hip for additional leverage. She pressed the nail gun against the wooden door. When she felt Mitch bump against it again, she pulled the trigger and fired until it emptied.

Boom-boom. Boom-boom-boom echoed in the room. The nails tore through the solid door.

Mitch screamed and went quiet.

She hoped he was down, but wasn't counting on it. Bowers dropped the empty Hilti and raced toward Bobby and the pipe bomb.

First she knelt next to the pipe and quickly examined the wiring. Anyone triggering the motion sensor on the garage door opener would set it off. The device on Mitch's lanyard was either a fake or he had been synced it with a different bomb elsewhere in the building.

She carefully removed an alligator clip from the bare wire and clamped it down onto the insulated section. That broke the circuit. If Mitch didn't look too closely, the wiring would appear intact.

Bobby watched her, wide-eyed. The grit from the cold concrete floor scraped against her palm as she scrambled toward him. While kneeling next to him, she pulled a bobby pin out of her hair and stripped off the plastic tip with her teeth.

"Look away. This is a skill you don't need to know," she told him.

While Bowers used the thin, metal tip to flip open the cuffs, she whispered to Bobby. "Don't move until I draw him outta here. Then run like your butt's on fire." She patted his shoulder and ran for the hallway.

Seconds later, she heard the door to the boiler room burst open. Over her shoulder she saw Mitch in the doorway.

"Bowers," he shrieked, "you're dead!"

The nails from the Hilti had mangled his ear and ripped gashes in the fleshy part of his upper arm and shoulder.

She raced around the corner. Almost immediately she felt the thump in her back and heard the shot echoing in the small space. It felt as if a giant sledgehammer had crushed her chest.

Her legs turned to rubber. Bowers careened into the wall. Searing pain ignited every nerve. The wind had been knocked out of her lungs. She put the palms of both hands on the cold concrete and gasped for air.

She grimaced and reached for the wooden handrail.

"Hurts, don't it?" asked Mitch with a slight West Virginia twang. "You're wearin' out my patience. Next time I'll be sure to land one where it'll really hurt."

Kill Notice

Bowers pulled herself up.

"Take off the vest," he ordered.

She ripped open the Velcro fasteners, hoisted the heavy vest off her shoulders, and let it drop to the floor so that her name badge was clearly visible on the breastplate. Riggs wouldn't miss that.

The weight off her shoulders relieved some of the pressure in her chest, but it also made her more vulnerable. Her T-shirt, damp with sweat, provided no protection.

A noise caught Mitch's attention. He wiped a bloody hand on his white undershirt and quietly crept backward toward the side door. His eyes and pistol remained fixed on her torso as he cocked his head as if listening.

A few feet from Mitch's boot, Bowers spotted the long, black tip of an under-door camera slowly emerging beneath the door as it inched along the floor. She showed no response, but she knew SWAT and Riggs would soon be pouring through each entrance with everything they had.

When Mitch took another step back, his boot came down on the camera. He jumped as if he'd stepped on a snake.

"Shit," he said. Mitch's scowl and blood smeared shirt and scars intensified his frightening presence.

Bowers swallowed hard and watched his every move.

"Looks like your FBI friend intends to join us. Upstairs. Go. Now!"

The rusted metal steps creaked and swayed as they scrambled to the second floor where many of the interior walls were open and unfinished. As if metallic ribs of a gigantic corpse, the bare studs stood dusty and decaying in neat rows. Bowers heard Bobby cough.

The moment she cleared the stairwell, she flinched when two nearly simultaneous explosions erupted downstairs. The doors had been breached. Hopefully Bobby had followed her advice and ran.

Mitch shouted at her. "Hurry! Corner room. Go, go, go."

He pushed her into the odd shaped room. Unlike the rest of the upstairs, great care had been taken to finish the walls. Carpenter horses were stacked in a corner. A demolition chute filled one of the windows.

The interior walls were brick re-enforced with metal plates. She had a few uneasy thoughts as to why he'd done that.

Knowing it would take time for SWAT to clear downstairs, she quickly scanned the L-shaped room for items she could improvise as weapons. The orange buckets and a six-inch wrench were useless, but to her left she spotted the sharp splintered ends of a broken broom handle leaning against a chest freezer.

Yelling and the explosive pops and crackles of flash-bang canisters roared downstairs.

Fortunately, Mitch had been so focused on her, that he didn't appear to have noticed her alteration of the pipe bomb or that she'd undone Bobby's restraints.

Bowers backed toward the freezer. Mitch broke to the right and stood maybe twelve feet from her. Despite the noise downstairs, he showed no visible signs of fear.

Instead, he contentedly hummed as he worked around a thick, brick barrier that extended four feet into the room and went all the way up to the ceiling like a mini fortress. There he propped his rifle against the corner, lined up a series of canisters, and opened a metal box filled with magazines ready to go.

Behind him, a dark, six-foot opening appeared to be some kind of chute. He stood next to the large opening and grinned at her. "That is why I chose this building."

GOING HOT

BOBBY ROSE to his feet and searched for the nearest door until he'd heard the blasts. He hit the floor and threw his hands over his head. He wanted to help Bowers, but the chaos of flashes and banging and pops and boots running had him all confused. His ears were ringing.

Dudes were yelling, "FBI. *Don't move!*"

Bobby couldn't argue with that.

Guys in serious gear stormed in around him. He saw the black letters, FBI, on the chests of their green vests and a bunch of scary looking ammo packed into the pockets. These dudes were badass to the max.

Bobby peered toward the back where four of them were approaching the garage door.

"It's a trap!" yelled Bobby. The next thing he knew, the men stopped and big hands lifted him to his feet.

"Bobby, I'm special agent Riggs. Do what I tell you." The man then eased over and examined the pipe bomb. "Bowers has been here," he told the man next to him. "It's disarmed."

Bowers could see Mitch had enough supplies to sustain a lengthy battle. That wasn't happy news.

Worse. The brick barrier not only blocked any clear view of him from the metal door, it also appeared to be re-enforced with a steel plate. Those factors alone gave him a considerable advantage, though she'd never tell him that.

Bowers backed into the large white freezer. The surface felt cold and smooth against her fingers. She glanced down at the words written in marking pen on the lid that read: "You shouldn't have left me with him."

"Who's in this one?" she asked.

"My mother," he said. Tears welled in his eyes. He shook his head. Seconds later, he began to laugh maniacally. The hair rose on Bowers' arms.

"What about your wife and children? Are they next?" she asked.

He blinked. "I watched them sleeping one night and thought about it, but I was busy enough. Killing is a lot of work, if you do it right."

"You botched the Keats scene. Left DNA all over it."

That drew a hateful glare. Just as quickly his expression changed to gloating. His mouth twitched. "I did think of adding your uncle Marvin to my collection and leaving a button on his wheelchair for you to find."

Bowers held her expression in check, but at her core she wanted to tear him apart in two-inch segments.

Bobby's voice in the distance drew her attention. She heard her name and something about "she's upstairs with that crazy dude."

"Mitch, it's over," she said. "In a few seconds they're going to be all over you. Give it up."

Showing no concern, he wagged his finger in the air. "This is checkmate. They just don't know it yet." He pulled out her Glock and sat it on a ledge with his ammo.

He gestured toward the shaft. "This dumbwaiter will take me to the basement in a flash. A tunnel from there connects to a shed hidden in the woods where a car is gassed-up and waiting for me."

Kill Notice

Bowers slid a few inches closer to the splintered broom handle and wondered if the detonator around his neck was real or fake. He glanced down and took it off and tossed it to her. "Do you want to press the button or should I?" He laughed. "Do it. Live a little. See what happens."

She threw it into the demolition chute. It clanked as it fell.

"You called my bluff. I thought you might." He laughed. "It's not my style anyway."

Mitch moved in close enough that she could feel the warmth of his breath.

"I like to watch," he said as he pressed the muzzle of his pistol under her chin. "But then you know that, don't you?"

She started to jerk her head away, but he forced her chin up until they were face to face. Bowers could feel those strange, black eyes studying her.

He glanced down at her T-shirt. "I've got a few moments. We could have a little fun, before I have to leave." With one hand, he took off her belt. The buckle clanked against the freezer and fell to the floor.

She held her breath as the fingers of his free hand slipped under her waistband.

"What color are they?" he asked.

Bowers glared straight ahead, but said nothing.

"I'm guessing black, maybe a thong." He tugged down the stretchy fabric of her pants and leered at her hips. "Black. I knew it." He slid his knife out of its sheath.

Goosebumps rose as the tip of the blade scraped over her skin. She flinched as he severed the black fabric on both hips.

"Get your hands off me," she said.

Mitch pushed the muzzle in harder, making it difficult to swallow. She gritted her teeth as he yanked her panties free. He stepped back and brought her underwear up to his nose.

Bowers pulled up her waistband while Mitch backed away and carefully draped them over a nail on the wall.

MARTA SPROUT

BOWERS HEARD SHUFFLING outside the room and knelt near a wall next to the door. Mitch ducked behind the cover of his personal fortress.

The door crashed open.

She caught a glimpse of a bulletproof shield. Her pulse pounded as a flash-bang canister rolled passed her and stopped. She turned her face away and covered her ears. A maelstrom of blinding flashes, pops, and crackles filled the room. It smelled like firecrackers.

Mitch let loose a torrent of rounds.

A bolus of adrenaline coursed through her veins.

SWAT returned fire. Bullets clanked against steel. Chips of shattered brick peppered the room. Brass casings danced like golden raindrops on the wooden floorboards.

Mitch stayed behind cover.

She glanced up as a big man took two steps into the room, dropped to his knees, and fell in front of her. Before he hit the floor, she knew that it was Riggs.

The entire room seemed to tilt. The sounds of shouting and gunfire seemed oddly far away. Rounds whizzed over her head.

"Hold your fire. Man down," Bowers yelled. Her actions were reflex. Muscle memory. Autopilot.

She grabbed Riggs by the straps on his bulletproof vest and dragged him away from the line of fire and next to the freezer. Her own breathing rasped in her ears.

Riggs coughed. He'd taken multiple hits. Blood had already started to soak his uniform.

She shoved a bucket out of the way, rolled him to his side, and made sure he could breathe.

Mitch tossed a few of his own flash-bang canisters into the hallway, and slammed the door shut. While he locked the door with a sliding bolt, he glanced at the man on the floor. "Well look who we have here," he shouted over the noise and snickered.

Bowers gripped the broom handle and rose. Mitch tried to slip

332

Kill Notice

around her, but she faced him and used her body and the broken handle to block him from reaching Riggs.

Something from outside thumped against the door. She knew SWAT would be setting up for a breach.

Mitch glanced at the broom handle in her hands and peered around her at Riggs. "I could put him out of his misery," he said with a cocky grin. "But he's finished anyway. Like I said. Checkmate."

Another thump hit the door.

"It's time for me to go," said Mitch. His voice sounded cold and inhuman as he pressed the muzzle of his rifle against her sternum. "I'll miss you, Bowers. Say goodbye."

With no forewarning, she flipped one end of the broom handle up, hard. A loud crack sounded as she knocked the rifle barrel away. Before Mitch had time to pull it back into position, she swung the broom handle like a baseball bat. The sharp ragged splinters raked across Mitch's throat.

"You're not going anywhere," she said.

The rifle fell to the floor with a clatter as he rocked back and grabbed at his neck.

"That was for Berti." Bowers tightly gripped the handle with both hands and lunged at him.

He pulled his Glock and fired.

Adrenaline drove her on. Bowers thrust the sharp ends of the broken broom handle under his chin and pinned him against the wall.

Mitch appeared stunned.

"This one is for Riggs." She drove the handle upward and back.

Blood arced from the wounds in pulsing streams. His pistol fell from his hand. Mitch clawed at his neck and then tried to grab the broom handle, but she drove it in deeper and held him there.

As she waited for shock to set in, Mitch jerked. He threw his hands around her neck.

"Big mistake," she said just before he squeezed down and bared his teeth in a ferocious grin.

Bowers took one hand off the broom handle. Her fingers found the worn edge of his thick leather belt and his knife. She pulled it from the sheath and drove it deep into his diaphragm.

His body quivered. His hands dropped.

She sucked in a deep breath and watched the pulse at the base of his neck racing in a desperate effort to compensate for his plummeting blood pressure.

His eyes grew wide and dark in stunned disbelief.

Bowers glanced down at his tan trousers and watched a large wet spot bloom at his fly. Mitch tried to cover himself with his left hand, but he had lost all control.

"Now who's vulnerable?" she asked as she pulled out the knife and waited.

He blinked once. Grimaced. Much to her surprise, abject humiliation seeped into his expression.

The room filled with the whine of equipment and pop of deforming metal. As the door came off its hinges, she held Mitch in place with the handle still embedded in his neck.

His arms fell limp. Time seemed to stop. Bowers felt him twitch and watched the life leaving his eyes.

Behind her the sounds of boots and hushed voices filled the room. Within seconds she felt the arm of a big man in full SWAT gear around her. "Bowers," he said, "we've got this. Let go." His voice sounded gentle and assuring.

She released the broom handle and allowed the man to pull her back. Mitch's body crumpled to the floor with a thud.

Bowers took a few steps. The burning pain in her hip told her she'd been hit. She ignored it and sunk to her knees next to Riggs. Her mouth went dry.

"Bowers, you all right?" asked the SWAT doc as he put his fingers on Riggs' neck.

"Take care of him. He's hurt worse," she told him.

Riggs lay limp on the floor. The memory of his touch made it hard to breathe. Never had she felt this helpless.

Bowers sat on the floor and refused to let go of his hand. When his fingers relaxed she saw her name written on the palm of his hand.

BADGE OF HONOR

A MONTH LATER, Bowers watched the bright headlights passing by. She stood on the sidewalk in front of The Old Ebbitt Grill. Over the last few weeks she'd wondered if she'd ever come here again, but here she stood. On the other side of the glass door stood Riggs, wearing a sly grin.

He opened the door.

Bowers took a deep breath and went inside, where two guys from the bar helped Riggs up the steps. Their favorite bartender, Rachel, had saved them seats. When Riggs slid onto the barstool, cheers broke out. The bartender put a Heineken and a Negra Modelo in front of them. "Your drinks are on the house," she said. "These rabble-rousers are picking up the rest of your tab."

"Hoorah," said a man with a bushy, red mustache. The rest of the guys at the bar lifted their glasses in a salute.

Riggs nodded and raised his bottle. "It's good to be back."

Bowers found herself staring at him. Seeing Riggs sitting there was another sight she'd thought she'd never see again. He'd been shot three times. One bullet had gone through the armhole of his vest, resulting in a chest wound. Another had hit him an inch below his vest. He'd called it a "rude appendectomy." The last one had nicked his thigh.

"You're damned lucky," she said.

"Speak for yourself." He took a long draw from his bottle of beer. "How's the hip?"

"Flesh wound. It's healing." She shrugged it off.

Riggs grimaced. "It looks like we survived another one."

She hadn't yet found the right words to tell him that she had resigned.

"You get your rifle back?" he asked.

She nodded.

"We found Bobby's phone," said Riggs. "It was at the warehouse. The kid had been in the park taking surveillance videos of the corner."

"So that's where Mitch found him," said Bowers. "Anything good on the videos?"

Riggs nodded. "The first one was so blurry it was useless, but the other one showed a kid named Jimmy Hill selling dippers on the corner. He's behind bars."

Bowers put a napkin under her glass. "How did Papa G feel about that?"

Riggs shrugged. "Haven't seen him around. Hasn't been back to the sub shop. I think he's lying low."

Bowers watched a couple take a seat at the bar.

Riggs nodded to someone behind her. "I think you have a visitor."

Bowers twisted in her seat.

Jayzee stood a good ten inches above everyone else in the crowd. She couldn't miss that big, toothy grin as he brought Bobby up the steps. She hardly recognized the boy. Bowers slid off her stool. "Look at you," she said, "all dressed up so fine."

Bobby stood tall. He'd cleaned up nicely. The fresh haircut and a new set of clothes had transformed him.

"Let me see your wrist," she said.

He held up his arm and let her inspect the wound. It was still red, but it had healed.

"It makes me look tough," said Bobby. He glanced at Riggs. "Some dude told me that scars meant we've survived."

Jayzee put a hand on Bobby's shoulder.

"Bowers," said Jayzee, "Thank you for clearing my name. I'm still on the team, sponsors are coming back, and I got some sense knocked into me, too. So I wanted to give back, you know?"

He peered down at Bobby. "I've got an extra guest cottage on my property. This dude is now my residence manager. We got a deal. He does good in school and keeps an eye on my place when I'm gone, and he and his family can live there on me."

Through the glass wall, Bowers saw Bobby's grandma and brother outside on the sidewalk. Tommy held Bo's leash.

Bobby seemed happier than she'd ever seen him. "Jayzee's been teachin' me to throw a football. Oh and I have something to show you."

He pulled out a folded paper and proudly handed it to Bowers. It was an algebra test with a B written on the top. She and Bobby bumped fists.

"I'm proud of you," she said.

Bobby's brows bunched together and his eyes watered. "I'm sorry about all this."

"Hey," said Bowers as she hugged him. "You did what you could. Most kids your age would've buckled. You didn't."

Bobby hugged her back.

"You're strong," she said. "I believe you will do just fine."

She shook Jayzee's hand. "Thank you. This means a lot."

As they were about to leave Bobby dropped a keyring in her hand. She stared at the small, silver compass dangling from the ring. "Bobby, you didn't need to—"

"Paid for it myself," he said, "Wit' honest money, too. I got one for me, too. I don't wanna lose my way ever again."

"I don't know what to say." Bowers tried to swallow the lump in her throat. "Thank you."

Bobby wiped his eyes. "I owe you my life. There ain't enough words in the whole world to thank you for dat."

"Then go do something good with it."

"Yes, ma'am."

"It's Bowers," she said.

"Yes, ma'am, Bowers." He grinned at her, and followed Jayzee outside.

She watched him join his grandmother and brother, and felt Riggs' hand at her waist. "Our table is ready," he said.

The head waiter escorted them to table 306. As usual they slid into the same side and faced the door.

Dinner came. It was delicious as always.

She toyed with her fork and could feel Riggs' stare.

"I told you I'd take a bullet for you," he said.

"But did ya have to take three?" She nudged him under the table. "Damned over-achiever."

She listened to Riggs' laughter. They talked about his surgeries and when he might go back to work. It was hard for her to concentrate on small talk.

"What about the Detective of the Year Award?" he asked. "They sure as hell couldn't give it to Mitch."

"The chief posthumously awarded it to Paul Green. His brother accepted the award for him."

"Your chief's a good man." Riggs pushed his plate away.

She played with his fingers. Every time she glanced at him, he held her gaze.

"When are you gonna tell me what's really on your mind?" he asked.

"I resigned," she said.

"I know." He gripped her hand. "I meant what I said about a space being there for you at the Bureau."

"I need time to reset."

"I know," he said. The way he tried to smile tore her to pieces.

"Riggs—"

He put her hand between his palms and kissed her fingertips. "Bowers. You're not broken."

338

Kill Notice

She rested her head on his shoulder. "I need to get away for a while."

"I know." He rose to his feet, albeit slowly, and pulled at her to follow. "Come."

She strolled with him out to the side exit. They stood in the hall. The moment felt awkward, until the warmth of his hand touched her face.

Images of the night they'd had together rushed through her mind. Jumbled in with it were the memories of waiting in the hospital with Uncle Marvin at her side and not knowing whether Riggs would live or die.

She felt his kiss and blinked as his breath washed over her. It moved her in a way hard to define. He touched her cheek. "I'll be here," he said.

Her emotions ran in circles until she decided to face the truth about how she really felt. "I meant what I said. I do love you. This is just a vacation."

"I know," he said. For a few seconds, the way Riggs held her made her feel as if she were the most precious thing on the planet. Then he kissed her forehead and let go.

"You know where to find me," he said.

PERSONAL EFFECTS

OWERS' FOOTSTEPS echoed in her empty apartment. Everything she owned had been put in storage or was still locked up in Magrath's evidence lockers, including her favorite mug.

Other than clothing, there had been little to pack. She did the final walk-through. The fresh paint on the bedroom door felt like an encrypted message only she understood. All traces of the black fingerprint dust were gone. The notes and buttons were part of her memories.

Bowers returned to the kitchen. The entire apartment had been wiped clean. The only evidence that anything had ever happened here were the new windows and door. Despite all that, the silhouette in her living room and the sound of the lamp crashing into the wall were as vivid as they had been on that dark morning.

Of all the things that haunted her from this case, she remembered his eyes.

She stopped at the breakfast bar where he had lined up her hollow-points in a neat row. A folder containing her underwater photos lay there now.

On the way out the door she picked up her folder. As she locked

Kill Notice

the front door, she stood eye level with the spot where she'd left her message: *I will find you.*

Mitch had thought her mistaken. He'd thought he'd never be caught. She bumped the door with her fist and left the apartment behind.

Ahead lay a narrow concrete path toward the parking lot. Bowers stopped at the bench where she and Riggs had sat that night.

The bench felt cool and firm when she took a seat. She sat back, pulled out her phone, and sent Riggs a text: *I will be back. I promise.*

A moment later he responded: *I know.*

TWENTY MINUTES LATER, Bowers parked her car in front of the Metro PD on Georgia under the big oak tree. She stood next to her car and took in the white-and-blue sign and the big windows. Behind them were the people she knew she would miss.

After locking the car, Bowers headed toward the front door. It felt strange, entering as a civilian. Above her the tall, graceful transmission tower soared high above the building.

The guard stepped out the front door and waved her inside. "They're waiting for you," he said.

Upstairs, she got off the elevator and found Johnny pacing the floor. Part of her wanted to stay and see him through a meaningful career and keep his ass out of hot water. The other part knew she had to put some time and distance between what had happened here and whatever the rest of her life would entail.

She made one last stop at the breakroom and found Magrath waiting for her. "I knew you couldn't resist one last cup," she said.

Bowers glanced at the Styrofoam cups and shook her head. "I hate disposable cups."

Magrath pulled Bowers' mug out of her bag and handed it back. "I don't need this anymore. Thought you'd want it."

Bowers ran a thumb over the FBI logo on the front and fought the knot in her throat. A second later she felt Magrath's arms around her.

"Honey, I'm gonna miss you," she said.

Bowers blinked. "You aren't getting soft on me, are you?"

Magrath laughed and wiped her eyes. "Let's go get some cake."

Bowers filled her mug with coffee and followed Johnny and Magrath down the bright hallway to the briefing room. Before entering, she heard her colleagues chattering away as always. Cops never seemed to run out of things to talk about.

Mike whistled when she strolled through the door. Loud clapping and boisterous cheers broke out. She'd already turned in her badge, uniforms, and weapon and hadn't expected all the well wishes or a farewell party.

Perez limped forward from behind the conference table. Voices in the room fell silent as his arms engulfed her in a hug. "Thank you," he said. "I owe you."

"I'll settle for a beer," she said as she patted his shoulder. "It's good to see you up and around."

They spent the next half hour eating chocolate cake, teasing the crap out of each other, and talking about the good times. Clawski wolfed down two pieces of the cake. Perez wore a huge smile as his colleagues greeted him. No one said anything about Mitch. They celebrated Johnny's news that he had bought a house and that he and his wife were expecting a baby.

Clawski wandered over, after pocketing a hunk of cake for later. He wiped the crumbs off his mouth and reached out to shake her hand. "You're all right, Bowers."

She laughed and gave him a hug. "Stay outta trouble, will you?" He popped his gum and grinned as always.

The chief quieted everyone down. "Well, I guess this is it," he said. "What you did was an act of extreme bravery and dedication to duty. And to show our gratitude, we think you should keep this." He handed her Glock back to her.

"May it protect you," he said. His eyes grew misty. He cleared his throat and shook her hand. "If you ever wanna come back, we've got a place for you."

Kill Notice

"I appreciate that, sir." She took a deep breath. "Don't make me go all girl on you now." She wiped her eyes. "Thank you all."

When the party ended, she stuck her empty mug into her bag. Johnny escorted her to the elevator. Mike hurried to catch the next ride down. Bowers couldn't help but notice the box in his arms labeled–CHARLES MITCHELL.

Bowers frowned. "What's that?"

Mike wore a sour expression. "His wife is downstairs to pick up his personal effects. She refused to come upstairs, so I was tagged to play delivery boy."

The door opened and Mike got in. "You coming?"

"Not yet. I need a minute."

When the door closed, and she faced Johnny. The two of them stood in silence as if neither knew what to say. Bowers reached out to shake his hand. "You're going to do fine," she said. "Just keep your temper under control. I want to hear when you make Grade 2."

Johnny hugged her.

Bowers hugged him back. "See you, partner."

The elevator doors slid open. Bowers entered and held the rail. As the doors closed, she waved goodbye.

One the ride down, Bowers stared at the polished metal and fought to contain the waves of relief and regret and appreciation rolling around inside her. She took a deep breath as the elevator bounced to a halt and the doors opened on the first floor.

On the way out of the front door, she waved at the guard, who offered a salute. That did it, she had to get some fresh air.

Outside, Bowers skipped down the steps and hopped into her car. Leaning back in the seat, she took one last view of the station.

Through the windshield, she spotted Mike trudging back into the building and leaving a dark-haired woman who was a little on the heavy side at the curb. Bowers watched as Mitch's wife put the white box in the trunk of her blue sedan. Her body language seemed to oscillate between anger and embarrassment.

Mitch's daughter waited in the back seat while his son stood on the lawn, staring at the police station.

343

The boy mirrored his father. Tall with dark eyes. He seemed fascinated by the men in uniform passing by. Bowers wondered how he would turn out. She hoped he wouldn't follow in his father's footsteps.

The mother called the boy, and they both slipped into the front seats. Plumes of white spewed from the exhaust pipe when she started the engine.

Bowers glanced at the back seat and saw the daughter staring back at her. The girl's face was smooth and soft, like children are at that age, and yet there were those same black eyes she'd seen on Mitch's face.

The hair went up on Bowers' neck.

The girl held something up against the window.

The car rolled forward, and the mother waited for a break in traffic.

In the back seat, a kind of glee lit up the girl's eyes as she flicked a lighter and held an orange flame up next to her face.

ACKNOWLEDGEMENTS

RECENTLY A FRIEND of mine quoted his father by saying, "The turtle didn't get to the top of that fence post by himself." I laughed, but the point was made. While writers do spend weeks and years alone at their keyboards, we all were inspired by others and benefited from the sound advice and insights of many. In doing the research for this book, I must thank The Office of Public Affairs, FBI; former FBI profiler Mary Ellen O'Toole, Metro PD Homicide Detective Bill Xanten in DC, retired FBI agent Mitch Stern, and Captain David Cook of the Corpus Christi Police Department who shared their time to make this a better story.

A great deal of gratitude goes to my friend and mentor, Dave Farland, who has always been there for me. One can't help but be inspired by this exceptional man who tirelessly shares his immense knowledge of story with writers at all levels.

My remarkable editors are Dave Farland, Diann Read, and Nick Mills. I also must thank Kevin J. Anderson, Jonathan Maberry, Mitch Stern, and the other writers and reviewers who have been so quick to offer their take on KILL NOTICE. A heart-felt thank you goes out to Kevin J. Anderson and the fine tribe of writers who meet each year in Colorado Springs.

The people who have inspired me are many. One day I hope to meet Stephen King and thank him – he doesn't know it, but he was the first to teach me the finer points of writing. My friends at International Thriller Writers represent an army of encouragement: Kathrine Ramsland, Jeffery Deaver, John Lescroart, David Morrell, Lee Child, Sandra Brown, Robert Dugoni, R.L. Stein, Heather Graham, Stephen Hunter, John Sanford, Steve Berry, and so many others. A special nod goes to Michael Connolly who encouraged me to get in the trenches with law enforcement and get the details from those who do the job.

Finally, I must thank my best friend, co-adventurer, and husband Dennis and my family and friends for putting up with my latte-driven obsession to write.

ABOUT THE AUTHOR

MARTA SPROUT

That I write thrillers is no surprise for those who know me. I teach at the police academy, do training scenarios with cadets and the SWAT Team. I spend time on the firing range with a wide variety of weapons, and routinely consult with law enforcement and those in the military.

Why? The answer goes deeper than authenticity. It's about a profound regard for life and the tense line between those who exploit others and those who take a stand to protect the innocent.

As a teen, one incident rocked my world. I drove to Hollywood long before sunrise and got hopelessly lost. I parked near a driveway in a gated community to read a map. After I drove home, as I walked in the house, I saw that driveway on the news. It was Sharon Tate's home. I'd been there just before the bodies were discovered.

Today, writing thrillers gives me a safe way to unravel why some are violent, to honor the brave, and wonder what you or I would do in the shoes of a hero.

Made in the USA
Columbia, SC
17 January 2020